"Yo...
You...
So...
Before the night is old,
Ride hard and strong and swiftly,
For in your hands resides
The fate of every Byrnian
And Mharian besides."

Instrument of Fate

"Christie Golden takes familiar, beloved elements of heroic fantasy—elves, tricky human/elf relations, bards, and dark magic—and gives them teeth by virtue of the compassion that she evokes for her characters. This is fantasy in which the fears are as real as the beauties—and even more believable. Fantasy with teeth."

—Susan Shwartz, author of *The Grail of Hearts*

Instrument Of Fate

Christie Golden

ACE BOOKS, NEW YORK

This book is an Ace original edition,
and has never been previously published.

INSTRUMENT OF FATE

An Ace Book / published by arrangement with
the author

PRINTING HISTORY
Ace edition / April 1996

The Putnam Berkley World Wide Web site address is
http://www.berkley.com

ISBN: 0-441-00322-2

ACE®
Ace Books are published by The Berkley Publishing Group,
200 Madison Avenue, New York, NY 10016.
ACE and the "A" design are trademarks
belonging to Charter Communications, Inc.

PRINTED IN THE UNITED STATES OF AMERICA

10 9 8 7 6 5 4 3 2 1

To Katherine Kurtz
Inspiration, mentor, and friend

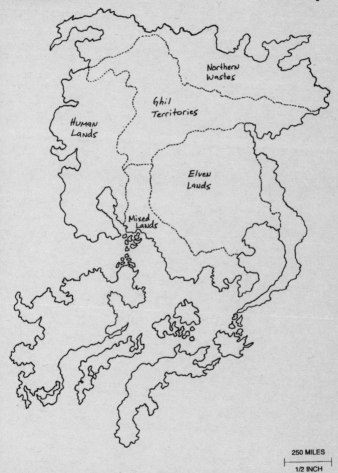

Northern
Wastes

Ghil
Territories

Human
Lands

Elven
Lands

Mixed
Lands

250 MILES

1/2 INCH

PROLOGUE

They had not spoken for over an hour, the large, strong wizard and the slim, elegant bard, and the silence lay heavily between them. Calleo paced back and forth, his human heritage of emotion revealing itself in every line of his ample body. His big hands clenched and unclenched, and he occasionally rubbed one palm across his bald pate, as if to smooth down hair that had not been there for decades.

Jencir permitted himself a touch of quiet humor. "Careful, Master Calleo," he warned. "You might rub away what little is left."

Calleo glared at the elf. "Curse the day anyone ever introduced elves to humor," he growled without real malice, then continued his pacing.

Jencir smiled, pleased that his teasing had been appreciated, and bent his head over his harp, his own golden hair as thick and full now as it had been for the last six centuries. Slim fin-

gers floated over the strings, coaxing soothing music to fill the
tense silence in the room.

The two were waiting for Prince Liandir, who had instructed them to meet him in his private quarters. The room
was large and airy. Its floors, ceilings, and walls were made of
the beautiful milk-white quartz that formed the palace, home
for centuries to Falarah's ruler, King Cynor, and his family.
Liandir's own personal touch was evident in the bright colors
of bed linens, draperies, carpets, and tapestries. In addition to
exquisite elven carvings, there were also the works of human
artisans. A small pool graced with a carved dolphin served as
home to water lilies and small, brightly hued fish. The large
window was open, and an early summer breeze made the sap-
phire-and-silver drapes swell and billow. The room accurately
reflected its tenant—a mixture of old and new, human and
elven, inanimate art and life's own works of beauty.

Lovely as his surroundings were, and soothing as the music
he produced might be, Jencir's thoughts were with Prince
Liandir. Away from the secluded peace of his private cham-
bers, the youthful prince of Falarah now sat at King Cynor's
side at the Council of Elvenkind. Under debate was what was
pallidly called "The Human Question," dealing with the mortal country of Byrn, just across the Falaran border. There
would be no shouting, no name-calling, no half- or completely
drawn weapons, things Jencir might have reason to expect had
the meeting consisted of volatile humans. No, the elves, by
their very nature rarely able to feel deep emotions, would simply talk.

Some wished to close the borders, have no further contact
with humans. Others, like Liandir and Jencir, had learned to
appreciate and enjoy mortals. Still others wanted extreme
measures, to halt what they regarded as "contamination." If
the extremists carried the vote, Jencir wondered, would he
and his friends—human and elf, prince and minstrel and
Court Wizard—pay the price? They had reached past their
own deep-bred prejudices, but clearly others could not—or
would not.

Jencir's sharp features saddened, the music he played shifting to a minor key.

Falarah was the most populous of the four elvenlands. Liandir's father, King Cynor, was among the oldest and most respected rulers. When, two centuries ago, the elven goddess known as The Lady had reduced the mountains between Byrn and Falarah to mere foothills, the Falarans knew that Her desire was for peace, not war. It was simple, logical, obvious; so obvious that Lord Cynor betrothed his daughter Ariel to the human prince Tach. Though Tach had died long ago, Ariel yet lived in her husband's country, the honored Queen-mother of Byrn, she and her part-elven descendants a living tribute to interracial peace.

The Falarans were proud of her, of the elven blood that mingled with human in Byrn. Others, including King Kertu of Sali, found such a union obscene.

"If you ask me," said Calleo, though no one had, "King Kertu and the Sa elves shouldn't have any say in what to do about the border. It's Falarah's border, not Sali's."

"Theoretically, you are correct. But the elves have thought and moved as one for millennia. Two centuries of contact with humans is not likely to change that."

The door opened, and Prince Liandir entered. Jencir leapt to his feet, and Calleo stopped in midstride. Liandir closed the door behind him and did not speak for a moment, but his sorrowful expression told his friends what had happened.

"Sweet Lady Death, they're going to war, aren't they?" exclaimed Calleo.

Liandir held up a slender, beringed hand. A faint smile tugged at his weary face. "Patience, friend Calleo! It is a good thing indeed that we elves do not often have strong emotions. There would be none of us left if we all fretted as you do!" There was only affection in his voice; the rebuke was friendly.

The prince walked slowly into the room. The highly formal robes he was required by etiquette to wear to the Council, heavy, fur-trimmed, and embroidered, threatened to overwhelm the elf's slender frame. He shrugged off the cloak, laying it on the bed. His prince's coronet, encrusted with rubies and one great, winking sapphire, blatantly declared his nobility to those who could not see it, far more subtly stated, in his kind face. Sighing, he rubbed at his eyes, eyes that were gray as a morning mist and half again as large as a human's. Handsome in a race that was, to an individual, uncommonly beautiful, Liandir would have seemed the perfect Falaran prince of legend had it not been for the unnatural weariness and pain on his face. He suddenly looked old, Jencir thought; as old as King Cynor.

The bard and the wizard waited, the former with the patience of his race, the latter with the agitation of his. Liandir's voice was deep with regret when he at last spoke.

"The Sa carried the vote. Falarah was the only elvenland willing to actively protest King Kertu's desire. The Kir did not wish to become involved and yielded their vote. And the Ilsi!" Liandir's musical voice grew rough with displeasure. "The Ilsi are too afraid of the big, blundering mortals to—how was it phrased?—risk contact with them. They think Kertu's desire to show a hostile mien will discourage humans from traveling to our lands. They do not see that if this road does lead to war, then they may get far more human contact than they expected."

Calleo's bearded face flushed and he swore violently. Jencir shook his golden head sadly. He hadn't cared for humans when he was younger, but two centuries of contact had worn down his prejudices. Now, he found he enjoyed the company of the blunt-spoken, lively Calleo, and others of his race. The thought that Kertu would prefer to murder humans rather than try to understand them—

"How long do the humans have?" he asked.

"Long enough, perhaps," Liandir replied. His face was thoughtful, his gaze directed inward. Jencir recognized that look. It meant the prince was planning something. "Kertu first wants to assemble an army of elven troops along the border between Byrn and Falarah, where the Kyras used to be. 'We no longer have a wall of stone,' said he, 'so we shall make a wall of steel.' Then . . . I do not know. Perhaps he will openly attack the Byrnians."

"Elves will lose a war against humans," advised Calleo. "We've got the emotions, remember. We know how to hate, how to channel bloodlust properly. You elves don't have that. And Byrn has a standing army, well trained and used to killing. Those damned Ghil in the north provide mighty fine practice bodies."

Liandir turned his gray eyes to his friend. "Perhaps Kertu is not capable of true hatred, my friend. But he does believe in the purity of elven bloodlines, and in the wrongness of associating with humans. And the Sa have had as much practice in attacking the Ghil as have humans. It could be a closer battle than you think, and if the humans are not prepared, they might be the losers after all."

He glanced over at Jencir, hesitated, and then uttered the news that he knew would hit the performer the hardest. "Kertu and the Sa have officially stated that they do not believe The Lady partially destroyed the Kyras."

"No," breathed Jencir. "How can they?"

"Well, it's a big tale to swallow, if you didn't see it," commented Calleo. "And it was only the Falarans and the Byrnians who witnessed it."

Jencir turned to the wizard, his color high, filled with the closest approximation of fury he was capable of experiencing. "*I* saw it, Calleo! I was there, fighting against the dreadful things that the Nightlands King had sent against us. I was there, when the sun went out. I was there when She appeared to elf and human alike, promising a new chance at peace for all races of Aertha.

"I watched as the mountains crumbled before Her words. Crumbled to bring humans and elves together, to learn from each other. And if Kertu and the Sa deny this, then they deny the lesson She was trying to teach."

"I pray it will not come to war, but . . ." Liandir's voice trailed off.

"If it does, will the other elven nations fight with Sali?" asked Calleo.

"I do not believe so, but I could be wrong. Most likely, Sali will stand alone."

"Will it?" pressed the wizard. "What about the People of the Sea? They have little reason to love my race."

"But they will not fight you," countered Liandir. "The conflicts of those on land do not much concern them."

"What about the Changers, or the Hidden Folk?"

"Changers? I have not heard of anyone encountering one in my lifetime," replied the prince. "They may not exist any more. Even if they do, they have never sided with elf or human in any struggle. There is no reason for them to do so now. And as for the Hidden Folk, they are as shy as the Ilsi. No, we have little fear that Kertu will find allies for actual warfare."

Jencir spoke up. "But the Sa alone, as Liandir said, will be formidable enough if they are allowed to surprise the humans."

Liandir took a deep breath, and shook his head. "This is wrong, terribly wrong. I know it. We must warn your people, Calleo. They must know what is going on *before* Kertu has a chance to gather an army. Could you perhaps send a message to Queen-mother Ariel?"

Calleo reluctantly shook his bald head. "My strengths lie in hand magic, not mind magic."

Liandir sighed in exasperation. "I would go myself, but I would be recognized, and Kertu will be watching me."

They sat in distressed silence, their minds working furiously. Suddenly an idea occurred to Jencir.

"Highness . . . *I* could carry a message for you."

Both Liandir and Calleo stared at him.

"I am but one of many bards in the castle," Jencir pointed out, "and it is not uncommon for us to travel to other cities, even other lands. If you, or Calleo, or even a royal squire were to attempt to carry a message, he or she would be suspected at once. Music, however, knows no borders."

"It damn well knows the Byrnian border, as far as Kertu and his ruffians are concerned!" Calleo exploded.

Gently, Liandir touched the human's sleeve, and Calleo composed himself.

Jencir was touched by the wizard's concern. "There are

ways for one lone musician to slip past the Sa border guards," he insisted.

Kertu's plan must not be allowed. All it could possibly lead to would be horrifically high casualties on both sides, casualties that called to the bard's mind song and tales of centuries before, in which both human and elves nearly slew one another down to the last child. . . .

Jencir had been witness to the most recent war between the races. It could not be permitted to happen again.

"I could take some kind of message that might be passed along to the Queen-mother even if I am stopped," Jencir pressed. "Come, Highness, you know this is the only way to save *all* of us!"

"Yes," said Liandir, his beautiful face lighting up with a new sense of hope. "And perhaps Calleo *can* help."

Two pairs of gray elven eyes fastened on Calleo. He was confused at first, but when Liandir began to explain, the wizard started to smile.

It just might work, after all.

Raise thy voice in songs of praise, for music greatly pleaseth the gods.

—from *Opening Prayers to Light*

CHAPTER ONE

The Borderlands regional bardic competition, held in the small town of Hallenore, was starting to wind down. The weather had cooperated, granting a cool morning and now a glorious, sunny afternoon. The more than half a thousand souls who had attended the annual event sat together in sweaty but jovial proximity, listening to the performers with avid interest. Filling every inch of the town square and taking up room on the steps of the buildings that surrounded it, they were by and large a genial crowd. They had come to listen to fine music and enjoy the day, not to drink, carouse, or pick fights. The Kyras in the east gazed benevolently down upon the scene, a constant presence in this town that was nestled against their rolling foothills.

A handsome young man finished a heartbreaking ballad, and was rewarded with enthusiastic applause as he bowed and descended the rickety stairs of the makeshift stage.

Jencir suppressed a shudder as a chill swept through him. He leaned with feigned casualness against a column that supported a building called Holding House. He pretended interest in the performer, but his sharp eyes were constantly scanning the crowd, searching. The elf wore only a nondescript linen tunic and simple breeches. In his arms he held a lute, wrapped for the moment in a protective covering of cloth. Jencir was glad for the press of people. The presence of so many witnesses would make a murder attempt far less likely. Not that it mattered much now. Chances were he was already dead.

He shuddered as the pain racked him. His muscles ached constantly, their protest increasing by the minute. Breathing was becoming agony. Despite the mild temperature, sweat broke out on his pallid face and trickled down into the collar of his tunic, which was damp from a hundred such paroxysms over the last agonizing day and a half. Angry heat radiated from the inflamed wound on his shoulder. His enemy had struck a glancing blow, inflicting a comparatively light dose of poison. Only that had allowed him to live this long.

Liandir's plan to warn Queen-mother Ariel had been put into action. Jencir had come with the warning that Ariel, indeed everyone in Byrn, desperately needed to receive if war were to be prevented. It had been a good plan, though, Jencir now realized with uncharacteristic bitterness, terribly naive. The three had assumed that no one would suspect a bard carrying nothing but the instrument of his craft.

They had been wrong.

The enemy's poison blazed its path through Jencir's once-numberless days as a fire burns kindling. Again salty liquid trickled into Jencir's mouth and he sucked on his bleeding gums. Inside, he knew, he was also bleeding—part of the poison's deadly effect. He could have halted it, could have cured himself, had he done what his body had, over centuries, been taught to do. All that he needed was to simply lie down, close his eyes, and let his body shut itself down while it healed. It was a powerful, primal physical reaction, and it was what enabled elves to live so long. Only beheading could kill an elf outright. For all other injuries and illnesses, the body went into what was known as Resting for as long as was necessary to heal, sometimes for years at a time if the wound was serious enough.

But Jencir had a task, a task his friend and prince had charged him with—a task that he owed The Lady Herself. So he had denied his body's cry for Resting, fighting the instinctive drowsiness and forcing himself to continue. He had never heard of anyone delaying Resting for more than a few hours. He suspected that he had already delayed too long.

Jencir squinted up at the sun, now well in the west. Even now, the shadows of the shattered mountains were creeping over the scene. Only a few more hours until sunset; only a few more hours of relative peace. With the night would come the enemy—a relentless, nameless pursuer who had a limitless array of disguises at its disposal, who had been hard on Jencir's heels since he had left Falarah, who had slain his beloved steed and who had, in the end, slain Jencir himself. The elf simply hadn't had time yet to die.

He shifted the lute in his arms and applauded politely as another bard finished, but did not watch the performer depart the stage. His eyes were on the crowd, still searching.

Lady, I pray You . . . just a few hours more . . .

His mouth began to tingle. The poison was spreading.

He was here, in open view, because he was supposed to meet a contact in Hallenore at this competition. The contact had been intended as a precaution. Traveling alone across what remained of the Kyras was always risky, and the dire nature of Jencir's errand made it more so. If he were injured, or someone were following him, the contact would bear the message to Ariel. Jencir's increasingly weakened condition cast a new sense of urgency over the scheduled meeting. This contact, whoever he or she was, must be the one to take the message to Kasselton. By morning at the latest, Jencir would either be Resting—or dead.

But where was he—or she?

Jencir wished that Liandir had told him whom he was supposed to be meeting. He could have at least had a description, to aid him in recognizing this person. But Liandir had not been sure whom he would select when Jencir had left. "Someone will be sent," the prince had assured his friend. "I have . . . friends."

Dimly, Jencir heard a faint buzzing sound. He realized almost at once that it was not coming from the bard currently performing. The sound was in his own ears. Fever raged through him. He forced himself to inhale, to loosen his restricted chest. When Jencir shifted position, he realized that his fingers, his long, clever minstrel's fingers, were slow and clumsy. It was the first stage of paralysis. The elf swallowed hard, fighting to stay alert and attentive.

A sharp sense of desperation grew inside him as he scanned the crowd for the hundredth time, searching for someone who would perhaps meet his eyes and nod almost imperceptibly. Or who would vanish, only to reappear, ready to take the precious message on to its final destination.

Where? If he could not put the message into safe hands, the enemy would win. No matter what, Jencir, his body preparing to shut down for healing or death, had lost.

Lady . . . please . . .

Alarmed, Jencir shook his head. His mind was wandering. Another few hours and he would forget his mission entirely as his body, unable to resist, would succumb to the Resting. His consternation increased when he realized that the shadows were far longer than they had any right to be. What he had taken for an instant of inattention had actually been over an hour. He closed his eyes, fighting the pain as another wave of torment crashed and broke over him.

"My lords, my ladies, pray you welcome Gillien Songespynner to our competition!"

The elf glanced without interest up at the stage. The final competitor was moving to take her place, and Jencir felt a touch of pity for the girl. Songespynner, was it? Clearly a stage name, and not an overly original one at that. She was also clearly not up to following with any success the outstanding performances he'd heard today. The new minstrel was tall and very slender, and her long, dark hair fell unbound to her hips. Her mauve-hued overdress modestly covered her throat and arms, though Jencir noticed that the sleeves fit closely. It was logical. No performer wanted to risk an ornate sleeve getting tangled in an instrument.

But her movements were awkward and jerky, and her sharp features betrayed her discomfort. She ascended the stage with exaggerated care, lifting her skirts almost indecently high. She clutched her mandolin, an instrument similar to a small, flat-backed lute, to her chest in an almost defensive pose. Idly, Jencir wondered just how bad the girl would be. It was a shame, he mused, that the last song he heard would be performed by an amateur.

Then she took a deep breath, and positioned the instrument comfortably against her body. Strong fingers—minstrel's fingers—curved about the slim neck and positioned themselves on the strings. Before Jencir's gaze, the awkwardness fell away from her as if it were a cloak she had casually dropped. Her eyes remained wide and her expression vulnerable, but as she sang, it became apparent why she had adopted the guise of a bewildered, innocent maiden.

> Twelve months ago I came here as
> A young and blushing bride.
> This handsome man had chosen me,
> And I'd stand by his side.
> 'Fore gods and men, I took the vow
> To love him faithfully.
> But a year has passed; I'm virgin still;
> My husband wants, but wants not me.
>
> 'Twas on our wedding night he said
> He loved his first wife still.
> Her death had left a void behind
> Which I could never fill.
> "This house is thine, and all within,
> Do with it as you may,
> But my bed I cannot share with you."
> And so, alone, that night I lay.
>
> She is gone, but not forgotten,

And she haunts my husband's hall,
And her portrait smiles sweetly
From the cold and stony wall.
And he hears her footsteps in the night
And he starts at every sound,
Even though he knows she's buried 'neath
Six feet of cold and stony ground.

Jencir stared, his attention completely seized, his pain for once forgotten. The girl, what was her name—something Songespynner; ah, Gillien, that was it—was magnificent! He had never heard the song before, and suspected she had penned it herself. It was encumbered by none of the stilted, formal refrains that unfortunately seemed common to Byrnian music, and the lyrics, as performed by this sweet-voiced child-woman, were heartbreaking. From the silence around him, Jencir knew that he was not alone in his appreciation.

I thought to give him time to grieve,
And patiently I'd wait.
Then welcome him back to my arms
And truly be his mate.
But time has passed, and here I lie,
A wife in naught but name:
The seasons come, the seasons go,
But winter in his heart remains.

I fancied I'd a lover take,
But 'twas a foolish whim,
For as his heart is bound to her,
So I cleave unto him.
There's none can stir me as he did
When courting me so fair;
But, oh gods, dear gods, it's killing me,
And my soul is lost unto despair.

She is gone, but not forgotten,
And she haunts my husband's hall,
And her portrait smiles sweetly

From the cold and stony wall.
And he hears her footsteps in the night
And he starts at every sound,
Even though he knows she's buried 'neath
Six feet of cold and stony ground.

A soft sob to his right distracted Jencir. A girl, a few years younger than Gillien's eighteen or so, stared at the singer as tears trickled down her soft, rose-colored cheeks. Not for the first time, Jencir wished that he had the gift for emotions that humans had. It was as if, to make up for their candle-flame brief lives, they felt everything with an intensity at which Jencir could only marvel. Gillien, the audience firmly in the palm of her hand now, continued. The last two verses were sung in a voice laced with torment and brushed with feather-soft insanity.

There is no anguish like the pain
Of loneliness in bed.
He scorns the warmness of his wife
And yearns but for the dead.
And celebrations hollow ring,
For distant is mine host,
And my ladies slyly laugh at me,
And they say I'm jealous of a ghost.

The first snow of the year has come
And lies like feathers white.
And from atop this parapet
Shall I fly down this night.
For though it is a fall indeed,
The flagstones are but down—
And surely soft white snow I'll hit
Instead of cold and stony ground.

She paused, stringing out the moment with unbearable tension, then repeated the chorus with a slight but sinister change in the wording that made even Jencir's skin prickle.

We are gone, but not forgotten,
And we haunt our husband's hall,
And our portraits smile sweetly
From the cold and stony wall.
And he hears our footsteps in the night,
And he starts at every sound,
Even though he knows we're buried 'neath
Six feet of cold and stony ground.

There was a silence as the last note of her mandolin faded and died. Then the spectators erupted with applause, leaping to their feet and crying their approval. Gillien started to bow, like a boy, which Jencir thought was odd, then turned the movement into a clumsy curtsey as awkwardness returned to her. Her face flamed at the applause. A tentative smile played about her lips, then the young minstrel surrendered to it. Her grin was crooked, but utterly sincere. Still grinning, she clattered down the steps to the area behind the stage.

Finally, the clapping died down, and the audience began to chat and mill about. The competition was over; all that remained was to announce the winner. Some crowd members left to purchase food from a few vendors who had shrewdly set up temporary shop near the square. The judges left their raised dais to the right of the stage to meet in private and discuss their opinions.

Jencir stayed where he was, his gaze prowling restlessly over the dispersing crowd. He would not tax what little energy was left to him by moving for no purpose. His innate elven patience warred with the pain and the Resting reflex it was causing. Now, surely, the contact would approach him. He was well above the crowd, clearly visible to anyone who might be searching for him—friend or foe.

Torches were lit at various points around the square and on some of the nearby buildings. Dusk was near.

Where was the contact?

As they moved past him, the Hallenorans glanced at the elf with polite curiosity. This close to the Falaran border, humans were not unfamiliar with Jencir's race, though elves were still far from common in Byrn. He knew that they were contrasting their own appearances with his, as he had done the first time he had seen a human. Mortals seemed to have universally dark hair and tanned skin, whereas the Falarans were fair of face and tress. Elven builds were far more slender than the powerful frames of humans, even those of females. And, of course, humans had those peculiar rounded ears. None of the gazes, though, were hostile to Jencir. He smiled with equal politeness, hoping for a sign of recognition from someone, but nothing came.

Pain descended again, and Jencir leaned for support against one of the courtyard arches. Blackness followed. Jencir almost collapsed. He bit hard on the inside of his cheek, and swam out of the near-faint. He tasted blood, but whether from his bitten cheek or his bleeding gums he wasn't sure. Dimly, he heard an announcement, and fought to understand the words through his torment and dangerous lethargy.

". . . have decided. Will all the competitors please come forward?"

Twenty-three musicians, carrying various instruments and ranging in age from child to old man, obligingly assembled onstage. Jencir spotted Gillien. She was shyly trying to hide in the back, but was tall enough that her ploy didn't work. The man who had the honor of announcing the winner was Kalaman Herrick, Reeve of Hallenore, an elegantly handsome man in his mid-forties. His face was alight with pleasure. Jencir had observed the reeve watching the competition with more than polite interest, and knew that the man's love of music was sincere.

"As most of you know, the minstrel who wins here tonight will go on to represent the region of the Borderlands in the final round of the annual Byrnian Bardic Competition. This competition, for those of you who are willing to travel that far, will be held three weeks from now in Kasselton, where King Evrei and the rest of the royal family will select the talented man or woman who shall carry the title of Bard of Byrn for the next year."

He paused, and stood up even straighter. "No Borderlander has ever won that title. But I think I speak for all of us when I say that, this year, that may well change. My lords, my ladies, I pray you, give all honor unto the winner of this year's competition—Gillien Songespynner!"

Even in the midst of his distress and physical pain, the elf allowed himself a pleased smile. Gillien was parchment pale with surprise. Even from where Jencir stood, he could see that the girl was trembling violently. Reeve Herrick motioned to her to come down from the stage and accept her just reward—prize money and a beautiful pendant to wear about her neck when she performed before the royal family. Gillien moved slowly past her fellow musicians, who, to their credit, seemed to be genuinely pleased that she had won. She tucked her mandolin under her arm, gripped her skirts, and began to carefully walk down the stairs.

Not carefully enough, though. As the crowd watched, adulation turned to sympathetic horror as Gillien stepped on her dress, stumbled, caught herself for a heartbeat, and then pitched forward down the stairs. She disappeared from view. There was a sharp cracking sound, then Gillien's voice came loudly to Jencir's ears, harsh with her embarrassment.

"I'm not hurt, I'm—*oh, no!*"

The words turned into a sharp wail, and when Jencir could next see her, Gillien was on her feet. She did indeed seem unhurt by the tumble, but her face displayed naked horror. Clutched in her hands were the broken, jagged bits of wood that represented all that was left of her mandolin. She looked as if she were fighting tears, and Jencir could not blame her.

Reeve Herrick lost his composure and stammered for a moment before he regained it. "Ah, but my lady Gillien, surely you can make or purchase another instrument? This should help," he added a bit indelicately, shoving the small purse toward her.

From somewhere, Gillien managed a smile as she accepted her rewards from Reeve Herrick.

"Certainly," she said. "I shall without a doubt perform before Their Majesties, as I have been tasked." But the desperately unhappy look in her large blue eyes gave the lie to her brave words.

Jencir felt terribly sorry for the girl. She might be able to acquire a new instrument, yes, but three weeks was not a very long time. If only—

The elf's gray eyes widened as a plan, so brave and reckless and dangerous that he caught his breath, began to take shape. Did he dare do it?

Did he dare *not* do it?

Lady, have You given me a sign? I pray that I am doing the right thing!

The darkness was descending. Jencir made his decision.

Mortified by the incident, the new Borderlands Regional Bard was trying to plow through the crowd as quickly as possible. Some respected her discomfort, but others were too anxious to congratulate the girl on the victory to give any thought to her own rather obvious desire for privacy. Jencir threaded his way through the crowd himself and sidled up to her as she tried and failed to make her way through the press of people to a place of solitude.

"My lady Gillien," he said, his musical voice carrying clearly through the chatter of the throng. "A word with you, if I may?"

Gillien's eyes widened in mild surprise as she saw who —or rather what—had hailed her, but she recognized a diversion when she saw one.

"Yes, indeed, let me speak to my fellow minstrel, please," she stammered, angling her shoulders and at one point literally pushing an eager young admirer out of the way. She had barely reached Jencir when the elf's hand seized her own and tugged.

Clearly a little worried now, she nonetheless followed him past a row of small shops and into the shadowed doorway of a bakery. Though the baker had closed for the evening, the scent of bread still lingered. Gillien looked at him, curious but unafraid. Jencir thanked The Lady that elves had achieved a reputation for benevolence here in the border towns. At least, he thought bitterly, elves would have that reputation until Kertu's warriors unexpectedly bore down on the trusting Byrnians like a storm from the east.

"Lady Gillien, I shall speak quickly and frankly. I witnessed your unfortunate misstep on the stage."

Gillien turned crimson, and a flicker of spirit shone in her eyes. "If you have gulled me here merely to insult me, Master Elf—"

He held up a placating hand. "Let me finish. I will do you a favor if you will do me one. This instrument," he said, reaching to free the lute he carried from its protective swaddling of cloth, "is one of the finest in Falarah. Its music is sweet and pure, and when combined with your own talents, will, I am certain, win for you the title of Bard of Byrn. I shall loan it to you."

Forcing his increasingly numb fingers to cooperate, he held out the lute. It was a beautiful thing. The wood out of which it was made was a creamy, light-colored hue and seemed to radiate a cool glow in the orange-yellow light. Its back curved softly into a pear shape and the front was flat and smooth. It looked to have been inlaid with swirls and decorative patterns of gold, and small jewels winked and shimmered as they caught the torchlight. The keys that tightened the strings were made of mother-of-pearl.

Gillien gasped aloud, and slowly, as if she were aware of her own movements, she reached to hold the lute. Not without a pang of regret, Jencir yielded it to her. She held it cradled against her small breasts as she gently ran her fingers over the smooth, highly polished wood. Maneuvering it into proper playing position, she plucked a chord, and a smile of sheer delight spread across her face as the sweet music floated upward.

"Oh," she whispered, "it's beautiful!"

"Then we are agreed."

"Oh, no, I couldn't—"

"You must!" Jencir realized that urgency had crept into his voice, and he brought it back under control. "Perform in front of the royal family, and win the competition. When you have done so, to thank me for the gift, present it to Queen-mother Ariel."

"Why don't you give it to her?" Gillien continued to tenderly coax music from the instrument. The lute obliged.

Jencir lowered his gaze, lest she read his own knowledge of his impending death in them. "My path does not take me there. Yours does. Come, lady, you need an instrument with which to play, and I need the lute delivered safely. There is no answer save yes. You know it as well as I. Lady's blessings upon you, child." Unable to help himself, Jencir reached and brushed her soft cheek with one finger, then dropped his slim, fine-fingered hand to caress the instrument one last time. The chord Gillien played changed subtly, dropping from major to minor key at the elf's touch. Then Jencir turned and hurried down the little alleyway, vanishing into the crowded courtyard, now illuminated only by torches.

"Wait!" Gillien cried, but the elf was gone.

*And thou shalt have no fear of death, should it chance
to come to thee, for thou shalt always be with Me, and walk
by My side, and in My grace, in dreams of peace and beauty
that none but My people can know.*

—from The Book of The Lady

CHAPTER TWO

After a moment's stunned hesitation, Gillien ran after the
vanished elf.

"Wait! I can't accept—"

But he had completely disappeared. As she turned the corner she found herself back in the milling confusion of the town
square, face to face only with total strangers, who smiled at
her with overly familiar grins and congratulatory pats on the
back.

Suddenly a strong hand seized her arm and spun her around.
Gillien gasped and formed a fist. Her nerves were frayed and
she was ready to land a good punch, "femininity" be damned.
She felt her tight sleeve tear where it joined the shoulder from
the force of the movement, and groaned inwardly. This *always*
happened when she wore dresses.

Her tense anger dissolved at once, as she recognized who
had laid such familiar hands on her. It was her twin brother
Kellien—"Kellien Steadyhand" when he was performing. The

two were the same age almost to the minute—Gillien was the
elder, but not by much—and of an appearance that had been
almost identical when they were children. Now, of course,
Kellien's shoulders were broader, and Gillien had a clearly
feminine curve to her body. But they had the same eyes, the
same sharp features, the same unruly brown hair, and the same
lively expressions. Kellien now was beaming, his face alight
with pleasure.

"We're all so proud of you!" he crowed, hugging her
fiercely. "And Mama says don't worry, we'll find a way to get
you a—" He broke off in midsentence and pulled back. His
blue eyes went wide with shock and appreciation as he examined the lute clutched in his sister's right hand.

"Well, well! It seems that you've already gotten yourself a
new instrument. And by Love's grace, a beauty, too! Who'd
you have to kill to get *that*, Gilly?"

"Hush," whispered Gillien in a fierce voice. Kellien's un-
guarded exclamation had already caused a few heads to turn in
their direction. And she didn't like the looks on their faces—
looks of suspicion, covetousness, and hostility. How quickly
people changed, Gillien thought bitterly. She'd been their dar-
ling a few moments ago, when she had no instrument. Now
that she had acquired one, especially such a remarkable one,
she realized that she had suddenly been transformed into an
object of jealousy and malicious talk.

"Let's get back to the caravans. I have to talk to you. And
no more jokes, all right? Bards have got a bad enough reputation as it is, you know."

Kellien obligingly shut his mouth and steered his sister
through the celebrating throngs that clogged the streets of Hallenore. As they went, Gillien wrapped the precious instrument
in the covering in which the Falaran had carried it. The fewer
people who saw her with this thing, she thought fearfully, the
better. Kellien's comment, while clearly intended as a jest,
could have been taken very seriously indeed by some of the
more mistrustful inhabitants of Hallenore. Minstrels who were
strangers in a town, even participants in the Borderlands regional competition, were regarded with suspicion. Many

seemed to think that "minstrel" was just a strange spelling of "thief."

She brought the bundle protectively to her breast, using both hands to cradle it. Forgetting about her long skirts, she tripped, as she had earlier on the stairs. Only Kellien's sure grip on her arm prevented her from stumbling and perhaps crushing the instrument, a second time in one day. Angry at her clumsiness in the hated female clothes, she shifted the lute to one arm and gripped her skirts with her free hand. To cover her embarrassment, she whispered to her twin, "Your brain and your mouth obviously have no connection. If anyone from the law had heard your comment, you'd be spending all my winnings trying to get me out of jail by now."

Kellien, only an inch or so taller than his sister, merely laughed. They had left behind the town square, and the crowds were thinning. Now they moved past private houses whose shutters were closed and whose occupants were either asleep or reveling with the crowds in the noisier sections of town. Gillien began to breathe easier. She didn't like crowds at the best of times, and now, with so valuable an instrument in her arms, she disliked the press of people even more.

The two were silent, walking down the cobbled street that led out of the town. Though Hallenore was a walled city, with gates that could be securely closed and fastened at night, the guards seldom bothered to do so. Hallenore might have been the site of criminal activity in bygone days, but now, even at the height of its festival, it was fairly tame. The gates stood open and unmanned, as usual. Kellien turned left, heading toward the grassy meadowlands where the various bards made their temporary encampments, but Gillien halted where she was.

The soft night breeze blowing from the west, pregnant with the sweet, clean scent of wildflowers in bloom, stirred her long hair. Even from here, she could see the warm orange glow of campfires, see the dark shapes that were her family's caravans silhouetted against the night sky. She glanced around, trying to see if anyone was watching them. She felt silly, but the precaution seemed necessary. Satisfied that they weren't being observed, she unwrapped the lute.

The night was damp, but not too chilly, and a slow, soft mist was rising. The moon was only a sliver and they were well away from the torches of the town, but still, the instrument seemed almost luminous. Its gems, particularly the large sapphire at the base of the short neck, winked like living things.

Gillien gazed at it, then sighed deeply. She handed it to Kellien.

"Here," she said, a trace of regret in her voice. "I want you to have a chance to play it before I give it back."

Kellien stared at her, the wondrous instrument temporarily forgotten in his shock. "What? Dear gods, Gillien, you didn't *really* steal it, did you?"

"Of course not!" Gillien rolled her eyes and took a deep breath. "There was a visiting elven bard in the crowd, and—"

"An elf? You saw an elf? Death's breath, you have all the luck, Gilly! Was he as pretty as they show them in the tapestries?" He slipped the strap over his head and arranged the instrument.

"Yes, yes, now be quiet and let me finish! He told me he felt sorry for me when I broke the mandolin, and he gave me this to use when I play before Their Majesties. He had only one condition—that when I finish, I give the lute to Queen-mother Ariel. It seems he was trying to get it to her and couldn't."

Kellien placed his left hand over the strings and plucked with his right. As before, the sound that emerged was uncannily pure. Kellien's teeth flashed white in the dim light, and he proceeded to play and sing:

> There is a young lady, or so I am told,
> Whose dress and whose manner is overly bold;
> She merrily flirts, then loosens her skirts,
> And she'll do you all night till you cry
>   that it hurts—

"Damn it, Kellien, can't you *ever* be serious!" The last thing Gillien wanted at this moment was for her ever-playful twin to go through all twenty-two verses of *The Saucy Wench of Winterfield.*

The merry music modulated into a slow ballad. Kellien spoke as he continued to play, and this time his voice was devoid of mirth. "All right. Seriously, if you want my advice, I think you'd be a fool to return this lute."

"Kellien, I didn't do anything to deserve it. Our family is anything but wealthy, and if anyone notices a girl practically in rags playing an instrument as fine as *that,* we'll either be jumped on by real thieves or locked up as suspected ones."

The music continued, soft and sincere, as Kellien replied, "Our family is poor because we've been trying all our lives to get even a little of the kind of money that you got tonight. My tumbling and knife throwing, Papa's escapes, Mama's dancing—we're good, sometimes damn good, but none of us has your talent. You've got a gift, Gilly, a great, true gift, and with that gift comes a responsibility to use it wisely. It sounds to me like your elven admirer was sincere. Nobody held a knife to his throat to make him give this to you, did they?"

"No," said Gillien, a touch sulkily. "But—"

"And if your conscience is bothering you so much, then do as he told you to. Go ahead and give it to the Queen-mother. But at least perform with it, won't you? This thing practically sings by itself. With that voice of yours accompanying it . . ." Kellien finished the final few chords, then reluctantly handed it back to his sister. The silence seemed suddenly very loud. "Well, I know what I'd do, but I'm not you."

Gillien felt terrible. It was not unusual for her and Kellien to get embroiled in a discussion of ethics. Gillien had reached young adulthood as something of a hoyden, running around with her brother dressed in his clothing (so much more conducive to adventures than dresses) and getting into all sorts of scrapes. She, however, had always confessed any transgressions, with the result that they were punished with alarming frequency. She felt now as though she were six again, and Kellien was urging her to steal apples from a farmer's orchard.

Only this apple was far more precious, and its allure infinitely greater, than any that grew on a tree.

Why couldn't she be more like Kellien? His outlook on life was so much simpler than hers. He never had these battles with his scruples. He would have cheerfully taken the instrument, played it, and then simply "forgotten" to give it to the Queen-mother. Gillien couldn't even take it for the night. She wrapped it back in its cloth, feeling a strange pang as its smooth pear shape was engulfed by the material.

At last, straightening her shoulders, she looked her twin squarely in the eye. "I have enough money with my winnings to buy another instrument, and there are at least two more towns between here and Kasselton. I simply can't keep this, Kelly, you know I can't."

He gazed at her for a long moment, then sighed heavily. "I know. I knew what you would decide, the minute you started talking. Mama and Papa would be proud of you. Can you at least bring it back to show them? The music—it's so lovely . . . " His voice was wistful.

But Gillien was shaking her head. "I have to return it tonight. I'm getting far too attached to it already, and if I wait until tomorrow, well . . ." She forced a grin. "I just might 'forget' to give it back."

"That's not such a bad idea."

"Kelly!"

"I'm only teasing you. Well, go on then. Hallenore's safe enough for you to go around by yourself, I suppose. You do have your knife, don't you?"

Gillien gave him a withering look. "I haven't been without a knife for ten years, simpleton!" And she would have no scruples using it, either, should some male get amorous ideas. A woman who was neither maid nor married was less than nothing in Byrnian society.

Kellien spread his hands in an I'm-just-looking-out-for-you gesture. "Forgive me if I like to make sure!" He dropped the injured brother look and continued in a normal voice. "Mama's got a special supper cooking and Papa has invited some of the other bards to a celebration in your honor." Gillien's face fell. "But, I'll tell them that Reeve Herrick and some other nobles in town asked you to perform for them. That's likely enough that I don't think anyone will suspect."

Gillien thought to herself that with Kellien spinning the falsehood, it would certainly be believed. She felt a rush of gratitude mixed with equal parts annoyance at his flair for lies and simple brother's love. Impulsively, she hugged him. Her torn sleeve ripped some more, but she didn't care.

"Thank you, Kellien. I'll make a deal with you. If the elf again insists that I take the lute, I will. But I want to at least give him the chance to change his mind. And besides," she grinned, "he might teach me a new ballad or two. Elven songs would, I imagine, go over very well with Queen-mother Ariel."

Her twin grinned in return. "That's my Gillien," he said. "Here." He removed his cape, placing it over her narrow shoulders and fastening the clasp at her throat. "Take this. You don't know how long this will take, and the nights turn cold around here. Try not to be gone too long, or all the supper will be eaten."

"By you."

"Of course!"

He winked at her, smiled, and sauntered off toward the meadow, whistling *The Saucy Wench of Winterfield*. Gillien watched him go, his limbs moving easily and gracefully, vicariously enjoying the freedom her twin had in his carefree manhood. He stopped, and picked a few of the wildflowers whose fragrance had so teased her nostrils. For their mother? she wondered. No, far more likely for Kellien's newest female friend. A ghost of a smile curved her lips, vanishing as she resolutely turned around to face the gates of Hallenore. There was no smell of flowers coming from the town; only smells of smoke, sweat, and the stale odors she associated with cities of any sort.

She again checked to make sure the lute was covered from prying eyes, then headed back toward the center of town. It was only then that she realized she did not know where the elf was staying—if he was indeed staying in town—nor even what his name was.

Her spirits crashed to her toes and she uttered a harsh, colorful curse. Kellien would have approved.

The night wore on as Gillien continued her search. At first, when it was still early in the evening, she confined herself to roaming through the crowds, looking for an inhumanly fair face with pointed ears and eyes half again as large as hers. She thought she saw him once, but then realized that it was another Falaran, equally handsome but a stranger nonetheless. She queried, but the elf knew nothing of his countryman. Gillien thanked him, disappointed, and continued.

After a couple of hours, her stomach audibly reminded her of the delicious meal her conscience had forced her to forego. She silenced the demanding rumble by purchasing a half-chicken from one of the vendors who was still open and taking advantage of the hungry crowds. Leaning against the stone wall that encircled the town square, she ate as quickly and daintily as she could, blowing on the hot meat and taking small bites. As she chewed, her eyes flitted from face to face. Strangers, all of them, even the bards against whom she had competed this afternoon. She'd have been welcome enough, had she played and sung as some of the others now did to the delight of the onlookers. But Gillien didn't dare even display her particular instrument, much less perform with it.

The hurried meal consumed, Gillien wiped her greasy hands on Kellien's cape and continued her quest. Now she went to the several inns in town and began to ask about the elf. Every hostelry in Hallenore was booked solid, but none was playing host to a visiting Falaran. More wasted hours crawled by as she followed up uncertain suggestions and still did not find the strange bard.

At last, tired and discouraged, she began to visit some of the lesser establishments in the more unsavory parts of town. Gillien knew that she was not conventionally pretty; she was far too tall, lean, and muscular for that. Yet she occasioned some less-than-polite looks in some of the smaller inns as she entered.

One of these was a small, dark, dirty little hovel that bore the incongruous name of The Castle. As Gillian entered, making as little noise as possible, she found the main gathering room more than usually dark and smoky. She stood by the door for a moment, blinking and letting her eyes—and nose—grow accustomed to the place.

The only light, it seemed, came from a large fire at the back of the room. No one was near the hearth, for it was far too late in the season to truly enjoy a fire's warmth, even at this hour of night. The patrons, whoever they were, were shadowy shapes huddled in corners. The dim light caught the flickers of belt buckles and studded leather—and the glint of weapons as well. There was silence, both before and after Gillien arrived, and despite the almost oppressive warmth in this dark room, she felt a chill. The air was thick with smoke and stale sweat.

She was grateful for the small knife at her hip; more grateful still that, unlike most women her age, she knew how to use it.

She glanced around for the innkeeper, but didn't find him at first. It was only after she had stood in the doorway for several long minutes, wondering if perhaps Kellien hadn't been right after all, that one of the shapes in the shadowy room stirred and hailed her.

"It looks like a fish out of water, lads!" he guffawed as he rose. "Well, my *lady*," he said archly, "how may I be of service?"

"I'm looking for someone," Gillien began in a shy, hesitant voice.

"Right here, darlin', I've got what you want!" came a hoarse voice. Whoops of harsh laughter and enthusiastic table-pounding ensued. Gillien cringed a little, swallowed hard, and drew herself up to her full stature.

"I'm looking for a Falaran elf." She kept her voice strong and steady this time. "He's a bard, I believe. Is he lodging here?"

The innkeeper had approached her, and now peered intently

into her face. Up close, the man was hard-faced, but not unkindly.

"Why, you're but a few moments behind him. Now there is an odd fellow, even for an elf," he said. "He's paid up for three months, on condition no one bothers him. Very insistent on his privacy, that one."

Gillien's heart sank. "But I have to see him. It's very important."

The innkeeper grinned, exposing brown teeth. "Aye, I'm sure it is," he said in a voice that implied just the opposite. "I daresay his desire for privacy didn't extend to the fairer sex. I know *mine* never does!"

He laughed loudly at his own joke, and Gillien winced at the fetid odor of his breath. "Ah, go ahead, missy. I'll let you see him. Down the hall there, third door on your left."

Gillien forced a smile. It was late, her feet hurt, and she cautiously permitted herself to hope that, finally, she had found the right Falaran elf. Eagerly leaving the main room and its thinly veiled hostility behind, she hurried down the corridor. This, at least, was lit by a single torch in its sconce. The light fluttered as she hastened by, casting grotesquely dancing shadows.

Gillien reached the third door on the left and tapped cautiously. Silence. She felt her spirits droop, and wondered with a sudden burst of irritation if the innkeeper had deliberately lied to her. She knocked again, harder.

"Why are you bothering to even knock?" came a faint voice. "You know what you have done to me. I shall not waste my strength to usher in my doom."

The words chilled Gillien. Who in all of Verold could the elf have been expecting? The voice was frail—was he ill, then, and having waking nightmares?

"Master Elf?" she said. "It's Gillien Songespynner. I've come to return your lute."

There was a silence on the other side of the door, then Gillien heard footsteps—slow, hesitant. The elf's voice came again, directly behind the door.

"If you are indeed Gillien, answer me this. I charged you with a task. What was it?"

"You gave me the lute and told me that I was to play in front of Their Majesties," Gillien replied, a bit confused. "And when I was done, I was to give the lute to Queen-mother Ariel."

Silence again. Gillien began to grow truly alarmed, and was seriously considering returning home and forgetting about the whole bizarre affair, when the knob turned. She was startled when the door opened slightly to see not the elf's face but a flaming brand. She drew back from the crackly heat with a startled cry.

"Show me your hands," the elf demanded.

"What?"

"Your hands, show me your hands!" She could see the elf's face now, eerily lit by the dancing flame. His eyes were dark, enormous, and terribly intense.

Utterly confused for the second time that night, Gillien obliged, extending first one hand and then the other, turning them over and even wriggling her fingers. Perhaps the elf thought she was carrying weapons. That made sense in this sort of a place, she had to admit.

"It is you, then!" The elf reached and tugged her inside, slamming the door after her and locking it at once. "Why in the name of The Lady have you returned, child?"

"I—I—" Gillien stammered, words failing her as she stared at the elf. He looked terrible. He had been pale and drawn when she had spoken with him several hours earlier, but now he appeared emaciated. His face was a white oval in the light of the burning stick he held, which he now tossed back into the fire. Cheekbones that would have been dramatically high now looked skeletal, the cheeks beneath them sunken in. Sweat poured down his face, making it shine unhealthily, and he trembled violently, although he was wrapped in nearly all of the bed linens. He turned back as if to sit on the bed, but stumbled. Gillien was there, a strong hand under his elbow. He caught her eye, gave her a quivering smile, and sank down.

"Well?"

"I thought you might have changed your mind—about the lute, I mean."

The elf's expression shifted from concern to something resembling horror.

"You brought it here? Now? Oh, child, what have you done?"

"I—I meant only for the best . . ."

He sighed and nodded. "I know. It seems humans do the worst damage for the best of reasons." A low groan escaped him as his body suddenly trembled violently. He gasped softly, and his hands on the blankets clenched hard.

Compassion rose in Gillien. This shabby, dirty room, with its unswept floor and its lumpy pallet, was ill suited to the lingering grace that showed on the sick elf's face. Even as she stared at him, worried, a thin trickle of blood escaped his mouth. He moved to wipe it away quickly with clumsy fingers, his eyes not meeting hers, as if he were embarrassed by his visible sickness. She had to get him out of here.

"Master Elf," she began, "I think you're very sick. Please, let me take you to a Healer."

The elf started at her words, shaking his head violently. "No! Your heart is kind, child, but I am far beyond anything your human Healers can do for me. Gillien, you must flee as I instructed you. Take the lute, guard it, give it to Queen-mother Ariel. Hurry!"

With more strength than she would have given him credit for, the elf seized her arm and propelled her to the window. He opened the wooden shutters and peered outside, his large-eyed gaze taking in everything. Turning to Gillien, he quite literally shoved her up against the sill, pushing her outside. She had to follow his direction, or fall. She obliged, swinging her legs over the sill. Poised half-in and half-out, she turned to the elf.

"What about—"

"*Go!*" hissed the elf. "Take the lute. Be safe, be careful, trust no one, and live, my child, live to write a glorious ballad about your adventure."

Gillien swung her other leg over the sill and stepped gingerly onto the darkened street. She had just turned to ask another question when a strange sensation shuddered up her arm. She stared down at the lute, open-mouthed and shocked into silence. The sensation, warm and tingly, came again, and suddenly Gillien felt as if someone had seized her and shaken her.

Caution!

The lute was sending her a warning! It was as clear, as obvious, as if it had been spoken, but she knew there had been no sound. Only a taut sense of readiness, emanating from the instrument, that communicated itself to her through a means she did not understand.

Gillien was no fool, though, and she stayed silent. She immediately dropped to her knees and edged away from the window, whose shutters the elf had not yet closed.

Not a heartbeat later, she heard a loud crash from inside. She gasped, and resisted the urge to look in the window. Instead, obeying the unspoken suggestion from the extraordinary instrument, she flattened herself against the stone exterior of the inn. Its cold seeped into her back. She clutched the lute to her breast, and *felt*—there was no other word for it—that it was trying to comfort her. She strained her ears, listening with every fiber of her being.

"Greetings, Jencir," came a voice. It was male, strong, and unspeakably arrogant, and Gillien disliked it at once. "You've led me a merry chase these last few weeks, but the game is over."

"It was over when you first poisoned me," came the elf's— Jencir's—strained voice.

"Was it? Your kind have a tendency to heal if left undisturbed. You were quick, Jencir, and did not get a full dose of my poison, else this chase would not have happened."

"It was . . . enough," sighed the elf.

"So it seems, in the end," agreed the stranger. "And now, I have half of what I was sent to find. I have you, the messenger. But where, errand-boy, is the message?"

"I do not understand what you mean."

"Oh, I think you do." The voice was soft, deceptively so. The more Gillien listened, the more it seemed familiar, but she couldn't quite place it. "As messages go, it's easier on the ear

than most, isn't it? The lute, Jencir. I saw you disappear behind the stage this evening and return empty-handed. Therefore, it must be the lute that is valuable, not your worthless
self. You had to have done one of two things—you must have
either hidden it or given it to someone."

"You are right. I did hide it. And you will never discover
where."

The stranger laughed. Gillien was shaking with terror, and
clutched the lute so tightly that she thought she might break it.
It continued to emit a sense of caution, and she bit hard on the
inside of her cheek to stifle any traitorous whimper of fear.

"You did not hide it. Careful as you were, some did notice
the transaction and were happy enough to point the way toward
the bardic encampment. But it was not there. And believe me,
I looked. Quite thoroughly."

Contempt laced the elf's voice. "I well know of the thoroughness of your kind." Then, Gillien heard a soft gasp of
pain, and winced in sympathy for the elf.

"Who did you give it to? Tell me! *Who was it?*"

Unbelievably, Jencir began to laugh. "Do you think I am as
feeble as that? I have seen The Lady! I have seen mountains
crumble at Her command! I have watched generations rise and
fall, and my will cannot be bent. You cannot hurt me anymore.
Torture me as you will, I am as silent as the grave to which I
shall shortly go. And when I have passed on, I shall walk with
The Lady in Her peaceful forests, while your kind has only
eternal nothingness awaiting you."

The stranger in the room snarled with anger, the sound suddenly mutating, becoming deeper, harsher. Despite herself,
Gillien gasped softly. Her panicky intake of breath, though,
was not heard above the terrible sounds that followed. The
stranger's voice was now low and guttural. There were words
in his speech, but they were garbled and incoherent.

Jencir shrieked once, a high, keen sound that sliced through
Gillien. The lute kept sending its silent messages of calm, but
she could no longer sense them. She would have thrown caution to the wind and plastered herself against the window, her
desperate need to know what in the Nightlands was transpiring

in that deceptively ordinary inn room outweighing her sense of
safety, had she not been literally paralyzed with fear. The horrible, unidentifiable noises continued—growls, hot, tearing
sounds, and a strange hissing noise. Then, all at once, they
stopped.

The silence was deafening.

Gillien breathed shallowly through her mouth, her heart racing furiously. No attack came exploding at her through the
window, as she had half-feared. The stillness from inside the
room stretched out into seconds, minutes.

She glanced down at the lute. It was no longer sending her
any feelings at all.

Licking her dry lips, Gillien forced her limbs to move. She
rose to her knees and crawled toward the window. For an instant she closed her eyes, gathering strength, then she slowly
brought her head around the corner and risked a glance into
the room.

She stared in numb horror at the atrocity that met her gaze.

She had expected to find Jencir dead, either murdered by
the interloper or else felled by the strange poison that was
clearly destroying him by the minute. She was prepared for a
corpse, perhaps even a savaged corpse.

She was not prepared for a clean-picked skeleton.

Jencir lay as he had fallen, his skeleton still intact, as if
someone had painstakingly laid him out for a burial. He lay
facedown, the skull resting on one bony cheek. The tiny, complex bones of one hand still curled around the hilt of his
sword. The other hand reached out, as if trying to claw its way
to freedom. Two rings glittered in the firelight, still poised
atop the finger bones they had decorated in life.

His clothes were gone, as was the leather that had com-
prised his pouch, though its contents were piled at his side.
The top of Jencir's skull had been removed and lay nearby,
like a shallow bowl. The inside of the skull was as clean, as
empty as if the bones had been a hundred years old.

Jencir had not simply been murdered. He had been *destroyed.*

Gillien turned away from the scene and vomited onto the

street. She began to sob, wiping at her mouth and futilely trying to muffle the telltale cries with her hand. And then the full
realization of what had happened hit her like a blow from a
mailed fist.

The stranger—the bastard, the monster or wizard or demon
who had done . . . *that* . . . to Jencir—he had been to her encampment.

The nightscape swirled before her for an instant, then a
cold, calculating reason took panic's place. Swiftly, Gillien
seized the hem of her despised skirts and tucked them into the
belt that encircled her waist. Grabbing the lute, she began to
run. Her strong legs, now unencumbered by heavy folds of
graceless fabric, took long, smooth strides across the uneven
earth of the narrow, litter-cluttered alleyway as Gillien, her
mind and purpose as clear as the night sky, raced toward her
encampment and the people she loved best in the world.

•

*When you've lost everything, then you've got nothing
to lose.*

—Byrnian folk saying

CHAPTER THREE

Gillien stumbled to a halt outside her family's encampment
twenty minutes later, her lungs laboring and her legs rubbery
with weakness. She felt giddy with relief; nothing looked out
of the ordinary. The fire had been properly extinguished, the
coals stirred and separated and covered with a layer of cooling
earth. The four ponies were tethered to the tree as they always
were this time of night. Her favorite, the trick pony Humble
whom she had trained herself, whickered with recognition and
tossed his dapple-gray head. The three caravan wagons bore
no sign of forced entry. The encampment was still, quiet,
peacefully asleep. Lanterns hanging on hooked bars shoved
into the ground illuminated a small patch of earth in front of
each caravan. The twinkling little flames inside looked like
captured glowflies.

She leaned forward, her hands on her bent knees, and

gasped in air. She let the lute tumble from suddenly nerveless fingers, and it bounced harmlessly to the earth. Her thudding heart slowed, and she was aware that she was grinning crazily. *Thank you,* she prayed in silent gratitude to the youthful god Hope. That god's sinister aspect, the crone Despair, had apparently averted her gaze tonight.

As soon as she caught her breath, she approached her own wagon. The emotional turmoil she had suffered through tonight had left her drained and exhausted. Sleep, untroubled by fear, in her own bed had never seemed so appealing to her as now. Gillien ascended the rickety steps, withdrew the lock-pick that was as constant an accessory as her knife, and swiftly picked the lock on her door. Her father, "Lev, the Man No Lock Can Hold," did not believe in keys. Each of his children knew the basic skills of lockpicking. "You never know when it might be useful," Papa had replied when Gillien asked him about learning such a dubious skill.

She eased open the door. "Dear gods!" she gasped.

In the dim light that came in through the partially opened door, Gillien saw that her neatly organized area had been utterly ransacked. Clothing, tools, what little jewelry she possessed, had been flung ruthlessly about. The feather mattress, Gillien's one true luxury, had been savagely torn open by a sharp knife, and gray-and-white goose down lay like a thick layer of snow atop the wreckage.

The peaceful scene that had greeted Gillien a moment ago when she had returned to her encampment had been a lie. This was the truth—the merciless chaos that had been her sleeping place. Unwanted, the words of the man who had murdered Jencir came back to her: *Believe me, I looked. Quite thoroughly.*

And if he had looked here with such brutal thoroughness . . .

Gillien backed out too quickly and tumbled down the stairs. Ignoring the pain of a bruised hip, she scrambled for the lantern. She seized it from its place on the iron hanger and raced toward her parents' wagon. Her tongue cleaved to her

suddenly dry mouth. Fear closed her throat. She could not call
out to her family, but at least she could act.

She clattered up the stairs, fumbling with the lock as she
cried silently, *no, please, no*! The door to the second caravan
gave way, and the pitiless lantern light revealed a scene of dis-
array similar to her own caravan—but with a horrible difference.

The block in Gillien's throat gave way to a hoarse sob of
shock and pain. Among the broken vases and furnishings, the
slashed pillows and mattresses, her parents lay where they had
been carelessly thrown, their bodies poised in unnatural an-
gles.

Gillien's knees gave way. She sank onto the floor, staring,
shaking her head in denial. A crooning, whimpering sound
came from her.

Mama . . . Papa . . .

She felt suddenly, dreadfully cold and began to shake un-
controllably. Finally, she steeled herself to look, to discover
how her parents had been slain. She found she could not rise.
Instead, she crawled on hands and knees until she knelt beside
her mother's body. Gingerly, she touched it. The flesh was
cold, rigid. They had been dead for some time.

Bile rose in her throat and tears threatened her vision. But
she had to look, to see what that monster had done to them.
She rolled her mother's corpse over to face her.

Astonishingly, the expression on the dead woman's face
was utterly peaceful. Her eyes were closed, the long dark
lashes brushing high cheekbones. Her face was in deep repose.
A thin line beneath her pointed chin and the sudden blackness
of a great deal of blood encrusted on her sleeping chemise revealed the manner of her murder.

Gillien scuttled back, tearing her disbelieving gaze from her
mother's body. She stared at her father. He lay on his side, but
his face was every bit as tranquil as his wife's, his throat just
as ruthlessly violated. Her parents had been murdered as they
slept.

The tears came then, mercifully dimming the terrible images. Gillien recalled her mother's fluid dancing, the way her

dark hair flowed about her slim, strong frame; she heard again her father's warm, comforting voice, felt his strong arms hugging her before she went onstage. She stumbled heavily, gracelessly, to her feet and fled before she could fling herself, sobbing, on their corpses. Her throat closed again as she clattered down the stairs to stand in front of the caravan belonging to her brother.

She knew now, beyond doubt, what awaited within. More than anything, she wanted to walk away without opening the door, but a desperate hope forced her to insert the lockpick in this, the third and final lock.

It turned, clicked. Gillien took a deep breath, and pulled open the door.

Something tumbled out on top of her. The lantern was knocked from her hands and went out as it hit the ground. She screamed, squirmed, shoving whatever it was away with stiff, frantic arms. It was only after she had wriggled out from under the weight and turned back, dagger in hand, that she realized that what had fallen posed no threat.

It was Kellien. He, too, was dead. Gillien grabbed for the one remaining lantern, knelt beside her brother, and shone the light into his dead face. His eyes were open, unseeing, fixed forever in a defiant stare of hatred at his murderer. He had clearly died fighting. Not for him the clean cut of the throat in the depths of sleep. Dark splotches on his clothes were mute testimony to a struggle; he had been stabbed several times. Gillien only prayed that her beloved twin had had the chance to strike a few blows of his own before Lady Death had come for him.

Overcome by loss, Gillien knelt by her brother's side. She stared at the lithe muscled frame, unwilling to believe her own eyes. Never again would Kellien sneak back into camp after dallying with a local girl to find that Gillien was waiting, ready to play a practical joke. Never again would those strong, slim hands toss a knife with uncanny accuracy, or coax music from an instrument, or gather wildflowers, or deliver the playful punch to her arm that signaled love. She had loved his laughter, so free and joyous. She couldn't believe that she would never hear it again. Kellien, so active and restless in life, was eternally still now.

Slow, deep anger started to burn in Gillien's heart, anger for the sheer senselessness of the three deaths. She was certain that the monstrous killer she had heard in Jencir's room was the one who had wielded the fatal knife, but the true reason for their deaths lay outside, resting quietly on the ground. Her face suddenly flushed with wrath, Gillien flung herself away from Kellien's side and seized the lute—the beautiful, unnaturally sweet-toned lute.

"He was looking for *you*!" she shrieked. "You gods-cursed, miserable thing, *you* did this to my family!" She raised it high over her head, about to slam it down on the stony earth, forever destroying its evil. But the instrument, clearly magical, stopped her.

No.

The simplicity and sincerity of the denial tingled up her arm. The lute was not afraid of its imminent destruction. It was merely communicating to her the simple fact that the deaths of her family were not its fault.

Gillien's anger dissolved, and she lowered her arms slowly. She stared at the instrument, then took it in both hands. "You are m-magical?"

An affirmation.

"Did . . ." Her voice thickened, but she continued. "Did you belong to the person who did . . . this . . . to my family? Are you his?"

NO!

The thought of any connection between itself and the murderer obviously offended the lute. The disavowal was so strong that Gillien nearly dropped the instrument.

Then its feeling changed. The instrument was sympathizing with her. Gillien's breathing hitched in surprise. She felt as though invisible arms were tentatively embracing her. The lute was doing its best to give her some comfort.

Her arms folded about it unconsciously and she sank slowly to the earth. It seemed warm to the touch. Her breathing hitched again, and then she cried bitterly. Hoarse sobs racked her frame and shook her slim shoulders. *Mama . . . Papa . . . Kellien.* Gone, all of them, their lives taken from them by some unknown brute.

Gillien sat and cried for a long, long time, cried until she had no more tears left, at least for the time being. Her face was hot as she reached to wipe away the final few tears that dripped down her cheeks into the high neck of her gown. She took a deep, shuddering breath. She was exhausted, drained, but felt a little better. A very little better. The first paroxysm of grief was gone and a welcome numbness was starting to replace it in her heart. She knew that in time the grief, the pain, would come again, but for now, she was able to think.

Trying to return the lute to the elf had saved her life—but had it cost her her family? She rejected that thought almost at once. Had she been here, playing the instrument and entertaining her family with its wondrously sweet music, the murderer would simply have killed her too and taken the lute. Her presence would not have saved them.

Gillien gazed down at the lute, aware that its mood had changed somehow. Responding to it, she felt a vague prickling of unease, and for a moment couldn't think why. Then her eyes widened and she caught her breath as she understood.

The lute was trying to remind her that her family had been killed for a reason. Someone wanted this lute so badly he had been willing to kill four people, including Jencir. But her being here now could be dangerous—very dangerous indeed.

"I need protection," she said aloud. And, she needed to report the murders. Feeling a little silly, she voiced her plan to the lute. "I'm going to turn you over to Reeve Herrick and tell him about the man who . . . who k-killed my f-family. Then I'm going to go to the nearest town . . . and try to forget all this."

The lute did not approve.

"But Reeve Herrick will know what to do better than me," Gillien protested. "And you would be safer with a soldier than a minstrel girl any day!" The lute still did not agree.

Her patience exhausted, Gillien rose and swung the lute over her shoulder. She had made her decision. Steeling her-

self, she reentered the caravans, trying to ignore the silent re-
proaches of the corpses within. Swiftly, she began to pack
everything she might need on a long journey: extra clothes,
dried meats and fruits, her lockpicking tools, jewelry for bar-
tering, her brother's throwing knives. She paused as she
grasped the little purse of coins that had been her prize at the
competition—gods, was it only a few hours ago? She felt as if
a lifetime had passed since that moment. She felt old, unspeakably tired, and dreadfully alone.

Not alone.

The lute, the strange, magical device that had cost her so
much, was with her, at least for right now. Oddly, she felt
comforted by its presence.

She transferred the lute to her right hand and swung her
makeshift pack over her left shoulder, then left her caravan for
the last time. She did not glance back.

Humble whickered in a friendly fashion as Gillien began to
saddle him. She spoke quietly to him, checking the girth and
then strapping her pack and, as an afterthought, the wrapped-
up lute to the beast. She wanted badly to carry the instrument
herself, but to have it on such display would draw unwanted
attention. She would leave the other horses and what was left
in her family's caravans for the town's use. Her immediate
destination was a place called Holding House, home of Reeve
Herrick. She gazed up at the stars, noting their position as her
father had taught her. They had traveled quite a way across the
sky; dawn wasn't too far away.

She had barely swung herself into the saddle when she
heard voices. Gillien's first thought, sending her stomach scut-
tling up to her throat, was that she hadn't been swift or clever
enough, that the killer who was after the lute had found her.
Then she realized that the voices were familiar ones. Her body
trembled with suddenly released tension. Taking a deep
breath, she squeezed Humble into a trot to greet the approaching figures.

By the light of the lamps they carried, Gillien saw that she
had indeed been correct. Heading straight toward her encampment was no less a figure than Reeve Herrick himself, along

with two of his reeve-men. Herrick had been, up until tonight, a jovial fellow, full of smiles and good wishes. Now his tall, lean frame sat arrow-straight in his saddle, and the expression on his face was grim.

Had someone heard something? Gillien wondered as she drew closer to the three mounted constables. That had to be it. Why else would Reeve Herrick have come here this time of night?

She leaned her weight back in the saddle slightly, and the obedient Humble halted. The night's strain showed on her face as Gillien waited for the men to draw up beside her. She opened her mouth to greet them, but Herrick's words snatched her welcome away.

"That's the girl. Arrest her."

Gillien stared, dumbfounded. It was only when the two men reached to pull her roughly off of Humble that she found her voice.

"Reeve Herrick! What are you—I was coming to find you! Someone killed—"

A hard, open-handed slap across her face knocked her into stunned silence. Her cheek smarted from the leather of his riding glove, and tears of mingled pain, incomprehension, and anger welled up in her eyes.

"I was here earlier," the reeve snarled, his handsome face drawn with disdain and rage, "to *congratulate* you. Imagine my surprise when your brother, dying in my arms, named you as his murderer!"

"No!" gasped Gillien. "That's not true! Take me to a Blesser and I'll prove it to you!" Gillien knew that many of the Blessers of the seven gods had the gift of mind magic. Some of them could read the thoughts of a willing volunteer. One might be able to block one's thoughts from a Blesser, but one could never create false images. Many towns Gillien had visited had Blessers come in routinely to examine witnesses—and suspects—for just such examples of truth.

"Silence, girl," growled the reeve. He turned his attention to her scanty possessions, rooting through the lumpy pack, while his reeve-men seized Gillien's hands and bound them behind her back. The knots were tight, too tight, and Gillien felt her hands beginning to tingle. Soon they would lose all feeling. She gritted her teeth and tried to twist her bound limbs into a more comfortable position as she continued to protest.

"Reeve Herrick, give me a chance to prove my innocence! I love my family." A lump rose in her throat, making it difficult to talk. "They're—they were—all I had. Why would I kill them?"

"Over *this*!" Triumphantly, the reeve produced the lute and brandished it accusingly in her face. "When you stole it, your family wished you to return it to its rightful owner. Instead, you silenced them to keep it. I know. He told me, Gillien. I went to get reinforcements, and conveniently found you returning to the place where you committed this atrocity."

Gillien could only shake her head at the lies the man was spinning. "No," she muttered. "I—

"And this is what you killed them with," continued Herrick, grasping Kellien's throwing knives. Gillien saw with a sinking feeling that she had, in her haste and confusion, packed them away still smeared with Kellien's lifeblood.

"You'll spend the night in prison and swing by the time the sun's fully in the sky."

"Take me to a Blesser!" Gillien demanded. "I have a right to prove my innocence and receive blessing!"

One of the men, a youngish fellow who had been watching the argument in silence, now spoke up. "The girl does have a right to speak to a Blesser within an hour of arrest, sir. It says so in—"

Irritated, Herrick waved a gloved hand dismissively. "There's no need for her to see a Blesser when I've heard a dying man's confession naming her as the killer."

The man frowned. "But, sir, you always—"

"Am I reeve here or you?" Herrick shot back. The man's eyes widened in surprise and he shrank from the anger in his superior's voice. Herrick gentled at once. "Apologies, Edel, but you didn't see what I saw—hear what I heard. The crime is brutal. Go and see for yourself if you wish."

Edel did as he was told while the third man, clearly unused

to searching female criminals for weapons, awkwardly patted Gillien's waist. He found none; Gillien's weapons were all in her bags. He searched no further and thus failed to find the small pouch Gillien wore on a thong about her slender neck, hidden under her dress. For that she was grateful; her sharp mind was already plotting an escape.

Edel returned, stumbling slightly, his face milky-pale with horror. Gillien, though she knew she was innocent, nonetheless felt her heart sink into her boots under the shocked gaze of the reeve-man. His lips moved, and Gillien realized he was murmuring a prayer: *Sweet Lady Death, come not so for me.*

"I did not do it," she said in a low voice.

Edel seemed not to hear her. He stared at her, stared through her, and kept repeating, "Sweet Lady Death, come not so for me."

"Now, Edel, you understand," said Herrick. Edel nodded. He seized Gillien in his strong arms and hoisted her into the saddle, not caring if he bruised her. Gillien bit her lip against the bumps. Clearly, protest was useless. She sat silently, encircled by the reeve and his men, as the group made their way toward Hallenore and Holding House.

Holding House was Hallenore's legal center. In its previous existence it had been a winery, when Hallenore had been a simple farming community and the vines had yielded their nectar to grace the local lord's table. Two hundred years ago, when war had broken out between the humans and the Falaran elves, local crops had been destroyed. The lord had donated his lands for His Majesty's use, and the area briefly played host to hundreds of soldiers who amassed here at the border before pushing on over the now-shattered Kyras into Falarah. By the end of the war, the vineyards had been damaged beyond repair. Some of those soldiers stayed after the war, and gradually the town of Hallenore came into being.

The winery had served as the headquarters for the area during the war. It continued in that function now, although on a far lesser scale. Only a dozen or so men patrolled the little town. Reeve Herrick lived here, presiding over the comings and goings of his constabulary and keeping watch over the small local armory, also located in Holding House.

The building was at one end of the town square, and Gillien had passed it often. Now she gazed at it as she approached, not from the front stairs as a guest, but from the underside, into the cellars, as a prisoner. The heavyset guard standing his watch at the thick wooden door looked up inquiringly at her, and she averted her eyes.

"What's she in for, sir?"

"The murders of all three members of her family," Herrick replied shortly. As had Edel before him, the guard took another shocked look at Gillien. This time, she didn't even try to defend herself. These men had already condemned her in their hearts. She kept her eyes on the sloping, hard-packed earth that led up to the cellar door.

The guard threw the bolt and Gillien was dragged off Humble. "The stolen property will be held until its rightful owner can be found," said Herrick. "The city of Hallenore confiscates all your other possessions, including your horse. Your purse," he added, holding up her winnings of just a few hours ago, "will pay for your keep while you are here."

He shepherded Gillien inside. Trying not to appear too obvious, Gillien cast a hawk's eye about her prison. Flickering torches in sconces lined the walls, providing only enough illumination for her to get a general impression. Most of the place was swathed in shadow. Despite the passing of two centuries, the bowels of the former wine cellar still smelled faintly of fermented grapes. The old fragrance mingled with the newer scent of musty straw that crunched slightly beneath their feet.

Ahead loomed a wall of stone, obviously built at a later date than the rest of the house. Herrick, his left hand gripping Gillien's right arm firmly, steered her down the corridor formed between the newer stone room and the old stone of the original building, then turned left. Ahead was a small set of stairs that Gillien assumed led up to the main part of the house. Several large casks lined the walls. Some of them might still hold ale and wine, as they surely would have a few centuries ago, Gillien supposed. Most of them, though, probably contained other goods. Above the third cask, mounted on a simple hook, was a ring of skeleton keys. Gillien's attention narrowed from observing everything to focusing only on the keys. She watched, silent and feigning dejection, as the reeve plucked the ring from the hook.

From this side, Gillien could see that there was something behind the newer wall. The entrance was by way of a large wooden door, with a small latched trap door cut into it at about eye level and closed from the outside with a lock and a heavy wooden bar. Herrick lifted the bar up, inserted a key and twisted. The door didn't open. The reeve frowned and tried another key. There was a click as the key turned in the lock this time and the door opened.

Well oiled, Gillien thought to herself, though clearly Herrick doesn't perform this job often enough to know which damned key opens which door.

Herrick shoved her inside a narrow corridor lined with three cells on either side. He picked the middle one on the left, opened it after two tries, and motioned for her to enter. Gillien did so obediently, her mind racing even as she pretended fatigue and resignation. The room was small, only about eight feet by ten, she guessed. The door was heavy and wooden, with no bars to see through. In fact, there were no windows anywhere in the cell. There was no bed, either, and the chamber pot in the far corner smelled like it hadn't been emptied within recent memory.

Herrick began to close the door. "Wait!" Gillien yelped. "Aren't you going to untie me?"

The reeve gazed speculatively at her. "Why should I?"

She gave him a harried look. "Where am I going to go?"

"But why do you need your hands free?"

She wanted her hands free to pick the lock, of course, but she could hardly say that. A more obvious, more embarrassing, response suggested itself, and a blush rose to her cheeks as she spoke.

"I'll need to relieve myself. I can't—men don't—I have clothes in the way," she finished.

A cruel grin spread across Reeve Herrick's face. "Soil yourself, bitch," he said pleasantly, then slammed the door closed.

Gillien jumped, both at the coarseness of his response and the unexpectedly loud sound of the slamming door. The darkness pressed in on her like something physical. Gradually her eyes adjusted enough so she could make out the thin yellow line that marked the door's location.

Moving slowly, quietly, Gillien backed up until her bound hands, palms out, could feel the stone. She swore under her breath. It was quite smooth. Moving along, she patted the chill, damp stone gently, hoping for a rough spot upon which she could fray the rope. Her foot came into contact with something small on the stone floor. Before she could halt the motion, and just as she recalled what it was, she had kicked over the contents of the filthy chamberpot. The stench wafted upwards.

Coughing, Gillien stumbled to the opposite corner. Her boot squelched; she'd stepped in the foul little pool. She swallowed hard, determined not to add the contents of her stomach to the noxious mess on the floor.

Moving as far away from the spilled puddle as she could, she sat down and rolled over onto her back. Kellien had often teased her about the almost boyish slimness of her hips, but now that source of embarrassment became a blessing for the young prisoner. Like her sibling, Gillien also knew tumbling and acrobatics, and that flexibility came into play as she slid her hands down past her hips and buttocks, bringing her knees close to her chest. It was not an easy task, nor a swift one. Twice Gillien felt her joints seize up and was convinced that the guards would find her in this compromising—and screamingly painful—position in the morning. Sweat broke out on her brow despite the damp chill of the place. She swallowed hard, ignored the pain and forced herself to relax. Each time, she was able to press on.

At last, after what seemed an eternity, she was able to draw first one leg and then the other through the circle of her arms. She gasped in relief and stood upright. Now it was merely a matter of twisting and chewing. The sweat she had worked up

was useful, as it made the bindings slippery. She twisted, remembering the hundreds of times she had watched her father
escape from knots far more complex than these, until finally a
strong tug pulled her right hand free.

Gillien wanted to cheer, but concentrated instead on pulling
off the cursed rope from her left wrist. She let it drop to the
floor and an instant later regretted the decision. She might
need that rope before the night—morning?—was through.
Bending to pick it up, she paused suddenly as she heard the
door to the outer wall swing open.

Quickly, she grabbed the rope, put her hands behind her
back, and braced herself for the sudden opening of her own
door. It did not come. Instead, another sound pierced the darkness—a hoot of drunken laughter and snatches of a song. Unexpected and unwanted tears filled Gillien's eyes yet again as
she recognized the tune: Kellien's favorite, *The Saucy Wench
of Winterfield.*

"Come on, Aldo, you know what you're supposed to do,"
came the guard's voice. He did not sound particularly irritated.
The guard and the singer were approaching Gillien's cell. She
tensed, wondering if she was going to have company, but the
guard opened the door in the cell to her left.

"Ah, yes, th' usual abode," slurred the drunken man. "Goo'-
ness me, it's nastier than it was las' time I was here."

The guard laughed without any real malice. "In you go, old
man." Gillien heard the door clang shut.

"Wai' minit. Where's m' food?" the drunkard demanded.

"You'll eat at daybreak, Aldo."

"Wan' eat *now.*"

"You want supper, you need to get yourself arrested before
midnight. After midnight, you wait for the morning meal.
Now, get some sleep. There's time for a quick nap before
dawn."

The guard left, closing the outer door behind him and dropping the bolt back into place. Gillien waited a few minutes,
then continued with her plan. Her fellow prisoner began to
sing again, and Gillien winced. At least, if he kept this up, he
would drown out any noise she might make.

Tucking the rope under her arm, she withdrew the small pouch that hung between her breasts. It contained two lock-picks, one short and one long. The minstrel took a deep breath to steady herself, tried to block out the racket Aldo the drunk-ard was making, and stepped forward. She patted the door, lo-cating the lock in the darkness with no trouble. Inserting her little finger, she felt about for what information she could dis-cover; her eyes were of no use here. She'd have to work by feel.

Gently, she inserted the slim pick and began to work it about. It stuck unexpectedly. She applied more pressure, and suddenly the pick fairly leaped out of her hands. Nerves frayed raw, Gillien almost started to cry. More long minutes ticked by as she felt about in the straw for the little pick. As she searched, she felt a vague discomfort nagging at the back of her mind, as if there was something she couldn't remember. At last, she located the pick, stood up, and tried again.

The lock wasn't the worst one she'd encountered, but it was bad enough. Her concentration wasn't all it might have been, either. Her hands were starting to go numb with the chill dampness of the cell; and what with the singer in the other cell, listening for the approach of the guard and . . . something else . . .

She paused, remembering to keep a firm grip on her tools, and concentrated on that other thing. Suddenly, she realized what it was.

The lute was calling to her. Somehow, even without physi-cal contact, it was crying out for help, making her feel tense and worried.

"I'm coming," she whispered under her breath. "Now just hush and let me concentrate, will you?"

Hurry . . . danger . . .

"Damn it, I've gathered that already," she muttered, throw-ing her full attention into the task at hand. She insinuated the second lockpick and jockeyed it around for a second or two, then, holding them both firmly in place, twisted them simulta-neously. There was a click, and the door swayed forward an inch.

"Thank you, Papa," Gillien said softly to her father's spirit, then pushed the door open the rest of the way.

She blinked even in the dim light of the torches and paused, waiting and listening. The only sound was her neighbor's raucous singing and the constant, inaudible pleading of the instrument. Gillien pushed the door closed and moved quickly down the corridor. This one, she mused to herself, was going to be a problem. The lock itself would probably yield without too big a fight. But how to lift the beam that held it closed on the other side of the door?

She was glad now that she had kept the rope. Perhaps she could snake the rope down, get a hook around the beam somehow, and yank it up. Perhaps. But with what? Gillien refused to sacrifice either of her lockpicking tools; they had more than proved their worth. She stood on her tiptoes and pushed open the little trap-door window, to see if there was anything outside that might prove useful—and gasped.

Gazing back at her with mild curiosity was a pair of wide brown eyes. "Good morning," said the stranger on the other side of the door.

*And the Lord descended into the Nightlands, where
things born of fear and hate guard him, repaying his evils
with their own.*

—from *The Book of The Lady*

CHAPTER FOUR

Gillien was so shocked she couldn't speak. She simply
stared, her eyes enormous. In the back of her brain, like the
scrabbling of a kitten trying to claw its way through a closed
door, she felt the lute still calling her. She had to escape, *had*
to, but by all the gods she could not think of anything to do.

"Eh, there, is that young Cadby?" came the voice of the
man in the cell, halting his drunken singing for the moment.

The brown eyes on the other side of the prison door crinkled
as their owner suddenly smiled. They looked kind, Gillien
thought distractedly.

"Yes, indeed, Aldo. I hear you've learned a new song since
our last meeting." The voice was kind, too, hinting at mirth.

"Ah, if it's Cadby, then t'day mus' be Lisdae," said Aldo
smugly.

Now the owner of the friendly brown eyes laughed aloud.
"Aldo's way of reckoning the week, I'm afraid, hinges on
which Blesser comes to get him out of prison on which day."

Hope washed over Gillien in a wave so powerful that her knees buckled. She reached and grabbed onto the wooden frame of the tiny window.

"You . . . you're a Blesser?" she said weakly. She thought she might faint from relief, and indeed, her voice sounded very small and distant, as if it came from far away. Swiftly the stranger, the Blesser, placed his strong hand over hers to steady it. That hand felt warm and comforting.

"Yes, indeed, child, Blesser Cadby of Light's Temple." He spoke clearly and slowly, for which she was grateful. "Today is Lisdae, so I am here at Light's hour of dawn. Tomorrow is Losdae, and Love's Blesser will come to visit the prisoners at midmorning, and so on throughout the week."

Gillien nodded and took a deep breath.

"And you must be the little murderess the guard warned me about." She glanced up at him, fear in her eyes. Would he, too, condemn her out of hand? But the kind face was smiling a little. "You don't look like someone who could murder three people without raising the hue and cry, I must admit."

"Oh, Blesser Cadby, I didn't!" New strength flooded her and she clutched hard at his hand. "Reeve Herrick . . . said I'd swing today . . . said I couldn't see a Blesser, and I didn't do it, I didn't kill them, oh, gods, someone has to believe me . . ." Gillien was aware that she was becoming hysterical, but she couldn't stop it. She could be brave in the face of encroaching death, but this unlooked-for hope had completely undone her.

Blesser Cadby was frowning now, anger sitting awkwardly upon a face clearly more used to gentleness.

"What? Denied you access to a Blesser? What in the name of Light was he thinking of? No, no, child, no one in Byrn *ever* is denied Blessing before death. You are telling me you didn't kill your family?"

Gillien blinked, frantically trying to clear her vision. The lute hummed at the back of her mind. She tried to shut it out. She couldn't retrieve it unless she was free, and in order to win her freedom she had to convince Blesser Cadby to let her out.

"No, I did not," she stated. "Blesser—can you read thoughts?"

"Part of my training, child—what is your name, anyway?"

"Gillien Songespynner."

"Very well, Gillien Songespynner. If you'll relax your death grip on my hand and move your face a little closer to the window, I'll see what I can do to help you prove your innocence."

Gillien blushed and immediately loosened her grasp. She took an unsteady step forward and placed her forehead against the small aperture.

"Have you ever done this before?"

"No. But I've heard about it."

"Well, try to calm yourself, if you can. Close your eyes— that's the girl. I'm going to touch your forehead—like so," he said, and Gillien felt gentle fingertips brushing her temples. "Good, very good. Calm . . . calm . . . that's it."

The minstrel felt her heart slow, felt the frantic fog that had clouded her mind evaporate. The plaintive call of the lute did not cease, but she was able to push it aside under the calming voice of Blesser Cadby.

"Now. Where were you at the time of the murders?"

Murders. The word made her tense, but she started to answer. "I was—"

"Shh, shh," Cadby soothed, "don't tell me—picture it in your mind."

She did, and suddenly she was back outside Jencir's door. She saw again the dark hallway, the rough wooden door. Gillien gasped, but did not pull away from the Blesser's cool fingers. The image in her mind was so real, so clear, it was as if she were actually reliving the incident. There was one major difference, though. This time, she was not seeing the scene through her own eyes, as it had really happened, but from an outsider's viewpoint. She assumed that the eyes through which she was now seeing belonged to Cadby. Gillien saw herself, tired and disheveled, clutching the lute with one hand as she tentatively tapped on the door.

"Why are you bothering to even knock? You know what you have done to me. I shall not waste my strength to usher in my doom."

Jencir's voice. Gillien, her eyes still tightly closed, winced a little. She dreaded going through this whole terrible night a second time, even though she knew it was the only thing that could save her life.

"Master Elf? It's Gillien Songespynner. I've come to return your lute."

Her own voice, sounding higher, sweeter, than it sounded in her own ears. The scene continued as it had a few hours before, and Gillien watched herself enter the dingy room, converse with the ill Falaran. Her heart hurt in sympathy for him, knowing what was about to happen to him. She saw herself shoved out the window to cower outside, heard the noises of the disaster within. Dimly, she heard Cadby's swift intake of breath as the Gillien of memory surveyed the ghastly scene of Jencir's gruesome death.

Then, oh, then, the seemingly endless run home, the false relief, the discovery of the bodies, ending with Gillien arrested and imprisoned by the man she had turned to for help.

Then, abruptly, the image was gone. Cadby had broken contact. Gillien blinked, slightly dazed, and glanced at the Blesser.

The young man's amiable face was covered with tears. Gillien was surprised. She had expected the Blesser of Light to be horrified, but Cadby was actually sobbing. He saw her reaction and swallowed hard. Haltingly, he explained.

"I didn't just watch what happened," he managed, wiping his face with his hands. "When I read thoughts, I become the person I read. I felt all your pain . . . I felt the lute . . ." He took a deep breath and regained a semblance of calm.

"I like and respect our reeve, but tonight he was a fool. There was no need to inflict more suffering upon you, Gillien. Sweet rays of Light, you've undergone more than your share tonight. Where are the—there they are."

Gillien heard the key turn in the lock, and wondered if she'd ever heard a sweeter sound in her life.

"You . . . you believe me?"

The look Cadby shot her was actually harsh. "It's not a question of belief, it's knowledge. I *know* you're innocent—I was there. Come. I don't think Herrick's awake yet, but the least I can do is rouse him out of bed after what he put you through."

He pulled open the door and Gillien got a full look at her savior. His attractiveness extended beyond pleasant features to a tall, slim, strong body that was modestly covered by his clerical white robe. She wondered if he was much older than she; he certainly didn't look it. For the moment, though, despite his tear-streaked face and reddened eyes, he was completely in charge. Gillien didn't protest as Cadby seized her hand in a firm grip and led her up the stairs.

"Will you take the lute to Kasselton?" he asked as they took the stairs at a quick pace.

"I . . . I don't know."

A few hours ago, she had fully intended to turn it over to Reeve Herrick, but the man had proved vindictive and untrustworthy. The lute had formed some kind of bond with her, of that she was certain. She wasn't so sure now that she was ready to entrust it to other hands. If a guard went with her, to protect her, though . . .

"Yes," she decided.

"May I make a suggestion?"

"Please. I need all the help I can get."

"Don't take the King's Road straight north to Kasselton," Cadby advised. "It's the most direct route and your—your enemy will probably expect you to go that way. Take the Queen's Road south instead. It's more circuitous, less traveled. And it'll take you west, through the town of Riverfork. When you're there, seek out Blesser Lucan of Light's Temple. I was a Tender under him. Tell him I sent you, and he'll help you."

Gillien listened with only half an ear. As if the lute knew she was on her way, its call increased in intensity. Cadby led her down a corridor and rounded a corner. He stopped so abruptly that she bumped into him, then peered cautiously from behind the Blesser.

They were standing in the doorway of what was clearly Reeve Herrick's personal quarters. In the center of the room, a

small brazier emitted what felt to Gillien like a great deal of
heat. A pallet, neatly made, stood in a corner. Clearly, the
reeve had not yet been to bed. Fresh rushes were strewn over
the wooden floor. Tapestries, not very ornate but thick and
warm, lined all four walls to cut the damp chill of the place. A
plain chest was shoved into one corner, and an empty chamber
pot sat in another. A simple table and chair were the only other
furnishings besides the pallet. At this table sat the Reeve of
Hallenore, the lute and Gillien's sack of belongings in front of
him.

Herrick stared intently at the lute, then reached to touch
it. He must have heard Cadby and Gillien's arrival, for they
had made no attempt at stealth, but he ignored them completely. The lute's plaintive, silent call to Gillien doubled,
trebled in intensity, but she held her tongue. Cadby was her
voice now.

Silently she willed him to speak, but clearly he was waiting
for acknowledgement. She kept quiet, following the Blesser
like a second shadow as he moved forward to stand in front of
the reeve's table. She kept her eyes on Herrick, and wondered
how he could possibly not feel the lute's distress.

Something else about him bothered her. Something had
changed from when she had seen him a few hours earlier. Part
of her training was in observation of people, their behavior,
their looks, their manner of dress. Often, it prompted a song
that would elicit smiles and coins. What was different about
Herrick now? He wore the same clothes—

Her eyes flew wide. He wore the same clothes, yes, but he
had removed his riding gloves. Gillien clearly remembered the
sting of that leather as he had slapped her across the face.
Now, as Herrick ran his fingers over the smooth blond wood
of the instrument, Gillien saw that his hands were . . . there
was no other word for it, *deformed* in some bizarre fashion.
The palms and undersides of the fingers had no lines. They
were completely smooth, with none of the telltale creases and
whorls that Gillien's mother had taught her to read. Idiotically,
Gillien wondered what Mama would have done had Herrick
presented his palm for a fortune telling. Probably have said

something like, "I see no troubles in your future." She always knew the right thing to say.

Now Herrick raised his head and stared at Gillien in frightening silence. His eyes were cold, impersonal, and as hard as stone. Her heart began to race again, and she thought she could surely see trouble in her own future, palm creases or no.

"Reeve Herrick," began Cadby, "I'm afraid you and your men have made a grave error in arresting Gillien Songespynner for the murders of her family. I have read her thoughts and—"

As far as Herrick was concerned, Cadby might have been no more than a fly buzzing about in midsummer. His gaze never left Gillien's face.

"Tell me about the lute," Herrick said in a flat voice.

Dear gods, what does he know? Gillien wondered, suddenly knowing how the rabbit feels when the fox's breath is hot on its heels. The lute hummed in her head, also concerned. She summoned all her theatrical ability, which was considerable, and looked innocently confused.

"What about the lute? I didn't steal it, Blesser Cadby can confirm that."

"Yes, I—"

Herrick interrupted the Blesser as if he hadn't even spoken. "What do you know about it? What was your link with Jencir? Why was the lute so important?"

She shrugged her shoulders, feigning ignorance. "I don't know anything about it. I'd never met Jencir before. It's just a simple instrument . . . isn't it?"

But under the reeve's unblinking, almost dead gaze, her confidence began to waver. She took a slight step backward, toward the door.

Faster than she'd ever seen anyone move, Reeve Herrick leaped from his desk—leaped *over* his desk—to block her way, slamming the door shut and leaning on it. Cadby's hand clenched hers tightly, grinding the bones together. She glanced at him. She didn't need to read thoughts to know that he was frightened and angry.

But his voice revealed nothing. "Gillien, get behind me, child," he said in a shockingly tranquil tone.

The lute's cry was nearly deafening now. She couldn't take it any more. Gillien looked from the priest to the reeve to the lute, and made a mad lunge for it.

A terrible cry silenced the lute's plaintive call and Gillien's heart thumped wildly in her chest. She froze midway to the table, transfixed, her eyes on Herrick. That horrible sound, a nightmarish combination of growls, hisses and guttural croaks, was horribly familiar. Gillien wondered if she would ever forget the dreadful noise. She had first heard it the evening just past, emanating from Jencir's room.

But this time, the harrowing sound came from Reeve Herrick.

Gillien's mouth went dry as old bones, but she could not tear her eyes away from the hideous transformation that was taking place. As she watched, mesmerized with horror, the tall form that was Reeve Herrick began to shift. Like wax melting from a candle, the handsome face mutated into a grotesque visage, part animal, part insect, and part insanity. A mouth, fully half the size of the face and crammed with an unimaginable number of needle-like teeth, opened and closed. Yellow ichor dripped from the monster's maw and sizzled as it hit the floor. It began to foam and burn tiny holes right through the wood.

The girl stared blindly at the hissing holes. Hadn't Jencir said something about poison? All this time Gillien had thought that the elf had been murdered by a human being—an evil one, but human nonetheless. Dear gods, dear gods, she knew better now.

A second head erupted from the thing's neck. This one was similar to the first, but in an advanced stage of decomposition. As it shrieked angrily, part of its forehead sloughed off, spattering on the wooden floor before eating through it. A third head twisted its way out of the thickening neck. This was utterly skeletal. It made no sound as it opened and shut its mouth save the *click-click* of that dreadful mouthful of teeth.

The transformation shuddered along Herrick's body, distorting it, bloating it, covering it with furry scales and strange, claw-covered paws. A barbed tail lashed, poison dripping from its stinger.

She knew what the creature was. It was a Nightlands Demon, a thing literally born of someone's fear-fraught dreams. Gillien wondered wildly what terrors had plagued the unhappy person who had dreamed up the thing that now stood before her.

The transmutation had taken only a few seconds. Now, its change complete, the Nightlands Demon swiveled its three ghastly heads in Gillien's direction. Four eyes and two empty sockets gazed at her, and then the beast began to lumber towards her.

She might have stayed there, hand frozen in the act of reaching for the lute, eyes wide with sheer terror, and let the beast come for her. But the lute apparently recovered faster than she, and sent a final, demanding shriek into Gillien's brain.

She started. The thing was big, and deadly, but it was slow, as slow in this form as it had been swift in the guise of Reeve Herrick. Her heart in her mouth, Gillien lunged for the lute and her bag of possessions, seized them, and raced for the door.

The demon stood between her and the door, almost but not quite blocking her escape. It was so large now that its head, stinger, and dangerous appendages were only a few feet away from her as she dashed past it. The thing moved to intercept her, two heads bellowing angry cries while the third skull clicked its displeasure.

"No!"

In her terror Gillien had forgotten about the young Blesser of Light. Now Cadby charged forward, distracting the dreadful creature for the precious seconds she needed to reach freedom. Cadby shrieked, his voice treble with agony, as the monster's spittle splattered on his upturned face. The vicious fluid greedily ate away at the youth's handsome features.

"Cadby!"

Gillien clutched the lute, torn between loyalty to the instrument and responsibility for the one who had freed her.

"Run, Gillien!" screamed Cadby. "Grant me thy Light, O god!"

Blind and in agony as he was, Cadby was still able to make a gesture with his hands. Light, brighter than the sun at full height, flooded the room. The monster emitted a terrible cry, shrill and piercing. Gillien screwed her eyes shut against its radiance, but red and blue patterns continued to dance behind her closed lids. She opened them a slit and saw the monster writhing in agony.

Its dreadful form began to dissolve, turn into a puddle of brownish-green goo. Its upper torso with the three malevolent heads simply collapsed, falling directly on top of the unfortunate Blesser. Cadby's screams were suddenly muffled as melting flesh, his own and that of the creature, filled his mouth and dripped down into his lungs.

Gillien threw herself upon the door. Reeve Herrick—the Nightlands Demon—had not locked it, thank the gods. Her hands were sweaty with terror and it took a few seconds before she could get a good grip on the knob. The lute's cry and the dreadful noises behind her frayed her already strained nerves to the breaking point. At last the knob turned and Gillien bolted through the door.

She skidded to a halt before the door to freedom. Unable to help herself, she risked a glance back at the reeve's quarters.

She could no longer hear Cadby's piercing screams, and for that she was grateful. His suffering was over. The monster, though, seemed to be in pain itself. It had no shape whatsoever now; it was merely a foul pool of thick sludge. The light conjured by Cadby had destroyed it.

Then, no longer supported by the dead priest's will, the sunlight called by the Blesser faded, like an abrupt sunset. And to Gillien's unspeakable horror, the puddle bubbled, shifted, and began to reform. The face of Reeve Herrick stared furiously at her, grotesquely perched atop a serpentine neck.

A sudden grab at her back made Gillien stumble forward. She whipped her head around and encountered the angry visage of a guard. He must have heard the cries from inside and come to investigate.

"What in the Nightlands—" his voice broke off as his gaze left Gillien's ghost-pale face and he saw the atrocity that was reforming by the minute. "Death's breath!" he cried. All the color had drained out of his own face, and he stared, riveted by the spectacle before him.

Gillien didn't wait to see if he would attack or flee. She ducked under his arm and was out the door, racing as fast as her legs would carry her, toward the stables.

Dawn was well and truly here now, and she had no problem seeing where she was going. The stables were directly across from the door to Holding House. She could even see the shapes of the animals within, made ghostly by the dim light of the early morning.

"Humble!" she yelled. There was no use being surreptitious anymore. From the noises behind her coming from Holding House, she knew that the guards were fully roused. She hoped the monster would keep them occupied while she fled.

She had no such good luck. Barely had she reached the open stable door than an angry male voice cried out for her to stop. She ignored it, running down the corridor between the stalls. Gillien slipped on the muck-filled straw; apparently the stables of Holding House were not kept as clean as they ought to have been. The hard-packed earth rose up to meet her with staggering speed.

Gillien knew how to fall properly. Tumbling was another skill that had been shared by the whole performing family. When she planned it, Gillien could flip off of Humble, turn over three times in the air, and land easily on her feet. Now, however, her long legs betrayed her, tangling up with one another with inevitable results. The one thing she could and did do was raise the lute out of harm's way just before the impact of her fall knocked the air out of her lungs with an abrupt, painful *whoosh*. She lay there for an instant, her body refusing to listen to her brain's command to rise and run.

She heard steps behind her. Forcing herself to inhale and

move, Gillien rolled over. The guard was a dark silhouette in
the doorway.

"Now, girl," he said in artificial tones of concern, "if you've
done nothing wrong you've got nothing t' be afraid of. Come
on out."

Dear gods, he can't think that *I'm* responsible for all those
guards howling in there! Gillien thought, shocked. She took
another painful, forced breath and stumbled to her feet.

The guard was moving slowly down the corridor. She could
see him better than he could see her in the dimness of the unil-
luminated stable.

"Nothing t' be afraid of," he said.

She dropped to one knee and began to rummage through her
pack. Her frantic hands discovered no weapons, only what
seemed to her at this instant like a dreadful amount of clothes,
dried fruit and other completely useless items.

If she were just on Humble, she—Gillien gasped as an idea
came to her. It could work! At any rate, it was her only
chance.

"Why look, Humble," she said, standing up straight and
making deliberately broad gestures with her arms. The pony
whickered at his name and turned to look at her.

Please, gods, let there be enough light for him to see me!
Gillien prayed. The guard stopped, confused. Gillien continued.

"It's that time of year," she bellowed. "It's time to pay the
tax collector. I don't like him—do you, Humble?"

The dapple-gray horse, recognizing the routine, shook his
head and whickered. He waited, ears pricked, for the next seg-
ment.

The guard dropped his patient tone. "Tax collector? Are you
crazy as well as a killer, you little bitch?" He started towards
her again, but would have to pass behind the pony to get to
her.

Gillien waited, though every second was an agony, until the
guard's progress brought him directly behind Humble's gently
swishing tail. "I think he's a *horse's ass* and ought to be

kicked out of office!" Gillien cried, making the wild gestures that cued Humble as to his next course of action.

At the signal, Humble obediently raised his hindquarters and kicked out violently with both rear feet. They connected soundly with the guard's midsection. Gillien heard an audible crack as the man's ribs gave way beneath the power of the trick pony's iron-shod hooves. The force threw him backward into the rear of another horse. Startled, this beast kicked out too, and one hoof landed solidly on the man's helmeted head. He grunted, and went down.

Humble craned his neck to look at the commotion behind him. He whinnied, confused, and looked to Gillien. There had never been anyone standing behind him before when he performed this trick.

Gillien felt weak as she realized her plan had worked. For a long moment, she couldn't even speak. "Good Humble," she said aloud at last. "I think you saved my life, fellow." She moved forward slowly, cautiously. The guard did not stir. "Oh, dear gods, Humble . . . I think we killed him!"

She knelt in front of the prostrate guard. At first he didn't seem to be moving at all, but then Gillien detected a faint rise and fall in the chest. She closed her eyes in relief. Humble's kick had clearly broken ribs, but the second kick from the other horse would surely have killed him without his helmet.

"I'm sorry," Gillien said to the unconscious guard, and she meant it. "I just have to leave . . . there was no other way . . ." Blinking back tears of contrition, she slipped into Humble's stall and untied him, patting the beast as she did go. Humble, too, clearly felt remorse. His brown eyes seemed to say to her, *that wasn't supposed to happen.*

"I know, I know," she soothed. The pony's bit and bridle were in place, but his saddle had been removed. There was no time to saddle Humble herself; she would simply have to ride bareback. Gillien led her mount carefully around the fallen guard. Humble picked his way delicately, having no desire to tread on the man in addition to having kicked him.

When they reached the door, Gillien mounted. No sooner

had she slung her pack and the instrument up in front of her
than the door to Holding House burst open. What emerged
looked like a scene from a Nightlands gate.

Men in various stages of disintegration stumbled out. Some
had no arms. Some had only parts of their bodies left. Some
were corpses, caught up and borne outside in the frantic wave
of escaping guards. Behind them all, still wearing a mask of
Reeve Herrick atop its monstrous body, came the nightmare
creature. It reached the doorway, saw its prey about to escape,
and bellowed in rage. It moved toward her, and then halted
abruptly, shying away from even the dim early morning's
light.

Gillien fled. Humble needed no urging. The smell of the unnatural beast filled his nostrils and the horse bolted down the
street, turning onto the main square and galloping as fast as his
legs would carry him to the nearest gate.

No one stopped them. Few were even awake at this hour,
and those who had the power to interrupt the fleeing bard and
the terrified animal were fleeing in terror themselves, pursued
by a creature that simply ought not to be.

Once out of the city, Gillien turned without hesitation to the
lesser-traveled Queen's road, following Cadby's suggestion.
Her mind had, at last, been firmly made up. Turning to the law
for help had proved to be an unmitigated disaster. She was a
wanted woman now, as far as Hallenore was concerned. She
could not rely upon anyone there to get the lute to its proper
home.

She knew now that she had to carry out Jencir's plan. The
elf knew what he was fighting, and had entrusted the lute to
Gillien and no one else. He must have had confidence that
she could carry out her mission. He had died in that trust,
and she was not going to let his memory down.

A grimness came to her face as she crouched low over
Humble's neck and let the pony run. Others, too, had died for
the lute: the guards, Reeve Herrick, Blesser Cadby, and most
importantly to Gillien, her own innocent family.

She would never, ever let the monster that had worn Reeve
Herrick's body like an abominable costume have the lute. Her

family had died for it, and by all the gods, Gillien was going to
make those needless deaths count for something. She would
take the lute to Queen-mother Ariel, or die herself in the attempt.

As if it could read her thoughts, she felt the lute across her
thighs express gratitude and pleasure.

*A girl-child? Why, she'll bring thee naught but pain
an' suffering, an' a brood of ill-got brats. A boy-child's
what the gods send when they're smiling upon thee, and a
boy-child is what thou shalt pray for.*

—from the Byrnian folktale,
The Goodwife's Prayer

CHAPTER FIVE

The scent of Humble's fear was rank as it rose from his sweaty neck, but Gillien continued to crouch low over the horse as he put panic-driven miles between them and the Nightlands Demon. Though she knew the hard pace would eventually tire Humble far more than a steady, mile-eating canter or trot, she made no attempt to slow him down. She shared every bit of the horse's terror and desire for flight. In his blind fright, he would not have obeyed her, anyway.

They clattered over the bridge that crossed the river Leti and up the other side, keeping the mountains on their left. And Humble was still going strong when Gillien yanked his head hard to the right, where the road branched off to become the Queen's Road. It was only when her hand, clutching the lute in a death grip, actually began to spasm with cramps that she decided to try to slow Humble's pace.

"Easy, boy," she soothed, shifting her weight backwards and pulling gently on the reins. Her leg muscles, gripping the

horse's body without benefit of stirrups, screamed in protest as
she moved. Humble complied after a few moments, slowing to
a canter, then a trot. He was panting, making unhappy little
grunting sounds, and was so lathered with sweat and foam that
his light dapple-gray coat had darkened to nearly black.

Gillien, too, was bathed in sweat, a combination of terror,
physical exertion and the heat of the deceptively mild morning. She winced as Humble jounced along at a trot, the most
uncomfortable of gaits for the rider. He needed to cool down
gradually, though, so she gritted her teeth and endured. She
craned her neck and glanced behind them down the Queen's
Road. No sign of pursuit at all.

"Maybe the guards captured the demon after all," she
mused aloud, but she didn't really believe it. She suspected
that the thing she had seen was more than a match for any
human force. She shuddered, feeling a cold chill even through
her heat, and forced her mind away from the creature that
wanted the lute. With an effort, she relaxed a little, forcing her
tense muscles to loosen. Humble sensed the change in his
rider, and seemed to relax a bit himself.

They walked for a time, Gillien trying to think of nothing
much at all. Her stomach rumbled, demanding attention.
Squinting, she raised her hand to shade her eyes and glanced
up at the cloudless blue summer sky. By the sun's position, it
was well into midmorning. No wonder she and Humble were
both worn out.

Horse and rider both needed to rest and eat. Gillien, daughter of a pair of traveling performers, was familiar with most of
the main roads in Byrn. The next stop along the Queen's
Road, which wound in a southwesterly direction, was, if she
recalled correctly, Riverfork. Cadby, that poor, brave Blesser,
had told her to seek out Blesser Lucan once she reached the
town. Again, Gillien searched the sky, sighing to herself.
Humble was a good, brave little horse, but he was no en-
durance champion. Riverfork was at least twenty-five miles
away. They wouldn't make it there before nightfall, probably
not until early morning.

Her stomach rumbled again. "All right, all right," she told

her growling belly. She pulled gently on the reins again and coaxed Humble into a brisk walk while she surveyed the surrounding countryside.

Humble's terrified speed had left Hallenore and its environs far behind. They were well and truly into farming land now. To her right stretched a golden, waving field of wheat, which grew thick and high. The farmer who owned the land to her left, it would seem, was not as fine a custodian of his lands. If this ever had been a field of any kind of cultivated crop, there were no signs of it now. Flat and crawling with weeds, wildflowers and stones, the earth offered no sheltering trees or even large boulders in whose shadows Gillien could seek temporary comfort.

"Besides," she said glumly, "if anyone's following me, they'd see me in a heartbeat." She debated disappearing into the waving wheat, then decided against it. A crunched-down trail of trodden wheat would advertise their presence as well as sitting by the side of the road.

Sighing, Gillien slid off Humble. She bit back a cry as her legs, furious at her mistreatment, buckled underneath her and she fell to her knees.

"Death's breath!" she groaned. Gillien gripped her aching limbs and massaged them, swearing loudly. Humble whickered and brushed her cheek with his soft muzzle. Gillien staggered to her feet, cringing with every move, and with her left hand reached for the animal's reins directly below his chin. Her right hand groped along the horse's broad back, finding the lute. For an instant, she wondered how the thing had kept from falling off Humble's back right along with her, but then let the question go. The lute was extraordinary, and that was all the explanation she needed.

She gripped the precious instrument, still wrapped in cloth, in her left hand while she led Humble down the road with her right. The horse clopped contentedly beside her. Despite the pain, she knew that walking would stretch some of the stiffness out of her tortured muscles. Besides, it was better than continuing to ride.

The sun beat down on Gillien's unprotected head. She was

growing thirsty, her mouth getting drier by the minute, and too
late she realized that she had neglected to pack a waterskin
along with food.

"I," she said to Humble, "am an idiot. Did you know that?"

Humble swiveled his ears in her direction, listening politely.
At the same instant, she felt a tingling from the lute. It was a
clearly sent negative reply to her statement. Surprised and unexpectedly touched, she glanced down at the instrument.

"Why, thank you. Though I doubt my thirsty horse will
agree with you."

A hint of gentle amusement, then the lute became quiet
again.

They walked on for perhaps another mile, Gillien constantly
scanning the countryside for any kind of shelter. The heat de-
creased slightly. Glancing up, she saw that the sun's rays were
starting to be blocked by a gathering of clouds. Her spirits rose
a little. No dark, threatening thunderheads, not yet, but rain
would be coming within a few hours.

"I never thought I'd be happy to be rained on while on the
open road," Gillien said to the horse and the lute, "but rain
means water for us both, Humble. And it'll help hide our
tracks." She had observed that Humble's iron-shod hooves had
left definite prints on the seldom-traveled Queen's Road, still
soft in places from the spring rains.

At last, she made a decision, and turned Humble's head to
the left, in the direction of the nonhusbanded field. The terrain
was starting to rise and fall in gentle, sloping hills. It would
provide at least some cover from the road, she thought to herself. And there was really no choice—she and Humble both
needed to rest and eat.

She noticed small areas of what appeared to be dark brown
earth among the weeds, and a few paces brought her close
enough to discover what it was.

"Animal droppings," she said, "not from horses, though. I
wonder . . ." They continued on over a sloping rise, and then
Gillien got a pleasant shock.

The hill was deceptively gentle. After rising to a barely per-
ceptible crest, it plunged away on the other side into a small,

grassy valley. In the valley was a little pond, surrounded by grass and a great deal of animal droppings. A few feet away from the pond was a small hut, simply made of a few wooden boards and covered with a thatch roof.

"Sheep!" Gillien exclaimed so loudly that Humble started. "This is a shepherd's watering hole! Come on!"

She pulled her pack off the animal's back and released Humble to make his own way down the slope. She then hastened down herself. The walking had loosened her stiff muscles, and the sight of shelter gave her spirits a lift. By the time she made it to the little hut, Humble had plunged his head into the water and was drinking thirstily.

"Not too much, greedy, or you'll get sick!" she chastised the horse, yanking his head up from the water. Humble whinnied and shook his head, sending drops spattering across her face. Gillien laughed—a sound she had not made in what seemed like forever.

She led the horse over to the hut and peered inside. "Something for you to eat and me to sit on," she commented to the horse, gazing gratefully on two bales of hay. A quick glance around showed that the hut, though not a master builder's dream, was solidly constructed. Pitch sealed any cracks, and the inside was dry. Gently, Gillien laid the lute on a bale of hay.

"I'll be right back," she promised, then set about seeing to her horse.

Lacking any kind of grooming equipment, she had to rub Humble down with handfuls of hay. He obediently stood still, and if he missed his stiff brush, he gave no sign of it. Gillien ran a hand down along Humble's slim, strong foreleg, urging the pony to lift his right hoof for her inspection. It was fine— caked with dirt, yes, but free from stones. Gillien scraped out the encrusted earth as best she could with her fingers. When she had a moment, she'd grind down one of her throwing knifes to sufficient dullness, and use that to clean Humble's hooves. "No foot, no horse," was a common motto in the Borderlands, and now was not the time to have her mount pull up lame.

The left foreleg and right hand leg were also free of stones, but Gillien winced in sympathy as she examined Humble's fourth hoof. A pebble, no bigger than her thumbnail, had gotten lodged in the frog, a V-shaped cleft of sensitive tissue. Gently, Gillien reached her thumb and forefinger into the cleft and worked the obstruction free.

"All right, fellow, go and have your supper," she told Humble, rising and giving him a gentle slap on his hind-quarters.

Humble neighed happily and began at once to crop the green foliage that grew in the moist soil by the pool. To supplement the meal, Gillien pulled loose a small armload of hay and dropped it by Humble's head. The gray ears swiveled forward as Humble's soft muzzle turned to the new treat.

"Now, my turn," said Gillien as she trudged to the water's edge. Her mouth was full of road dust, but she hesitated before cupping a handful of water, and gazed at her reflection.

She looked exhausted. That was no surprise. The eyes that met hers in the water were encircled with dark shadows, and looked wary and furtive—the eyes, she thought bleakly, of a hunted beast. Her cheeks seemed sunken, and her dark hair was a wild, stringy cloud that hung down nearly to the water.

Sighing, Gillien rinsed her dirty hands and then drank her fill. She splashed some water on her face, and felt a little refreshed. Wincing as she rose, she went back to the hut. A little rummaging in her pack yielded an apple and some dried, chewy meat. She ate quickly and in silence, content to sprawl on the cushioning hay and watch Humble crop grass. From her vantage point, she watched as the clouds she had spotted earlier turned darker and more threatening. When her stomach was satisfied, she fed the apple core to an appreciative Humble, then removed her filthy clothes. Eagerly, she padded naked out to the small pool. Just as she stepped cautiously into the water, the rain came.

The drops were cool and clean, splashing around her as she waded into the tepid water. It felt heavenly. She closed her eyes, leaned her head back, and opened her mouth to the rain. The water wrapped itself around her, soothing her aching muscles and cooling her sunburned skin. Gillien swam a few lazy strokes, then floated on her back. The raindrops tingled and tickled a little as they fell on her stomach, breasts and face, washing away sweat, dirt and tension. She took a deep breath and dove, arching her body and keeping her legs together, pretending that she was a fish, a dolphin, one of the magical People of the Sea, here in the cool dark depths where the burdens of the Land People ceased to have any meaning at all.

But too soon the air in her lungs began to burn and she was forced to surface again. She gasped in the rain-scented air, catching her breath. The rain was falling harder now, and Gillien shoved her sodden mop of hair out of her eyes to watch Humble enjoying the rain as much as she was.

Even as the sight of her horse, her friend, her companion on this desperate journey made her smile, it also reminded her of just why she was here. And the pain, temporarily banished by the cleansing water, suddenly flooded back. Treading water, Gillien choked on a sob, then gave in to the hurt and cried for a time in the rain. She made no attempt to wipe her face, but let the shower do it for her. When the tears stopped, and rain alone made her face wet, Gillien dove one more time and then reluctantly left the water's embrace.

Dripping, she hurried to the shelter of the hut. She leaned over and began to wring out her hair, not bothering to dry herself. For one thing, it was hardly chilly. For another, her dirty clothes smelled of that filthy cell still, and she had no desire to dampen what few dry clothes she had brought. She glanced over at the lute, still wrapped up and waiting patiently for her. She shook her hands, drying them as best she could. Cautiously, so as not to get a damaging drop of moisture on the instrument, she unwrapped it.

"Hello again," she said softly, keeping one dry finger on its smooth wood.

She felt it greet her, and she smiled a little. "I feel a little . . . well . . . like a simpleton, talking to an instrument."

The lute hastened to reassure her. Gillien sighed. "Well, I used to talk to my instruments anyway, even when they *weren't* magical, so I guess this is all right. Besides, no one's around to hear me except for Humble, and I talk to him, too. I used to give my instruments names, you know. I think all musicians do. Do you have a name?"

She felt a tremor of something . . . was it mirth? Then a negative response. It seemed to be nameless.

"Well, would you like me to name you? Seems like you ought to have one if an ordinary old mandolin did."

The lute appeared to want a name.

"All right. Let me think about it." Gillien turned her attention to her pack, searching through it until she found one of her throwing knives. Gingerly, she tested it on the inside of her forearm. It nicked a clean slice with barely any effort, and she flinched. "Ow! Well, I guess it's sharp enough!"

Placing the knife carefully on her bare thighs, she leaned her head to the left, gathered her wet hair together, and twisted it tightly. She took the knife in her right hand. Grimly, her lips pursed in a thin, unhappy line, she began to saw through her thick mane of hair.

"We're running away from two sets of enemies now," she explained to the lute as she cut through her hair bit by bit. "First is Reeve Herrick, or the demon, or whatever it was. The one that killed your friend Jencir, and killed . . . we're running away from him. It. That's obvious. The law is going to be looking for us, too, if the guards of Hallenore somehow think that I killed all those men and poor Blesser Cadby.

"The advantage—ow!—is that they're going to be looking for Gillien Songespynner, female bard." A long clump of hair fell in a twisting coil to the hard-packed, straw-covered dirt. Gillien put down the knife and regathered her hair. Wet dark strands clung stubbornly to her fingers. She tried to wipe them off, but they clung to her damp torso and legs. This was going to take longer than she thought.

"So they will *not* be looking for Garen, a youth who is simply traveling to Kasselton to see all the bards." She glanced over at the lute. "I'll keep you wrapped up as much as I can, don't worry."

More hair fell. "Papa always loved my hair. Said it was beautiful, so thick and long, just like my mama's when she was my age. . . . But anyway, I've traveled enough to know that one girl by herself just isn't safe. I hope I could hold my own in a struggle. I mean, I can throw a knife well, and Kellien certainly taught me some interesting ways to fight!"

A smile flickered, faded. Dark, damp tresses were severed by the bright blade.

"But it might not be enough. And I've heard talk about slavers. You always hear that, I've heard it since I was a child, but there might be something to it. And I hear that what they do to women . . ." The thought of losing her maidenhead made her feel physically sick. She'd lost so much already. An unwed woman who was not virgin was, quite literally, nothing in Byrnian society.

"No, this disguise is best. It has its own risks, though. It's against the law for a woman to wear men's clothes. Isn't that ridiculous? Well, I'll just have to make damn sure that no one ever finds out that I'm a woman, that's all."

She was silent for a while, cutting her hair at what seemed to her a soggy strand at a time. The rain fell steadily outside, in a hard patter on the earth, making only soft whispering sounds as it fell on the waterproof thatch roof. Gillien gazed at the gray rain, at the gray horse that cropped by the silver-gray water. She shivered a little, feeling chilled for the first time.

"I wonder if that thing really was a Nightlands Demon." Her eyes were distant, recalling the creature in minute detail. "I know they're all unique, each being born of a nightmare, but I've never heard of one that could change its appearance. Or escape from the Nightlands."

Now that she was restored slightly by rest, food, and bathing, the crippling intensity of Gillien's fear started to recede and her sharp mind began to gnaw on the problem.

"It did *look* horrible, like a Nightlands Demon ought to look, but then again, it had also looked like a person."

A dreadful thought occurred to her and she gripped her hair hard enough to bring tears to her eyes.

"It looked like a person," she repeated, enunciating each word carefully. "Dear gods . . . could it look like *any* person? Any . . . *thing*?"

Fear rose up in her again, and she began to shiver in truth. If the thing that was after the lute could assume any shape it wanted, how would she know friend from foe?

"No, no, don't think about it, Gilly," she reprimanded herself in a voice that quivered. "You think about it too much, and you'll curl up in a little ball and stay right here for that thing to find you." She took a deep breath. "Concentrate on what you know. It doesn't like light, so you're probably safe during the day. And it's probably got some kind of injuries from the guards, enough to maybe slow it down. Concentrate on the details, that's the girl. See what else you can remember."

She thought hard, sawing away at her tresses, and recalled a fair number of things. It had managed to poison Jencir and dissolve Cadby's flesh, so if it ever came upon her again, she knew to beware of its insidious poison as well as its more obvious attack. There was something else. . . . What was it?

"The hands!" she yelped. Jencir had made her show her hands to him before he would let her into his room. At Holding House, Gillien had seen why. The shapechanger's hands had been utterly blank. Knowing that she had one certain way of identifying her pursuer sent a wave of intense relief washing through her. She smiled a little, and was able to let it go for the time being. Renewing her attack on her locks, she finally finished and felt mingled triumph and regret as the final thick lock parted beneath her knife.

She fluffed her hair vigorously with stiff fingers, combing it through. "So little left," she said softly. Her hair, which had once tumbled to her waist, didn't even reach her shoulders now. Gillien dug in her pack and found a chemise and a floor-length overtunic of cotton. She examined them critically, trying to see if anything in the design or decoration of the garments bespoke feminine rather than masculine or, at the very least, neuter. Nothing did. Gillien's family couldn't afford fine fabric or expensive decoration on clothing, except for performing pieces. Save for the length, Gillien's tunic would not have looked out of place on Kellien's young, male body. As for the chemise, it could easily be cut to shirt length, and she'd buy a pair of breeches in Riverfork. Gamely, Gillien took another knife, tested it for sharpness, and went to work altering the chemise. The cotton fabric tore easily, and she didn't care that it was ragged and unraveling. Shirts could be tucked in.

The blue cotton tunic, however, was more difficult. Made of a thicker, tougher fabric, it did not yield as easily as the chemise, and Gillien had soon made rather a mess of it.

"Damn it, why didn't I take a pair of shears?" she grumbled, venting her increased frustration as the blue cotton tunic ripped in unwanted directions. "Mama always did the sewing," she explained to the lute almost apologetically. "Me, I never knew the threading end of the needle from the point, except when I jabbed myself." At last the task was done, and the tunic ready to wear.

She slipped it on and surveyed the damage. It now fell raggedly to her knees, exposing slim, decidedly feminine legs.

"Hose," she said firmly, reaching for the items in her bag. She slipped first one and then another on. She tugged on her boots, and smiled. There was now no exposed leg at all. "There, that's better, don't you think?" She wasn't touching the lute, so did not expect a reply.

Gillien had sometimes played a boy in skits the family had performed, and now she adopted the swaggering, head-high pose she'd learned by imitating Kellien. It felt good—liberating. She'd never felt like holding her head high when she was just being herself, except when she had gotten caught up in the rapture of performing.

"Only one thing wrong," she said, sighing and pulling the tunic off over her head. "Well," she amended wryly, "two things." Reaching for the rags left over from her inexpert trimming job, she began to carefully wrap them around her small breasts. She needed to bind them tightly but not painfully, as she didn't plan to unwrap them often. It would be easier, and more convincing, to keep her chest bound. Carefully, she wound layers of material around her upper chest, taking care to build up her shoulders as well, in search of a believable, albeit slim, male torso.

This final task accomplished, she donned the tunic. "It feels . . . very strange," she confessed, wishing the rain would let up so she could survey the effect in the pond. "But if it works, then it's worth it. Now," and she reached eagerly for the lute, anxious to play it, "what about you, hmmm?"

She plucked a few notes and winced. The dampness had affected the instrument's sweet tone. She tuned it string by string, cocking her newly shorn head and listening for the tone. Fortunately, part of Gillien's gift had been perfect pitch. When the lute was tuned to her satisfaction, she settled herself on a bale of hay and began to play. She was not paying attention, merely enjoying the sound of beautiful, random chords, when a song suddenly popped into her head. Obeying the impulse, she began to sing along with the lute.

> Your horse is strong beneath you,
> Your heart is brave and bold,
> So ride, O ride, brave Deveren
> Before the night is old,
> Ride hard and strong and swiftly,
> For in your hands resides
> The fate of every Byrnian
> And Mharian besides.
>
> One foe of yours is human,
> One foe of yours is not.
> And everyone you love most dear
> In their dark web is caught:
> Your brother fights for freedom,
> At perhaps a bloody cost,
> But it's here in these dark streets tonight
> That the war is won or lost.

Gillien repeated the chorus, wondering what on earth had brought *Deveren's Ride* to her mind. It was nearly always a success with the crowds, for it was an exciting song, but it hardly ranked as one of Gillien's personal favorites. Mentally shrugging, she continued on.

In your hands you hold the secret,
In your hands you bear the cure
For the deadly sweep of pestilence
That slays with its allure.
O Deveren, with dawn will come
The triumph of the Dark
Unless you—

She suddenly gasped with comprehension and nearly dropped the lute. Gooseflesh erupted along the entire length of her body.

"Dear gods!" she cried, her eyes wide. "*You* wanted me to play that song!"

Agreement from the lute.

"You—I—" For a moment, words failed her. She took a deep breath and continued in a calmer tone of voice. "You suggested the song to me as a way of telling me something, right?"

She was right.

"You are comparing Deveren's ride of five hundred years ago with *my* taking *you* to Queen-mother Ariel?"

Again, she was right. She did not want to be. "You're trying to tell me that if I *don't* get you to Queen-mother Ariel, something very, very bad is going to happen."

Yes, indeed, the lute was positively insistent that such would be the case. Gillien's heart sank even further, if such a thing was possible. Comparing her to Deveren, and the lute to the precious information and blessing Deveren had borne, meant that she would be responsible for the lives—or deaths—of hundreds, perhaps thousands of innocents.

"You know, I was going to go through with this anyway. I didn't really need to be burdened with this new information," she said wearily.

The lute appeared to be contrite.

"All right," she sighed, maneuvering it into playing position again, "can I just play something light and distracting? Please?"

The lute assured her that a light tune would be welcome.

Gillien, relieved, launched into one of her favorite songs, *Safe Harbor*. It suddenly seemed very appropriate.

As she finished up, she noticed that the rain had nearly stopped. Her sense of responsibility resettled upon her falsely broad shoulders like something physical.

"Well," she said to the lute, "Kellien was right. You do practically sing by yourself. Shall I call you Singer?"

The lute seemed quite pleased with the name. "All right, Singer it is. Come on. With the fate of the world resting on how many miles a fat trick pony can cover in a day, we'd better get going."

This journey is but one of a lifetime.

—motto of the god Traveler

CHAPTER SIX

The day grew hotter, the air thick and sticky from the earlier rain shower. The clouds did not disperse, and more than once Gillien heard threatening rumbles and glanced up anxiously, expecting a downpour at any minute. None came, though, for which she was grateful. More rain would only drive the humidity up and drench the only dry clothes she had left. And she couldn't count on finding shelter a second time.

The new haircut she sported felt wonderfully cool. Never having worn her hair short before—the only time women were permitted to have their hair shorn was either in penance or sickness—she decided that she liked it. That and being able to wear the more comfortable masculine clothing reinforced her notion that her decision was a good one. The one exception to physical comfort was the binding she'd wrapped around her chest. It did not permit her upper torso to breathe at all, and that area of her body was soon stifling hot.

Humble began to flag as the afternoon wore on. Glancing

up at the sun, which made infrequent appearances from behind
the wall of gray clouds, Gillien saw that the daylight hours
were waning. She urged Humble on, but the best she could get
from the exhausted horse was a halfhearted shamble. Even
that only lasted a few minutes before Humble, frothed and
panting, slowed down to a walk and refused to go faster.

Finally Gillien dismounted, tying the pack securely to the
horse and carrying the wrapped-up Singer herself. She nibbled
at some dried fruit as she walked alongside her tired mount.

"I don't want to be mad at Humble," she told the lute, "but
the day's nearly over. We're nowhere near Riverfork. And I'm
just as tired as he is." She stopped, aware that her voice had
taken on a petulant tone. Gillien hated complainers, and was
embarrassed that she was so close to becoming one herself.

The thick, hot air around them began to cool gradually.
Gillien welcomed this at first, then began to worry as she noticed their shadows lengthening.

"Nearly twilight," she said somberly. She brought the horse
to a halt, and gently touched the back of his foreleg. Humble
immediately knelt, letting his mistress vault onto his broad
back. "I know you're tired, boy, but we've got to keep going.
It's getting cooler," she added, hoping to sweeten the pot.

Humble's ears flicked backward at the sound of her voice,
and when she squeezed her knees tight he obligingly moved
into a loping, rolling trot.

Humble was no steed of the gods, though, able to outrun the
sun as one fleet-footed, magical mare had in an old folktale.
He was just a simple, rather fat trick pony, lumbering along at
what was for him a furious pace. The light grew dimmer, until
Gillien could barely see the road ahead. No stars were visible;
the thick blanket of clouds overhead had obliterated their
friendly presence from her view.

Fear began to press on her. Her heart beat in quick, hard
hammers, and she started to glance anxiously behind her
every few minutes. No one was there, though she knew she'd
hear hoofbeats long before she could see anyone in the twilight. She felt the comforting mental touch of Singer, trying to
calm her.

"I know, I know," she replied, "but I can't help thinking about that . . . thing . . . and know that it likes the darkness as much as I dislike it!"

Singer had nothing to counteract the simple logic of Gillien's statement, and they fell into a troubled silence. The twilight faded into an almost complete blackness. Gillien debated leaving the trail, but decided to press on. Humble had keener senses than hers; surely he would be able to smell the creature if it were near.

And then she wondered if the monster, in addition to looking like anything it wanted to, could also *smell* like anything it wanted to. The thought unnerved her so totally that a small, frightened sob escaped her. Singer sought to soothe, and Humble picked up the pace a little, but unreasoning fear had gotten its talons into Gillien and she kicked the horse furiously. Humble leaped into a startled canter.

It was then that she saw the small light bobbing up and down on the road ahead. It swung back and forth, like some kind of drunken glowfly, but it was clearly heading in her direction. Gasping, Gillien jerked on the reins. Humble skidded to a confused stop, prancing nervously. She froze, uncertain as to what to do, where to go. What in the name of the gods was that ahead?

"Traveler's blessing be upon you, wanderer!" came a friendly male voice as the bobbing light grew closer.

Gillien knew the greeting, and as she watched, she saw that the light was nothing more than an oil lamp, carried by a man in his middle years. He wore a gray cloak over gray, mud-spattered clerical robes. The hood of his cloak hid his face at first, but as the Blesser of the god Traveler drew closer, he reached and pulled it down. His thick, dark hair was touched with white, and his face was lined beyond his years from a lifetime of exposure to the sun. He carried a medium-sized pack on his back and walked with the aid of a thick, sturdy staff. The smile that he turned up to Gillien was full of genuine pleasure.

The Blesser's hands, Gillien noted, were bare, and as he reached up to pat Humble's neck she caught a glimpse of the

man's palm—hard with manual labor, calloused, and quite full
of the normal lines and folds of any human hand. The fear
bled out of Gillien and she slumped in the saddle, giddy with
relief. She smiled back at him.

"Greetings, Blesser," she responded, keeping her voice as
deep as she could make it.

"You're out a bit late, aren't you, young—" he peered up at
her, and Gillien held her breath "—fellow," he finished. She
felt a quiet flicker of pleasure. Her disguise had passed its first
test.

"Yes, Blesser. I was hoping to make it to Riverfork tonight,
but it seems my horse wasn't quite up to it."

"Well, you might be able to make it—it's only another hour
or two—but I wouldn't advise traveling alone after dark.
There's a Lamp of Traveler just up ahead, about another mile
or so. Why don't you rest there for the night?"

Gillien's spirits began to rise. She knew about the Lamps of
Traveler, although she and her family had never made use of
the hostelries. Run by the Blessers and Tenders of the god
Traveler, the Lamps were small buildings where one could eat
a simple but solid meal, sleep one night in a rough but clean
bed, and leave refreshed the next morning. The Blessers demanded no money for their hospitality. Traveler, the patron of
all wanderers on the road, wanted his pilgrims to be safe and
healthy. One donated what one could. Wealthy travelers often
left large sums of money. The very poor sometimes could
offer up only heartfelt thanks. Both gifts were considered
equally precious to the Blessers of the most carefree and jovial
deity of the human pantheon.

Gillien's mouth watered at the thought of some real food.
And as for a safe place to sleep— "Do you run this Lamp,
Blesser?" she asked politely.

The Blesser shook his head, laughing. "Nay, child, I'm of
the Roving order." He gestured with his hands. "This is my
bed, and the stars my ceiling." He paused, glanced up at the
overcast sky, and amended with a chuckle, "Providing that
they're out, of course."

Gillien laughed with him. She'd never heard of the Order of

the Rovers, but it seemed appropriate. Traveler wouldn't want all of his Blessers to be stay-at-home innkeepers, vital though that task was.

"But, Blesser, you said yourself you wouldn't advise traveling alone after dark," she said, concerned for his safety. She knew, as he could not, what dreadful thing might be soon be coming along this road. "Aren't you worried?"

The Blesser threw back his head and laughed aloud at this, a hearty, carefree sound that seemed to Gillien to echo in the darkness.

"My young sir, I've been on the road since I was little older than you. Years in the sun and snow may have aged my appearance, but believe me, my body is strong and fit. And this," he added, gesturing with the staff, "is an old friend. We dance beautifully together, my staff and I, and often our audience has regretted asking us to perform!"

She saw now that his lower arms were powerfully knotted with muscles, and guessed that the rest of him was likewise lithe and strong. He stooped and picked up a rock from off the path. As Gillien watched, curious, he cradled the stone loosely in his palm and murmured a few words under his breath. Closing his fingers over the stone, he passed his staff over it.

Gillien gasped, entranced. As she watched, the rock in the Blesser's hand began to move. A soft glow emanated from it, and as Gillien continued to stare the rock was transformed from a simple stone into a small oil lamp similar to the one the Blesser himself carried—complete with oil and dancing flame atop the wick. She had heard of this type of magic, known as hand magic, before, but had never seen it being worked. Like all four of the magic types—head, hand, heart and spirit—it was rare. Not as rare as spirit magic, generally considered to be miraculous and a sign of divine intervention, but rare nonetheless.

The Blesser saw her rapt face and smiled a little. "Here, son," he said, "may Traveler light your path tonight, and bring you safely to a Lamp of another sort."

Gillien accepted the lamp gratefully. "Thank you! Now I'm sure not to pass by it in the dark!"

They both laughed then. Cautiously, Gillien said, "I'm hoping to meet a friend of mine in Riverfork, a young woman by the name of Gillien Songespynner. She's a bard. Have you by any chance encountered her on the road?"

The Blesser shook his head. "Nay, son. I'd remember a bard, too, for I enjoy a pleasant song now and again."

This answered Gillien's real question—if anyone had begun asking questions about her, or if reports of the calamity at Hallenore had reached this wanderer. Satisfied, she again thanked the man, bid him farewell, and rode ahead with a considerably lighter heart.

Despite the little oil lamp she carried, she almost did pass by the hostelry in the dark. It was the honking noise of a gaggle of geese that drew her attention to the building. The Lamp of Traveler was set several dozen yards away from the road, and the light from its surrounding torches and open windows seemed very dim in the thick, starless dark. She was unable to see the pen that the housed the geese, but their distinctive sound made her smile. Geese were sacred to Traveler—it was believed he had created them to provide food for his followers—and it made sense that the Blesser in charge of the Lamp would have a few. She tugged Humble's reins sharply to the left and hurried over, more than eager to leave the night's mysteries and fears behind.

As she rode closer, she saw that the temple, for such it was, was of a fair size. Two torches, blazing steadily in the still air, stood firmly embedded in the earth three yards away from the door. By their light, she could just make out the image of Traveler himself, carved onto the heavy oaken door. A few yards away, behind the temple, she saw the dim shapes of large fowl milling about in the shadows. They were quiet now; whatever goose debate had been going on had obviously been settled.

She swung her legs off Humble, wincing again at the pain in her abused muscles. No sooner had her feet hit the ground than a boy perhaps a year or two younger than she approached from behind the building. He was slim, about her height, and wore a scaled-down version of the vestments she'd seen on the

Blesser she had encountered earlier. He had an enormous number of freckles and an open, friendly expression.

"Traveler's blessing be upon you, wanderer!" he said, smiling.

"Many thanks," she replied. "I take it you're the Tender here?"

The boy nodded. A rogue thatch of curly dark hair fell into his eyes at the gesture. He flipped it back with an unconscious gesture. "One of them, anyway. Tender Benean at your service. Please go in and get yourself something to eat, sir. I'll tend to your horse." He reached for Humble's reins.

"If you have any hot mash for him, I'll pay for it. I've ridden him hard today and must get up early."

Benean gave her a quizzical look. "You've never visited a Lamp before, have you?"

"No," she replied, wondering if somehow she'd inadvertently offended the god, or at least the Tender.

"We give all our pilgrims the best that we have—food, drink, shelter. You don't have to pay for any of it. If we have hot mash available, your horse will get some."

Gillien felt herself blush. "I—I'm sorry, I didn't mean . . ."

He grinned at her again. "Of course you didn't. Just letting you know how things work around here, that's all. We'll take good care of—what's his name?"

"Humble."

Benean laughed at that. "Traveler would enjoy that! He'll eat well and sleep with friends tonight, sir. You go in and eat something hot yourself."

Without another word, Benean left, leading the obedient gelding around back to where Gillien assumed the stable was. The geese set up another chorus of honking, then subsided. The unexpected friendliness of the boy, a stranger, touched the exhausted girl nearly to tears. She blinked them back, hard, and went to the door. Hot food sounded wonderful.

As she reached for the door, she smiled a little. She could see the carving of the god more clearly up close. The gods of Verold were all very human in appearance and behavior, except for this one. Traveler was not nearly as imposing a deity

as the dark Vengeance, or Death, or even Light, despite the
fact that he was far less human in appearance than any of the
other six gods. He was depicted as tall and thin, almost
gawky-looking, with a goose matching him step for step. His
face, had it been frowning, would have been terrifying in its
ugliness. But it was split by an amiable grin, and the sharp
teeth somehow didn't seem at all frightening. His four arms
were occupied: one hand clutched a pack, the other held a
walking stick, and the final two were occupied with playing a
small lyre. The ugly visage and the overabundance of limbs
was deliberate. Traveler was the patron not only of those who
wandered; he was the protector of those who had been born
malformed.

Beneath him, Gillien knew, although she could not read the
writing, was inscribed his traditional motto: "This journey is
but one of a lifetime." She leaned forward, kissed the ugly god
as a sign of respect, and entered the Lamp of Traveler.

The fragrant smell of cooking stew and hot bread hit her
nostrils almost at once. She closed her eyes and inhaled happily, then entered and closed the door behind her. This area
was what passed for a dining room. A second Tender was
busily stirring a huge pot that hung over a cheerfully burning
fire. Beside him, propped snugly against the wall, was a sideboard that held a pile of wooden bowls, mugs, and several
small loaves of bread. The picked-over carcass of a goose,
roasted earlier that day, kept the loaves of bread company.
Four or five earthenware jugs and two plates full of chopped
vegetables occupied the far end. Her mouth watered in anticipation as she stepped forward.

"Um, greetings," she said hesitantly.

The young man glanced over at her, flashed a quick smile,
and returned to his task of stirring the pot. "Greetings, pilgrim.
If you're hungry, please help yourself to a bowl and I'll ladle
some stew for you."

He was her age or maybe a little older, and dreadfully handsome. He had high, fine cheekbones, and dark eyes that
seemed to see straight into her soul without posing the slightest threat. A sudden fit of embarrassment at her filthy appear-

ance welled up in the bard and she broke eye contact at once, making for a spot against the wall where she set down her sack and the precious Singer. Walking over to the sideboard, Gillien felt her customary coltish awkwardness enshroud her, felt her spirit almost physically withdraw into herself, and was not surprised—merely mortified—when she tripped over her own feet and almost went crashing into the sideboard. She was saved by the Tender's quick, strong hand on her arm. Her face flamed as she glanced up at him.

"We just put some fresh rushes on the floor," he said, politely covering her clumsiness. He pointed at his own foot, and Gillien could see that, even encased in boots, one was obviously deformed. "I have to watch my step all the time because of that, and you look very weary, my friend." He was poised and friendly, far more polished than the outgoing young Tender who had taken care of Humble. No doubt he was the one chosen to succeed the present Blesser, in due time. The twisted clubfoot, a horrible blight on anyone else, merely emphasized how fit the youth was to follow Traveler. It had become a blessing rather than a curse. This young man reminded Gillien vividly of Cadby, and guilt and pain rushed to close her throat.

Gillien suddenly remembered who—or at least what—she was trying to pass herself off as, and nodded a brusque thanks. She pulled herself up straight and took bold strides over to the sideboard. To her surprise, she didn't stumble a bit now. Acting like a man seemed to put a spell of surety over her untrustworthy feet. Helping herself to a loaf of still-warm bread and a bowl, she silently handed the vessel to the Tender, who, in equal but amiable silence, ladled her a steaming helping of the appetizing fare.

"The jugs hold wine and water to cut it with, if such is to your liking," the Tender told her. Gillien glanced down at her occupied hands, one holding an almost-too-hot wooden bowl of stew and the other clutching the loaf of bread. Two trips, then. She'd never manage to juggle bread, bowl, and mug without dropping something. She padded over to her spot, set down the bowl first, and placed the crusty loaf carefully over the side of the bowl. Gillien had barely risen when she was face to face with the handsome young Tender, who smiled as he gave her a mug of wine.

"Here, friend," he said. Silently—she did not trust her voice to speak—she accepted the mug with a fleeting, cautious smile of her own. "I'm Tender Konal. Please let me know if you need anything more." The youth did not linger, but turned away immediately and limped over to the sideboard. He picked up the plate of chopped potatoes and carrots in one hand, a jug of water in the other, and deposited the contents of both vessels into the pot, which he began again to stir.

Gillien turned her attention to the food. It was worth paying attention to. Simple fare, yes—roots and vegetables with just a hint of meat for flavoring, but it was hot and delicious. She used the bread as a utensil, scooping up chunks of the stew and devouring them. She had barely swallowed her third mouthful when the door opened.

Her heart began to pound like a smith's hammer. Suddenly the good fare felt like a tasteless lump of clay in her mouth. Gillien froze, her eyes riveted on the opening door. Chatter and laughter met her ears almost immediately, and she relaxed a fraction. She was expecting a lone enemy, not a group of them.

The newcomers were all of a size: big, brawny men with sunburned faces. There were four of them, and they made the roomy area seem abruptly cramped.

"Good evening, pilgrims," Tender Konal greeted them. "You look like fellows with hearty appetites. There's plenty here for all of you. Please—help yourselves."

Three of the four men needed no second urging, seizing loaves of bread and biting into them. The fourth, clearly the leader, addressed the Tender.

"We're traveling to Riverfork with crops to sell at the market tomorrow, and one of the wheels broke clean off," he said without preamble. "Don't suppose there's a wainwright closer than Riverfork?"

"I'm sorry, no. But you'll find several honest fellows in town who would be happy to help you in the morning."

The man swore, then suddenly remembered he was in a holy house. "Pardon, Tender," he apologized gruffly. "Well, is there room for us here tonight?"

"Plenty," Konal replied. "When you've eaten, just go straight through that door to the sleeping area. You and the young sir here," and he gestured at Gillien, who kept her eyes on her food, "are thus far the only ones gracing us with your presence at the Lamp tonight, so there should be plenty of pallets."

"Thank you, lad," the farmer replied, taking a bowl and loaf of bread for his own. His men were already hard at work making inroads in the food, sitting cross-legged on the rush-strewn floor and chatting companionably among themselves.

"There are two doors in the sleeping area," Konal continued, pitching his voice slightly louder. "The left one leads to the sleeping quarters of the Blesser and the Tenders. If there's a problem in the night, please come rouse us. The door at the end of the room leads to the altar, where you may thank the blessed Traveler for his gifts."

Gillien smothered a grin. No wonder the youth had raised his voice on the last sentence. He'd gotten the point across without being too pushy.

The statement seemed to sober the head farmer, although his compatriots did not appear to have heard. "Oh, aye," he said, as if the thought had just occurred to him. "Tender . . . would Traveler be likin' some fresh berries?"

Konal grinned. "Not even Blesser Rufiel can speak for Traveler, but on behalf of Traveler's servants, fresh berries would be most welcome."

Gillien had been trying to hurry up, finish her meal, and head for the safety of the sleeping room, but now she paused in midchew. The men had been talking about such things as crops, harvests, livestock, sexual prowess, and other things of no interest to the young woman. Now, though, the drift of conversation changed as the head farmer went outside to bring in the promised berries.

"I always hate leaving th' wife and young ones," one of them mumbled past a mouthful of bread. "No telling what might happen nowadays."

"Ah, your wife'd be a match for a whole pack o' Ghil, 'specially if they trod in her precious berry patch!" laughed one. The third laughed so hard he almost choked, and driblets of stew came spewing out of his mouth. Inhaling, he whooped with mirth and dragged his sleeve across his bearded face.

"Well, that's true enough," grinned the first man. "She took a hoe to me, once, when I was young and foolish enough to step on one o' those damned plants." He scooped up some stew with a hunk of bread, chewed, and swallowed. "Still, I just don't like it."

"We're way too far south for those overgrown rats to be a problem," the third one insisted.

"It's not the Ghil I'm worried 'bout. It's the damn human filth as does their dirty work for 'em."

Gillien had forgotten to eat, so engrossed was she in the conversation. Had slavers dared come this far into civilized territory? One heard the odd rumor now and again, but . . . She forced herself to continue to eat so as not to attract attention.

"Ah, that's what you tell your wife so's she'll cuddle up with you," the second one laughed. This time, though, his companions did not join in.

"Why in the name of the Nightlands King do you think Jarin asked the three of us t' come along to Riverfork?" the first one growled. "I can bring my own supplies well enough, but there's strength in numbers. Slavers like strong men—they do the hard work that the damn Ghil would just as soon not do. You think the vermin get their gemstones by askin' 'em t' just jump out of the ground?"

The other two fell silent. Their leader, Jarin, reentered with a small basket of berries, which he handed to Konal. The youth accepted graciously, and went outside, presumably to wherever the kitchen was located.

"I been talkin' with the Blesser," he told them as he began to eat. "He says we're smart to be careful. Seems that there was a caravan that used to trade with the Falarans that stopped here every year, and he ain't seen breath nor whisper of them. Another caravan got stopped at the border and had to come back with all their goods. You boys got trustworthy men lookin' after your folk?"

The three nodded. "Good," Jarin approved. "Slavers like finding women and children. Spoil 'em and sell 'em, that's their motto. Filthy bastards."

The mirth had fled from the conversation, and even in this most welcoming of places, Gillien felt a chill. *Spoil them and sell them.* Unconsciously, she reached one hand over to where Singer lay swathed in fabric. Like the touch of a trusted friend, the lute's mental reassurance comforted her.

The men finished their meal in silence, returned the bowls and mugs to the sideboards, then went through the door into the sleeping area. Gillien finished her own supper, using the final bite of bread to sop up every last drop of the herb-flavored broth. She drained the mug—the wine was delicious, cut enough with water to make it a good drinking beverage without having it go to one's head. The fine, robust flavor complemented the stew perfectly. She rose, placed her dishes with the others, gathered up her possessions, and entered the sleeping room.

It was dim enough for sleeping, certainly, but not completely dark. A fire, large enough to provide a bit of light but not enough to heat the place to the point of discomfort, burned steadily at the far end of the hall. A second fireplace, which would be employed in the winter months, was cold. Eight pallets, complete with pillows, lined the walls. The four farmers had chosen theirs, and were already starting to drift off. Low conversation could still be heard, but one of them was definitely snoring.

Gillien picked a pallet as far away from the farmers as possible, and sat down. As she'd expected, the rough mattresses were stuffed with straw and simply laid on the floor. The pillow, she discovered as she prodded it experimentally, was another subject altogether. It was soft and filled with, not unexpectedly, goose down. No wonder Traveler liked the evil-tempered birds so much. They had so many uses.

She was achingly tired, and her lids were already starting to droop. But unlike her fellow travelers, she was determined to thank the god who had provided for her. She took Singer, still wrapped in concealing fabric, with her. She could spare no money; all she had to offer was her song. Gillien eased open the door that led to the altar, wondering what she would find.

The light was dim, dimmer even than that in the sleeping room. Gillien stepped quietly inside, closing the door behind her. She blinked, letting her eyes adjust to the faint illumination provided by the single candle, then smiled at what she saw. The floor was strewn with earth and leaves, representative of the roads that Traveler walked. In the center of the room was an altar fashioned from tree branches and stumps. It was there that the single candle burned.

A small bowl sat on a pedestal of wood at Gillien's left. A few coins, jewels, and trinkets of worth only to the giver and the god lay on the polished wooden bottom. To Gillien's right was a small font of water. She hesitated, not knowing for certain what it was for, then cupped a hand into the water and drank a little. The water was cool, earthy, and oddly sweet.

She felt a faint tingle of mirth quiver up her left arm, a message from Singer, and she blushed. Apparently, she'd just taken a draft of holy water, meant to purify the worshipper, not slake his thirst.

"Well, I've never been in a place like this before," she hissed to the lute, covering her embarrassment with irritation. "How was I supposed to know?" She glanced up at the altar a few steps ahead, and mumbled, "Sorry. I meant no disrespect."

Singer felt certain that none had been taken.

Gillien sighed; she'd gotten off on the wrong foot yet again. She stepped forward and seated herself cross-legged—so much easier to do in a short tunic than a long, hindering dress—and placed the instrument in her lap.

She plucked on Singer softly, humming a little, searching for the right song. She found it, and smiled to herself.

"I want to thank you for your hospitality," she said aloud, feeling awkward. "I'm in a lot of danger, and a safe place . . . well, it's something very special to me now. I'd like to ask your blessing for the rest of my journey. It's really important that I carry out my task successfully. But I guess you know that, you're a god."

She began to sing, softly, so that she would not be heard by the slumbering farmers, but clearly. The song was an old, old traveling song, and she was sure that the god had heard it a hundred thousand times before, but she had always loved it. Gillien and her family had always made a point of asking Traveler's blessing and singing this song before embarking on a new journey, and it had worked for them . . . until the monster came.

Her voice caught as her thoughts drifted away from the lyrics to the thing that was pursuing her. Deliberately, she forced them back to the song, and concentrated on the sense of freedom, adventure, and quiet confidence the words always imparted. She strummed the final chord, then sat in silence.

"Last time I heard a boy your age sing soprano, he'd had a very nasty accident," came a rough voice laced with humor.

For a wild instant, Gillien was certain that the god himself had spoken, then logic asserted itself. She twisted around violently to see the Blesser standing behind her, leaning against the doorway.

He was as unlike the handsome, gentle Cadby as could be imagined. This man was big, well over six feet, with powerful arms and a deep chest. Hard lines were grooved on his face, and his eyes were sharp and piercing. He had almost no hair; what little was left was iron gray. Big hands with powerful fingers were incongruously engaged in drying a bowl. The sleeves of his gray robe had been rolled up, revealing a griffin tattoo on his inner left arm. As he finished up his task, she saw his palms, creased and worn, just like they ought to be.

He was no Nightlands Demon. Still, if she had encountered him in ordinary clothes outside the temple, she would have fled. But a closer look showed her that the expression on that hard, roughed-up face was every bit as friendly as that on young Konal.

"So, my young lass, who are you, and what are you doing dressed in that fashion?" he asked, subtle as a charging bull.

She could continue the fabrication no longer. "Blesser—do you have mind magic?" It would be easier to show her trouble than tell him about it.

The big man shook his head. "No. No magic at all. I serve Traveler with the sweat of my body. And a good, strong body it is too. I used to be a cook in His Majesty's army until I heard the call, in case you're wondering what a hulking bear like Rufiel is doing posing as a holy man."

There was no mistaking the friendliness and humor of Blesser Rufiel, and Gillien relaxed. "My name is not important," she said. "The important thing is, I'm in a lot of trouble, and the less you know about me the better."

A thundercloud of anger settled on the craggy face. "Is someone trying to hurt you, child? An angry husband or father?"

"Kill me, actually. And anyone who stands in his—its— way." She paused, wondering if she ought to drag this good-hearted man into the puzzle, and opted for partial truth. "I wish it were something as simple as a jealous husband, Blesser, but I'm all tangled up with something even I don't understand. All I know is, you mustn't tell anyone about me. I mean, you can say a young boy stayed here one night, but don't tell anyone I'm a girl, or that I play an instrument. *Especially* that I play an instrument. And look out for their hands. You see anyone with palms that aren't lined, please, please be very careful."

The Blesser was about to laugh, but saw the deadly earnestness on her pale, dirty face. "An illusionist?" Some kinds of mind magic could make the practitioner appear to be anyone he wanted. It was always a he—the only magic gifted to women was heart magic. Men alone could practice mind and hand magic.

Rufiel's guess was good enough; no need to complicate things with Nightlands Demons or whatever it might be, Gillien thought. "More or less. Please, Blesser Rufiel, you and your Tenders be very careful."

Rufiel stared at her a moment longer, then stepped over to the offering bowl. His thick fingers plucked out several coins, and without a word he handed them to the young minstrel.

"You'll need this," he said.

"Oh, no, those are for Traveler and running the Lamp, I—"

"If you're in danger, miss, I would be no priest if I didn't do everything I could to help you." The voice was hard, but not cruel—just determined. "I'll speak to my boys. Someone may have seen you come in here, but by Traveler's staff, they'll not learn anything more about you from us."

"A Blesser of Light tried to help me this morning," she said, her voice thick, "and he wound up dead. I don't want—"

"I will say a prayer for your friend, child, but I have no plans to join him."

The coins, gold, copper and silver, still glittered in his big, callused palm. Gillien reached out her own small hand and accepted the gift.

"I don't know how to thank you."

"Oh, yes you do. When this is all over, you come back to the Lamp and sing us a song all about it. Traveler loves songs of adventure. And so do I. Go get some sleep, now. I will keep watch tonight. When do you wish to rise?"

"I'd like to be in Riverfork by dawn."

"I'll wake you when it's time. Sleep now, child. This is a house of safety. Nothing ill will come to you, unless it manages to make its way past me." He smiled, revealing several missing teeth. "And nothing yet has."

Gillien obliged, returning to her pallet and falling asleep almost as soon as her head hit the pillow. Her dreams were light and pleasant, and bore no hint of the nightmare that haunted her waking moments.

Most blessed are they who willingly sacrifice so that others might live. They are the holiest of holy mortals, and all the gods—yea, even dark Vengeance and Lady Death—give them honor.

—from The Seven Levels of Holiness

CHAPTER SEVEN

Gillien was instantly awake, her eyes wide and darting about in the darkness as she inhaled swiftly through her nostrils. One big hand was clamped firmly over her mouth. A second hand had her wrist in a lock that was not painful, not yet, but promised to be if she moved a fraction of an inch.

"It's Blesser Rufiel," hissed a soft voice in her ear. Gillien went limp with relief. "Thought I better make sure you woke up quiet. With all you'd been through, you might wake up fighting."

Gillien saw the logic in that, even as she was annoyed with Rufiel for his tactics. She nodded her comprehension, and he released her. Her heart was still thudding painfully even as she trembled with the release of tension. She found that she was indeed wide awake, despite having only a few hours' sleep. She supposed that she ought to thank the Blesser for *that,* too, but at this instant did not feel terribly inclined to do so.

"What hour?" she whispered, rising. The pain of stiffened

limbs assaulted her, and she stretched out her aching body with caution.

"Three hours before dawn. You should make Riverfork just in time for sunrise. Do you have friends there?" asked Blesser Rufiel. She could just barely make out his shape in the dim light of the fire. He was a huge, dark figure, hulking above her, yet he caused no fear. She trusted him.

"I . . . well, I hope so," she answered.

"If you need help, come right back here. You know the way. Tender Konal has packed some food for you and Tender Benean has your horse ready." He reached out a hand and placed it gently on her forehead. "Traveler's blessing be upon you, child."

Before she could thank him, the big man had turned purposefully away and lumbered back toward the dining area, closing the door behind him.

Gillien began to gather her belongings. She paused for a moment, then, unable to resist, slipped her hand inside Singer's swaddling and caressed the smooth, cool wood.

"Good morning," she said softly.

The lute welcomed her touch. She smiled, happy to reestablish contact with the magical instrument. It hoped she was well and expressed a hint of concern.

"Yes, we're still all right. Back on the road again, though, I'm afraid."

Singer did not mind.

She rewrapped the instrument, heaved her pack over her shoulder, and left the Lamp of Traveler.

Dew hung in the air like something palpable. Gillien felt the damp coolness on her face as she stepped outside, closing the door behind her. As Blesser Rufiel had promised, Humble and Benean were waiting for her. The young boy grinned.

"All ready for you, sir. You'll want to stick this in your pack," he added, extending a wrapped bundle in her direction. "There's some bread and fruit in there for you to eat. I noticed you didn't have a waterskin. I know it can get thirsty on the road, so I gave you one of ours."

"Tender Benean, you and everyone here have been so kind to me, I hardly know how to thank you," Gillien replied.

"We have but served our god well. He'll show his pleasure soon enough. He'll send some fat merchant through here or something like that." The boy grinned, and Gillien felt a kinship with him. A smile tugged at her own lips, and she surrendered to it. Without another word, she touched Humble's foreleg, and jumped up onto her mount's back as he knelt to accommodate her. A few soft words and gentle pressure with her leg turned the horse back to the road, and Gillien lifted a hand in farewell to Benean.

The open courtyard that was the public area of worship in Light's temple was not as crowded today as it had been yesterday. Blesser Lucan was not surprised. Riverfork was not an overly devout town, and that even some folk made time in their schedule to worship each god on his or her holydae was commendable. Yesterday, Lisdae, had dawned on a fairly good showing of worshippers in the temple. Today, Losdae, Love's service was held at Love's temple at the other end of the city, and did not begin until midmorning. Those who were able to slept late. Others were busy tending to their duties. In Riverfork, as in every town in Byrn, faith ranked below getting food on the plate.

Blesser Lucan observed that there were a few here today, though, seated patiently on the smoothly carved wooden benches. As he stood before them, one eye on the sky awaiting the right hour, he noticed that several were strangers. This was to be expected in a merchant village like Riverfork.

The courtyard was about fifty feet by forty. Low stone walls provided a symbolic enclosure, but not a practical one. Plants sacred to Light blossomed in a garden that lined the wall: sunflowers, marigolds, daisies, heliotrope, and others. The courtyard itself was nothing but earth, baked hard by the sun. At the far end of the courtyard was Light's temple proper, constructed of light-hued wood and fitted with many windows made of real glass. Some of the glass windows were stained, and at night, illuminated from within, Light's temple was even more beautiful to behold than during the day.

The sky was slightly overcast, but Lucan had been performing this ritual daily for twenty-seven years. He kept his eyes on the mountains that were the best landmark in Verold. He knew the predawn sky well enough, even in the pouring rain, to know when Light showed his face to Verold.

The moment came. At that instant, Lucan's gaze dropped to the candle placed in the direction of east. He gazed at the unlit candle, letting his eyes softly unfocus. Then he waved his hand, gnarled and liver-spotted yet still strong, over the lifeless wick, and conjured fire. The wick sprang to life just as the sun appeared in the east. Later in the day, when the sun, traveling on its daily rounds, was fully at its apex, the Blesser would light the candles to the north and south. Precisely at sunset, the candle in the west would be lit. All four candles would then burn steadily throughout the night, signifying that Light was present, even in the darkness. Only at the still, quiet hour right before dawn would they be extinguished, to be relit in the presence of those who worshiped this powerful, benevolent, yet unpredictable deity.

Lucan turned and smiled gently at the small gathering that sat before him. "Light shall never fail us," he said in the Low Tongue so that all might understand. High Speech was reserved for ceremonies confined to Blessers, Tenders, and those educated enough to be able to comprehend the far older, more complicated language. "Behold, even when we cannot see his face, he provides illumination. What is his message to us, children of the Light?"

"Illumine," the little congregation replied.

Lucan nodded his gray head, pleased. Even the strangers present here today seemed to know the answer to that one.

"Illumine," he repeated. "Illumine not only with the tools that we know and can feel and see—with sunlight made welcome in our homes with open shutters, with candle flame and lamp flame, with torch and hearthfire. But illumine with the greatest light of all—the light of knowledge."

Some of those assembled began to stir. Lucan smothered a

slight smile. It was easy to acknowledge the power and importance of Light during the day, when the god was in his ascen-
dancy, and at night, when his absence prompted other forms of
brightening a room or an encampment. But the second defini-
tion of the god's creed was never as favored among the general populace.

"Listen to the elders, in home, in village, in city. Observe
the beasts of field and forest, for they have inner knowledge
that the gods have granted to them that we poor humans must
learn for ourselves. Hear what the elven folk have to teach, for
their days have been many, and Light has shone upon them far
longer than upon us." This was a fairly new addition to Lucan's daily blessing, and a fairly daring one as well. Despite
the passage of two centuries of peace and interchange with the
Falarans, not everyone had overcome the ancient, inbred hatred and fear of the immortal race. A few people stirred un-
comfortably at his words, but no one seemed too upset. He
continued.

"And finally, listen to the inner wisdom that blossoms
within every one of us. For unlike the beasts of the forest, we
have the ability to learn and grow, to take the light that shines
within and show it to all we meet. Light has come to us for another day. This day is new. Go now with Light's blessing upon
you, and make of this fresh beginning what you will."

They bowed their heads as Lucan, his white robes swishing
gently, walked among them. He laid a hand upon each wor-
shiper, silently asking Light for his blessing. In silence, after
they had received the blessing, each person rose, looked sky-
ward, placed his hand upon his heart, then left quietly.

One person remained, Lucan noticed. A youth, perhaps fifteen or so, stayed seated on the bench. Lucan felt amusement
brush him, for even though the boy pretended to be wrapped
in prayer, his dark, shaggy head still bowed, Lucan could see
the glimmer of his eyes beneath the almost-closed lids. And
those eyes were fixed on the Blesser.

"Well, my lad," said Lucan as he sat down beside the boy,
"What can I do for you on Light's beautiful new day?"

The boy raised his head. He was a pretty youth, his features fine and delicate, his lips almost too full for a boy. He glanced around uneasily, then said in a low voice, "Blesser, I have news for you. Is there someplace where we can talk privately?"

The twinkle in the old man's eye dimmed. The young man's voice was quiet, but earnest. Whatever the news, he seemed to think it was of great import.

"Aye," said Lucan. He glanced up and gestured to his three Tenders, young boys about the same age of this visiting youth. "Lads, I'll be in my quarters. Can you tidy up for me?"

"Certainly, Blesser Lucan," responded the boys, who immediately set about picking up the benches and placing them to one side. Lucan rose, and indicated that the youth should follow him into the temple.

"I'm Blesser Lucan. What's your name, my son?" asked Lucan as he led the boy inside.

"Garen," the youth replied.

Despite the overcast sky outside, the many windows inside the temple made it brighter than any other comparable room. The main room was far smaller than the courtyard, as generally the only ones admitted here were the Blesser and his Tenders. A single table and benches were set up, covered with the remains of a simple meal to break the fast.

Lucan noticed the untidiness and apologized. "People often stay to talk privately with me on Lisdae after the morning ritual, but not often on the other days of the week. Please excuse the mess; I wasn't expecting you."

"You may wish you'd never met me before this is all over," murmured the youth. Lucan turned sharply to gaze at his visitor, who hunched over his bundles of personal belongings.

"You seem distressed." He opened the door on the far end and motioned the boy through. This was his private room. A small, simple pallet on a rope bed, a single chair and a roughly carved wardrobe were the only pieces of furniture. A personal altar had been set up, facing east.

"It's not lavish, but it is private, and that's what I believe you requested. Now," and he seated himself on the bed, leaving the chair to the boy, "what is your news, my young friend?"

Garen did not answer at once. He went to the window and peered out, careful to not disturb the altar. Satisfied that there was no one about, he sat down in the wooden chair. Several times Garen opened his mouth, then closed it again. The Blesser waited patiently. Illumination, he had learned, occasionally took time.

At last he looked up, and met the Blesser's curious gaze with level blue eyes. "You'd probably get the news in a few hours anyway, but I got here first. At least I hope I did. I'm very sorry to tell you this, Blesser Lucan, but . . ." he swallowed hard, then continued. "Your friend Blesser Cadby is dead."

Lucan felt as though someone had punched him in the stomach. His heart contracted with an almost physical pain, and tears dampened his brown eyes.

"Dead? Oh, Cadby . . . but . . . but he was so young, only a little more than a boy himself, he . . . how did this happen?"

Garen licked his lips, and replied hesitantly. "He was killed . . . killed defending me. He gave his life to save me. I'm so sorry, I wish it could have been different."

"Wait a moment." Lucan held up a hand, trying to sort out the cold information from the heat of his own feelings. "Let me see if I understand you correctly. Cadby died saving your life?"

"Yes."

"Then he died in all grace, and Light will surely number him among the Bright Ones." It was a standard phrase, and in truth he *was* happy for the spirit of the youth who had been like a son to him. But selfishly, Lucan knew he would have denied the boy such immediate grace had he been able to buy Cadby a few more years here on Verold. When he spoke next, his voice was thick.

"How did my young friend die? What peril did he face?"

Garen was silent for a time. When he spoke, he did not directly address Lucan's question.

"Blesser, for various reasons, I'm afraid I can't let you read my thoughts to prove the truth of what I say."

The Blesser smiled wanly. "It would do me no good. Light granted me the gift of hand magic, not mind magic. I can light a lamp in his name, but I can't create the illusion of a sunny day. But I'm curious—why do you think I would doubt you, son?"

"Because what I'm going to say, I think any sane person would disbelieve." Garen leaned forward, his eyes snapping intensity. "But I swear to you, Blesser Lucan, by all the gods and in the memory of those who have died because of my mission, what I say to you is the absolute truth." He swallowed again. "I've lost loved ones too, you see."

"My sympathies, child. Go ahead, then, and tell this tale you don't expect me to believe." He had recovered somewhat, and knew where his duty lay. He had taught Cadby to be selfless, and the boy had taken him at his word, it would seem. Lucan knew he could do nothing less. If Cadby had thought this youth important enough to give his life for, then Lucan could at least hear Garen out.

Gillien gazed at the man, sizing him up. He was everything an elderly Blesser ought to be, apparently. From his gray hair to his kind eyes, from his gentle hands to the genuine love in his voice when he spoke of Cadby, he appeared to be trustworthy. So had Blesser Rufiel, and he had proved her faith in him. But Rufiel was not privy to the sort of strange and sinister tale Gillien was about to relate to Lucan. If there was only a way she could prove the truth of her story!

She was holding the lute in her lap, her pack at her feet. Without realizing it, she slipped a single hand through the fabric, nervously rubbing Singer's smooth wood. At that moment, she felt it contact her. She started.

"Are you all right, Garen?" the Blesser inquired.

Gillien nodded, and started to smile. Singer was right. There was a way to prove at least some of her story, after all.

"Blesser Lucan," she said, unwrapping the instrument, "everything ties in with the importance of this instrument. It's a message—what message, I don't know. But I know that it must get to Queen-mother Ariel as soon as possible."

The Blesser began to frown. "I don't understand," he began, but Gillien cut him off.

"Take the lute. Its name is Singer. Hold it, and then you'll understand."

The old man leaned forward, accepting the beautiful instrument, and rested it in his lap. He touched it with the cautious but curious gracelessness that marks those who have no familiarity with instruments. Suddenly his eyes flew wide. "It . . . it speaks to me!"

Gillien nodded. "In a way, yes. What is it telling you?"

"I'm . . . I'm sensing urgency, a strength of purpose. Something very, very important." He shook his head, as if clearing it of unnerving thoughts, and handed the lute back to Gillien.

"Here, boy. It's too strange a thing for the likes of me. But after that, I'll tell you, I think I'd be willing to believe you if you said you came from Light himself."

"Nothing so noble, I fear." Amusement left Gillien's features, leaving them dark and somber. In a quiet voice, she told of Jencir giving her the lute, but did not mention being the performer who had won the competition. She was certain that once Cadby had been missed, queries would come to Riverfork, and the name Gillien Songespynner would be well known. She spoke of the murder of the elf and her family, of her imprisonment, of Cadby's courage and subsequent death. She told of the monster, taking care to leave nothing out that might alert the Blesser should the creature come to Riverfork in pursuit.

"So you can see," she finished, "why I thought you might not believe me."

Blesser Lucan was silent for a long time, his eyes distant. At length, he spoke.

"Yes, Garen, I understand your concern. And I must say, even now, though I do believe you, it seems preposterous. But so is a magical instrument, and I've felt that with my own hands. Cadby's behavior as you have related it to me is utterly in character for him. That poor, brave boy. I had such high hopes for him. He had great courage, Garen, and an even greater gentleness about him. I'm sorry you didn't know him better."

Gillien lowered her gaze. "I could see his courage and his gentleness, Blesser. Anyone could. I—I wonder . . . do you blame me for his death?"

She had to know. If he did, she would move on. She was not about to thrust herself on a grieving man who blamed her for the death of one who had been his best and brightest Tender.

Lucan shook his head slowly. "No. We all do what we must, do what we are born for. Cadby was born to Light's service, and he died carrying out his charge. I don't know what you were born for, child, but right now it's clear that your errand has an urgency that won't be denied. I find it commendable that, even with the deaths of your whole family weighing on your heart, you strove to do what was right. Cadby did no less. That he is dead and you are alive, well, that's for the gods to sort out."

A weight was lifted from Gillien's heart. Only now, when she had been absolved from blame in that good man's death, did she realize how heavy a burden guilt had been.

"Thank you, Blesser."

"Now," and Lucan sat up straighter, shaking off his sorrow, "what do we do with you and Singer now, hmmm?"

Gillien was confused. "I take it to Kasselton, of course."

"Well, it's clear that that instrument belongs in the hands of our Queen-mother. But do you really think you're the right one for the task?"

Gillien's brows drew together as indignation flooded her. "I've done a good job keeping it out of the hands of that monster so far," she snapped, hurt.

Lucan laughed and held up his hands in a placating gesture. "No, child, it's not your ability that I doubt. I just think that you may be in grave danger. The Nightlands Demon, or whatever it is, now knows who's got Singer. It—he—damn it, the creature—won't just be looking for the lute. He'll be looking for *you*. Wouldn't it be wiser to give the lute to someone else

to take for you? It might create a diversion, throw him off your
trail."

Gillien considered this, still holding Singer in her lap. Jencir
had thought that passing the lute along would buy time, and he
had been right—to a point. Transferring Singer to the care of
someone else had thrown the monster off the lute's trail, but
not Jencir's. In the end, the lute was safer, but the elf was just
as dead as he would have been had he not surrendered the instrument.

She tasted bile in her mouth as she recalled the clean, white
skeleton of what had once been a Falaran. The lute sent her a
calming message.

And in a way, she thought, she *had* passed the lute along
to "someone else"—to Garen, the wandering young man. If
that had not confused the creature enough to buy her at least
a little time, then handing it over to a stranger wouldn't, either. And even if it did, Gillien realized that she most definitely did *not* want to die. She didn't know if she had that
kind of courage—the courage that Jencir had, continuing to
press on knowing he was dying of poison, or that Cadby had
displayed when battling a monster straight out of someone's
worst nightmares.

Singer thought she did, and she smiled a little, caressing its
almost baby-smooth polished surface. *At any rate,* she thought
to the instrument, *I don't really want to find out.*

Besides, she realized now that she didn't want to part with
the instrument. She was surprised at how fond she had become
of the inanimate object—though, truth be told, it was far more
than a simple construct of wood and string. She was very protective of it, and the thought of entrusting it into anyone's care
other than her own was abhorrent.

"No," she said slowly. "I think it'd be best if I kept on carrying the lute."

"Will you at least allow someone in town who has mind
magic to read your thoughts, to see what you might have over-
looked in your encounter with the creature so that you will be
better equipped to fight it?"

"No!" Gillien yelped. Her voice rose several notes, and she

brought it back down to as masculine a sound as she could manage. "No. I can't, Blesser, you have to trust me on this." If someone read her thoughts, they would know her true identity as a woman. And she just couldn't picture the kindly Blesser Lucan agreeing to send a maiden into such certain peril. If she wanted to keep Singer to herself—and as her hands curled around the neck, she admitted that she very much did want to—she would have to keep her identity secret for a bit longer.

Lucan sighed. "As you will, child. I am not permitted to force you to undergo such an intimacy, much though I think it would benefit you." He rose, all brusque efficiency now. "I think you need food, a hot bath, and some rest in a safe place, yes?"

A wan smile curved Gillien's lips. "Why, Blesser Lucan," she joked, "I thought you said you couldn't read minds!" It was good to laugh again, at least a little. The answering smile on Lucan's face reassured her that her humor, despite the tragedy that had brushed both of their lives, was welcomed in this holy house.

Fresh bread, greens from the garden, and fruit were Gillien's repast. She ate in the main room, listening to Blesser Lucan talk about Cadby. The topic of conversation saddened her, but she was glad to hear more about her rescuer. And it seemed to help Blesser Lucan work through his grief. By the end of the meal, he seemed reconciled to the younger man's death, reassured by the thought that the termination of Cadby's life had been for a great and admirable reason—to save another. Gillien felt humbled.

While she ate, the three Tenders lit a fire in the hearth and set pots of water to boil. One by one, the pots were removed from the heat and a Tender, carrying the heavy pot of water carefully, trudged off in the direction of the Blesser's chamber. When Gillien had finished her simple meal, she stayed and chatted with the Blesser for a while longer. At last, one of the Tenders poked his head into the sitting room.

"It's ready for the young sir, Blesser," he said.

"Excellent. Thank you, my son. Garen, you know the way to the room. I'll leave you to your ablutions. Time for me to be about my business; I've let the Tenders run nearly everything this morning and Light alone knows what mischief they've done." He winked in an amiable fashion at the boy in the doorway, who grinned broadly. As she had noticed with Rufiel and his Tenders, Gillien observed that the relationship between Blesser and Tender was not that of noble and servant, but more akin to master and apprentice—perhaps even father and son. There was a great deal of mutual affection between the youths and their master, and much mutual respect, as well.

The Blesser rose and without another word went into the courtyard, where he began inspecting the flowers. Silent as a shadow, the young Tender followed. Gillien fairly raced toward the Blesser's room and the luxury that awaited her.

Closing the door behind her, she turned and grinned at the sight of the large oaken tub filled with water that still steamed slightly. She tried to lock the door, but it had none. Gillien would just have to hope that the Blesser and his Tenders respected the privacy of their guest. She went toward the window, trying not to violate the sacred space of the altar. Her intent was to close the shutters. But she soon realized, to her consternation, that there was none to shut.

"Of course," she said aloud. "No temple to Light would have shutters on its windows."

Could she cover the glass pane with the bedding? She wanted to, but decided against it. She was imposing enough on Blesser Lucan's hospitality as it was. To unmake the bed, hang the sheets over the windows, and perhaps knock down something on the Blesser's private altar would be rude at best, a desecration at worst. She gazed outside, relieved that this window faced only the more functional garden of the temple, and not another house or the busy street.

Resigning herself, she turned to the bath. Quickly she undressed, taking off the sweat-stiff clothing she'd worn for two days and dropping it on the floor. She grimaced; she was filthy and the scent of her own sour sweat assaulted her nostrils. With a final, nervous glance outside, she unbound her breasts and sighed with relief at the liberation.

Across the tub was placed a wooden plank, atop which

rested a cake of soap, some sweetmeats and a glass of wine. As if she'd still be hungry after that meal! A towel lay folded on the bed. With sweet anticipation, Gillien stepped into the water.

It was still pleasantly hot, and as she eased herself down, noting with pleasure that her bare and delicate backside came into contact with a linen pad rather than splinter-filled wood, a sigh of pure contentment escaped her lips. For a few moments Gillien simply soaked, enjoying the feeling of warm water on her weary limbs. Then she dunked her head in the water and used the soap to work up a lather. She was still staggered by how little hair she had left now. By the time she had finished lathering her body with the soap, her hair was almost dry.

She stepped out of the tub onto a mat of woven rushes and began to towel herself dry. Glancing at her filthy clothes, she wrinkled her nose in disgust. The thought of dressing herself in the soiled clothes was offensive, but she only had one other change of clothing. And surely, there would come a time when she'd want fresh clothes more than she did now.

Grimacing, she rebound herself, wrapping the sweat-stiff fabric around her body, until she could once again present a passible male silhouette. Then she shrugged into the cut-off chemise and tunic. The hose and boots, though, could wait.

Gillien unwrapped Singer, and then stretched out on the bed. She wanted to play a few songs, she really did, but she was so tired. Last night she had gotten only had a few hours of sleep, hardly enough to make up for the harrowing long hours of terrified flight she'd endured. She rolled over on her side, cradling Singer to her as, when she was a child, she had cuddled her favorite doll. Within moments, she was fast asleep, utterly secure as the sun's light bathed her face and body, promising protection.

The Seven Gods of Mortal-kind,
the Humans that they lead and blind;
The Fala, the Sa, Ilsi and Kir,
The Lady's people, races fair.
Just as fair, their forms more free,
Swim the People of the Sea.
Demons made from darkest dreams
Guard the Night King as he schemes.
Last and least, the angry Ghil
Lurk and envy, stalk and kill.
But there are more who linger here
Than Demons dark and gods to fear;
More than elves and more than men—
Aertha's kind are one and ten.

—"The Naming of the Kinds" from
The Book of The Lady

CHAPTER EIGHT

Among themselves, the beings had no words to describe who or what they were; for among themselves, the beings had no words.

But those who spoke with voices and who used words to communicate had many names for the race. The Ghil called the creatures *t'chk taa,* the Swallowers, when they spoke of them at all, and spat to cleanse their mouths of the hated word. For though the ratlike Ghil had enemies aplenty, the amorphous beings were the only ones who fed upon them. The Sa, the beings' unlikely allies at the moment, called them the *keshiim,* the Changers. The Fala had a long, involved name for the entities that translated into mortal tongues as "those without souls who slay without remorse." The humans, who until two nights ago had never heard of the shapeshifters, had no word for them at all, though "monster" was what the Changer named Va'kul had heard the dying mortals cry.

It had been little more than a fortnight since Kertu, king of

the Sa, had sought out the Changers to beg their aid. His messenger had been courteous, and the Changers had been curious
enough to listen. They set the terms of the meeting, and Kertu
had agreed.

The night was clear, with only a half-moon to provide illumination. Kertu came as promised, bringing only two other elves
as an honor guard. The two elves carried, respectively, a sword
and a spear—token weapons against shapechangers, but showing a willingness to fight if threatened. Kertu himself bore no
weapons at all. The three Sa climbed the steep mountainside to
the plateau that the Changers had agreed upon as the ren-
dezvous point; if they were weary they did not show it.

Kertu's eyes and crown glittered in the moonlight as he
glanced around, puzzled at first. There were no Changers to be
seen. His face registered displeasure.

Kertu stood up straight, planting his fists on his hips. The
faint light turned his waist-length silver hair to white as he
tossed his head. Every line in his slim form bespoke elegance—
and arrogance.

"I have come, in the dark of the night, with no lights and no
weapons, as the Changers had requested. Do they not honor
their word?" he asked loudly, his musical voice carrying in the
stillness.

There was no answer at first. Then, before the startled elves'
eyes, the scraggly bushes, rocks, and weathered stumps of trees
that dotted the plateau began to shimmer and change. They
widened, lost their clear planes and contours, melted into
rounded forms that were vaguely sand-colored and glistening
with moisture. As one, they quivered. One of them began to
shift yet again, growing taller and slimmer. Legs, arms, and a
head formed, assumed detail and color. In less than five heart-
beats, what looked like a male Sa elf stood before Kertu and his
honor guard.

The "elf" bowed. "King Kertu shows bravery. His people like
the light; ours can be slain by it. He has kept to the terms
agreed. Such courage pleases us. This one," and the Changer/Sa
tapped his chest, "has taken your form, so that you may more

easily communicate with us. This one is called Leader. Sit, and speak to us. We will listen, Kertu of Sali."

And they did. But in the end the Changers, who communicated telepathically, agreed that what Kertu said was nothing much after all. When Kertu had finished, Leader spoke. It was clear that he, and his people, were unimpressed.

"Your fight does not concern us. This Falaran elf—what do we care if he reaches the humans?" Leader waved a slim, pale, unlined hand in disgust. "For longer than this world has been, we have watched you shapelocked beings battle among yourselves. We have never intervened before. Why should we risk one of our own for you now?"

A crafty smile settled on Kertu's sharp face. "Because the humans are your enemies as well as ours," he replied.

The seventy or so shapeless lumps, the slickness of their skins shiny in the starlight, quivered at this answer—their way of showing amusement to the shapelocked. Leader, having taken elven form, had the proper equipment to laugh in disbelief. It was a sight not often seen, for few elves had been gifted with the ability to laugh with real mirth.

"Our enemies, Kertu? How can that be, when they do not even know of our existence?"

"They do not need to know of the existence of predators to wipe out their prey," Kertu replied softly, his intelligent eyes focused on Leader.

Abruptly Leader's laughter ceased. Anger suffused and twisted his face—another strange sight. Swift as a thought, Leader's most trusted and efficient warrior moved beside Kertu. Its form was still mostly without shape, save for one deadly detail. A giant stinger had emerged from the amorphous being, and that stinger was poised within easy striking distance of Kertu's torso. Crying aloud, the elven king's honor guard rose to their feet, their weapons at the ready.

Kertu knew, as all the elves did, about the Changer's poisonous touch, and raised a hand in command.

"Do nothing rash, Taran, Casnar. Put away your weapons."

Reluctantly, the two elves did so, but remained standing and tense.

"Explain your words, elf," spat Leader.

"The humans hate the Ghil. They are presently engaged in an ongoing battle to exterminate the species. Left alone—left *undistracted*—they might well succeed.

"Join with us. Let us prevent this Falaran from warning the humans, so that we might take them by surprise. Lend us one of your warriors to track him down and discover what message he bears."

Leader was clearly upset by the sudden threat to the Ghil, their sole source of food.

"But . . . why can you not send your own people?"

"The humans do not know our race well, which is as we have wished for many centuries. Even Falarans are far from common sights in Byrn. The sighting of even a single Sa in Byrn would be cause for much discussion—much attention. And that is precisely what we do not want."

Kertu paused, brushed a lock of his flowing silver hair out of his purple eyes, and continued.

"But a Changer can look like anyone, anything, it desires. Your race is possessed of the ultimate disguise."

He reached out his hands imploringly. "Help us track down the Falaran bard. You will not only aid us—for which we shall be grateful—but you will insure your food supply, so that your . . . young . . . may flourish."

Leader considered, "listening" to the advice from all his people assembled at once. For the complex Changer brain, it was no difficult task. Some of them were afraid that interfering would bring the wrath of the humans down upon them. If humans ever knew of the Changer susceptibility to light and fire, they could use that knowledge against them, potentially destroying the entire race. The human penchant for burning forests and fields for their crops, some pointed out, had, all unknown to the humans, already forced the Changers out of their original range.

Others thought Kertu was lying. Still others, outraged at the thought of slow starvation, were more than ready to make an alliance, and offered to go as Kertu's weapons.

Leader listened, and thought. At last he spoke.

"We see reason in your request, Kertu. But we will send no

more than one of our kind to do your task. Should it fail to return, then we will not again venture into human territory. They are little known to us; we would not willingly become the objects of their persecution. I shall send my finest warrior, my cleverest Shifter."

He pointed to the Changer sitting beside Kertu. "Prove your worth to the Sa king, and he shall give you a name by which he will know you."

The being's form began to shudder and pulsate. Protrusions burst out of the shimmering wet mass and began to carve themselves into arms and legs. A knob formed on the top of what was rapidly becoming a slender elven torso. Nose, ears, eyes, mouth took shape and color. A final shudder, and what had seconds ago been a shapeless mass was now a twin to a surprised but pleased Kertu—a perfect, nearly flawless replica down to the last point on the delicate, pale ear and the least detail of the elf's clothing.

The resemblance ended when the Changer's mouth curved in a wide, decidedly un-elven grin of cold pleasure. Only the hands were pale and as unmarred by creases as the curve of a baby's cheek.

"Name me, Kertu, King of the Sa," said the Changer in a voice identical to Kertu's.

"I shall call you Va'kul," said Kertu. "It means Many Faces in our tongue."

Va'kul inclined his head. He found he enjoyed the sound of the name as well as its meaning. He was highly intelligent, and in a few hours had learned and internalized everything the Sa knew about human customs and behavior.

Early in the game, Va'kul had come startlingly close to completing his mission, surprising the foolish Falaran crossing the Kyras alone. The elf Jencir had fled on foot, leaving his battle-trained horse to bravely carry on the fight, delaying Va'kul while Jencir put distance between himself and the Changer. Unfortunately for Va'kul, the tactic had worked. Dawn had come too swiftly, and the wily elf had managed to bear his precious burden into the Borderlands of Byrn while his enemy, fuming at the near-triumph, had to wait out the hours of deadly daylight.

But, Va'kul reminded itself as it galloped along the Queen's Road in the form of a horse, it had managed to poison Jencir nonetheless. The blow had been glancing—a strike rather than a full piercing of the elf's body—but Va'kul had secreted enough poison into Jencir to suffice. The elf had tried to trick Va'kul, buying more hours, but had eventually lost the battle. That had been a good thing; Va'kul had discovered that it could feed on Falaran flesh just as well as upon Ghil flesh. Such was valuable information, for this quest looked as if it might take longer than Va'kul or Leader, and perhaps even King Kertu, had expected.

It had been easy to find out where the girl, Gillien Songespynner, was camped in Hallenore. Va'kul, after carefully observing many humans, had donned what its kind called a NewShape, an appearance fashioned out of the creature's imagination rather than being based on any particular person. He had gone to "congratulate the minstrel" while posing as a traveling peddler. That had given him the chance to visit the family. How pathetically easy it had been to pose as one or the other of them, slip into the caravans, and slit their sleeping, exposed throats with the tools of their own trade! Only one, the boy, had woken and given Va'kul any difficulty at all.

And how furious Va'kul had been when he discovered no lute at the encampment.

The black horse that was the Changer snorted and tossed its mane angrily. Its hooves flew with tireless speed, devouring the earth, drawing closer to where it had assumed Gillien Songespynner had fled.

Drawing closer to the lute.

Knowing that the murders would be discovered, Va'kul had slipped into the home of the head law man of Hallenore, Reeve Herrick, and silently snapped his neck as the man lay sleeping. His best hope was to pose as the reeve, for no doors would be shut to his inquiries. With the face of such an authority as a mask, Va'kul had located Jencir quickly—but again, not quickly enough. He finished the job of slaying the elf, engulfed the corpse with his shapeless body, and absorbed all soft organic material—flesh, clothing, leather. When he had finished, he had simply walked out the way he had come. Va'kul had deliberately murdered Gillien's family in a normal, human fashion rather than engulfing their remains so that he, as Reeve Herrick, could "investigate" the murders and track down the "killer," Gillien.

How obliging of her to show up and deliver herself into his smooth, unmarked hands—with lute intact! But the lute would not reveal its message, and things had suddenly gone very, very wrong. She had escaped him a second time, even sent him on a false trail up the King's Road for several miles.

But now, the great horse Va'kul was on her trail. Now, it would—

The black stallion clattered to a sudden stop, its nostrils flaring wide. A human, up ahead. Gillien? Perhaps. Perhaps not. In an instant, the horse's body twisted and re-formed itself into the innocuous-seeming peddler whose shape had lulled Gillien's family into a false sense of security.

At once, Va'kul lost the animal's heightened senses, and could no longer scent the mortal. But a small pinpoint of light was drawing closer, bobbing and weaving a few feet off the ground. Sound floated to his ears; the human was singing a walking song.

> Walking and wand'ring, wending my way
> By sun or by starlight, by night or by day.
> With many companions, or all on my own;
> With Traveler guarding, I'm never alone.
>
> Here is a tavern, here is a town,
> Here is a king, and here is a clown;
> Here is a mountain, here is a stream;
> Here I shall rest me, here I shall dream.
>
> Sun on my face, my god in my heart,
> Here's to beginnings, here's to good starts;
> Blessed be the traveler, long may he roam
> And blessed be the traveler, coming safe home.

> Walking and wand'ring, wending my way
> By sun or by starlight, by night or by day.
> With many companions, or all on my own;
> With Traveler guarding, I'm never alone.

The singing traveler wore what Va'kul was coming to recognize as holy vestments, though these were of a different hue than those worn by the young man who had dared stand up to him back at Holding House. This man approaching was also older. He carried a small lamp and used a walking stick.

"Good evening, Blesser!" Va'kul called, raising his hand in a gesture he had observed being used as a welcome.

"Traveler's blessing be upon you, wanderer!" the Blesser called cheerfully in return. As he drew closer, he slid the hood back off his face and bared his teeth in the gesture that Va'kul recognized as friendly among humans.

"It's a bit late to be out alone on the road, friend. It's getting on toward the mid-night."

"I am pleased to have encountered you. Is there a place where one might rest anywhere nearby?" If there were an inn or tavern, Va'kul realized his chances of finding Gillien were better. She would be afraid to travel alone at night—afraid of him.

"Not for many more miles yet, I fear, unless you wish to retrace your steps and lodge back at Hallenore."

Va'kul was disappointed, but not discouraged. "Do you think this road safe, Blesser?"

"As safe as any road in these times, I would say. It is not as well traveled as the King's Road, but that may be good or ill luck. Where are you heading?"

"Wherever people will buy my wares." He indicated the pack he carried. It bulged, but with nothing at all. It was late, and no one would ask him to unpack at this hour, with no light by which to see. "I sell trinkets, carvings, such things."

The Blesser smiled indulgently.

"May your pack soon be light and your pockets heavy," he said graciously. "My path takes me northeast, else I'd accompany you. Travel safely." He bowed and made as if to move on.

Va'kul hesitated. "Blesser . . ." It was risky, but not terribly so. If this plan failed to work, he could kill the Blesser easily enough.

"Yes?"

"My young daughter has recently come this way, planning to meet me in Riverfork. Perhaps you have seen her? Her name is Gillien Songespynner. She's about so tall, with long, dark hair. She plays a lute."

"Ah, now that must be a popular lass," replied the Blesser. "You're the second one has asked about her since I've been on this road."

Instantly, Va'kul was alert. "And the first?" He fought to keep his voice casual. There was more to be gained by probing the Blesser for information than in attacking him.

"A young man on a dapple-gray pony. Said the girl was a friend of his."

"When was this? And what did this boy look like?"

A shadow of consternation crossed the priest's face. "Oh, dear, I hope I haven't wandered into a family quarrel."

Va'kul seized on this opening. He worked his face into sorrow overlaid with a hint of anger.

"You have forced the truth from me," he said, making his voice catch. "My daughter ran away. I fear she may have eloped with this young man. Pray, before it is too late, tell me what he looked like, and where I might find him."

"Be not too harsh with the lad," the priest urged. "Remember how hot the blood flows in young men of that age."

Va'kul, who had never felt blood, hot or cold, flow in his own body, nevertheless nodded.

"I wish to talk with him, that's all."

"I was with him only last night. He is as tall as your daughter Gillien. His hair too is dark, but rather curly and short. He rode a dapple-gray horse, and his clothes were untidy. He seemed pleasant enough. I gave him a light to travel by, and sent him on to the Lamp of Traveler, several miles southwest. I doubt you'll reach it before morning, and I fear your bird may have flown by then. If he was meeting Gillien in Riverfork, he would have been on his way early this morning. He would not have tarried at the Lamp."

Anger flooded Va'kul. He felt his control over this form start to slip, and he tightened his hold on his appearance.

"Then I must find him in Riverfork. And, I hope, my wayward daughter. Goodnight, Blesser." Without waiting for an answer or a blessing, Va'kul strode into the darkness.

After he had put a safe distance between himself and the Blesser, he again transformed. This time, he shunned both the human form and the equine.

Va'kul's guise of a peddler melted and turned in on itself. The arms thickened, grew longer, as the human body shrank and compressed into a giant black bird, which ruffled its feathers and then sprang into the sky, its powerful, shiny wings beating with purpose.

There was no need for Va'kul to confine itself to the earth anymore. It did not think it would encounter Gillien on the road before reaching Riverfork. Another human had ventured into the Changer's plans; another complication in a hunt that had already gone far too wrong for the hunter's liking.

Who was this mysterious young man? Was he indeed simply a young lover, or was something more sinister afoot?

Was there another hunter in this chase?

Riverfork might indeed be many miles to the west. Va'kul the peddler might have taken many hours to reach it—even Va'kul the horse. But it was not far, as the crow flies. Not far at all.

Within three hours, the shapeshifter had reached its destination. Riverfork, nestled in the V formed by the junction of the rivers Myr and Ullan, was a fairly large community, the largest human town Va'kul had yet seen. Uneasiness stirred within it as it flew slow, lazy circles over the place. Gillien could be anywhere. Va'kul cocked its head and rolled one eye toward the moon, whose waxing brightness silvered the landscape and town beneath. The white orb had traveled far since nightfall, and Va'kul knew that dawn would be on the way in just a few hours. It assumed that Gillien had arrived here shortly after dawn on the day before, which would mean that she had had the entire day to search out shelter.

It was best to try to find news of her, Va'kul decided, rather

than search for the girl herself. Besides, Va'kul was growing
hungry. Assuming so many different forms used much energy.
It folded its wings and plunged silently earthward, alighting
well outside the city limits. Once on the ground again, it assumed its peddler shape and began walking toward the town.

At Riverfork's main gate, he was met with a challenge. Two
guards, large men in leather armor whose drawn swords indicated they meant business, stopped him.

"Who comes to Riverfork at this hour?" one demanded.

Va'kul bowed obsequiously. "Only Erstan, a humble peddler.
I pray you good sirs, the night is damp. Will you not admit a
simple wanderer?"

The second one stepped forward. "Unpack your goods, peddler," he demanded.

Va'kul had expected as much. His sack was now loaded with
what appeared to be an array of children's toys—carved
wooden soldiers, a stick with a horse's head on it, a smiling doll
made of cloth. As the first guard approached, carrying a lantern
to inspect the sack, Va'kul tensed. The toys were of course part
of himself, as were his clothes. Nothing on him, clothes, toys, or
packs, was removable. If the guards wanted him to empty the
sack, he would have to transform quickly and kill them both.

Fortunately, the hour was late and the guards less than thor-
ough. They were not interested in an old man's wares, only in
his possible weapons—which Va'kul had deliberately not "created." The guard glanced into the sack, felt around the bottom
with his hand, then nodded.

"Welcome to Riverfork, old man," the second guard said. He
turned to face the large door and pounded on it. "Open."

There was a moment of silence, then a creaking sound as the
gates were slowly opened. Va'kul nodded his thanks and
slipped into the town of Riverfork.

At this hour, the streets were deserted. Lamps burned along
the main streets, providing smoky illumination, but most of the
shops were closed. Far down the main road, Va'kul could see
the glitter of lanterns and dimly catch an echo of music laced
with human conversation and laughter.

Va'kul was pleased. A tavern. It was, he was learning, a place where humans gathered to drink and talk, where tongues were loosened and unsavory deeds went less noticed than in other, brighter, less heady places. A place where the lonely—or the frightened—might go to find company.

Va'kul looked down at his hands with a trace of irritation. No one among his people knew why they could not replicate the unique patterns of the hands and feet. The Sa thought they knew. According to Sa mythology, the whorls on the hands and feet were where humans and elves kept their souls. Since the Sa felt that the Changers had no souls, it was logical that they could not forge the complicated patterns.

Irritation grew into anger. Va'kul was the finest among his people in shapechanging. Yet not even he could make his palms and feet display anything other than a smooth, pale surface. Now he gazed at the stiff, thick fingers of the peddler he feigned to be. As he watched, the fingers grew softer, longer, the hand smaller. The nails, cropped to the quick, began to lengthen into carefully trimmed ovals.

The change continued, reshaping the gaunt, tall peddler into a statuesque female. The gray, sparse hair thickened, tumbling down in a lush black wave to the Changer's slimming waist. Clothes, too, appeared, turning Va'kul's rags into attractive, form-fitting feminine attire. Gloves, having the appearance of soft, supple leather, began to cover the delicate fingers.

Va'kul tossed her thick mane of hair and fluffed it with her gloved hands. She wished she had what humans called a mirror, to see if this NewShape was as attractive as she was trying to make it. She ran her fingers over the oval face, full lips, and long throat; down full breasts and trim waist.

She sighed, a sweet, musical sound in the quietness of the dark hour. It would have to do. She needed to find sustenance soon, or else she would not be able to hold this form for long.

Drawing her shoulders back and fixing a slight smile on her face, Va'kul entered the tavern in search of prey.

For it's drink, drink, drink,
And pass around the bottle-O
Don't think, think, think,
Upon what you've just seen.

The clink, clink, clink
Of blood-red wine-filled glasses O
Will sink, sink, sink
The thoughts of pain so keen.

—Byrnian soldiers' drinking song

CHAPTER NINE

The goblet provided by the tavern, a poor, cheap wooden creation, still held a glimmer of ruby liquid in its depths. Beside the shoddy chalice sat an equally poor bottle of wine, still mostly full.

Daric Rhan stared as if hypnotized by the glint of red within the goblet, then his gaze wandered to the bottle. His tongue crept out to lick his lips, tasting what lingered of the vinegary beverage. It did little to complement a meal, less as a thing to be enjoyed on its own merits, but Daric seldom drank wine for its flavor.

He took a deep breath, held it for a second or two, then let it escape slowly through his nostrils. It was a trick he'd figured out long ago, something to make his tumbling thoughts slow, become less urgent. Sometimes it worked. Other times, like tonight, it didn't.

Daric was a large, well-muscled man. Dark brown hair was pulled back into a small ponytail, and women had once been easily seduced by his rumbling laugh and flashing brown eyes. He had not laughed in a long time, though, and his dark eyes were more often circled from lack of sleep than glimmering with passion or mirth. His face, as he stared at the bottle, seemed decades older than his mere twenty-four.

He felt a gentle touch on his broad shoulder. Soldiering instincts instantly alert, he whirled, dagger already partly drawn, to see the smiling face of a beautiful woman.

"A handsome man like you shouldn't be sitting alone," she purred in a slightly husky voice. "May I join you?"

Her hair was dark as midnight, tumbling down her back, and her tight-fitting garments left little of her womanly curves unrevealed. But there was something in her eyes, her manner, that Daric didn't like. Something cold, almost predatory. She was too certain of victory, and that sat ill with him. Tonight, of all nights, he didn't want to engage in any kind of struggle—even a friendly one that took place in bed. Besides, he didn't have the sort of money that a woman this beautiful would demand for her attentions.

He dropped his gaze to the cup. "No," he growled. "Find easier prey tonight, whore."

The hand on his shoulder tightened. Her nails dug into his flesh even through the fine leather gloves she wore. Daric glanced up at her again, his eyes narrowed. Her lovely face, almost too lovely, too perfect, had gone hard and angry. Then, like a curtain falling across a bed, a smile replaced it. The woman nodded acknowledgment, and moved on. For a moment, Daric watched the alluring sway of her hips as she went to another corner of the dark, smoky tavern. The men sequestered there welcomed her presence with lewd, raucous remarks. The woman smiled, and seated herself in the lap of one of them.

For a moment, Daric envied her. She was so certain of her purpose in life—of her skills, her talents, and how to apply them to get exactly what she wanted. Once, he too had been that way. Once, he had been a decorated hero in His Majesty King Evrei's Army of Byrn. Once, he had been an officer, leading men to fight the pervasive but—he thought—unintelligent enemy the Ghil. His unit of warriors had cleared out the entire Northwestern Section of the foul vermin. Dozens of them a day fell to his sword and those of his men, once they had found and conquered the hidden burrows of the creatures.

Then the quake had come, as unexpected and as impossible to fight as the wrath of the Nightlands King himself, trapping Daric's unit within the earth. With an equal suddenness, the tide had turned. Humans were the quarry now, frantically battling time and the Ghil in order to escape with their lives. Some escaped to safety; some escaped to death. And some— Captain Daric Rhan among them—were trapped like mice by the cat and put to work, overseen by monsters and, far, far worse, men who behaved like monsters . . .

A deep shudder passed through Daric as he shut his eyes against the memory. He thought he groaned aloud, and his eyes flew open. Had he? Was anyone . . . did anyone hear or see . . . But the tavern inhabitants were intent on their own troubles or pleasures, and cared not for the painful reminiscences of one formerly gallant captain.

Seven months. That's all it had been. Just seven months lost to sweat and darkness and pain. How in the Nightlands, Daric wondered with a fresh burst of despair, could something that had lasted so brief a time in days, hours, and minutes continue to secrete poison for four long years?

His hand closed around the bottle. For an instant, Daric wanted to give in, as he had done time without number before. It was such an easy escape. Wine, or ale, or cider—the type of alcohol mattered little—was cheap and easily obtained, and the oblivion it offered beyond price. Daric lifted the bottle . . . then set it down again.

An easy gesture, physically. The bottle itself weighed hardly anything at all. But Daric felt cold sweat dot his forehead and trickle down the back of his neck, and the strong hand that held the bottle of forgetfulness was trembling violently. Slowly, deliberately, he clenched his fist closed and brought it down to his lap.

Oh, yes, the former warrior thought to himself with a hot wave of self-loathing, the bottle brought forgetfulness. It also brought destruction, and too often, after the forgetfulness had fled before the cold light of morning and reason, the ruins of what it had caused him to do remained to reproach him.

A bottle near enough to this one to be its twin had rendered him drunk when a raiding party of the Ghil had descended, two months after his rescue. He had been less than useless. Only the courage of his men kept him from being recaptured and flung into a Veroldian version of the Nightlands a second time. Red wine had lost him his position then. And last night—or was it the night before? Daric wasn't sure—beer had lost him even a poor job as a night watchman for the city of Riverfork.

A slow flush darkened his already tanned, stubbled face as he recalled the shameful incident. The unkind liquor had not allowed him to draw the veil of forgetfulness over *this* particular disaster.

Drinking on duty was, of course, forbidden. But for the last few months, Daric had managed to elude detection when he filled his waterskin with wine, beer or whiskey. He'd tried not to take too many sips, but the night air was dry, and his partner more inattentive than usual. Daric found himself intoxicated faster than he had expected, and when he heard the screams for help, he couldn't make his legs move properly. His partner reached the scene of the murder before he did, and when the criminal fled with Daric's partner in pursuit . . .

The blush deepened. Daric had, in his drunken haze, leaped on his own partner and allowed the criminal to escape. Some merciful god had been looking out for him then. His violent punches had only injured his shocked partner, not killed him. Daric's condition had been obvious, and that night he had sobered up behind a locked prison door.

Now, he was no longer employed by the city. Now, he could drink any and everything he wanted, as long as the money in his purse lasted. Now, Daric Rhan could become what he seemed destined to be—another homeless, drunken idiot who huddled in the forgotten corners of Riverfork, accosting strangers and begging for money with which to get even drunker.

Or he could leave the town and its shameful memories behind. Byrn was a big country, and strong men willing to work hard could always find employment, legal or otherwise. There was only one thing standing in the way of a fresh start, and it seemed to smirk at him from the table.

The goblet bore mute testimony to the fact that Daric had already sampled the wine. He had to. It was the wrong season to request "new" cider, freshly bottled apple juices that had not yet reached the full power of their fermentation. Well water was hardly potable, and to select that or, gods forbid, goat or cow milk as his beverage would draw unwanted attention. There were enough in the tavern as it was who knew him, and who occasionally favored him with disgusted glances. Daric would not inform the strangers present of his weakness by so publicly admitting that he, as large and powerful a man as he was, had no head for liquor. He had ordered a bottle of wine and a pitcher of water to lessen the liquor's potency. It seemed to work well enough. Thus watered down, and used to wash down the tavern's pitiable excuse for a meal, it lacked the power of straight drink. And its flavor, poor to begin with, had no appeal when served this way.

He could do it, maybe. In his own time, and his own way, letting no one in on the shameful secret that alcohol had as sure a grip on him as Death's spirit wolves on a dying man's soul. Then, he could get—and hold—a position of respect. He could think clearly again, as he had done before . . . before . . .

And then the memories would have not even the slightest veil, some perverse voice in his mind told him. *Are you ready to remember, Daric Rhan? To recall just what was done to you when—*

Abruptly, Daric made his decision. There could be no job that paid well enough, that offered his soul enough peace and activity, to make it worth permitting the memories to resurface.

His handsome mouth compressed into a grim, determined line. There was enough money in his purse to get well and truly drunk tonight. Tomorrow, and all the other tomorrows, could take care of themselves. He'd not see them again, save filtered through the comforting haze of forgetfulness. He reached for the bottle.

Without warning, a slim, gloved hand closed on his wrist. Before Daric could react, the hand was gone, and its owner had slipped into the seat opposite the startled warrior.

"I have a better proposition for you than what lies at the bottom of a bottle, my friend," the slim, cowled stranger said in a soft voice. Utterly shocked, Daric, one hand on his dagger, stared into huge, purple eyes that unmistakably marked the stranger as a Sa elf.

"Call on what training you remember, warrior, and keep your tongue still," the elven stranger continued, his voice soft and sweet. The purple eyes glittered in the slight light of the single candle on the table.

"I have a proposition for you, one that I think you might find advantageous indeed."

Still Daric stared, wondering which of the emotions warring within him was the appropriate one. He was stunned to see a Sa elf on this side of the border. The Sa were known to dislike humans, and to the best of his knowledge none had ever even ventured into Byrn before. Wisely, the elf had cloaked himself from head to foot, covering the silver hair and telltale pointed ears with a voluminous cowl. His hands were likewise covered with gloves. Their paleness in comparison with the darker tones of mortal skin would have been noticed and remarked upon. Only the eyes, twice again as large as Daric's and a startling, cool shade of violet, betrayed the being's race.

Besides the shock of simply seeing the elf, Daric found that he was furious at what the Sa had implied—furious because it was the truth. He had been about to drown himself in the red tide of alcohol, but it shamed him to the core of his being that anyone, particularly such an alien being as a Sa elf, should know of his secret shame.

He did not want to listen. He wanted to grab the bottle, raise it to his lips, and drain it dry. But Daric had not lost the curiosity that had once made him a brave and adventurous soldier, at least not quite. He quelled his itch for the drink and forced himself to be civil.

"Who are you?" he demanded, though remembering to keep his voice soft.

"Guard your face as well as your tongue, mortal," the elf sighed softly, pouring himself a glass of wine from the bottle. "There are eyes and ears everywhere, none of which ought to see or hear what I have to say. Smile, and greet me like an old friend. Or at least a new one."

A hint of a smile touched the elf's own thin, pale lips.

"To answer your question, my name is Taran. More, you do not need to know. I am looking to hire a strong man who knows how to use a sword." He gestured to Daric's attire, the sword propped up against the table within easy reach, should it be needed by its master.

"You seem to meet the requirements, at least the outward appearance. Your mien, your build, the tools of your trade— even a stranger to your land such as myself could hardly fail to discern your occupation." Taran took a sip of wine, and made a face. "Hardly quality fare, but no matter."

Daric's mouth thinned as his temper rose.

"I need no further employ," he said shortly. "I would ask that you leave my table."

A faint smile showed on the sculpted features.

"Ah, but I disagree. You *do* need it. If I may speak frankly, I noticed that you chose the least expensive wine and meat for your meal. And your clothing . . . well, it is hardly what a swordsman who has a high position would choose to wear, is it?"

The voice was cool, and never varied in its soft, polite tones. Daric knew that the vast majority of elves had only moderate emotions and mockery was not something they tended to engage in, but he felt himself the butt of some Sa joke. He fought to contain his anger.

"The quality of my sword speaks of my training, and the quality of my food speaks of my fall from grace, is that it?"

The words were hard, bitten off, but he kept his voice quiet. Taran raised a silver eyebrow in approbation.

"Precisely. Do I take it that you are interested in hearing more?"

Part of Daric wasn't. Part of him wanted to take the bottle, drain it, then crack it over this arrogant elven bastard's fragile skull. But another part of him was glad of the intervention, and was curious. He could always drink later.

"Go on."

"I need to know about you first. Do you have any family?"

"None."

The elf nodded. "That is well. What is your view of your king and country?"

Daric's dark black eyebrows narrowed in a frown. His brown eyes flashed.

"I may not serve my king and country directly anymore," he growled, "but I'm no traitor to either, if that's what you're asking."

"Would you slay such a traitor?"

"If I had enough proof and the crime warranted it, yes," Daric replied. He was fully alert now. Whatever Taran wanted, it was certainly not going to be some petty lark.

"You are not afraid of killing, then."

"I've done it before."

"Does the blood of innocents darken your blade?"

Daric again felt anger well up inside him. "I have killed Ghil, criminals, and men who wanted my life. But I have never raised my sword against woman or child, or man, without cause. If you're looking for a hired killer—"

"Have you heard rumors of the slave trade?"

The question jolted Daric as if he'd been slapped. *The slave trade.* Taran's face was as calm as ever, though his eyes were watching Daric's reactions with the keenness of a hawk. For a moment, Daric's mouth worked, but no words came.

"It pays well, I understand. Would you be interested in joining if you were so approached?"

Words hissed out between Daric's gritted teeth. "You asked who I'd kill earlier, elf. I'll tell you. I would kill slavers with as little qualm as I'd kill a rabbit for my supper—and with a far greater sense of justice. Rabbits, at least, derive no pleasure from torturing and betraying their own kind."

Taran made a slight gesture, indicating that Daric should

lower his voice. A few seconds later, Daric saw the woman who had approached him earlier sweep past without looking at him again. She was hanging on the arm of a foolish-looking older man, one delicate, gloved hand caressing his cheek. The old man was beaming happily. He'd wake up sadder but wiser in the morning, Daric thought to himself.

He discovered he was sweating again. Taran had moved the bottle out of his reach, whether by accident or calculation, Daric wasn't sure. Gods!

The slave trade ... "Trade." As if it were a craft, like smithing, or carpentry.

Ah, gods, his mouth was dry ... But the elf was speaking again.

"Soldiers need to be strong, need to be immune to temptation or bribery. Yet I know that all men have weaknesses." He leaned forward, his voice soft, almost a caress on Daric's ears.

"Where is yours, Daric Rhan? Do you crave the glitter of gold? The curve of the body of a woman? Or perhaps it is your own sex that excites you, that could tempt you from the task I might set you." His overlarge purple eyes never left Daric's. "Do you wish to bask in the bright light of fame? Or is the key to your soul the contents of ... a wine bottle?"

Fury rose in Daric like a sudden storm. For a moment, the wave of rage was so strong he couldn't speak. He made as if to rise, his right arm already curling into a huge fist, but the gentle, feather-light brush of Taran's hand on his arm stayed him long enough to listen to the elf's placating words.

"The questions served a purpose, Daric Rhan. I needed to know just what kind of man you are. It would be easy enough to hire a swordsman, but I need more. I need someone that I can trust, and that is far more difficult to find. You, my friend, are not like the others I have seen here tonight. You are, I believe, what is called a 'good man' among your people. Please, I shall not intrude further into your privacy. Calm yourself, and hear what I have to say. Perhaps this will sweeten your temper."

Daric felt something brush against his thigh. Slowly, he relaxed back into the chair and unobtrusively extended a hand

under the table. Taran placed a small pouch in his palm. It was
heavy for its size, and through the supple leather Daric felt
several coins. He raised an eyebrow, indicating that he was
impressed with the fee.

"This is your payment in full. There will be a sizeable
bonus waiting for you when your assignment is completed.
Does that seem fair?" asked the elf.

"Depends on what the assignment is," Daric replied.

"It is a simple one. There is a young woman who is traveling to Kasselton. Her name is Gillien Songespynner, and she
is a performer. She has cropped her hair and passes for a
youth; I know not what name she uses in this guise. No doubt
she is safer traveling alone pretending to be a young man, but
the roads of Byrn are no place for a woman alone under any
disguise. I am certain you share my sentiments. She needs an
escort, and that is why I have hired you. Bring her safely to
Kasselton. I will meet you there, and take over care of the girl.
You will receive your bonus at that time."

Daric waited. For the sum of money the elf had agreed to
pay him, surely there was something else. When the elf spoke
no more, he asked sarcastically, "Is there something you're not
telling me? Something you've left out? Is this girl a runaway
princess, perhaps?"

A thin smile curved the elf's lips. "The girl is exactly what
she seems—a bard en route to perform at the yearly festival.
Nothing more, nothing less, I assure you."

"But you're willing to pay very well for her safety."

The purple eyes hardened.

"Yes," stated Taran. "I am. And that is all that should concern you. What will it be, my swordsman with a conscience?
Do you take the job, honest work for honest pay, and protect
the child from ruffians . . . or slavers? Or have I merely been
wasting my time and," he grimaced at the bottle of wine before him, "torturing my palate?"

"You must have a patron to whom this girl's safety is vital."

The elf smiled grimly. "You are not a fool, whatever else
you may be. You are quite right. I do indeed have a
patron . . . though you would never guess his identity. Come,

Daric, you could keep me here all night trying to worm my secrets from me, and you would be none the wiser and considerably poorer in the morning for your efforts. Take the task and the money I offer, or free me to look elsewhere!"

Daric considered. The money was good—very good. Good enough to confirm his suspicions that there was something more to this task than appeared on the surface. He had no doubt but that there would be risk involved. But what did he care? What, by all the gods, was there for him to lose by accepting? His dark gaze traveled to the wine bottle, lingered there for a moment. If nothing else, he thought grimly, it would be solid motivation to keep the cursed liquor from his lips, give him new memories to cover the old. That alone might be worth taking a risk.

He weighed the little purse in his hand again. He did not dare bring it out and count it, not here, not in public. For all he knew, it might be filled with coppers. But somehow, gazing into the alien eyes of the beautiful yet totally inhuman creature who sat across from him, he didn't think so. Taran's cloak was well made, of dark wool trimmed with fur. His movements had afforded Daric glimpses of the clothing and jewels that lay hidden by the enveloping, and no doubt stifling, fabric, and they bespoke wealth and position. The offer was genuine and fair, as far as he could tell.

It looked as if he were being hired to undertake something adventurous. And adventure—even including danger—certainly provided as fine a distraction as intoxication.

"Very well. I accept."

And when the last drop of blood was shed upon the sorrowing earth, and when the final blade was sheathed, then The Lady banished Her beloved to the Nightlands—a place where She forbids Her son Light to enter, and a place that She keeps guarded by dread things born of hatred and nightmares.

—from *The Book of The Lady*

CHAPTER TEN

Gillien woke to the warmth of sunlight hitting her closed lids. For a moment, she panicked, unsure of her surroundings. Then memory came, and with it the dreadful recollection of her aching loss. She was safe in the temple of Light, had been fed, looked after. But she was alone, save for the lute; alone with a long, hard road still ahead of her, and something dreadful dogging her steps. She felt the temporarily banished knowledge resettle on her shoulders, and she sagged with the weight of her grief.

Sighing, she sat upright, forcing the dark thoughts aside. She felt stiff and physically well rested, although the brightness of the room told her that she couldn't have slept more than an hour, if that.

"Well, a little sleep is better than no sleep," she murmured to Singer, which lay beside her in the bed, "and I must say, this little sleep has been wonderfully refreshing. But I'm hungry again. How is that possible—I ate like Humble!"

She blinked sleepily, and ran her hand along Singer's smooth, sun-warmed wood. She gasped, and snatched it back almost immediately, staring at the lute.

"What . . ."

Singer's wood was hot! But a quick examination of her hand showed no burn, not even a reddening of the skin. Wide awake now, she reached with one finger and touched the strings. Again, she felt the sensation of heat coursing along her hand. This time, though, she realized that it was not a true, physical heat, any more than Singer's "voice" was an audible one. She was sensing some sort of energy from the instrument.

"What is it, Singer? What's wrong? Don't burn me again, all right?"

A third time, she placed a hand on the magical instrument. The heat didn't hurt this time, but the intensity still lingered.

Singer wanted, needed, to be played. A slow smile spread across Gillien's face.

"Oh, is that all?" she reprimanded it teasingly. Taking the lute, she swung her legs over the side of the bed and settled the instrument in her lap. She plucked a string; the note was still sweet. Apparently the lute preferred the comfort of the indoors to a rainy day outside, just as she did.

She was about to start playing when something about the room caught her eye. She blinked, looking around. Something was not right. It took her a moment to realize that the tub had been taken away, and a basin and pitcher of water set down beside the bed in its place.

"I must have been dead asleep," she said to Singer. "I didn't hear anyone come in! Here, give me a moment. I'll play you better when I'm awake myself."

She had just poured some water into the basin and splashed it on her face when she heard a knock on the door. Remembering to pitch her voice low, she called, "Come in."

"Well, well, Light's greeting to you, sleepy one," said Blesser Lucan cheerfully as he entered. He was carrying a large armload of bulging sacks, which he set down with a sigh of relief.

"I took the liberty of purchasing a few things for you in town yesterday."

Gillien frowned in incomprehension. "Yesterday? But—" she glanced outside. Lucan laughed heartily.

"Yes, it's only about an hour after dawn . . . on Healsdae!" In answer to her startled look, he said, "Son, you've slept for almost a full day. How do you feel?"

"Wonderful," Gillien was forced to admit. "Blesser, I'm so sorry . . . I kept you out of your own bed! I didn't mean to—"

"Hush, Garen. You obviously needed the sleep more than I did. And besides, sleeping in the stable occasionally is good for my young Tenders. It reminds them how pleasant their life here really is." His old eyes twinkled.

"Now," he resumed, beginning to unload the sacks, "here's what I got for you in town. First, I purchased tack for your horse—saddle, bridle, and so forth. Riding bareback no doubt has its rustic appeal, but you'll need a sure seat to keep ahead of that . . . thing that's following you. Secondly, I obtained some clothing for you. Nothing fancy, but fresh clothes will come in handy, I'm certain."

He began to lay the objects out on the bed, and Gillien felt tears of gratitude start in her eyes. She saw two cotton shirts and breeches, a pair of hose, rope, dried fruits and meat, a comb for her wild hair, and tools to groom the hardworking Humble properly. The final parcel the Blesser unwrapped nearly broke her self-control.

"And here are your knives. I've had them sharpened. A dull weapon is no weapon at all, and I want to see you safe, lad." It was a statement, not a maudlin hope, delivered with gentle brusqueness.

"Blesser Lucan, I can't possibly pay—"

There was a flash of anger in Lucan's normally bright eyes, and his expression hardened ever so slightly.

"Cadby gave his life so that you and that lute would reach safety. Surely I can part with a few paltry coins to honor his last wish!"

There was no reply to that, and Gillien was silent.

"Well, you must be hungry," he said, changing the subject briskly. He stepped forward into the altar area and opened the window. A fresh breeze entered and filled the room with the scents of earth and plants. "There's food to break your fast waiting in the main room as soon as you've packed."

"Thank you, Blesser. I'll be there right away."

But she wasn't. After the Blesser had gone, she busied herself with packing the goods the Blesser had obtained for her. She accomplished that task quickly, but when she laid a hand on Singer's neck to wrap the lute, it reminded her that she had forgotten a promise.

"But, we really should get on the road . . ." The lute's need was real. "Oh, all right."

Sitting down on the bed again, she pulled the lute into position.

"What would you like, sirrah?" she asked. She waited for Singer's response, then began to play and sing a song she had learned many years ago and had all but forgotten.

> Children together, with flowers all a-blooming,
> Raised in Falarah, in Falarah, the Fair,
> They played in the forests, with trees all a-budding,
> The daughter of Cynor, and King Camar's heir.
>
> Elf-maid and princeling, they grew, all a-laughing,
> Till darkness and death cast a shadow on play;
> Till lies and till falsehood, with tales all a-spinning,
> Turned lovers to strangers on one darkling day.
>
> Ariel and Tach, mere players in the dance,
> Pawns in the hands of a deeper, darker foe;
> Reaching for the Light, not giving in to chance,
> Holding onto love, it's the only truth they know.

It was a sweet song, and despite the thread of melancholy that wafted through it, the ballad had a happy ending: Prince Tach and Princess Ariel had indeed wed and borne children. Tach had crumbled to dust over a century ago, but his legend lived on as the greatest wizard-king Byrn had ever known. Tach had been the only wizard in Verold's history who possessed all four types of magic—hand, mind, heart, and even spirit magic.

As for Ariel, she continued to dwell in her adopted homeland, unaging and serene, adored by human and Falaran alike as the honored Queen-mother. As she sang, Gillien wondered what this elf-woman would be like when she finally met her.

From his place in the garden, pulling up carrots by their leafy green tops, Lucan straightened, hand on his stiff back, and listened. A slow smile spread across his face. He'd assumed that the boy was merely in possession of the magical instrument; he had no idea that Garen knew how to play it. And such a sweet voice! The pure tenor, almost a falsetto, merely confirmed what Lucan had suspected. Garen had not quite yet reached adulthood; he was younger than he feigned to be.

"Well, son," he said to himself as he returned to his task, "I hope that when your voice breaks it's still as sweet as it is now."

The three young Tenders, in their various places about the temple, also heard the singing as it flowed out of Gillien's open window. One of them, busily doing the week's washing, snickered and made a rude comment about Garen's masculinity to the other, who was wringing out the wet, clean clothes.

"Quiet!" the other boy reprimanded. "Blesser Lucan says that some boys mature faster than others. You are a perfect example, with that kind of comment!"

The younger boy stuck out his tongue, proving the older Tender's point.

The song ended, but others came, for a good quarter of an hour. The inhabitants of Light's temple that morning were serenaded, and when at last Gillien reluctantly packed Singer away, everyone was disappointed.

Others, too, heard the singing. Passersby pricked up their ears and smiled for a moment, before returning their minds to their more mundane concerns.

Gillien's voice and Singer's pure notes carried farther still, and something else rejoiced in the sound as well. Something that lurked, safely ensconced at the bottom of a pile of discarded rubbish. Mixed in with rotting food, contents of chamber pots, and other refuse were white human bones; all that remained of the man Va'kul had lured from the safety of the lighted tavern into the darker parts of the city, slain, and fed upon.

Va'kul was in its natural form—a round lump of glistening sand-hued substance. This was its least taxing form, and Va'kul wanted to conserve all the energy it could. It was safe, here in the refuse pile. The dreadful stench ensured that.

Pleasure shuddered through the Changer. It knew that voice, though it had never heard its owner sing; it knew the tone of that instrument, though it had never heard it played properly. Once heard by Va'kul, a sound was never forgotten. It had heard Gillien speak; it had thrummed the lute itself, in the guise of Reeve Herrick. It had been right. Gillien was here indeed, and she had foolishly revealed her exact location. Pleasure was replaced by a sensation of dissatisfaction. If only its people were immune to the scalding light of the sun, Va'kul could go now and claim its victim. If only—but they weren't, so it must huddle here, and wait until the soothing shadows of dusk laid their cool fingers upon the land.

It could wait. Va'kul knew where its quarry had gone to ground now, and night would come soon enough. The girl and the precious burden she bore would not escape it again.

Gillien ate the bread, still hot from the oven, and washed it down with goat's milk. Simple fare, but how wonderful it tasted after a night—and day, she chastised herself—of deep, restful sleep. After such a rest, playing Singer and eating, she felt as if she could fight off an entire army of shapeshifters.

She beamed broadly as Blesser Lucan came to see her off. His eldest Tender had groomed Humble until the dapple-gray gelding's coat gleamed like satin, and the new saddle and bridle fit the horse well indeed. Humble, too, was the better for a day of rest and good food. His ears pricked up and he whinnied happily as the Tender led him up to the gate outside of the courtyard.

"I can't begin to thank you for all you've done for me," Gillien said, patting her animal's glossy neck.

"No need to," the Blesser replied. "I am doing what anyone would do."

"I doubt that very much."

Gillien was torn. This man had been so kind to her. He reminded her of her own father, in attitude if not in age and appearance. She longed to embrace him, to show just how important his help had been. But she dared not. Her plan hinged on how effectively she portrayed herself as a boy, and she'd risked that enough already by playing the lute and singing this morning. She knew from experience that Byrnians did not look kindly on tough, masculine-appearing or -behaving women. And she had learned by keeping her sharp little ears open that they were just as scornful and hostile toward feminine men.

She couldn't risk it. When this was all over, she'd come back and thank both him and Blesser Rufiel . . . provided, she thought gloomily, that she was still alive to do so. Instead, she thrust out a hand toward Lucan. The Blesser clasped it and shook it heartily. Then, sobering a little, he extended his other hand and placed it on her brow.

"Lord of Light, Illuminator of the dark places on Verold and in the depths of men's souls, protect this boy. Shine your light upon him, by day with the sun and by night with the stars. Keep him safe, and give him wisdom to choose the safest path to his destiny. So shall it be."

Suddenly, Gillien was seized with apprehension. She didn't want to go. Lute or no lute, magic or no magic, she wanted to stay here, where it was safe, where there were no shadows to dog her footsteps. She was sickly aware that tonight, she would have to camp alone on the road. The nearest town was many miles to the north, and she'd not reach it for several days. And according to Blesser Lucan, there was no Lamp of Traveler for many miles.

She felt Singer send her a comforting wave of reassurance.

And Gillien knew, as she swung herself into the saddle, that she could not refuse the gentle imploring of the magical instrument.

She did not trust herself to speak. Instead, she waved goodbye, and turned her horse's head to the main road.

Lucan watched Garen go, and sighed heavily. He glanced up at the sky. There were a few more hours until the sun was at its height, and he had much to do before then. The sudden coming of the youth and his vital task had disrupted the temple's cozy, uneventful schedule. It was past time to return to the normal, peaceful pace of life.

Because the boys had worked so hard during Garen's stay, stepping in to do extra chores without complaint, Lucan decided to give them an evening free. They could go visit their families in town and, for a little while, simply be young boys in the summertime. His reward for his charity was immediate. The Tenders' faces lit up and they grinned from ear to ear. Content as they were serving Light—most youths their age had far harder jobs such as farming or other physical labor— they were, in the end, still children. He enjoyed letting them play for a time; it made them happier when they served.

Alone that evening, Lucan lit the final candle in the west as the sun sank slowly to its nightly rest. For a moment, he gazed at the four candles.

"You are born and die each day, just as the sun does," he said softly, to no one in particular. "How reassuring to those of us with mortal flesh."

He went into the main room and ate a light repast. With the three eternally famished youths gone to devour their mother's home-cooked food, there was little need to prepare a meal for himself. He found that his appetite waned as he grew older; he needed less and less to sustain him.

Perhaps that is the way with all things, he thought; as we near the twilight of our lives, we consume less, do less, partake of life just a little less than before. Perhaps this is a way of readying ourselves for the inevitable departure.

Then he berated himself for his uncharacteristically melancholy thoughts.

"It must be Cadby's death," he concluded, speaking aloud in order to hear some kind of sound in the unusually quiet room. "I am dwelling overmuch on such things. Perhaps I shouldn't have let the boys go home for the night—" Lucan shook his gray head. "I'm getting old, lonely, and a bit soft in the head."

He distracted himself by throwing himself into his evening chores. Light's temple was always brilliantly illuminated through the night, to show to the inhabitants of the town that Light was never fully gone from their lives. Lucan built up the fire in the main hearth until it was blazing cheerfully, something that was done faithfully each night, winter or summer. He placed candles in each of the many windows and lit them, using the power of his mind and a wave of his hand, respectfully invoking the god as he did so.

He had just ventured outside to light the torches that marked the perimeters of the courtyard when he heard a noise coming from inside. At once, Lucan tensed. It was probably nothing, he told himself: one of the boys back early after an argument with a sibling, perhaps, or the temple's cat, endured as a pet because she kept the mice out of the crops.

He heard the sound again, and suddenly was aware of just how old he was—old and unarmed, save for the power his god granted him. Lucan tried to still his rapidly beating heart and took a calming breath. Then he turned and went into the temple.

"Who comes to the temple of Light?" he demanded, keeping his voice strong as he stepped into the main room.

The blazing fire and dozens of candles made the room nearly as bright as it was in the daytime. Yet Lucan saw no one. Surely, it was the heat from the fire and candles that made sweat break out on his forehead.

"Come out, friend. All are welcome here."

He stood, tense and apprehensive. There was another sound, and someone stepped out of Lucan's bedroom.

"Greetings, Blesser," said the girl. "It's just me, Gillien. Guess you didn't hear me."

Lucan stared, utterly confused. The young woman before him was terribly, frighteningly familiar, although Lucan had never seen her before in his life. Her face and expression were those of Garen's, right down to the crooked smile and bright eyes. But she was no boy. Her small breasts were clearly defined by the snug fit of the mauve-hued, floor-length gown she wore. Long hair fell unconfined to her slim waist.

She held in one strong hand what was unmistakably Garen's precious lute. There could be no twin to the instrument, and this was Singer, down to the last ivory tuning peg and inlaid jewel. The priest continued to stare, trying to mentally clothe that feminine figure in ill-fitting boy's clothing, crop that long, thick hair.

"Sweet beams of Light," he whispered. "Garen?"

The girl's smile faltered.

"It's Gillien," she repeated. This time, her voice lacked its musical quality. There was a cold edge of anger to it, like the glint of suddenly bared steel. "I know you recognize me!"

And so suddenly it almost made him faint, Blesser realized who—what—he was facing. Blackness whirled before him for an instant, then he regathered his courage. Stepping closer to the fire, he challenged the beast.

"Begone, foul creature! No denizen of the Nightlands has a place in Light's temple!"

The girl-child, so pretty and yet so dangerous, stared at the holy man with her inhumanly evil gaze a heartbeat longer, then acknowledged recognition.

"Aye, Blesser," she growled, her girlish tones dropping seven octaves, "I am indeed a creature from the lands where Light is afraid to go. But though your god may challenge me, his mere mortal representative may not! Know you not that I have slain and devoured one of your brethren before now?"

Gillien's shape split apart like so much rotten fruit. It turned in on itself, a horrible image of pulpy flesh and glistening organs, to become a reptilian, gray-scaled shape. But it kept the girl's face, distorting it as if it had been made of clay. Roaring its defiance, it twisted and writhed until it was an enormous viper, wearing the visage of a maiden.

Lucan cowered against the fireplace until the heat of the flames against his back was well nigh unbearable. He had seen many horrors in his lifetime, but no murdered corpse or hissing Ghil had prepared him for this monstrosity. The image that dominated all others in his mind was Cadby—stronger, younger, and certainly braver than himself, dying at the hands—claws? tentacles? talons?—of this abomination. He couldn't think clearly.

The demon, for so Lucan deemed it to be, continued to roar, nearly deafening the terrified Blesser.

"Where is the girl? The lute? Send me in their direction, pathetic mortal, and perhaps I shall spare your worthless life."

Through the red haze of fear, something managed to reach the Blesser's brain. The beast was not moving toward him. It continued to lurk in the doorway of the Blesser's private chamber, its sinuous, obscene snake-shape squirming and thrashing. Lucan heard a loud crash as the wardrobe toppled and fell; heard the musical tinkle as the ceramic pitcher and bowl were shattered.

But the thing did not venture into the main room, with its lit fire and dozens of winking candles.

Gods! the Blesser thought to himself in a stunned epiphany. There's too much light in here! It can't come in!

New courage flooded him and he stood erect, proud and confident once more.

"My god's power is too much for you, thing of darkness!" he cried, and now his voice was as clear as it had been that morning, when he had called Light's blessing down upon the worshippers.

"Come and get me and *make* me tell you what you want to know, if you dare!"

The thing's howl of outrage was like a knife in the Blesser's brain. But he held his ground, not even covering his ears lest the creature think it had gained an advantage.

"Yes, come for me, Nightmare creature, as you came for

poor Cadby. Only then will I betray my young friend—if you can make me!"

Concentrating, the old man summoned light. It came to his call, a gift from god to servant wielding the power in a righteous cause. Cadby had conjured the illumination of daylight with his mind magic, now Lucan's hand magic served him with light in a different way.

The door jamb, made of wood, suddenly burst into flame. All the candles flared to several times their normal light, blackening the stone walls. The rushes at the creature's feet sparkled and squirmed like living things.

The Nightlands Demon, or whatever it was, cried out again, but this time real pain was laced with its fury. Coils of snake-like flesh surged up to cover its eyes, and it retreated into the cooler, darker depths of the bedroom.

Giddy with triumph, the Blesser followed, but not too closely. He pointed his hand at his rope bed, and the straw within the simple pallet ignited. Tongues of orange-yellow flame licked hungrily up the walls, reaching as if guided—for they were indeed—toward the now-wailing monster.

The thing shifted, changed, and suddenly Cadby was standing there, his flesh blackened and blistering.

"Lucan!" Cadby cried brokenly, stumbling toward the other man. "He enchanted me—made me serve him—I'm not dead, I'm not, but I will be . . . halt your flames, I beg you, old friend! They will burn me as surely as they would you!"

Tears spurted into Lucan's eyes and sudden doubt made him reel. By the gods, that *was* Cadby in front of him. Had the girl lied? Was the younger man really in thrall to the monster as he claimed? These were Cadby's eyes, normally so merry but now filled with fear; the youth's handsome, kind face; his shape, his movements, now clumsy with pain and terror.

Lucan raised his hand and was about to banish the flames when he caught sight of Cadby's hands. They were reaching out to him, imploring, trying to grasp him.

They were also unlined, shiny, and blank as a sheet of parchment.

Lucan swore a deep oath, one that would require many prayers to erase, and envisioned the monster's clothing on fire.

The flames obeyed at once. What had appeared to be Cadby now shrieked, stumbled toward the window, and crashed through it. The Blesser ran to peer out. He saw nothing, and for a wild, heart-shaking instant wondered if the thing was waiting to spring for him. Then he heard a flapping sound, and glanced upward.

There, silhouetted against the pale light of a gibbous moon, he saw a giant bird speeding out of sight. The moonlight glinted on its black wings and eyes, as it turned to glare back down at him. It cawed, a sound a thousand times deeper and louder than any uttered by a natural raven, and then was gone.

Lucan's energy left him in a flood; he felt his knees give way. He made no attempt to put out the flames, not yet. He would let what was combustible burn on until the safety of the dawn. There would be no hint of darkness in Light's temple tonight. Silently, he said a prayer of thanksgiving.

He had loved Cadby, but had no wish to meet that man's fate. Enough to have looked on the face of the Nightlands, and survived. More than enough for one old man tonight. Lucan thought of Gillien, whom he had sent on her way alone under the delusion that she was a boy, and began to cry in hoarse, racking sobs. He had sent a good, sweet, brave child to her death. No ordinary human could face such evil and survive.

"May Light forgive me," he whispered. "May Light have mercy upon my soul."

The Blesser wept, tears making tracks down his soot-blackened face, while his holy house crackled and burned about him.

*And the gallant knight bore down upon the dragon, lifting
his mighty sword high in challenge. "Begone, foul wyrm!" he
cried. "Come thou not near the maiden!"*

*"Save me!" cried the maiden. "For the great monster hath
imprisoned me, and I dreamt not of rescue!"*

—from the Byrnian tale,
The Gallant Knight

CHAPTER ELEVEN

The horse had a stubborn streak a mile wide and loved to get
the bit between her teeth. Daric hadn't even graced the animal
with a name yet, thinking of it as That Damned Beast when he
thought of it at all. But the bay mare had been sound, her teeth
still fairly straight, and the look in her eye as she appraised the
former warrior showed intelligence even as it trumpeted her
strong will.

Daric had been paired with dozens of horses in his time, and
he'd yet to meet one who had gotten the best of him. But That
Damned Beast certainly seemed willing to try.

He had purchased her, along with traveling food, gear and
clothes, with the money the mysterious Taran had given him
the night before. Daric had been shocked when, a few hours
after the meeting, he had examined the contents of the purse
and discovered that all the coins were silvers or golds. Taran's
wildly generous payment had allowed him to purchase everything necessary for traveling, and then some. He had his sword

and dagger honed at the blacksmith's, then headed north on a stretch of the Queen's Road known locally as the Trail of Caves.

"The girl will be traveling along that route. She is almost a full day ahead of you, but her horse is not capable of intense, steady riding," Taran had advised him, that unflinching purple gaze never leaving Daric's face. "Find yourself a beast that will travel swiftly and steadily, and you should come upon her soon enough." The elf's face furrowed in what might have been a hint of amusement.

"Expect resistance on the part of the maiden. She has been able to hold her own so far and might not be as appreciative of a chaperon as she ought."

Daric had departed at midday on Healsdae, riding hard to make up for the day's lead Gillien had, and camped only when he and That Damned Beast were clearly in need of rest. He estimated that they'd put at least twenty miles behind them before stopping for the evening.

The night under the waxing moon was strange to him, it having been years since he had lain clearheaded under a starry roof. Daric lay on his bedclothes, the Beast dozing a few yards away. He gnawed on a piece of dried meat, substituting the chewy flesh for bitter-tasting wine. It was an unsuccessful ploy, for he found himself craving the drink. He hadn't gone a night in weeks without starting off the evening—or afternoon, or morning—with a drink of some sort, and his body didn't know how to shut itself down all by itself. He stared up at the stars, looking at the familiar constellations by which he had navigated most of his life.

There was the Elf Castle, the largest and best-known star cluster, with its eleven clearly visible stars outlining a fanciful palace. To the right, lower on the horizon, was Traveler's Lamp—a fixed-point star, larger than any others, that was the truest light in the sky for those seeking their way. Each of the gods had their own constellation, of course, though few of them seemed to be any kind of accurate representation of a deity, his or her symbol, or anything remotely connected with the god in question. It was as if, Daric thought cynically, all the priests were determined that their divinity have his or her proper place in the skies, and sometimes a stretching of the imagination was called for to see the pattern.

More clearly visible was the Sickle of the Ghil—the curved, nasty-looking instrument that the Ghil used to attack back in the times when their principal prey were farmers; before the disgusting creatures had learned that captive humans could make them better, finer weapons . . .

Daric felt nausea welling up inside him, and spat out the half-masticated mouthful of dried meat. Suddenly, its taste made his stomach roil. Gods, his mouth was dry. He should have brought a bottle, just one, to still the sudden shaking that seized him and ease him into a decent night's sleep.

But no, that was the coward in him talking. Daric had deliberately not brought any alcohol whatsoever with him. He knew the road well, and remembered there were many springs and streams from which he could slake his thirst. And if there was no bottle, why then, there would be no temptation to drink from the bottle.

He rolled over onto his side, pulling the blanket around him more tightly in the vain hope that his uncontrollable trembling was due to simple cold. But he knew it was not. He shook and sweated his way through the night until the chill dawn crept over the horizon and he had an excuse to focus his mind on other things.

It was Travsdae dawning, the most propitious day, according to popular belief, to get miles under one's feet—or under the hooves of one's horse. The Beast gave token protest when he tried to saddle her, but a sharp word and a well-placed *thwap* with a closed fist brought her around. She wasn't hurt, and they both knew it, but she fixed him with large brown eyes that accused even as they threatened.

He felt her inflate her belly as he brought the girth around. "Don't try that trick with me, you damned beast," Daric muttered as he fastened her girth. He leaned into her, heavily and unexpectedly, and she let out a surprised *whoof* as the air rushed out of her. Daric smiled a little to himself as he was able to pull the girth up two full notches. Horses loved to pull that

trick on unwary humans. They would swell their bellies so the
girth would not be cinched as tight, and the saddle would slip
off once the rider mounted.

"Think of some new ones, would you? I'd like a challenge,"
he said sarcastically, mounting and jerking her head up as the
Beast tried to snag a mouthful of grass.

She swiveled her ears back and flattened them slightly. He
sighed. Travsdae's good luck be damned. The first full day of
riding this recalcitrant animal would certainly be the hardest
one of the journey.

They made good time, although That Damned Beast tried to
knock Daric off by running under branches, giving him an ex-
tremely uncomfortable trot, and once even trying to buck, executing an unsuccessful little crow hop before he yanked back
hard on her sensitive mouth and swore blisteringly at her. Daric
seized up on the reins and used his legs firmly until she seemed
to surrender, at least for the moment.

The sun rose and the heat increased as the morning wore on.
There was no sign of the girl. He was just beginning to wonder
if the elf had been wrong in his directions when a shrill, soprano shriek rent the still air.

"Get your gods-cursed hands *off* of—"

The cry was cut off, but Daric had already slammed his heels
into the Beast's side and she was off with startling speed. He
sank into the saddle, keeping his weight low and balanced, and
drew his sword without even thinking about it. The Beast
climbed the slight rise at a swift pace and Daric saw, as he
crested the hill, the boyish-looking girl who was undoubtedly
the young bard he was after.

They were three against her. Although one big brute had already gotten her pinned beneath him and was trying to tie her
flailing, striking little hands, it was clear that Gillien Songespynner had given a good account of herself. Daric, his mind
clear and focused, took in the scene with his experienced eye
even as he bore down upon the ruffians.

The biggest one wasn't trying to hurt her, that much was evident. He swore as her blows landed, but managed to seize her
wrists and grappled with the stout rope he carried. One

clenched fist was inexorably brought to the other, and the man wound the rope around her wrists as if he were trussing up a colt for gelding. The girl writhed and fought, yanking back a hand and striking as curses poured from her mouth.

A second man had his right hand clapped to his bleeding side. Not two feet away lay a sharp dagger, of the sort that traveling performers used in their stunts. It was covered with blood up to the hilt. The man's free hand rummaged roughly through what Daric guessed was Gillien's pack. The man was frowning, his black brows drawn together on his leathery face, then suddenly he laughed.

Triumphantly he withdrew a gorgeous instrument—the lute that Taran had casually mentioned that Gillien played. It was clearly worth more than several of Taran's bags of silver and gold, and the thug cried out joyfully.

"Here's more than that boy is worth, Marton!" he crowed. "Let's take this and let him be!"

"You're mad! Strong thing like him would fetch me—gods curse you, bastard, let me go!"

Gillien had sunk her sharp little teeth in her captor's hands. He backhanded her with the other one. Her head jerked to one side, but she continued to fight.

The third man was attempting to capture a small dapple-gray gelding, who kept prancing just out of reach. The man made a lasso of his rope and tossed it. Gillien saw the movement and uttered what sounded to Daric and the other men like a totally nonsensical phrase.

"Humble! May I have this dance?"

At once, the horse reared and began to leap up and down, clearing the earth by two feet before landing on his powerful rear legs. The lasso fluttered impotently to the earth, and as the swearing rogue dove for it, the horse struck out at him. The hooves missed by a good several inches, but the movement startled the man and he fell.

All this happened in but a few seconds, as Daric raced toward the men. He knew them for what they were, vile slavers, and his rage drove him forward like one possessed. He was as silent as Lady Death, his handsome face fixed in a hard mask of hatred, his mouth a thin line. He was silent, but his horse's hooves rang out loud and clear. As one, the three men looked up, and their jaws dropped as Daric bore down on them.

He knew slavers to be the epitome of cowardice, and was not surprised—only disappointed—when they showed their true natures. He desperately wanted to kill them, but they clearly had other plans. Slavers acted in secret, by stealth, surprise and trickery. One lone "boy," albeit a feisty one, and a pony were no match for three large, bullying brutes. Daric, however, his dark hair flying behind him and his eyes as hard as black rocks, was more than they had bargained for. With a speed the warrior hadn't expected, they abandoned the girl and pony and leaped onto their own waiting mounts.

One of them, though, was determined to escape with some recompense for his injuries. Still bleeding from his side, he climbed aboard his horse and clapped his heels to it. In one hand, he carried the lute.

Gillien appeared as reluctant as Daric to simply survive the encounter with her life and freedom. She cried out angrily, a harsh, deep growl, and stumbled to her feet. Her hand went to her belt and emerged with a dagger identical to the one that had bloodied the man earlier.

"You son of a whore!" cried the girl, drawing back her hand and throwing the knife with practiced smoothness. It hurtled through the air and embedded itself in the fleeing thief's shoulder with an audible *thunk*. The man cried out. Involuntarily, his fingers loosed their grip on the instrument and went to clasp the injured shoulder.

The lute thudded to the earth. Daric expected the instrument to shatter on impact; it was a fragile-looking piece. Instead, it bounced a few times on the hard ground and came to rest, its curved back up.

Stumbling, blood dripping from her mouth, Gillien ran to the lute. She fell to her knees beside it and picked it up. Daric couldn't hear what she was saying, but she was holding the thing to her breasts as one might cradle a child. Since it was obvious she was all right, he turned his attention to the fleeing ruffians. He had just gathered the surprisingly obedient Beast beneath him and was about to launch her into pursuit when an angry cry startled him and the horse.

"And just where in the Nightlands do you think you're going?"

Daric turned just in time to feel a slight breeze as a dagger whizzed past his face with mere inches to spare. He was not a fool, and he halted the horse at once. The girl clearly knew how to use the weapons, and he didn't doubt for an instant that she had not intended the blade to strike him. It was meant as a warning.

Bitter disappointment welled inside him as he listened to the hoofbeats of the slavers grow fainter and fainter, until he could no longer hear them at all. He turned the Beast around to face the girl and glared angrily at her.

"I could have caught them! Why didn't you let me—"

"Who asked you to come play the rescuer?" she retorted. Another knife was in her hand—where did she get them all?—and the other fist was closed tightly, protectively, around the neck of the lute. Gillien was panting heavily and sweat poured down her face. Her lithe body was taut, ready to act, and emitted a tension that was almost palpable to the warrior.

She did look like a boy. Daric wondered if he'd have recognized the maiden for what she was had he come upon her accidentally. He decided not. She was far too slim and strong for a real woman, and no true maiden would dare act in such an unseemly fashion.

He took a deep breath, and reluctantly let the slavers go.

"Gillien Songespynner," he drawled, taking a perverse pleasure in seeing the naked shock on her face as he spoke her true name, "I was *hired* to be your rescuer."

The face, flushed just an instant ago, went deathly pale. Nervously the girl glanced up at the sky, then back at Daric.

"Show me your hands," she demanded.

"What?" Daric wondered if it was the sun or the attack that had addled the girl's brains. Perhaps they had already been addled. "Why should I—"

"Because I'll put this thing through your throat if you don't," Gillien said. The knife was still poised to be thrown. The arm that held the weapon was trembling, but there was a cold determination in the maiden's blue eyes. This was no bluff.

Mentally, Daric corrected his assessment of the girl. She wasn't addled, he decided in disgust. She was completely insane. Glaring at her, he stripped off his riding gloves.

"There," he said, showing her his hands. "Five fingers on each hand. Were you expecting six? Or claws, maybe?"

Gillien ignored him. Cautiously, she stepped forward and inspected his hands.

"P-palms up," she ordered. Her voice was controlled, but the unintentional stammer that escaped her revealed that she was very nervous about something. Daric rolled his eyes but obliged.

"Anything else, my lady?" he growled. "Care to see my feet? Or perhaps my—"

"Who sent you?" She had relaxed, but only slightly.

An overwhelming desire for a drink hit Daric. Gods, what had he been thinking? He was twenty-four now, far too old to play a hero in a situation that was rapidly becoming a scene out of a theatrical performance. He should never have let Taran talk him into this. No amount of money was worth being interrogated by this little manlike girl.

"I was hired by someone named Taran. That is all I am permitted to reveal to you, so I pray you, my *lady*, don't ask me any more questions. I might be tempted to truss you up to your horse's saddle and escort you to Kasselton with a gag in your mouth."

The girl's expression changed. Her eyes became distant, as if she were listening to something he couldn't hear. She put the knife in its sheath absently, and pressed the lute to her body. One hand gently stroked the smooth wood. Then, for no reason that Daric could fathom, the tension ebbed from her body, and she smiled a little up at him. He decided that she was rather charming when she wasn't brandishing knives and swearing at the top of her voice.

"Taran," she repeated. "Yes. I . . . I know Taran. Of course I do." She glanced down again at the lute. "And you say he hired you to escort me to Kasselton?"

Daric was still annoyed, but bit back his resentment. "Aye," he replied. "For a goodly sum, too. You must be important to him."

Gillien nodded slowly. "I guess I must be," she said. She winced, suddenly aware of the pain from her recent scuffle. Gingerly, she touched her bloodied lip.

Daric slipped off the Beast's back. "Don't suppose you brought any healing medicines with you?"

"Actually, I did," she replied, going over to her pack and laying the lute carefully down on the earth. She withdrew a small leather pouch and began sorting through its contents. At last she found what she wanted—a small, ferny leaf that she popped into her mouth and began to chew gingerly.

Daric was impressed. He recognized the herb; no battle-tested veteran would not. It was yarrow, long known for its value in stanching blood and healing wounds. She mistook his interest for ignorance.

"It's to stop bleeding," she explained. "It's also supposed to be good for toothaches. And I guess this qualifies on both counts." She paused in midchew. Pulling the leaf out, she spat into her palm and grimaced. In the puddle of saliva, blood and yarrow lay a single white tooth. Gillien swore, tossed the useless tooth away, and resumed chewing the healing leaf.

Unexpectedly, Daric felt a twinge of admiration for the girl. Most women he'd known would be sobbing hysterically at this point. To be struck in the face and lose a tooth was enough to destroy anyone's composure. For a woman—a girl—to have undergone what Gillien had and still remain calm was nothing short of amazing.

"So the mouth is taken care of," he ventured. "How is the rest of you?"

She shot him a swift, cautious glance.

"I'm fine. Bruised and sore, but nothing worse." Her words came out slightly mumbled by the swelling of her jaw and lips. Clearly, she hadn't made up her mind whether or not to believe his story. She did not thank him for his concern. In turn, he did not offer to help her gather up her belongings. He sensed that his offer would be at best politely refused, at worst haughtily rebuffed. At last she had her horse ready to go and swung herself into the saddle. She fixed him with an arch gaze.

"Are you coming or not?" she queried.

Daric frowned, and mounted his own animal. Unable to help himself, he said, "For you to have lost a tooth meant that blow was pretty rough. Are you sure you don't—"

"Oh, I've lost teeth that way before." Again, the words were slightly slurred as she edged them around her puffy face.

The warrior stiffened. "Who . . ."

"My brother." She didn't sound concerned, and squeezed her horse into a slow trot. "But that's all right. I broke his nose, so we were even."

Daric couldn't believe his ears. There was warmth and affection in her voice as she recalled the incident. Her eyes lost their hard wariness, and a faint smile touched her bloody lips before pain banished it.

"Must be one unique family you have."

The light faded from her face.

"I'd rather not talk about it," she said in a voice gone small and unhappy. Grimly, she kicked her horse into a canter. Daric, confused and still resentful, followed in silence.

The terrain was much rockier as they headed north, passing the intersection with the west-east Great Road. Small ridges rose on either side, and the steep path slowed them down. This road was not called the Trail of Caves without reason. Daric made note of the surroundings with a practiced eye. There would be ample shelter in any one of the many natural enclosures, but wood for a fire would be harder to come by. There were a few dead trees scattered here and there, their dried skeletons reached toward a sky that smiled down with an uncaring blue grin. Daric decided that when they stopped for the night, they would have to make sure there were such trees within easy reach for harvesting.

As the sun reached its zenith, he noticed that Gillien's mount was starting to tire. His own was still full of energy, though she was dark and glossy with sweat.

"Are you hungry?" he asked.

The girl's face had swollen even more, and he doubted she

could eat. He expected a sharp retort, but instead she replied, "I'm starving."

They dismounted. Daric staked the Beast's reins to the earth; given half a chance, she was likely to bolt back the direction she had come. Gillien, though, swung herself off her dapple-gray gelding, unburdened it, patted its neck fondly, and sent the animal off without a backward glance. Happily, the horse trotted off to one of the few visible patches of grass growing in a natural hollow created by rocks.

"Aren't you worried he'll wander off?" he asked.

Gillien shook her head and began to pull food out of her pack. "Humble would never leave me. I raised him from a foal, and besides, he's perfectly trained." She made for a flat, sun-warmed rock, and sat down to enjoy her meal.

There was a trace of pride in her voice and Daric ventured, "You trained him?"

Again, she nodded and began to cut an apple into bite-sized pieces. "He was the star of the dog-and-pony part of the show. Nobody had ever seen a horse do the sort of things Humble can do."

"Like dance?" Suddenly, Gillien's bizarre command to the horse—*Humble! May I have this dance?*—made perfect sense. As did the animal's subsequent prancing on his hind legs.

"Like dance." A shadow fell across her face. "That's not the first time Humble's tricks have come in handy recently." The girl eased a bite of apple into her mouth and chewed. She grimaced. "Gods, that hurts, but I'm so damn hungry!"

"And your skill with knives . . . you were more than a bard. Taran told me you could play, but I had no idea your talents extended beyond that." His earlier annoyance with the girl had vanished in the face of her obvious accomplishments. Daric was one to give credit where credit was due. He opened his own pack and took out a small loaf of bread. "What else can you do? You're full of surprises."

She shot him an appraising look. "You know a lot about me. What about yourself? Just who are you, anyway?"

"My name is Daric Rhan. As I told you, I was hired to protect you by Taran." He put a slab of dried meat on the bread, covered it with another hunk of bread, and bit into it.

"Singer said Taran was . . ." She fell silent at once. Alarm was written plainly on her face. What had she been about to say—or rather, he assumed, let slip? Daric swallowed, suddenly suspicious.

"Who's Singer?"

"Nothing. Just . . . I don't want to talk anymore, all right?" She put another bite of apple into her mouth and chewed painfully.

Shrugging, Daric returned his attention to his own meager meal. He washed it down with the last of the water in his waterskin. By his recollection, there was a spring a few miles ahead; they could stop and water the horses there.

After eating, Gillien rose and began walking toward a large boulder that jutted up out of the earth about ten yards to the west. Confused, Daric called, "Where are you going?"

She stopped in her tracks, her back straight and rigid. Coolly, she turned around, and although her words were calm and almost icy, she was blushing deeply.

"I am going to find a private spot to relieve myself," she said. "That is, if Daric Rhan the Hired Rescuer doesn't *mind*?"

Daric felt heat redden his own cheeks. He didn't answer, merely turned his back on her and began to repack. She emerged a few moments later, still pink with embarrassment. Putting the thumb and second finger of her right hand to her lips she emitted a loud, piercing whistle that made Daric jump. Almost at once, he heard a thudding of hooves as her horse returned from gods knew where.

"You do have him well trained," Daric said. He glanced at his own disobedient steed, who flattened her ears against her skull, whickered, and gave him glare for glare.

"It just takes a little patience," she replied, touching Humble's leg and climbing into the saddle as he knelt. "Maybe I could help you with your horse. Looks like you need some. Tell me, when you were in the army, were you a foot soldier? You don't ride like cavalry." She grinned wickedly, despite the pain to her injured mouth it must have cost her.

Daric was startled. He hadn't mentioned his time in the service . . . or had he? Damn girl was far too clever by half . . . too clever for her own good. He swung himself into the Beast's saddle, his mind working. She must have deduced it somehow. His bearing? No, that hadn't been military for some time now, he thought bitterly. His sword was his own, as was the scabbard he had lovingly made for it himself years ago. His clothes?

He glanced down at himself as he gripped the Beast's reins and struggled briefly with her to get her to shift into a trot. Of course. He had the tattoo of the Byrnian griffin on his inner left arm; a traditional device and place for a military man's tattoo.

"For your information, I was captain of a cavalry unit," he replied, slightly stung, as she had no doubt intended.

"So why aren't you in the army now? You're too young for retirement."

"What happened to your family?" Daric retorted. "Why are you traveling alone, disguised as a boy?"

The look she gave him was naked hurt, undisguised by her earlier insouciance. She did not reply, merely kicked Humble to a swifter pace. Daric felt suddenly and unaccountably ashamed of himself.

They reached the spring and stopped to let the horses drink, replenish their own supply of water, and take a short rest. Then they walked on until nightfall. Daric pointed out an area that had a good supply of dead wood and Gillien agreed that this was a wise choice for a campsite.

She seemed unaccountably nervous as the sun sank toward the horizon, glancing about as if she expected something to materialize out of thin air. Gillien helped him gather firewood and urged, "Stoke it well. I want a lot of light tonight."

He obliged, and by the time dusk had fallen they had a large fire blazing brightly. Daric staked the Beast again, removed her saddle and began to groom her. She kept twisting her head to try to nip him, completely ungrateful for his efforts on her behalf. He kept one eye on his strange young charge and absently swatted the Beast each time her teeth ventured within range.

Gillien groomed her horse with a great deal of enthusiasm

and affection. She talked to the animal and vigorously cleaned the caked-out sweat and dirt from his coat, brushing it until it gleamed. The white mane and tail got equal attention, and she squatted beside Humble without a second thought for her personal safety as she touched his fetlock and asked him to give her his hoof.

Daric eyed the Beast. The last time he'd tried to clean her hooves, she'd tried to kick him. Still, they had to be inspected, and he was able to get a quick glance at the delicate frog area of each hoof before That Damned Beast decided that was quite enough.

Gillien still squatted beside her horse, murmuring conversationally to him and carefully cleaning the dirt from his feet with a hooked pick. At last, she rose, but she seemed reluctant to join Daric at the campfire. He began to cook their supper, still watching her out of the corner of his eye.

She lingered with the horse, petting his velvet muzzle, then she suddenly hugged the creature about the neck. Before she buried her face in the newly combed mane, Daric caught the gleam of tears on her cheeks, illuminated by the fire's glow. He was surprised. She had taken a vicious blow without a qualm, but she was now weeping freely, her emotions naked on her sharp-featured face.

At last she came and sat down by the fire. Wordlessly, Daric handed her a bowl full of stew. It was nothing much—dried meat and vegetables boiled in water, but she ate steadily. The swelling in her face had gone down. She glanced shyly at him.

"Thanks for making soup," she said. "It's . . . it's not as hard for me to eat as something else."

That was the first kind thing that she had said. Confused, Daric nodded.

"I'm going to set some traps tonight. Tomorrow we should have some fresh meat. Think you'll be able to eat it?"

Gillien nodded absently, still staring into the flames, and took another sip of the hot liquid.

"What did Taran tell you about me?" she asked.

Daric shrugged. "Not much. He told me your name, that you

were disguised as a boy, and that you were traveling to be in the bardic competition in Kasselton."

She snorted slightly. "And you didn't wonder why he hired a professional swordsman to guard me?"

"I thought we saw the reason for my presence earlier today," Daric replied, blowing on the bowl before taking a sip of soup. "You fight well, little maid, but you're no match for three men."

"And you are?"

"With my sword, I am." It was not boasting; it was the simple truth.

She analyzed his expression, her blue eyes roving about his face as if she could glean answers simply by looking at him.

"Do you know what they wanted from me?"

He was startled. "What little backwards hamlet spawned you? Haven't you heard of the slave trade? You were lucky they didn't realize your true sex. Even boys . . ." his voice trailed off, and he realized his palms were suddenly wet. Dear gods, he wanted a drink. He'd strike a deal with the Nightlands King himself for just one goblet right now.

"Do you think they'll come back?" The idea apparently had not occurred to the girl before, and she looked alarmed. Daric forced himself to eat more of the soup before he replied.

"No. Slavers don't have the courage of rabbits when it comes to a fair fight. They want easy prey."

"And . . . that's it? That's the danger you were hired to face? Slavers on the road?" The answer seemed important to her, and he felt a vague trace of annoyance.

"Yes, yes, and yes."

She rose abruptly and unpacked the lute. Sitting on a stone across the fire from him, she held the instrument cradled in her lap, but did not play. Her slim, long-fingered hands absently caressed the smooth wood. For a long time, she said nothing. Various expressions flitted over her sharp features; she seemed to be waging some sort of inner debate. He finished the soup and began to unpack material for snares.

At last, she seemed to have reached a decision. She cleared her throat, and he turned around to look at her.

"Daric . . . there's something you have to know. Something you weren't told." She sighed, then looked him full in the face.

"I'm being followed by something a lot more dangerous than slavers. And I owe it to you to at least tell you what it is— though I think that once you know, you'll wish you'd never seen me before."

"Do tell me a story, little bard." The shakes were on him again, and he tried to hide them by busying himself with the snares.

"It's true. Listen to me!" Something in the tone of her voice made him look up, pause in his activity. Gillien was in dead earnest. Reluctantly, he rocked back on his heels.

"I'm listening."

And listen he did as her incredible story unfolded. She told of a dreadful nightmarish shapeshifter who had murdered her family and then tried to kill her. She spoke of the two Blessers, one who believed her and died protecting her, and one who believed her and at this moment might be in danger. More than her words, Daric harkened to her expressions, the tone of her voice, the nervous gestures she made from time to time. After many years leading men, Daric knew how to read people. This girl, at least in her own mind, was not lying.

"The one thing it doesn't appear to have control over are its hands," she finished. "That's why I demanded to see your hands. It can't seem to duplicate the wrinkles we have on our palms and fingers. And I think it's scared of light, as well, which is why when we camp, we have to have a fire."

This was no tale, told to scare him as a joke. The girl clearly believed her unbelievable story, and her obvious seriousness lent weight to the fantastic tale. The night was cool and dark, and the stones that loomed about them cast wavering shadows in the orange, flickering firelight. Daric felt the hairs on the back of his neck prickle.

Was it really possible that the girl was telling the truth?

Just as quickly he banished the thought. Clearly, Gillien had been through something dreadful. He believed her when she said her family was dead, but remained doubtful that the killer was a shapeshifter. It was too preposterous . . . wasn't it?

"Do you believe me?" she asked finally, breaking the silence that stretched between them.

"Let's just say that I consider myself warned. You get some sleep, Gillien. I'll keep first watch. And I'll keep the fire stoked, I promise."

She smiled uncertainly at him, then stretched out on the earth, covering herself with a blanket. Next to her, like a lover, lay the lute that was clearly so precious. Her eyes were bright, watching him watch her. She unsheathed a knife and laid it within easy reach.

"Don't touch my lute, don't touch my horse, and don't touch me."

Daric raised his hands in an age-old gesture that indicated his willingness to keep away from her. That seemed to satisfy Gillien. She closed her eyes. Within moments, she was breathing deeply and regularly.

Daric rose, and went beyond the ring of firelight to set his snares. The girl's tale had spooked him slightly, and he found himself glancing behind him now and then. When one of the horses blew softly, he jumped, then cursed himself.

A good tale. When Gillien reached the bardic competition, she'd have a fine one to spin. But a tale was a tale, and had no bearing on the realities of the fairly harmless creatures that lurked under the cover of a Byrnian night sky.

Nonetheless, he stayed awake longer than he had planned. He did not waken Gillien; there was no need to have "watches," despite what he had said. He would let the child sleep. He certainly couldn't, not for many hours, for surging through his veins was the craving for drink, and dancing through his mind were images of rocks transforming themselves into demons.

"Oh!" cried the lassie, pretty and flushed,
"Is that not your sword?" quoth she, and blushed.
"Aye," said the knight, "But a sword just for you,
So come here, my lass, and I'll prove that it's true."

—from *The Warrior's
Big Sword*

CHAPTER TWELVE

For a few sleep-clouded moments, Daric thought that the beautiful voice was part of his dream.

He had been on the battlefield, his sword slicing cleanly through the hordes of Ghil as they charged. He could smell them, feel their hot breath, hear the gnashing of their long, yellow teeth. He slew each one as it attacked, but still they came, as they always did in this dream, wave after wave of the foul creatures, until they triumphed by sheer numbers, drowning Daric and his compatriots in the crush of reeking bodies. In his sleep, Daric began to gasp for air.

But this time, the tide of Ghil suddenly began to recede, fleeing before a beautiful woman whose voice sounded like audible sunlight. The light that radiated from her nearly blinded Daric, but he knew enough to realize that this was The Lady, the strange and radiant goddess of the elvenfolk. She walked like any other mortal, on the ground, but the dark crea-

tures scurried away from her in terror. Her hair floated behind
her like a white cloud. As she passed, Daric caught the sweet
scent of a feast being prepared; his mouth began to water at
the smell of roasting meat.

The sound was achingly sweet; exquisite, pure, powerful.
He blinked himself awake, discovering that he was staring
right up into the newly risen sun. He was awake now, certainly, yet the dream music continued.

> For behold, the mountains crumble,
> You shall find the path is clear.
> And your feet shall never stumble
> If you venture without fear.
>
> So go forth and greet the mortals,
> And their wisdom they will teach
> For the Kyras are but portals,
> Lasting peace is now in reach.

No wonder he had dreamed of the elven Lady, with Gillien
singing the Falaran ballad *The Lady's Gift*. He'd heard the
song before, many times, but seldom with a clear enough head
to make out the lyrics.

More interesting than the song was the singer. He'd
watched Gillien closely all day yesterday. He'd seen a girl
with courage, fire, and vulnerability. He'd seen a girl who
seemed torn between a natural friendliness and an imposed
sense of mistrust. Yesterday, he would have called her
"feisty," or "stubborn," or "boyish." He would never have
thought of her as feminine, or beautiful, but here was the evi-
dence right before his eyes.

Gillien was facing him, perched atop a small boulder. Her
attire and outward appearance were exactly the same as yesterday. Yet now, singing quietly just for herself, she permitted
herself to relax as she had not done before in his presence.

Her eyes were closed, and her face was lit with a smile as
she sang. The features he had thought of as sharp now appeared delicate and sculpted. Long, slim fingers moved grace-

fully about the lute she held, coaxing notes from the strings with artless ease. When she was not holding herself rigid, with anger or mistrust, her body's natural poses revealed her inherent femininity.

There was nothing boyish or awkward about her now. She was all womanly grace and harmony. The Gillien who sat before him and sang the story of an elven goddess's miracle could never be mistaken for a youth, bound breasts and cropped hair or no.

Alerted perhaps by the feel of eyes upon her, Gillien opened her eyes. At once her face lost its look of inner rapture, became wary and furtive. She seemed to close in on herself, folding her arms protectively about the instrument and regarding him with tense attentiveness.

"I'm sorry if I startled you," he said. "You play beautifully."

A smile emerged shyly on her face. He was discovering that he liked to see her smile.

"Thank you. I'm sorry if I woke you. I tried to play quietly."

"Don't worry. It's time I was up." He stretched, and rose.

"I was up early, and I thought I might as well start cooking the rabbits. I mean, food keeps better cooked, and we can't always be sure of fresh meat and . . ."

Her voice trailed off. She drew her knees up to her chest, holding the lute close. Daric wondered just what the instrument meant to her. She seemed to regard it as something terribly precious, not just monetarily but emotionally as well. A gift from her now-dead family, perhaps?

"They smell wonderful," he said. "We can eat some now and save the rest for later. How many did we get?"

"I found two. I'm not sure how many snares you set." She slipped off the rock, all efficiency now, her gentle vulnerability cast aside. Once more, she was Garen, a sharp-featured young man. Daric silently marveled. The girl was talented, no doubt about it.

"I set eight. Come, I'll show you how to do it. You can help set them tonight, if you'd like."

"Oh, yes, I'd like to know how to do that." She followed him as he took her to where he had set the snares the night before. He pointed out the clues that had told him where he would be most likely to catch the rabbits.

"See those hard little pebbly things?" he said. "Those are rabbit droppings. They never soil their lair, so you shouldn't set a trap right where you find them, but it's a sure sign of their presence. And here," he stooped, brushing aside a small twig with careful fingers, "is a paw print. And you can see that what little there is of foliage has been cropped."

He was treating her as he might any young man he was traveling with, and she responded to his change in attitude by relaxing a bit. She was very observant and a quick learner. Once she knew what to look for, she was able to recognize the telltale marks. Soon, the rabbits were retrieved, cooked, and prepared for travel. The two travelers broke their fast, packed away their belongings, and took to the road again.

When they cantered or trotted, they did so in comfortable silence. But when they slowed their horses to a walk, allowing the beasts to rest a bit, the silence became awkward. Gillien unpacked Singer, and began to strum the strings.

She was not searching for a specific song, simply letting the instrument make whatever music it chose to. She was confused and puzzled. For the first time since the lute had stunned her with its magical ability to communicate with her, she was unsure of its intentions. She felt left out, somehow. When Daric had mentioned Taran, Singer had responded to that name with pleasure. But it refused to send her any kind of hints as to who Taran might be. No image of mighty warrior or noble priest appeared in her mind when she had asked it earlier that morning, "So who in the Nightlands *is* Taran?"

And no image came now. Singer expected her to trust its judgment. Gillien did, up to a point. Clearly, the lute had not expected Daric, but it seemed to want her to trust him, too, simply on the confidence it appeared to place in the name of that dratted, mysterious Taran.

She'd been scared when Daric first appeared, galloping over the rise like some warrior out of legend, his long hair flying in

the wind and his face as hard as stone. For all she knew, he
could have been one of the creature's minions, not a monster
himself but someone the creature hired to do its work for it
during the dangerous hours of daylight. Or Daric might have
been a slaver himself, or at the very least a self-centered
swordsman who'd been without female companionship for too
long. So she'd put up a tough semblance, using sarcasm instead of sincerity, silence instead of trust.

He had let her sleep in peace. Oversleep, even—he'd clearly
taken both watches. Whatever he was doing, he was not after
her or the lute. He'd had ample opportunity to take both, if he
had so desired.

Singer had insisted that the warrior know the true risks, so
Gillien had reluctantly told Daric about the Nightlands Demon
in pursuit. She hadn't expected to be believed, and though
Daric had been polite, it was clear that he had thought her
story just that—a story. That was fine with her. Just as long as
he continued to guard her, she'd keep an eye out for the creature.

Gillien shifted her fingers on the instrument's neck, changing the melody slightly. She glanced sideways at Daric. Handsome? He might have been, might still be if he could lose that
haunted look in his eyes. Now and then she noticed him trembling, though he fought hard to subdue it. She wondered if he
were ill. Some terrible burden sat on those broad shoulders—
something, perhaps, as terrible and tragic as what had happened to her.

Her gaze fell to his strong hands on the reins, lingered on
the griffin tattoo. She'd been deliberately insulting when she'd
teased him about his disobedient horse. Clearly, Daric Rhan
knew how to ride well. Equally clearly, the horse he rode had
more mischief and malice in her than most. Gillien suppressed
a chuckle as the horse suddenly stopped and put her head
down, but before she could execute any movement designed to
topple her rider, Daric sensed the change in his mount and reacted appropriately. The horse, slightly annoyed, deigned to
obey.

Gillien glanced down at her own horse, and smiled. Humble

was a horse in a thousand. Smart, sweet-tempered, and obedient.

"I still have you," she said softly, unaware that she was speaking aloud.

"Hmmm?" asked Daric, turning to glance at her.

Gillien blushed. "N-nothing. I just . . . would you like a song?"

Daric brightened, for an instant losing that shadowed mood that appeared to diminish his large frame.

"After what I heard this morning, yes indeed. Something lighter, perhaps. I'm not in the mood for a goddess right now."

"No goddess, eh? How about a wench?" Her long fingers swiftly located the right chords and she began playing *The Saucy Wench of Winterfield.*

For the first time in their journey together, Daric Rhan actually laughed. The shadow fled completely, though only temporarily, Gillien feared.

"How does a young maiden know that bawdy old tavern tune?"

"Ah, you forget, I grew up in a performing family. My brother—" her throat threatened to close, but she forced herself to continue. "My brother loved the song and wanted me to learn it. He said I did the best low-class Mharian accent he'd ever heard."

"Let's hear it."

Though her mouth was still slightly swollen from the blow she'd received yesterday, Gillien set her jaw in the frozen position that most Mharians seemed to use when speaking. "Ahyem, thir new, an' what's a feen fillow leek yarsel dooooin' on sach an eeel-taimpered harse? Sha'll booook ya reet aff, sha weel."

Daric laughed delightedly, a ringing, bold sound that was pure pleasure.

"Gods, Gillien, you're a wonderful little mimic. That sounds just like them! Go ahead, I've got to hear you do this song."

"All twenty-two verses?"

His eyes widened. "*Twenty-two?* I've only heard, oh, fourteen or so."

Her grin spread. "Oh, Kelly and I made up a few more."

"Somehow, that doesn't surprise me."

Gillien, her heart lightening for the first time in days, cheerfully launched into the song. Daric joined in on the chorus, shyly at first, then with more gusto as he grew more comfortable.

The rest of the day was spent in companionable talk and silences. They made good time. Daric's horse seemed to resign herself to obeying her rider's commands, and the gregarious Humble was happy for a fellow equine to keep him company. The riders, too, relaxed. The silences were no longer antagonistic; they were there simply because neither one had anything to say and they needed to gallop from time to time to keep up the pace.

When they halted for the midday break, Daric took the opportunity to give Gillien further lessons in wilderness skills. Some mushrooms, which he and Gillien gathered as they talked, would be delicious eaten raw or cooked in stews. Others, which he also pointed out, were deadly. He seemed able to discover clutches of berries and herbs in some of the most unlikely places, quickly harvesting and popping them into his mouth.

When they stopped for the day, Daric swung his pack off of That Damned Beast, who blew happily, and made no attempt to swing her head around to bite him this time. "We made good time today," he commented.

"We certainly did. If we can keep up this pace, we ought to make Woodhill Pass by midafternoon on Vensdae," said Gillien, carefully setting Singer down before removing the pack from her own horse.

"We'll see how the horses like that. Come here, and I'll show you how to make the snares."

Obligingly, Gillien plopped down beside Daric, gazing with curiosity at the twine he held in his hands.

"It's a little tricky, so watch closely." He demonstrated how to twist the twine just so, then set it up on a nearby bush. Carefully, so as not to spring it, he covered it lightly with dried earth. When he had finished, the clever little rabbit trap was nearly invisible.

"Let me try," said Gillien, eagerly snatching a length of twine for herself.

"You'd better watch me one more time," suggested Daric, grinning with just a hint of condescension at her enthusiasm. "As I said, they're tricky, and—"

"Like this?" Gillien showed him the twisted twine.

The patronizing grin faded. "Yes, that's right, but to set it correctly—"

Ignoring him, Gillien trotted over to another bush, this one several yards away from their camping area. Kneeling, she set up the trap as swiftly as Daric had done, meticulously sweeping just enough dried topsoil over the twine to disguise it, but not enough to trigger it.

Daric shook his head. "I give up. No sense in me trying to teach you anything. Next thing I know, you'll be beating me at sword fighting!"

"Oh, no," Gillien assured him hastily. "I've never held a real sword in my life—just wooden ones that we used for performances. I'm sure I don't have the wrist strength for—"

She stopped, puzzled. Daric was laughing at her! She sank back on her heels, confused and a little hurt. Seeing her expression of chagrin, Daric smothered his amusement and laid a friendly hand on her shoulder.

"Oh, Gilly, how you do make me laugh. I was only joking! Seriously, though, you have a very quick mind—and even quicker fingers. Did you supplement your family's earnings by lifting a purse or two?"

Gillien's brown eyebrows drew together in an angry scowl.

"How dare you even suggest that! We earned every damn copper that came our way, and don't you think we didn't! Yes, I bet if I tried, I'd be a marvelous pickpocket. I picked the lock on a prison cell in order to escape with my life, but the only reason I know how is because my father was an escapist. He could get out of *any* lock and he wanted his children to learn his skill." Still angry, she rose and stalked back to the encampment, unpacking her things with unnecessary vigor.

She heard Daric come up behind her, felt his tentative hand on her shoulder again. She didn't turn around.

"How *dare* you insult their memories. How *dare*—"

"Gilly," he soothed, pressing her shoulder and gently urging her around to face him. "I'm sorry. I spoke out of turn. I've never really known a traveling performer before, and, well, there are rumors about them just as there are rumors about professional soldiers. And I'm sure you've got the songs to prove just how bad my profession is, haven't you?"

Reluctantly, Gillien thought of the terribly bawdy song, *The Warrior's Big Sword,* and a smile touched her lips.

"Ah, much better. I like to see you smiling." His eyes were kind now, and she found that he was in truth quite a handsome fellow when he wasn't silently sulking.

"I like to see you smiling, too," she confessed, "and you don't do it often enough."

The words, which she had hoped would please him, had the opposite effect. The mirth and light left his face, and shadow shrouded his visage. He rose suddenly.

"I don't always have something to smile about," he said, his voice rough. "I'll go set the rest of the snares."

She watched him stride away, his pose stiff and defensive. Not for the first time, she wondered what it was that took the animation from his soul and replaced it with edgy melancholy.

She groomed Humble, then turned him free to graze. Daric returned and silently began to gather dead wood. She did likewise, helping him build the fire and prepare the meal. They did not talk much as they ate, and Daric turned in early. Sitting beside the blazing fire, Gillien watched him. He was not asleep. His body was too tense, too falsely still, for that.

She had seen him asleep, early that morning before she began to play Singer. Whatever haunted him during the day had full reign over him when sleep descended. He had cried out wordlessly, tossed and turned, whimpered and flailed.

It had made Gillien want to go to him and hold him, comfort him as she might a sick child. But she did not dare. It would no doubt embarrass him, and it would reveal her softer side—something she didn't want him to see right now. Tearing her gaze away from her guardian, she picked up Singer.

"Hello," she said, softly, so that Daric would not overhear.

Singer sent its welcome, but she sensed something else as well. The lute was unhappy about something and trying to hide it from her. Instantly, Gillien was alert. She strummed the strings, but Singer suggested no song to her.

"What's wrong?"

Again, a vague unease.

"Danger?"

Singer hastened to assure her that there was no immediate danger.

"Then what?" Fond as she was of the magical instrument, Gillien was starting to become slightly exasperated by it.

The lute seemed to banish its restlessness and suggested a cheerful song. Shrugging, Gillien obeyed, taking care to keep her voice and playing low so as not to disturb Daric. She played until she and Singer both seemed to have enough, then carefully wrapped the lute away from the dampness of the night. She stretched down beside it and fell asleep.

Daric was up first the second morning of their journey. He was brusque and distant, and Gillien was slightly intimidated. After a few attempts on her part to get him to relax, she gave up. They ate quickly, with little enthusiasm, downing bowls of hot mashed grains and breaking camp shortly thereafter.

Daric seemed to relax after a few hours of riding, and when Gillien played a few lighthearted tunes, he even joined in. The midday break was pleasant, and after making good time for the rest of the afternoon, they agreed to get a few more miles under their belts than they had originally planned.

"That sounds good to me—just as long as we have enough time to start a fire before darkness falls."

"Gillien, it's positively *hot* out, and will be quite warm enough for at least an hour past sunset," Daric observed.

She threw him an exasperated glance.

"Not for the heat, for the light!" she reminded him. "The demon doesn't like light, remember?"

He glanced away, but not before Gillien had seen him rolling his eyes.

"Damn it, Daric," she cried, suddenly furious. "What will it take for you to believe me?"

"Seeing the cursed thing for myself," he retorted. He kicked his mare, who lunged forward, startled by the gesture. "Come on, then," he called over his shoulder. "The next good deadfall isn't for another few miles, if I remember this route correctly."

Hurt and angry, Gillien swore and squeezed Humble's sides. The pony lurched ahead in a tired trot-shamble. She watched the sky anxiously. Rain was on its way, and the evening sky was rapidly becoming a dull, uniform gray that slowly darkened toward blackness as the minutes passed.

At last Daric's deadfall area appeared. He slowed down to ride alongside her.

"Over there is a cave," he said, pointing to a rock formation to the left. "It's big and roomy. Do you want to camp there or stop here? It looks like rain will be coming."

"If it rains, then we go to the cave. If not, let's stay here. I want to get that fire started now, not a half hour from now."

"Damn it, Gillien, it's just over that ridge! And if the rain comes, we'll have wet wood. A move in the dark—"

"It's almost dark *now*, Daric. If the demon is following us, it'll be on us before we can even reach the cave if we don't have some sort of light!"

Without another word, Gillien galloped up to the deadfall area and swung off her lathered horse almost before Humble had reached a full stop. Pausing only to relieve the dapple gray of the twin burdens of pack and lute, Gillien urgently set herself to the task of gathering dried wood.

Humble glanced reproachfully at her for a moment. Usually, Gillien attended to the horse before she did anything else. She felt a twinge of guilt.

"Sorry, Humble. I'll groom you as soon as I can, but if we don't get a fire started, we're all going to be in danger." The horse blew and stamped, annoyed, but walked off in search of grass to crop.

Daric pulled off his own pack. "You talk to the horse," he

said in an irritated tone of voice, "you talk to the lute—are you mad enough to think they'll understand you, girl?"

Gillien turned on her traveling companion. She noticed his face was pale and he was trembling as he staked his horse's reins to the earth, sweating slightly despite the cooling temperatures. But she was too annoyed to moderate her words out of pity for his strange malady.

"Yes, I talk to the horse, I talk to the lute, I even talk to myself. And you know something, Daric Rhan? All three listen to me better than *you* do."

They did not speak to each other for a while after that. Daric busied himself with setting the snares and Gillien began to light the fire using flint and steel. She felt relief seep into her bones as the kindling caught, a full, fine blaze following shortly. She raised her eyes from the dancing fire and looked about the area they'd chosen as their encampment.

The landscape was even stonier now than it had been earlier on their journey. The darkness was more stifling as well, due to the thick blanket of clouds that hid both moon and stars from her view. The fire, though strong, seemed somehow feeble to her, its orange glow the only thing holding back the press of night.

Something prickled at the back of her neck. She froze, senses alert. The sensation happened again. Gillien knew what it was. Her heart beating loudly, she ran to the lute and quickly unwrapped it.

"What is it?" she whispered, holding it and stroking its smooth wood.

Danger!

Gillien's skin erupted into gooseflesh and she dropped Singer. She almost cried out as she heard a sharp cracking noise behind her. At once, she had a dagger in each hand and whirled, her eyes enormous, her heart pounding.

"Sweet Lady Death, Gillien!" said Daric. "You're as nervous as a rabbit tonight. What's wrong?"

She still held her daggers at the ready.

"Show me your hands," she ordered, though her voice shook. She had been ready enough to kill Daric when she had first met him, thinking he was a pawn of the dreadful thing that followed her. Now that she knew him, would she be able to attack his form, should the demon choose to wear it? She didn't know, and she prayed to all the gods that she wouldn't have to find out.

Daric grunted in disbelief. "Not this nonsense again."

"Daric, I swear, I'll put this knife through your throat if you don't!" Her voice climbed higher in her fear and agitation.

Sighing with resignation, Daric stretched out his hands. They were creased and calloused—a swordsman's hands. Gillien's relief was so profound that her knees buckled and she sank heavily to the stony earth. Daric was there at once, his strong hands on her shoulders in a grip that was almost painful, yet oddly comforting in its power.

"I don't know what's happening with you, but you're scaring yourself like a child with a fireside tale," he said, his voice rough. Yet when she glanced up at him, she saw that his brown eyes were filled with concern. "Now calm down. I'll get dinner, you just sit there and calm yourself, all right?"

Gillien glanced over at Singer, her eyes narrowing. It still seemed distressed, but without touching it she could only sense its vague displeasure and worry. She wondered what was happening to it. The lute had been behaving oddly ever since Daric had joined up with them. She trusted Singer, but she was also learning to trust Daric.

She wished she could take the instrument in her arms, ask it just what in the Nightlands it thought it was doing scaring her like this, but Daric kept one eye on her as he went about preparing the meal. He thought she was peculiar enough as it was. She didn't want to see him engaged in an argument with a musical instrument. Confronting Singer would have to wait until later, perhaps when Daric was asleep.

In the meantime, she didn't want to just sit here. Gillien was used to activity. She got to her feet.

"Where do you think you're going?"

"I have to groom Humble."

"I have to groom That Damned Beast, too," he muttered, glancing over at the animal in question. The bay mare glared back at him, stamping one hoof impatiently. "When we're done eating."

"No, no, I'll do it now. It'll calm me down," she added pointedly. Daric shrugged and continued cutting up potatoes.

Gillien unpacked the grooming tools, went to the ring of fire, put two fingers in her mouth, and whistled. Almost at once, she heard an answering neigh and Humble came cantering up out of the darkness. He stopped a few feet from the fire. His ears were pricked forward and he seemed eager to see her.

"That's my good boy!" Gillien said. "You've been very patient, and I'm sorry I made you wait."

She continued talking to the horse, taking refuge from her nagging sense of worry in the familiar routine of grooming a beloved beast. Humble was caked with dirt and sweat, and she had to put a little more effort into her task than usual. She combed his mane and tail, enjoying the fluffy feel of the cleaned hair beneath her hands.

She put down the comb and picked up the hoof pick. Squatting down beside the horse, she tapped his fetlock, asking for his hoof. Obediently, he raised his leg. Gillien glanced down to see if there were any stones in the frog area.

She broke out in a cold sweat. Her heart began to slam painfully against her chest.

Humble *had* no frog.

The underside of his foot was a completely blank shade of gray-brown. It was utterly unpatterned—as Reeve Herrick's hands had been.

Her mouth was completely dry. She waited an instant or two, steeling herself for the horrific transformation, the sharp stab of a poisoned spur, the dissolution of her body into edible and inedible parts. But the monster wearing the shape of her adored trick pony made no move. It seemed completely unaware of her discovery.

And then the second realization slammed home, and she almost cried aloud. If the creature was posing as Humble, then almost certainly the pony was dead.

Humble! No . . .

No time to mourn now. No time to even be afraid, now. She

had to keep up the pretense that all was as it should be, that she was grooming a horse, not some unnatural beast clothed in its flesh.

She forced herself to breathe.

"Looks just fine," she said, and was amazed that her voice sounded completely normal. Her mind raced as she went to the other three hooves, pretending to inspect them. Why hadn't the creature attacked? It must not want to risk a counterattack with the painful fire. And why should it? All it needed to do was to wait until they were both asleep, then simply take the lute. It had been a brilliant scheme, felled only by its strange inability to replicate the patterns on hands—or in this case, on the bottoms of hooves.

Rising, Gillien forced herself to pat the creature. It felt just like horseflesh, and even whickered in a friendly fashion. She led it to one of the few trees still left standing and tied its reins tightly around the trunk and through the branches.

"Gillien! What are you doing? You never tie Humble," came Daric's questioning voice from the fireside.

The beast tensed. Gillien mentally cursed Daric a thousand times, then came up with an excuse.

"No horse likes thunder and lightning," she said. "I just don't want him getting spooked and running off, that's all."

The monster relaxed. "All right," said Daric affably.

As nonchalantly as she could, Gillien strode to the fire. She bent down and took hold of a branch, shoving it deep into the heart of the flame. Softly, she whispered, "Daric, it's here."

He glanced up at her. "What is?"

She squeezed her eyes shut, forcing back the terror that threatened to overwhelm her.

"The demon. It got H-Humble. It's taken his form. I saw its hooves—no frog, no shoe. . . ."

Daric sighed and shook his head. "Oh, Gillien," he began, in a voice tinged with pity.

"You don't believe me." It was a flat statement.

He hesitated, then replied, "No, I don't. I think you've been through a lot recently and—"

"You said the only way you'd believe me was if you saw

the creature yourself," she hissed, her eyes blazing as hotly as the fire. "Well, your wish is about to be granted."

She straightened up and suddenly ran for the creature, thrusting the flaming branch in front of her. Daric rose at once.

"Gods, Gillien, you're going to hurt your own damn horse!" He dove at her, but missed her by an inch.

The creature reacted a second too late. Crying out incoherently, Gillien shoved the fiery brand directly into Humble's sleepy-eyed, sweet face. It roared in agony, pulling back against the reins that bound it to the tree. Its equine face, scorched and burning, began to ooze over until it was devoid of features. Humble's strong, lean legs collapsed underneath him, becoming boneless yet deadly tentacles each equipped with a shiny, poison-slicked spike.

Behind her, Gillien heard Daric yell, first in shock, that she would so hurt a simple beast, then in horror at the sight he was witnessing. An instant later, though, he rallied. He stood beside her, big and powerful, his sword in one hand and a blazing branch in the other.

"Don't let it sting you!" she cried. "Poison!"

The demon-horse took a vicious swipe at Daric's face with its glistening appendages, but the swordsman's reactions were just as swift. Daric swung with the sword, lopping off a chunk of slimy flesh that hit the ground with a soft splat. At once, it lost all form and became a yellow-gray puddle.

With the same motion, Daric shoved the fiery brand into the creature's side. The entity screamed, an unnatural, metallic sound, and whirled around to face him. It was brought up short by the reins. Crying out in frustration, it pulled against its tether. There was a deep groaning sound. The old, dead tree was no match for the creature's strength. The roots erupted and the tree toppled even as the leather reins snapped.

The beast, free, sprang for Gillien. She flung the brand at it. It ducked, giving her just enough time to scramble back to the safety of the fire and get the flames between her and it.

The monster hesitated, loath to press its attack so close to the fire. In that brief pause, Daric renewed his attack. Cries of anger turned into shrieks of pain as the creature writhed and burned, transforming into a monstrosity of arms and legs and heads, all of which struck futilely in Daric's direction.

In the end, the pain and damage wrought by the humans was too much for the creature. Its grotesque form, now black and oozing, underwent a final transformation. It sprouted wings from its deformed, semi-equine shape and leaped for the sky.

Daric, panting, watched it go. There came a deep booming roar, and for a moment he thought it was the creature, returning for another bout. Then moist droplets pattered his upturned face, and he realized the noise was only thunder.

"The rain will put the fire out!" he heard Gillien shriek. "The cave, Daric!"

She had already reached Singer and had shrugged into the instrument's shoulder strap. The lute emitted a sense of urgency that the young bard felt all the way to her bones. With the lute safe, all Gillien could think about, all she could let herself think about, was light. She frantically grabbed handfuls of burning sticks and began to race for the cave Daric had pointed out earlier, the lute banging against her body. She heard Daric's running feet behind her as he overtook her and raced ahead. She followed.

She would never have found the cave had he not known where it was. He climbed up a small, sandy hill and seemed to vanish into the wall of rock. But when she got there herself, panting and damp with rain, she saw the entrance.

Daric had dropped the fagots. "Here," he gasped, "pile them on. You get the horse and our packs over here, I'll go for more wood."

"Gods, Daric, be careful!"

"I think it's gone, at least for the moment."

The next quarter of an hour, Gillien was never to remember. Somehow, she gathered up the packs, tied them onto Daric's mount, and galloped over to the cave. The horse refused to enter, so she staked it down where she could see it from inside.

When Daric returned, carrying a huge armload of wood, he found the girl sitting beside the fire, the lute at her side. She was thoroughly drenched, as was he. She held her knees to her chin, clasping her legs tightly with her arms, and rocked back and forth. Her eyes were blank, unfocused. Not even the light from the fire could make her skin look rosy.

Daric had seen that look before and come to dread it. He had seen it in the eyes of men who had lethal injuries, just before life left them. And more frightening, he had seen it in the eyes of men who had no injuries whatsoever, but who had witnessed more than their minds could bear.

He swore softly, piling more wood on the fire in the hopes that a brilliant, leaping blaze would somehow soothe Gillien. She didn't react at all. Finally, he sat down next to her and covered her with his cape.

"Gillien," he began, "I don't know what to say. I was a fool not to believe you, and I'm sorry. I wish it hadn't gotten Humble. I really do, but we both managed to escape with our lives. That's the important thing."

Her chilled lips moved, but no words came. Daric reached his arm around her, pulling her to him. Her body trembled violently, rigid within the circle of his arms.

"H-Humble," she managed at last. "He—he was all I had left. The last of my f-family. And that thing got him too. It got Mama, and Papa, and Kelly, and now it's got Humble, and gods, gods, Daric, one of these days it's going to get me too—"

"Shh, now," Daric soothed. "I'll keep you safe, I promise."

"*It got Humble!*" she shrieked, startling him. "Don't you see?" Her eyes were wild now, enormous and brimming with tears. "I have nothing left! It's taken everything that was important to me, everything I had, that I cared about." Her voice broke, and the tears came flooding down her cheeks.

"Nothing left . . . nothing . . ."

She sobbed wildly, and he held her tightly, laying his stubbled cheek on her wet hair. He closed his eyes in relief. "If one can weep, one can heal." It was a tired old saying, but he had seen enough pain in his life to know that it was true. He knew in his heart that was why he was unable to let go of the past.

He found his comfort in the liquid that came in a wine bottle, not in the drops that ran down one's face.

For a long, long time Gillien wept, her slender body heaving and writhing with emotion. Daric knew it was only partly for the loyal Humble himself. Even more, it was for all the horse represented. As she said, Humble was the last of her family. Now, Gillien knew herself to be truly alone in the world, and that knowledge was devastating. At last her sobs faded into soft gulping shudders, and then hitched breathing. He kept his arms around her until he felt the tension quietly slip from her body, and knew that she was asleep.

Daric moved only to toss more branches on the fire, keeping one arm securely around the exhausted young woman. Such courage, he thought to himself. Knowing that such a . . . thing . . . was after her, and still moving on. He was now thoroughly convinced that every part of her story was true—that she had indeed lost her family to a nightmare creature who could take any form it chose. Daric thought that if he had had to undergo such an ordeal, his sanity might not have survived intact.

There was no sleeping for him that night. He lay with the slumbering, brave young woman cradled against his chest. He stared at the fire and then past it, out into the blackness of the night, where his horse neighed and where that monster might still be lurking.

Unconsciously, his arm about Gillien tightened.

"I'll protect you, Gilly," he whispered.

Rule 12: Sleep is vital. So is the ability to fully awaken at need. One drowsy moment could mean one dead soldier. Sleep with your sword at your side, and practice awakening fully alert.

—from *Codes of Conduct for*
Byrnian Commanding Units, Section Four

CHAPTER THIRTEEN

It rained through the night and into the next morning, which dawned as gray and bleak as Daric Rhan felt. Gillien had slept the deep sleep of the totally exhausted. She had lain heavily in his arms, against his chest, sending his limbs to sleep beneath her slim, muscular weight. He now welcomed as a sort of penance the discomfort and needling pain that marked his limbs returning to life.

He wanted to apologize to the girl a thousand times over, but it would make no difference. It would not bring Humble back, would not take away the horrors the young bard had witnessed last night and over the last few days. He was grateful only that he and Gillien had survived the attack.

He gazed at the gray light at the mouth of the cave, which showed his horse sleeping with lowered head. The overhanging rock offered enough shelter for the bay mare to keep out of the rain, but little more. Daric had kept the fire well stoked throughout the night—the one feeble gesture he could make, he thought grimly, to atone for the danger that his closed mind had brought on the two of them. Now he let it burn down to embers suitable for cooking.

Daric longed to let Gillien sleep. There was no pain in sleep, unless one had nightmares, and the depth of Gillien's grief had taken her beyond such things. But with only one horse for the both of them, every moment of traveling time was precious. At least he could have breakfast ready and everything prepared for departure before waking her. As slowly and carefully as he could, he eased her limp form away from him, wincing as pain shot through his numbed limbs.

She mumbled something in her sleep, then started awake.

"Humble!" she shrieked, flailing. "Singer . . ."

"I've got your lute, here it is, it's right here," he comforted, quickly grabbing the precious package and handing it to her. She gasped and held it to her breast, closing her eyes and rocking back and forth.

Not knowing what to say, Daric averted his eyes and tried to stand. His leg gave out underneath him and he would have fallen had he not grabbed onto a rock outcropping. He swore violently.

"It happened, didn't it? It wasn't a dream?"

Her voice, normally bright and enthusiastic, was as bleak as the day and Daric's mood. He chanced a look at her face and saw that she was ashy pale, her blue eyes a dull shade of slate.

He licked his lips. Gods, how he wished he could contradict her. But he could not.

"Yes," he said. "It happened."

She nodded her cropped head, then rose and shuffled out of the cave, moving to a spot out of his field of vision. She made no attempt to cover her head, and indeed didn't even seem to notice the rain at all. Daric also badly needed to relieve himself, but he set about preparing the meal and waited until Gillien returned. Her hair was dripping and her clothing was damp.

"You might want to change into something drier," he suggested.

She turned her weary gaze onto him.

"Why bother?"

"You don't want to catch a chill." Inspiration came to him. "And you're dripping on the lute."

She wasn't, and it was an underhanded ploy, but it worked. Gillien started, as if she had just remembered something dreadfully important, and something like animation came back to her movements. Daric felt his spirits lift, just a little. At least there was still something the girl cared about.

He threw his cloak over his shoulders and went out into the rain to perform his own morning ritual. He lingered a few moments longer than was necessary to give Gillien time to change should she so desire, then went back inside. He felt a faint flicker of pleasure when he saw her fastening her belt around a dry shirt and pants. Her damp clothes were spread out on the rocks close to the fire to dry. Daric shook the moisture off his own cloak and spread it next to hers.

They ate and packed That Damned Beast, who seemed to sense that something was amiss. She whickered quietly as Daric loaded her up and did not once try any mischief.

"Are you sure she can carry us both?" Gillien asked, hesitating as she approached the horse.

"She's going to have to. And you don't weigh that much. Let me give you a leg up."

He made a cup out of his hands. Gillien placed her left foot in the cup and swung her right leg over, mutely holding out her hands for the lute. Daric handed up the wrapped bundle and she settled it between her legs, cradling it. He swung up in front of her and gathered up his horse's reins.

His mind raced with thoughts as they traveled steadily northward in the drizzle. They were both alive today, yes, but not because of anything he had done, not really. Gillien had told him the truth, right from the beginning, and he had refused to believe her. It was not his sword nor his courage, but Gillien's keen eyes and incredibly level head that had saved them both.

He had failed to protect her. That she was alive was entirely due to her own innate good sense.

But how could he possibly have believed the story? coun-

tered another part of his mind. It was ludicrous—exactly the
sort of mythic fabrication that a heartsick bard might be expected to weave. He'd been alert for real, logical danger, not a
nightmare sprung to hideous life. He'd wanted something that
could be fought and defeated by cold steel, not hot fire or
something as intangible as sunlight.

Daric's mouth was awfully dry, but water wouldn't quench
this thirst. Wine was what was called for to drown his guilt
and extinguish his anger. He'd done it often enough in the past
to know its qualities. Just one long swig of liquor might at
least take the edge off.

Behind him, he felt Gillien stir, felt the hard wood of the instrument poke him gently through its protective cloth. He
heard a soft sigh as her right arm fumbled for a better grip
around his waist. There had been no words of reproach from
the girl, though she might have been expected to let loose with
a volley of blistering curses. Daric almost wished she had.
He'd have felt better, a little less guilty, less impotent. But she
was silent, withholding blame and comment.

She didn't need to. He blamed himself enough for both of
them. And the numbness he craved would do nothing to atone
for his errors. A drunken warrior would be less than no use to
Gillien; he'd probably cut off her head before he hurt any
enemy. He wondered if she could feel him shaking where she
touched him. It would serve him right.

That Damned Beast proved to be a good horse in a crisis.
She carried them both with a great heart, but her pace was of
necessity slowed. Daric had hoped to reach Woodhill Pass by
midafternoon, but it was going well into twilight before they
even reached the forested hills that had given the town its
name.

"Should we stop? Make a fire?" It was the first thing Gillien
had said all day. Daric wasn't looking at her, but he knew
what he would see if she turned around: her aquiline features
tense and frightened, her blue eyes staring up at the darkening
sky.

"No," he answered, "it's not too much farther now. Maybe

five miles or so. I don't know if the inns are full or not. It's a busy time of year for Woodhill Pass."

"Is there a Lamp of Traveler?"

He hadn't been in a holy house for years, and the thought hadn't occurred to him. "Yes, there is."

"Can we stay there? I—I think it might be safer."

Daric was inclined to agree. He didn't know the full powers of the demon, or whether it was afraid to enter a holy house as many mythical beings were, but it certainly couldn't hurt.

"All right. The Lamp, then."

It was located right at the outskirts of the town, and they cantered up just as the last rays of sun turned to ashy gray. Gillien slipped down from the horse as a young man hurried up to take That Damned Beast's reins. She held Singer close, and kept her eyes on the ground.

Daric took charge. "Good evening, Tender. Is there room for two more at Traveler's Lamp?"

"There is always room at Traveler's Lamp for those who are weary," came a cheerful voice from the door. Daric glanced up from the boy to see the Blesser himself, a tall, thin man with dark ringlets of thick hair.

"Welcome, welcome. As it happens, you will probably be the only ones here tonight. So I may safely say there's plenty for all!"

His teeth flashed white as he extended his arms to heartily embrace first Daric, and then Gillien. The girl looked quizzically at Daric, who gave a slight shrug.

"Thank you, Blesser . . . ?"

"Jervis, and this is my Tender, Tavi." He laid an affectionate hand on the boy's shoulder. A skinny, gawky child whose eyes seemed too big for his face, the boy seemed to flinch away. Daric didn't blame him. Constant exposure to such effusiveness as the Blesser displayed would have irritated him, too.

"Tavi will take care of your horse. Please, please, bring your belongings in, and we will see what Traveler and I can do for you."

*   *   *

Gillien was glad the water was hot. She almost wished it were boiling, so that she could burn away what she had been through. As it was, she sat naked in front of the steaming basin, wrung out the washing cloth, and scrubbed furiously at her skin until it grew pink beneath the heat and friction.

She supposed she ought to be grateful that there was hot water at all, not to mention that she had a whole room to herself and therefore had the privacy necessary for her to enjoy a quick bath of sorts. After a day of riding hard, half of that time being rained on and the other half being soaking wet from said rain, it ought to come as a luxury. She found, though, that all it did was remind her of the bath at Lucan's temple. Thinking of the kind, elderly Blesser, she said a quick prayer that he had escaped the creature's notice.

She did not unwrap the sweat-stained cloth that bound her breasts, contenting herself with a less-than-complete ablution. She dried herself off with a rough towel that the silent, big-eyed young Tender had provided, then changed into dry clothes. They were the last clean clothes she had, but if all went well, she and Daric would be at Kasselton in two days. Then, she could give Singer to Queen-mother Ariel, who would understand whatever strange, dire message it had to relate to her.

The thought stabbed at her. She glanced over at Singer, who lay quietly on one of the four pallets in the room.

"I'm going to miss you," she said, walking over and taking the lute in her arms.

The lute, too, seemed distressed at the thought of parting with her. A sudden thought caused her to brighten.

"Maybe . . . maybe after you've delivered your message, she'll let me have you back! As a reward or something. That is," she added, blushing, "if you'd like to stay with me."

A sudden rush of affection bathed her in a warm tide. Singer cared deeply for her, it told her in its own strange form of communication. Perhaps such a thing could be. But beneath its eagerness Gillien sensed a sorrow, a reluctance, perhaps even a tinge of fear.

"Well," she said, "we'll worry about that later. Time

enough for figuring out what to do with you once we've gotten you to Queen-mother Ariel, right?"

Singer was forced to agree that she had the right of it. Impulsively she hugged the instrument. No, Singer wasn't a person, or even a pet like Humble had been. But it was clearly sentient, and Gillien had grown fond of it.

"Come on." She brightened. The hot water and clean clothes were working their simple magic upon her weary body and spirits, and she was feeling a bit better. "Daric's waiting for us, and I'm hungry."

The dining room was small. There was a single table, two wooden benches, and a large hearth by the fireplace. The floor was hard-packed earth. It was, if such a thing was possible, even simpler than the one Blesser Rufiel had run. Certainly, its smaller size and empty pallets indicated that it was close to taverns which undoubtedly proved more enticing to wandering travelers.

This suited Gillien just fine. She didn't want to be around other people tonight. Daric and Singer for company were more than enough.

The warrior was there before her, sitting on the hearth. He, too, had bathed and changed. There was something different about him, but she didn't know quite what at first. He turned and smiled at her as she entered, and then she realized that he had taken the opportunity to shave. His hair, too, was pulled back and tied in a neat ponytail.

He rose as she walked over. "The ghost is gone," he said.

She frowned at him, not understanding. "What?"

"The ghost in your eyes. It's gone." His smile deepened. "I'm glad. I was worried about you there for a while."

She dropped her gaze, suddenly shy. "When do we eat?"

Daric chuckled. "You don't waste words, do you? Well, perhaps if we sit down, we might get served."

He was right. No sooner had they taken their seats at the rough table than young Tavi came out with a loaf of bread and a pot of butter.

Gillien's eyes lit up. "Smells wonderful," she said, smiling at the youth. The boy didn't meet her gaze, nor did he answer.

He merely turned around and headed back into the kitchen, returning with two goblets and a bottle of wine.

"Thank you," said Daric, noticing the boy's silence. Tavi mumbled something. "What was that, Tender?"

"I said," replied Tavi in a voice barely above a whisper, "that Traveler provides." This time, he fairly ran back into the side room.

"Shy little fellow," said Gillien, opening her mouth and taking an enormous bite of bread thickly coated with butter.

Daric looked after the boy, nodding a little. "I don't think he's happy here."

Gillien started to reply, realized her mouth was far too full to permit communication, chewed a bit, and tried again. "Not everyone is destined to serve the gods."

"True. But most at least make a pretense in front of worshippers."

Gillien poured wine into her goblet. The scent was fruity and strong, the color rich and dark. Daric found himself staring as if mesmerized as the heady fragrance teased his nostrils. The wine smelled to be, if such a thing was possible in this unassuming little Lamp, of excellent quality.

The craving descended with all the force of a horse's kick. The warrior found himself clenching his hands in his lap in order to restrain himself from seizing the goblet and downing the contents at one gulp.

"Would you like some?" Gillien asked, her open face all innocently questioning as she held the bottle.

Daric knew that everything available for consumption would be brought to the diners at Traveler's Lamp; therefore, there was literally nothing else to drink.

"Yes, thank you," he stammered. His voice sounded taut and raspy even to his own ears, and Gillien shot him a curious glance as she poured the liquid.

It's a safe place, Daric thought to himself. It wouldn't be like getting drunk on the trail, where that monster might find us. Or even slavers . . . the word made his fingers itch to grab the goblet, but he restrained himself. It would be all right to get a little tipsy here—wouldn't it?

He reached out a hand that trembled and closed his fingers about the goblet's stem. Carefully, so that he wouldn't spill any, he brought the drink to his lips. Oh, gods, its call was as sweet as a woman's throaty cries of pleasure, and infinitely more desirable.

"Daric, are you all right?"

Gillien's question made him pause. His brown eyes met her blue ones as he looked at her over the red surface of the wine. He swallowed hard. There was no accusation in her expression, only concern. She'd probably never even seen a man in the grips of the need, as he was. What was she thinking? That he was sick? As soul-weary as she?

How in the name of all that he'd ever loved could he get drunk, knowing that she was relying upon him?

He'd betrayed her trust once, by not believing an admittedly preposterous tale. But he couldn't knowingly betray that trust again—not and still be able to look her in the eye.

He licked his lips. "I'm fine, Gil—er, Garen. Just as hungry and tired as you are, that's all."

Her face relaxed into a relieved smile, and she took a sip of the wine. Her eyes flew wide. "Mmmmm . . . It's good, but it's awfully strong!"

Daric was silently glad of the warning. He'd need all the help he could get if he could pass this test—drink the wine, yet not drain the bottle. His tongue tingling in anticipation, he took a swallow. Just one. Then he deliberately put the glass down.

She had been right on both counts. The wine was delicious—full-bodied, smooth, and far sweeter to him than she could possibly comprehend. It also was deceptively strong. He would have to pace himself carefully if he were to keep to his newfound resolution.

Gillien, under no such restraints, ate and drank cheerfully. The liquor seemed to flush away the last of her pallor, and by the second glass, she was her normal self again. Daric was grateful for that.

"Would you wish some fruit and cheese while we prepare your meat?" came Blesser Jervis's far-too-jovial voice. Startled, the diners glanced up at their host. He carried a tray of three types of cheese, along with apples, berries, and something that Daric didn't recognize at first.

Gillien did, though. "Pomma fruit!" she yelped happily. "I haven't had this for years!" She picked up the hard-skinned, lumpy black fruit and began to slice it open. The two halves fell to each side, revealing bright pink flesh inside.

The Blesser laughed indulgently. "We like to provide the best to our guests," he said, picking up the bottle and refilling Gillien's cup. "The meat will be out shortly." He smiled brightly and hastened back to the side room.

Gillien was by now well on her way to tipsiness. She handed Daric half of the pomma fruit and dove happily into her own, scooping out the sweet flesh with a spoon. She closed her eyes and savored the taste.

"Oh, these are wonderful," she sighed. "I could eat these all day."

Daric smothered a smile as he ate his own half. He had forgotten what it was like to be tipsy; he had too often drowned such lighthearted celebrations of the vineyard's fruit in bitter, angry, alcohol-saturated stupors. Gillien would hate it if she knew, but right now she was almost unbearably cute. She took another few gulps of her wine.

"Traveler loves a good tale. Tell me about some of your travels with your family," he said, hoping that the wine had dulled the pain enough for her to speak of them.

Gillien looked sad for a moment, then brightened. And the tales came pouring out. Many and varied they were, mainly humorous and always, always happy. She told of the tricks she had played on her brother Kellien—and, to be fair, those he had played on her. She told about training Humble, whose early tempers would have put That Damned Beast to shame. And she told of the tumbling and songs, tales and tricks that had become second nature. Daric could see Gillien's mother dancing, a whirl of dark hair and laughing eyes; could feel the music soaring up into the sky as the family sat of an evening and sang, just for their own pleasure.

Daric listened, drinking in her words rather than the wine. It

held his attention until the meat—a savory-scented leg of lamb
with potatoes and turnips—arrived, served by the silent, un-
easy Tender. They ate, Gillien managing to fit food in her
mouth between stories, until the wine truly caught up with her.

She was sagging in her seat by this point, her chin resting in
her hands, her elbows the only thing keeping her head from
hitting the table. Her eyes were half-closed, and she had a
ridiculously endearing smile on her face.

"I think," Daric hazarded, "that you're going to sleep very
well tonight, young man."

Her brows drew together. "Who're you callin' . . . oh." She
nodded, remembering just who and what she was trying to im-
itate. "Yes, I think so, too."

She got to her feet, wobbling a great deal. Daric quickly
rose and caught her by the elbow before she fell. "You don't
have a head for liquor, do you?"

Gillien blinked, trying to focus on his face. "No," she admitted. She pulled away from him, balanced precariously, and
then began to weave toward her room. "G'night," she called
back, waving at him.

"Goodnight," he replied, feeling mirth curve his lips. Poor
thing, he thought, you're going to have one terrible headache
in the morning.

He expected the Blesser or his Tender to come in and remove the plates, but no one entered. He assumed that they
were waiting for their guests to go to bed first before tidying
up. That was considerate, for Daric wasn't really in the mood
to make idle conversation with either the effusively kind
Blesser or his taciturn Tender. He sat by the fire, which had
burned down to embers, and analyzed his feelings.

To his surprise, he realized that he felt good. Very good.

He had won his first battle with the demon in the bottle
tonight. He had been able to resist the temptation to drink
deeply, had in fact finished barely half a glass of the delicious
vintage, if even that. He had slaked his thirst with the juicy
fruits instead, finding that once he had set his mind to the task
it had been fairly easy.

Of course, having such a pleasant dinner companion had

proved a wonderful distraction. He wasn't sure that he could
have resisted the call had he been dining alone.

But resist he had, at least this one battle, at least this one
night, and the victory was sweet. Tired and drowsy, he lingered a few moments longer, savoring the quiet this place offered. Tomorrow would provide new battles, new challenges,
but for now, for this moment, with his stomach full and the
warmth of a dying fire at his back, he was at peace.

He let his gaze return to the table, where the bottle sat, still
not quite empty. No, he mentally told it. It was then that he
noticed the lute. It looked rather forlorn, propped up against
the leg of the table with no one to hold it and make it sing.
Daric thought to himself that Gillien must have been intoxicated indeed, to have forgotten about—what was it she called
the lute? Ah, Singer, that was it.

He rose and picked up the lute almost gingerly. It felt just
like any other instrument he had handled. It was too late to
knock on Gillien's door and return it to her. She'd be sound
asleep by now. He'd have to guard the lute until morning for
her.

Carrying the instrument, he went into his own room. It was
small, with four pallets, a table, a chair, and a window. It was
warm in the room, so Daric went to the shutters and opened
them. He gazed out onto the night.

The rain had stopped. The silvery sheen of the nearly full
moon brushed the rocky, wooded landscape with a milky finish. It was quiet outside, and peaceful. Deceptively so, for
Daric knew that the darkness hid the monstrous creature that
had come far too close to killing Gillien and himself. His lips
tightened.

He turned away from the moon-glossed landscape and removed his shirt and hose. The puckered flesh of scars, from
battles with men and battles with Ghil, caught the moonlight.
Clad only in breeches, he lay down on the straw pallet. He
carefully placed the lute, which seemed so important to
Gillien, on the table where it wouldn't be accidentally trod
upon in the dark. His sword he laid beside the bed, within easy

reach. It might be a holy house, but Daric Rhan was going to take no chances.

He closed his eyes, and sleep overtook him.

His eyes snapped open, and Daric was instantly awake. For a moment he lay, keeping his muscles still, waiting to see what had awakened him.

The sound came again. The small, commonplace sound of dried rushes crunching beneath someone's feet. Commonplace in the daytime, but not at night. At the same time, Daric felt something rough brush his hands.

Swifter than a thought, he curled one hand into a fist and punched with all his strength. He felt cartilage give way beneath his knuckles as warm blood gushed down his hand. Simultaneously, his other hand found the hilt of his sword and he brought it whipping around in an arc of flashing silver.

The intruder cried out and stumbled backward, which probably saved his life as Daric's steel whizzed within an inch of his throat. He dropped the thing that had touched Daric's wrists—a stout length of rope. More rushes crunched, and the man was gone.

Daric was up and in hot pursuit, anger banishing every last trace of sleepiness as his feet hit the floor, smashing rushes of his own. He had almost reached the door when another figure rose out of the darkness, leaping at him with a snarl of anger.

But Daric was too fast. He whirled, bringing the steel with him. The blade flashed in the dim light. With a *chunk,* it bit deeply into the second man, who seemed to Daric nothing more than a human-shaped bulk. Daric's powerful arms kept the sword moving, pulling it through flesh and bone and sinew. The man's roar of rage turned into a gasp and wail of pain. The moment seemed to last forever. Finally, the sword, its polished gleam dulled by the black sheen of his enemy's blood, emerged.

The man crumpled and fell without a sound.

Daric forgot him at once. Single-minded of purpose, he continued his pursuit of the first intruder—the first slaver. Oh, he knew their methods. No simple thief would try to truss him up with cord. Only slavers did that.

In seconds, Daric came upon his man in the main room, just about to burst through the door to the anonymity of the night. Daric ran like a stag, clamped his powerful swordsman's hand on the other's shoulder and whirled him around.

It was Blesser Jervis, his nose broken and spurting blood from the blow Daric had dealt. Gone was the overly amiable host, all smiles and simpering courtesy. This man had hate and fear in his eyes, and snarled like a trapped beast.

Daric was so stunned that, for an instant, he almost missed the dagger that Jervis shoved toward his midsection. Years of reflexes stepped in, though, and Daric dodged the deadly point. He swung defensively, and for the second time in as many minutes his sword bit into and cleaved human flesh.

The slaver cried out and crumpled to the floor. His innards, shiny and slick with pumping blood, spilled out and splattered on the hard-packed earth. He twitched once, and then lay still.

Daric was panting, his broad torso slick with sweat. He glanced wildly about, sword still at the ready, but no more attacks came. Either all the slavers were dead or they had fled at the commotion.

Fled . . . with what?

"Gillien!" he cried, running toward her door. He grabbed the handle, turned it. It would not open. Swearing and calling her name at the top of his voice, he put his shoulder to the door. The lock was good. It took two tries before the door gave beneath the force of his fear, anger, and powerful muscles. He stumbled as it gave way, then looked wildly about.

The shutters of the room stood wide open. Moonlight flooded the room.

Gillien was gone.

*Anger twisted the Lord from the inside, so that he grew
hideous to look upon. He in his fury created the Ghil, who
know no love or kindness. Rather they are followers of Death
and Vengeance.*

—from *The Book of The Lady*

CHAPTER FOURTEEN

"Where is the lute?" came a smooth voice from behind
Daric.

The warrior whirled, arcing his sword around in the direction of the voice. An instant later, his brown eyes widened and
he tried to divert the blow.

Taran was quicker. He had his own slim sword up almost
before Daric had turned. The blades clashed with a ringing
sound of metal on metal. Then the elf moved his frame, far
slighter and swifter than Daric's muscled body, executed a
subtle movement with his wrist, and Daric's sword seemed to
leap from his hand to fly end over end through the opened
door into Gillien's room.

At once, Taran lowered his sword and raised his hand in a
placating gesture, fearing, perhaps not without cause, that
Daric would continue to attack in blind rage. But Daric was
himself again—although he was furious.

"Taran! Death's breath, you bastard, what are you doing here?"

The Sa met his hot gaze with cool purple eyes.

"I have been following you, of course—at a discreet distance. And it seems to be a good thing that I have. You have lost your charge, but that does not matter now. Answer my question, human—where is the lute?"

Daric couldn't focus on the words. He was battling a vicious combination of anger, fear and insult.

"You've been following us? For how long?" His voice rose, and his face grew flushed.

"Since the beginning," replied Taran. "I have never been more than a few yards behind you at any moment. But calm yourself. I have been a warrior and a hunter for over six centuries. No living human could have detected me. I reveal my presence now only because I saw that the guardian of the lute has been abducted, and—"

"You *saw*?" Daric advanced, his hands clenching and unclenching. He had at least a good foot on the elf and outweighed him by quite a few pounds. "You just stood there and *watched those bastards take her*?"

Taran took a step backward. He did not threaten the warrior, but kept his sword ready should Daric strike. His eyes were bright, alert, though his face remained devoid of expression.

"I am only one, and they were many," he replied, his voice calm. "My orders were to protect the lute. I did not see it on her person when they took her. Where is it?"

Daric still couldn't believe his ears. "Your orders? From who? Why do you want a damn instrument when Gillien is—"

"You stupid fool, can you not comprehend that it was never Gillien I wanted guarded? The lute is the vital thing! Now tell me where it is or by The Lady I shall run you through where you stand!"

Daric knew that the elves, by and large, were not capable of strong emotions. Still, Taran's irritation had threatened to spill over into outright anger. And Daric did not doubt the validity of his threat.

"The lute's in my room," he said.

Without another word, Taran turned and ran for the instrument. Alone, Daric felt the rage ebb from him, leaving him unexpectedly weak. He stumbled into Gillien's room to pick up his sword, investigating it perfunctorily for damage. It was fine. His legs felt as though they might give way beneath him, and he sat down hard on the pallet. His muscles trembled. He realized that his pulse was racing and his skin had gone cold and clammy.

Slavers. Gillien, that engaging little sprite of a girl, had been kidnapped by slavers.

A moan escaped his lips. Part of him was still angry, afire to leap onto That Damned Beast's back and charge after Gillien. But another part of him cringed from it. That part was still in thrall of sorts; it still languished deep in the heart of the Kyras Mountains, still felt the sting of the whip . . .

. . . *Crack.*

Daric gasped with pain, but pressed his lips together and said nothing. He would not give these gods-rotted sons of whores any satisfaction whatsoever. He was the "slave leader" of the group, the one who had to keep the men "in line." The least he could do for them was keep his own courage strong.

The welt on his back rose and began to sting as sweat trickled over it. It was cold this far underground, but the work was hot. Mining the precious stones that the Ghil used to trade for slaves and equipment took energy, especially when there were few breaks for water and no breaks for rest.

He tried to raise the pick, bring it down on the stone again, but the pain was too much. Daric paused, grunting, trying to summon the strength. Two of his men, their faces barely visible in the flickering light of the torches, glanced up at him, then away, back to their task. They did not want to feel the bite of the whip themselves, and Daric could not blame them.

The male Ghil leading Daric's work crew gave his inhuman approximation of a laugh. The whip cracked again. This time, Daric fell. Instinctively, one of the other slaves reached to help him up.

"Leave 'lone!" snarled the Ghil, his teeth flashing. When

the man continued trying to help Daric back to his feet, the Ghil grunted and the whip fell again—this time on Daric's man.

This man, unable to help himself, screamed aloud. The noises attracted the attention of another Ghil who was on general patrol through the tunnels. This one, a female, scampered over and spoke harshly to the first Ghil, her toothy mouth forming around human speech with awkwardness.

"Not whip for fun!" she chittered. "Decrease productivity!" Daric, getting his breath back as the pain began to ebb, chanced a glance around. His spirits lifted slightly with hope. It was always good when Ghil argued among themselves. It improved the chances of escape.

The Ghil leader, clearly annoyed at the interference, snarled back at his better. Aboveground, when the soldiers had slain the creatures at the rate of a half-dozen a day, they called them "giant rats." Now, belowground, encased in chains and at the whim of the foul-scented creatures, the soldiers deemed the Ghil far more sinister.

When the things stood erect, which was most of the time except when they were running for speed, the Ghil averaged a height of about five and a half feet. Their overall shape was in truth rodentlike, from the flat, clawed feet to the large, rounded ears set at the base of their elongated skulls. The beasts had hands of a sort—three stubby fingers and an opposable thumb that enabled them to handle human weapons with, if not grace, at least brutal enthusiasm. They were covered in thick, black, oily fur, though as of late they had taken to wearing bits and pieces of human clothing. Their eyes, huge and black and beautifully adapted to living in the dark, missed little, and behind those black eyes and beneath those naked pink ears sat a surprisingly complex brain, capable of great malice and cunning.

It was not surprising that the one in charge was a female. That she was of high rank as well was immediately apparent to Daric, even in the dim torchlight the Ghil reluctantly provided to the "blind" humans. Her abdominal pocket swelled and writhed with young. As she chastised her underling, one

*of the furless, ugly whelps poked its sightless head out and
hissed.*

*Daric felt his stomach churn. Of all the things that dis-
gusted him about the Ghil, this obscene way they carried and
nurtured their underdeveloped young in a pouch outside their
bodies revolted him the most. But the Ghil honored their females, especially those who bred prolifically, with high commands.*

*The female Ghil gently pushed her young one back into the
pouch with one hand. The other hand she clenched into a fist
and shook beneath the male's muzzle. Her long, scaly tail
thrashed behind her in irritation.*

"Not whip for fun!" she repeated.

"Bad humans!" the male Ghil protested. "Need whip!"

*The female hissed and took a swipe at the male. The male,
clearly having had enough, dropped the whip. His crest, several ridges of spiny fur that ran down the length of his spine,
rose in challenge. Daric continued watching, not bothering to
even pretend to work now. All around him, hammers and picks
fell silent as the other enslaved men paused, alert and watch-
ful, their gazes flitting from the fighting creatures to Daric.*

*The female hissed angrily. Black dewlaps curled in a snarl,
revealing orange teeth. Her own crest rose in response to the
male's challenge. Deep within her pouch, sensing the agitation of their mother, the little ones began to mew.*

*Then the male sprang. The female was ready for him. The
whip the male had carried and the short sword the female
wore at her hip were ignored. Such tools were only used fighting slaves, not for settling their own inner disputes.*

Now.

*Daric caught the eyes of two of his men. He nodded silently.
The man smiled a little, and nudged his compatriots. Their
chances had never been better. The two Ghil were entirely focused on one another. They assumed the men were still working—and as long as they thought that, they would not dare
remove their eyes from one another to make sure. Daric gritted his teeth against the pain, lifted his pick, and brought it
slamming down on the chains that bound his feet, not the hard*

*rock that they were supposed to be mining. The others fol-
lowed suit, working on their own chains. Daric could almost
sense the lightening in their hearts as the links began to give
way.*

*Clang. Clang. Snap. Freed, Daric turned his attention to
helping the others, bringing the pick down on their chains as
well. Some of them looked frightened, casting anxious glances
over their shoulders at the rat-things locked in deadly combat.*

*Enough men were freed. The Ghil were still fighting, but for
how much longer? It was time to take the chance.*

*"Run!" Daric hissed at those who could. They needed no
more urging. They grabbed torches and sped down the twisting tunnels that would eventually lead to the surface and liberation. Daric, though his chains were broken, remained behind.
Most of these men working with him today were his own men,
soldiers under his command when they had been free men
above ground, before the earthquake had trapped them here in
the dark with the Ghil. He had an obligation to them, had to
get them all free of their shackles before he himself could flee
with them.*

*The snarls and hisses, shrieks and thud of thrashing bodies
meant the two Ghil were still locked in combat. It was a terrible sound, but it was sweet to Daric's ears. As long as they
were engrossed in their hot, angry fight, they would ignore—*

*A sharp squeak, then silence. Daric froze, pick still in his
hand, his eyes riveted on the nearly severed chain. Only two
men remained. The man he had almost freed stared up at him,
weeping openly, but Daric could do nothing for him now. He
had been perhaps only a few more seconds from freedom, but
his opportunity had died along with the losing Ghil.*

*The female, triumphant, stood erect above her dead oppo-
nent. Her elongated head swiveled in Daric's direction, ears
flattening. She narrowed her beady eyes at Daric.*

*"Bad slave! Make trouble. Have to find others now. Time
lost!"*

*Daric charged her, brandishing the pick as a weapon, but
the female Ghil was far too agile. She leaped to one side,
using her powerful tail to land a solid blow across his midsec-*

tion. The limb struck Daric with all the force of a club. He was
knocked off his feet and went sprawling on the hard stone. The
female scampered to him, and dropped to all fours so she
could look him in the eye.

Painfully gasping for breath, he stared up at her, thinking
she might have cracked one or more of his ribs. She shoved
her muzzle to within an inch of his face. She smelled terrible.

"Made you slave leader," she reproached. "Good food. No
whip." Daric thought of the oversized grubs that had consti-
tuted his meals for the last four months and nearly vomited.
"You do this now," she went on. "Bad. Punish."

She clicked her teeth together several times, to further express her displeasure. Daric searched his dry mouth for what
moisture that remained and spat at her—a gesture that both
humans and Ghil had in common. He knew it would probably
mean his death, but it would buy precious time for the six men
who had managed to escape.

Her squealing cry of rage nearly split his ears. She fell
upon him then, biting and clawing. Daric cried out in agony
as dozens of white-hot wounds opened and burned along his
body. But he did not die; the female had enough restraint.
They were crueler than the males of their abominable race,
but more practical. Daric was too good a slave, too strong,
too useful, for her to kill simply out of anger. At last she sat
back on her haunches, panting in hissing, shallow breaths and
licking his blood from her hands and fur.

"Punish," she said, and this time the word was a low growl.
"Give you to slavers."

He saw her tail whip around and descend, but never felt the
blow.

Daric awoke to agony. His head and ribs ached, and for a
moment all he could do was lie still, trying to summon the
courage to move. Finally he tried, and discovered that he was
bound hand and foot.

His eyes flew open. There was ample torchlight, something
that was rare down below, but he was tied stomach down on a
large boulder. He felt the rough, rocky surface on every inch
of his skin, and realized the Ghil had removed even the token

*scrap of clothing that served as a loincloth. He craned his
neck, but could see nothing, no one.*

"I'm sorry you woke up."

A woman stepped into his view. She was naked, as was he,
but she aroused no desire in him. His pain pushed him past
such things. She ladled water from a bucket onto his face. His
tongue crept out to lick up the moisture. She refilled the dipper
and held it to his lips while he drank, easing his parched
throat.

"What . . ."

"This is the place of punishment," she said. Her voice was
dead, devoid of expression, as was her face. Her eyes were
sunken in her sharp-featured face, and her hair was a tangled
mat about her shoulders. She couldn't be more than twenty,
but her eyes were centuries old.

"I don't know what you did, but it must have been pretty
bad. Be quiet and they might go easy on you." She smiled with
no humor. "They don't usually get them fresh."

Another sound reached Daric's ears. It was the sound of
male laughter and coarse talk. The sound grew closer. The
woman immediately put the ladle back in the bucket. It
splashed quietly.

"They're here," she said, and without a second glance
turned and walked away . . .

Daric returned to the present, gasping. He was lying on the
pallet in Gillien's room at the Blesser's temple, curled up with
his arms around his knees. He blinked several times, trying to
force himself to realize that he was here, now, not in that
gods-forsaken cavern four years ago.

Slowly, he uncurled himself and glanced around. For the
moment, he was alone, and he thanked every god for that. Still
trembling, he rose and stumbled into the main area.

His eyes were drawn to the bottle on the table. Still partially
full, it sat there, mocking him. He closed his eyes and willed
the memories to go away, but they kept returning in bits and
pieces, forming some kind of obscene mosaic.

Agony. Helplessness. Rough hands, touching, squeezing,
forcing his body into various positions. Blood trickling down

his legs. The looks of comprehension, pity, and disgust on the faces of his men when he had finally been allowed to return to them, hours later. The searing shame that had burned hotter than the physical pain.

Daric staggered to the table. He seized the bottle, uncorked it, brought it to his lips.

And now Gillien was in the hands of the same kind of men.

With a low, angry growl, Daric spat out the tepid wine. He flung the bottle into the fireplace with all his might. It exploded into dozens of glass shards with a loud crash.

"There is a young man here with something to tell you," came Taran's voice.

Daric whirled to find the elf holding onto the arm of Tavi, the young Tender. One deceptively slender hand dug into the flesh of Tavi's upper arm. The other carried the lute by its graceful neck.

The boy actually seemed happier than when Daric had last seen him.

"My lord," the child began, "first of all I have to beg your forgiveness and mercy. I didn't want to do what I did. But he would have killed me."

Daric passed a hand over his cold, sweat-dappled brow. He wanted, badly, to go after Gillien, but the boy could have vital information. He swallowed hard, calmed himself.

"Tell me," he said simply. He gestured to Taran, and the Sa elf let go of the boy's arm.

"I really am a Tender of Traveler," said the boy. "But the slavers came about six months ago. They took the real Blesser and set up their own man in his place. I was known in town, so I was of some use to them in keeping up the pretense. People would stop here, thinking it was an ordinary Lamp. Jervis drugged the wine, and then the slavers would come and take them away." He had kept his eyes on the ground while he spoke, but now he raised them to Daric. They held pain and pleading in their brown depths.

"Sir, I—I had to go along with them. I didn't want to. They'd have made me a slave, too."

"Yes, yes," said Daric impatiently. He was grateful that he

ad not given in to the call of the wine. No wonder Gillien had
een so intoxicated. "Continue."

"It was a perfect ruse," said Tavi. His voice thickened with
emorse. "Everybody trusts the Lamps of Traveler, you see.
Nobody would think . . ." Tears filled his eyes, and he wiped
t them with the back of his hand. "It's my fault, in a way, and
need to atone. I need to do something to make Traveler for-
ive me."

Hope rose in Daric. "Tavi . . . do you know where they've
aken her?"

"Her? I thought . . . oh, no." Tavi's eyes widened in com-
rehension and pity. "No, I don't know where she is right
ow. I'm sorry, believe me. The slavers never travel a set
oute, to throw everyone off their trail. But I do know where
hey meet the Ghil to sell the slaves. They didn't include me in
heir plans, but I have sharp ears. Every quarter moon, they
neet with the Ghil. I heard them talk about that meeting place.
've been there, once. I can take you there."

Daric reached out to the boy and squeezed his shoulder gen-
ly. "You're a good lad. Taran—are you coming with us?"

The poised elf allowed himself a condescending chuckle.
'Of course not. As I told you, Daric Rhan, my orders are to
afeguard the lute, not the girl. If you wish to pursue her on
ome idealistic quest, by all means go ahead. My task, how-
ver, is to take the lute safely to Kasselton. And I will not do it
y way of a slaver's route. I wish you good luck, but I fear—"

The elf broke off. His eyes flew wide in astonishment, and
he stared down at the lute.

"What . . . but . . ."

"What in the Nightlands is going on with that damned
ute?" cried Daric, exasperated.

Taran ignored him. He brought the lute up to his chest,
holding it gently in his arms as one would cradle a child. Daric
emembered Gillien holding the instrument in just that fash-
on, and pain stabbed him.

At last, Taran raised his eyes to meet Daric's. His face reg-
stered utter surprise—and disapproval.

"The lute does not agree with me," he said. "It seems to

think it owes its present safety to your young friend, Daric,
and wishes to help you rescue her." The corners of his lips
went down. "I do not approve, but I will accompany you."

The boy stared at the instrument with a mixture of
astonishment and fear. "Is it—alive?" he asked, his voice
trembling.

Taran smiled indulgently. "It is a magical lute," he explained. "Now, Daric, can you see how precious a gift this is
and why it must be delivered safely?"

"I see that an inanimate object has more compassion than
you," Daric retorted. "Tavi—what about horses? Did the
slavers take them, too?"

The boy shook his head. "No. Jervis sold them to another
group of thieves."

"He had every aspect taken care of, didn't he?" Daric said,
not expecting an answer. He glanced over at the body of the
false Blesser, dead where he had fallen half-in and half-out of
the open door. "You bastard. I hope you're keeping the Nightlands King company tonight.

"Tavi, saddle the horses. We're wasting time."

The difference between a lady and a whore's but a drop of blood.

—overheard at The Castle Tavern

CHAPTER FIFTEEN

Gillien drifted from sleep to wakefulness in a jerky, clumsy transition. She felt the heaviness of her limbs as if they had been turned into stone, tasted the dry raspiness of her parched throat. Even the blood that pumped through her body seemed sluggish and congealed. Her dreams—her nightmares—had been vague and disjointed, filled with dark shapes, pain blunt and keen, and a lethargy that rendered her a passive observer rather than a participant to . . . what?

She tried to think, but couldn't. Her head was a dull nest of sullen hurt, and a sharper pain in her belly and between her legs cried out to be attended to. She seemed unable to will her eyes to open. And though she could hear male voices speaking words that she knew, she could not understand them.

Her lips moved, seeking moisture. She knew that she needed to slake her thirst, and that would require movement. By the time her impaired mental state had hobbled this far, she dimly remembered the events of the past night.

It must have been the wine. Stronger than she'd thought. Gods, *much* stronger. Now her bladder was adding its plaintive call, desperate to be voided. Was that the pain in her abdomen, that burned along her body? It did not seem familiar, did not feel like something she had awakened to before. This pain scorched, chafed, blazed.

Her eyes still closed, Gillien tried to move to alleviate pressure on the strangely sensitive area. Her movement was suddenly halted with a jingling sound.

Her drugged haze began to clear with a sudden, sharp, lucid stab of apprehension. Gillien opened her eyes.

She was not, as she had thought, safe in her pallet at Traveler's Lamp.

She was lying on a pile of animal skins on the bare earth. More skins covered her nakedness. Blankets draped over stout sticks served as a makeshift tent. At the far end of the tent sunlight poured in through the triangular entrance.

The girl gasped, tried to bolt upright. The movement was arrested at her wrists and ankles, and she saw that she had been manacled securely in both places. Each wrist and ankle was encircled by a metal cuff. The clanking metal chains fastened together left hand to right, left foot to right. A third chain, fastened to the length between her wrists, trailed off to her right, where she saw that it ended in a stake that had been driven firmly into the hard-packed dirt.

Where was she? What had happened? Where was Daric? Gillien panicked. Instead of trying to dig out the stake quietly, she began to twist with all the hysterical confusion of a trapped animal. The chains jangled noisily. She tried to stand but the chain to the stake wasn't long enough to permit it.

As she fell back down on the skins, she felt the pain between her legs and in the lower part of her abdomen. She twisted to get a look, to see if perhaps she had been injured.

Her flat stomach and thighs looked whole. But they were smeared with red fluid.

For an instant, her mind resisted the truth. Her first thought was that her moon time was not for several more days, and it had never hurt with this aching agony before.

Then her frightened gaze made out the red handprint on her belly, just above the thatch of black hair at the juncture of her thighs, and she screamed.

She had been kidnapped by slavers, and raped. Probably repeatedly.

She was now less than nothing.

Images paraded before her mind's eye. Her mother's troubled countenance when she had been alone with a young man for more than a few moments. The pride—and relief—in a newly married woman's eye when Gillien's family had performed at a wedding celebration. The knowledge that had been drummed into her head a thousand times over, from her family to the world in general, that her maidenhead was the dearest possession she had, worth far more than her skills or talents, and that without that fragile shred of tissue she had nothing left to offer.

She felt suddenly very cold, and sank down onto the pile of skins. Her body was numb, disobedient. It would not rouse and fight as part of her wanted to do. Instead, Gillien curled into as tight a ball as the merciless chains would permit and began to keen, softly and quietly.

Singer was nowhere to be seen. The beautiful lute whose feelings had comforted her so often over the past—gods, was it only nine days, or eight?—had undoubtedly been taken by the brutal men who had done . . .

She squeezed her eyes shut. Hot tears spilled out from under the dark lashes. The soft, animal sound continued to creep from her throat. She had no control over the noise at all; it was as if it came from somewhere deep inside, as if a separate entity was mourning its loss quite apart from Gillien's tumbling thoughts.

Jencir had trusted her with Singer's safety. The elf had deemed her worthy to bear the instrument, had died—horribly—to protect it and her. And she, foolish, weak girl, had carelessly let the magical instrument fall into the wrong hands. Just as she had . . .

She steered her thoughts away from the ruined entrance to her womb. How had the slavers found her? Had Daric betrayed her—or had be been captured, too? The questions were too hard and she averted her thoughts. Easier to hate herself, rage against her incompetence, her unworthiness, than to grieve or think.

Now, whatever message Singer had borne was silenced —or worse, in the wrong hands. What would happen now? What *was* the message that so many had died for, that she, Gillien Songespynner, she of the lost virginity and no worth at all, had heedlessly tossed away? Would someone—maybe several hundred someones—die because of her irresponsibility? Would kingdoms fall, and gods wreak vengeance upon Verold? Would the whole world be destroyed, made nothing, be completely without worth?

Would she even care?

She blinked, aware that something had changed. The makeshift tent was silent, though sounds still came in from outside. Through her red wall of pain, both physical and emotional, Gillien was perplexed. Something was not right, something simpler and more basic than the plain, brutal fact that she had been violated and enslaved and that her life was effectively over. Something small, but very, very bad indeed.

Her heart lurched and her stomach knotted. She suddenly knew what it was. Air was still rushing past her throat, pushed from her lungs by her misery and terror. But no sound was emerging.

Even her voice had deserted her. Gillien could not utter a sound.

She jerked fiercely as the revelation jangled through her head, trying to cry, to scream, to speak. Nothing. No sound. Only puffs of air, the sounds of her mouth and tongue moving with empty words, frantically trying to rip speech from a soul too shattered to give it.

The tears stopped as well, and she fell back on the furs. She closed her eyes and tried to climb inward, seeking a place of warmth from the cold outside, of quiet from the unendurable noise of her voice's silence. She was suddenly tired. She'd fought so hard, lost so much, rallied again and again and again in the face of terror, murder, loss, and grief. But Gillien had no more strength left to battle her own hurting body, her own weapons of self-loathing and shame, her traitorous voice. She surrendered, and why not? What awaited her, after all? Anything at all worth struggling for—or against—now that her family was gone and what they had died for lost?

Sleep. Quiet. It would be good, just to turn inward, and rest, and never have to climb out and battle anymore.

Rescue of a sort came only a few seconds later, in the form of a tall, rangy slaver. He stood at the entrance to the makeshift tent, silhouetted against the bright, uncaring sunshine.

"Well, well, there's my pretty little whore. I usually take the curvy ones, but I couldn't turn down a girl playing a boy. Too interesting. And now that you're awake," the man added, "time for some more fun. This time, sweet bit, you'll get to play too. How do you want it—are you a girl or a boy today?"

He advanced toward her, shedding his clothes as he came. Gillien stared at him, for a moment as transfixed as a sparrow before the snake. His smell preceded him—a sour, stomach-turning mixture of animal and human sweat, of cheap wine and old blood. The man was tall and solidly built, though not as cleanly muscled as Daric. His broad torso, crisscrossed by scars, was covered with thick black hair. He had an equally thick beard, small, cruel eyes, and a nose that looked like it had been broken countless times and was now merely a squashed lump on his face.

His nudity was no revelation to Gillien. She was a child of poor people who understood all the workings of the human body and made no attempt to hide them. She and Kellien had sometimes bathed together, sometimes talked about pretty ladies and handsome men while doing so. She was not afraid of the male body, whether in excitement or repose. So it was not the sight of her tormentor's nakedness and obvious arousal that galvanized her.

It was the shock of seeing that his nether parts were still encrusted with her virgin's blood as he advanced, leering, for another round of violence that made her erupt into action. He had not even bothered to cleanse himself before returning for more.

She went from a huddled lump on the furs into a whirlwind of anger. She had to crouch, for the chain that led from her arms to the earth would not permit her to stand upright, but she did so, heedless of her own nakedness. His eyes widened, but with lustful pleasure and not fear.

"Why, my kitten's a mountain cat. Good. I like it when they fight."

Secret pleasure surged through Gillien. This man, if he could even be called a man, had no doubt subdued hysterical women before. He was big and powerful, and she knew that if she had been another sort of woman—a softer, richer, more innocent sort of woman—he would have had her in a few moments and made her pay for her brief rebellion.

A hard smile twisted her silent lips. But Gillien *did* know how to fight, and how to fight effectively. She turned the harsh smile into a snarl and screamed curses at him, though they did not emerge from her still-silent throat.

He laughed openly and lunged at her, intending to bury her beneath his weight. It was a familiar move to Gillien, who had spent many playful hours tumbling and wrestling with her twin, and she countered almost without thinking about it. Swiftly she ducked and twisted aside. He stumbled, off balance. Gillien dropped to the floor, reached out with her manacled hands, and caught his leg in the chain that stretched between the metal cuffs on her wrists. She yanked up and he fell hard on his back.

As he started to roll over, trying to rise, she pounced onto his back, straddling him in a turnabout of what he had planned to do to her. Her wounded womanhood pressed against his skin, hurting. She ignored the pain. Snarling silently, she whipped the chain around his throat, crossed her wrists and yanked hard. The angle was not enough to snap his neck, but she knew she bruised it badly before he managed to struggle out from under her.

Gillien clamped her long, strong legs about him and tried to ride him like an unruly horse. She might have succeeded, but the chain embedded in the earth drew tight and pulled her off of him.

"Gods-cursed bitch!" he rasped, his big hand reaching to massage his aching throat. His grating voice was as sweet as music to her ears. She'd damaged him, at least a little; had taken his voice as he had taken hers. Gillien spat soundless words. He drew back his leg and kicked her before she could scramble out of the way. Groaning, she curled inward, trying to protect her vitals from a second blow.

Strong hands grabbed her wrists, shoved them fiercely over her head. Gillien writhed, but the slaver had her pinned beneath him now. Blind panic threatened to overwhelm her, to drown her in useless struggle instead of strategic fighting. Her dream, that she now knew was no dream at all, returned in full force. What was about to happen was nothing more than a reenactment of something her mind had witnessed while she was drugged, and then tried to consign to the realm of nightmare fantasy. The dark shape had been this man; her lethargy, the drug in action. He had thought her asleep, unconscious, as had she herself. Now she knew that at least part of her had been awake, aware, and had known the violation was taking place.

If it cost her her life, she was not going to let him do it a second time.

She forced herself to go limp. His lips traveled over her face, polluting her with foul kisses. She did not react. The pressure on her arms lessened and then disappeared as the slaver, engulfed in his passion, released her arms so as to fondle her small breasts.

Her fingers were the only part of her that moved now. She groped for something, anything, and found a small, discarded goblet. Disappointment sliced through her—how could such a thing be a weapon? Her fingers flew over the metal, searching for something that could make it more dangerous. The lip of the cup was thin, not thick, and hope flared anew.

His mouth found hers. She bit down hard. At the same moment, her hands came up. She grasped the goblet upside down, the lip pointing toward her attacker's head. Summoning all her strength, she brought the goblet down at an angle as hard as she could.

The narrow lip bit deeply into the man's skull. It dug a furrow in his scalp, and a flap of skin crumpled up into the cup as Gillien shoved down powerfully. Blood erupted and the slaver immediately released her, his hands rushing up to cover his wounded skull. He squirmed away from her and she at once rose back up into a crouch. The goblet was heavy enough for her to land a solid blow should he attack. It would be all she could do. If he should come at her again, she knew he would come for death, not pleasure.

He staggered to his feet, crying curses and spitting blood. She waited, poised, breathing heavily, her sharp-featured face as wild as an animal's. Her naked body was glistening with sweat and blood—some her own, some that of her attacker.

As he stumbled about and groaned, she saw the whiteness of his skull peeking from beneath the crumpled bit of skin and hair. At last he stood erect, and his face was twisted in hate.

"You bitch," he grunted, "I'll kill you for this. You bitch, you—"

A second figure appeared in the doorway. This man was smaller, slighter of build than the other slaver. His hair was gray and his eyes a piercing blue. Intelligence glinted in his weathered face and he took in the scene in a heartbeat. Just as the slaver, unaware of the second man's presence, prepared to lunge murderously at Gillien, the smaller figure seized his arm.

"Calm down, Barak," said the second man in an easy, comradely voice. "She ain't worth it."

Barak uttered a scorching epithet. "You see what she did to me, Carm?" he yelled, pointing wildly at his injured head. "You see that? Damn!"

"I see you were stupid enough to leave a weapon in the reach of a girl with a mountain cat's temper," Carm replied mildly. "Come on, leave it alone. Ain't worth it."

"I'm gonna *kill* her!" Barak raged, refusing to be calmed.

Gillien, still tense and ready for attack, glanced from one man to the other. Fury sang in her blood, temporarily eclipsing the shame. She wanted another fight with Barak as badly as the slaver wanted it. She tried to say as much, but words again refused to come when she summoned them.

Carm saw her attempt at speech and laughed. "She's dumb, Barak! At least she can't talk back to you like the last one did."

Barak was obviously beginning to feel the pain through his heated anger and winced a little, starting to calm down. "Yeah, I still say you should have let me cut her tongue out."

"And *I* say that the more disfigured a slave is when it reaches the Ghil, the less money we get for 'em." Carm was clearly the practical one in the group. Gillien didn't know which one she hated the most at the moment. Her own breathing was starting to slow, and her muscles ached from the tense posture she continued to hold.

"So," continued Carm, "is bashing her head in worth losing all that gold? For what she'll get us, you can bed that lusty little thing back in Kasselton for a week."

Barak brightened visibly at this. "I suppose you're right. Gods, but my head hurts . . ." He glared one last time at Gillien and spat bloody saliva in her direction. It landed on the furs, a good foot away from her body.

"You're one lucky whore, you know that? If you'd had a game leg or withered arm, I'd have beat you to a pulp by now."

Gillien narrowed her eyes, hoping the cold blue glare would say what her mouth could not: *Yes, and I'd have seen to it that you never lay with another woman again, you bastard.*

She watched, still tense, as the two of them left. Carm made reassuring noises, offering to stitch up Barak's injuries and promising him a more cooperative bed partner when Barak felt ready for another bout.

After a moment, Gillien sank down onto the furs. She shook violently with the sudden release of tension, and reached for the warmth the furs promised. She realized that she had Barak's second brutal assault to thank for her rejuvenation. Less than a quarter of an hour ago, she had been ready to sink forever into the embrace of utter despair. Not so now. Now she was angry, although each time pain shuddered through her crotch she felt a hot flash of shame.

She remembered an old folk saying: When you've lost everything, then you've got nothing to lose. It was true. She might as well live, she thought. Even with her minstrel's lively imagination, she couldn't conceive of anything worse happening to her.

Her mouth still tasted of Barak's blood. She swallowed, and allowed herself a vicious pleasure. Kellien would have been proud of how she'd acquitted herself today.

She started as Carm appeared in the doorway. He stood there for a moment, his eyes roving over her body. She sensed no desire from him, only appraisal. At last, he spoke.

"You're a fighter, ain't ya, little mountain cat?" he said, in a not unpleasant tone. "Big mistake. Barak was mighty taken with you. Said he wanted to keep you for himself. Now I think he'd fair *give* you to the Ghil, just to watch you suffer."

Gillien stared at him, ready to attack should this man take over where Barak had left off. He seemed to read her thoughts on her face and grinned.

"No, little lass. I don't like the ladies much. If you'd been the handsome boy you looked like, that would have been another tale. Now," and he stood over her, "you can cooperate, or you can get hurt. I'm going to bring in something for you to eat and drink, and then I'm going to put you in the cart with the others. You're lucky—don't have to gag you. Now, the Ghil don't like damaged goods, so we won't be able to hurt you too much."

Carm squatted down next to her. He smelled less bad than his friend; the fragrance of pipe smoke nearly masked the stale odor of sweat.

"Truth be told, I don't like to hurt my property much anyway. Some find that fun, but I don't. But I *do* know how to hurt without damaging."

Swift as a thought, he seized her hand in his. A quick turn, a subtle pressure on the web between thumb and first finger, and Gillien writhed in voiceless pain. It was sheer agony.

"Do we understand each other?"

Grimacing, Gillien forced a nod. The man let go and she gasped in relief.

"So, are you going to behave?"

A second nod. Carm grinned.

"Good girl," he approved. "I'd have hated to have to cut up that sweet face of yours. Now, let me get you something to eat and take care of what my overeager friend has done. Can't have you getting sick—Ghil don't buy sick slaves."

He left, whistling cheerfully. Gillien was confused. Carm did not seem like a cruel man, but what good person would deal in enslaving his fellow human beings? For an instant, she envied any handsome young men that the slavers might have gathered up. Surely Carm would be kinder to a bedmate than Barak was.

She shook her head, trying to shake loose that thought. If Carm had lain with her, she suspected he might have been gentle—and she would have hated him far less than she hated Barak. That hate was precious to her now. It was what had rescued her from yielding to her fate, had sparked her to fight . . . had restored her sanity.

Silently, she thanked Barak for the hatred that burned in her breast. That dark emotion kept her warm when Carm returned with water and some soup for her to eat. She devoured every mouthful, determined to keep her strength up. When she had finished, Carm handed her a bowl of water, a semi-clean towel, and a small jar of some white, creamy substance. Gillien looked up at him, confused.

He pointed to her crotch. "Clean yourself up and put some salve on. Skin's been broken and neither you nor I want you to get sick, do we?"

Shame reddened her cheeks, threatened to overwhelm her. His words were casual, careless, as if she had undergone nothing worse than an encounter with a thorn bush. *Skin's been broken*. It was true as far as it went, but there had been no part of Gillien's body, not even her bard's skilled fingers, that had been more precious than the thin membrane that had been so viciously rent.

She ground her teeth. *Skin's been broken*. Shame would not

keep her alive and sane. Practicality would, and Carm seemed to know it. He didn't even avert his gaze as she pursed her mouth in a grim line and gingerly bathed the wounded area. Neither did he watch with sadistic or lustful pleasure. He merely watched to make sure that she did it correctly, nodding approval as she scooped up a glob of the salve and applied it. At once, the stinging, burning sensation lessened. The internal ache remained, but there was nothing to be done about that.

Carm, convinced of her cooperation now, helped her into a makeshift garment that consisted of a square of cloth with a hole cut in its center. He draped it over her. She worked her head through, making no move to struggle as he tucked the fabric about her and left her chained arms free.

He led her outside. For a moment she blinked in the sunlight, dazzled after the darkness of the tent. When her eyes grew accustomed to the light, she analyzed the scene in front of her, her mind alert and analytical for the first time since the dreadful ordeal began.

She did not know who to blame for her abduction. The Blesser was a possibility; it would have been easy to drug the wine. But Daric also could have done so, and now that she thought about it, Gillien realized with a sick sensation that Daric had not drunk much of the wine at all. Perhaps they were both involved. Or perhaps he had been captured, too.

She looked around, pretending not to be interested in her surroundings as Carm led her over to the other slaves. Daric was not among them. Either he had been killed during the abduction, or he had been part of the plot. Slavers would not willingly lose a strong man like Daric. He would be very valuable to the Ghil. She felt a sharp pang. Either answer was devastating.

Though the encampment was clearly makeshift, it was equally clear that there was routine, skill and forethought in its erection. The slavers had the look of organized men about them in their attitudes toward one another, the practiced and perfunctory speed with which they broke the encampment, and the casualness of their poses. The ratio of slaver to slave was at least two, perhaps three to one. From the snatches of conversation, Gillien ascertained that this was a meeting place. Money was exchanged, slaves were herded from one group of men to the other. Carm, moving about with an air of sharp-eyed efficiency, seemed to be the leader of the group. Gillien had heard the tales of the ruffians who kidnapped innocents for slaves, but she had no idea that the slave trade was so well organized . . . so brutally productive.

As for Gillien's fellow prisoners, they looked much like her. There were twelve of them: four women, if Gillien counted herself among them; two men, and six children, ranging from the ages of about six to twelve or so. They were dressed just as she was, in clothes that protected them from the elements but did little more. Some of the children were crying softly, but most of the prisoners had the same dead, dull look in their eyes as Gillien imagined she had had.

She was probably the best "find" among them, Gillien mused darkly. The other three women were older and clearly not as strong as she. The two men were in their fifties, at least. And the children . . . would they survive, grow, reach maturity as slaves?

The twelve captives were forced to stand in a row. Each was chained hand and foot, and as Gillien watched, Carm and another man whose name she did not know began to tie the slaves together with ropes around their midsections. Gillien felt her resolution waver as she recalled cattle being led to market in just such a fashion.

Oh, gods, we're nothing but animals to them. . . .

The rope snaked around her waist now, binding her to a twelve-year-old boy who was a few inches shorter than she was. He was slim and handsome, and the dirt on his lean cheeks bore a clean furrow from eye to chin. He was not too old, it would seem, to weep. Now he stood quietly, his dark eyes glazed over. He didn't even appear to notice Gillien.

She glanced around to her other side as a small girl was led up to stand beside her. The child couldn't be more than six years old, Gillien thought with a stab of pity. She looked up at Gillien with imploring eyes as the rope went around her tiny waist.

"Please," came a rough, tired voice, "please let me be near my children." Gillien glanced around and found the speaker— one of the women, a few years older than she.

The little girl screwed up her face. "Mama!" she whimpered. The boy on Gillien's right tensed as well.

"We don't do that," came Carm's obscenely cheerful voice. "You won't be seeing him after we sell him to the Ghil. Might as well get used to separation now."

Gillien watched intently. The woman's face worked. Tears filled her eyes.

"We won't run," she begged, "we *can't* run, gods, surely you can see that! They're afraid, and—"

Carm stepped up to her, shaking his head sadly. "Those are the rules," he said. He raised his hands. In his left palm was a swath of dirty fabric. Casually, as if he were trussing a colt for gelding, he inserted the cloth into the woman's mouth and tied it behind her head. She began to struggle, but her panic was no match for Carm's cool practice. The only sounds she could make were slight muffled noises.

Gillien winced in sympathy. The woman's gagging touched off a response in her children, who both began to scream and thrash. At once, the big men were there, gagging them and putting extra rope on them to still them.

Carm glanced over to Gillien. Approval glittered in his eyes.

"Good little mountain cat. It goes easier when you cooperate, you see?"

Gillien dropped her gaze in feigned dejection. In reality, she did not want him to see her eyes—and the fiery hatred that burned in them. From beneath her lowered lashes, she observed that roughly two-thirds of the men were not planning on accompanying the slaves to be sold to the Ghil. Barak, cleaned up some but still looking the worse for their encounter, had mounted his horse and together with seven other men, was preparing to leave. He jerked his mount's head around and cantered up toward Carm.

Carm glanced up. "Back down to Woodhill Pass?"

Barak shook his head. "No. Too small t' hit twice a season. I'm for goin' straight through to Riverfork."

"Smart. You'd attract attention in Woodhill Pass, lookin' like that." Carm laughed a little, indicating Barak's clipped, stitched scalp.

Gillien's heart began to race, but she kept her head bowed.

Barak said something crude and spat at Gillien. "Get a good price for her, Carm. An' sell her to the meanest rat in the bunch for me."

"For you, Barak, of course. Travel safe."

"Travel safe, Carm." With a final, murderous glare at Gillien, Barak and the other seven men rode out of Gillien's field of vision. She hoped Barak's abused mount would throw him and snap his foul neck.

"Move," came Carm's voice.

Three groups of four trussed-up slaves were herded toward the waiting carts. Gillien, the twelve-year-old, the little girl and the man who was tied to the youth's right went in one cart.

"Lie down," Carm barked. They did so. At once Carm draped several blankets over them, tying it down securely.

It began to grow hot beneath the blankets. Gillien, her muteness absolving her from having to wear a gag, breathed in dust and heat, sweat, and the tang of fear. She closed her eyes; it was too dark to see clearly anyway, and she knew what surrounded her: two frightened children and one elderly man.

She heard someone shout orders, and the carts, drawn by two horses apiece, lurched into movement. The little girl tried to move closer to Gillien, and the bard heard soft weeping sounds, muffled by the fabric in the girl's mouth.

Grimly, Gillien took stock of her situation. Daric was gone, either dead or turned traitor. The lute was gone, destroyed or in the hands of the horrible creature who had already taken so much from Gillien and left only death and despair in its wake. Her virginity, the one thing beyond all others that reckoned her of any worth in her society, had been rent asunder.

She had left only her hands and her head. She knew what the Ghil were, what they wanted. Her body was strong and agile, and her hands were clever. They would not want music. They would want her hands to help make weapons, to mend what passed for clothing, to tend to their wounded.

And because her body had value to the Ghil, it had value to the slavers. They might torment mother and child by separating them, but they would not injure any of their "property." That would work to her advantage.

As the heat rose under the stifling blankets, Gillien listened with sympathy to the mourning sound of children and began to plan her escape.

CHAPTER SIXTEEN

The uprooted tree lay stretched out, like a fallen corpse, its roots bare for all to see in the moonlight. The torn earth was still fairly fresh, a brown gash in the hard-packed, dry surface. Strips of leather hung from the tree's branches. They had once bound a dreadful thing masquerading as a pony, but they bound nothing now. A few feet away lay the remains of a fire, made cold and dark by recent rain.

Several dozen yards away, the moon's radiation illuminated the pearly skeleton of what had once been a faithful horse. There was no trace of skin or sinew on the white bones. Anyone who happened upon it would have thought that it had lain there for weeks, perhaps months, and that the scavengers of the plains had done their jobs well. Few would have suspected that the animal had been dead for a mere three days.

Near the remains of the beast, the ground atop a newly dug hole began to quiver. A giant, flat paw resembling a shovel broke the earth. It was followed by a second clawed paw, then a small, sharp snout. The oversized mole emerged quickly, shaking itself clean of the debris that still clung to its velvety fur.

Va'kul was ravenous. The energy provided by the pony had long since been exhausted. It glanced up at the sky, but the form it had chosen, perfect for digging, had weak eyesight. It was tired and feeble from the three days spent healing itself from the unexpected attack the girl and the warrior had perpetrated. It took a moment to think, and to consider its next change carefully. Shifting its shape drained it when it was this hungry.

It had not expected the girl to see through its disguise as her pony. She and the warrior had been clever, and brave—far too much so. The fire they had brandished in its face, or what had passed for its face, had done more damage than they could have guessed. Va'kul had had to go to ground immediately, resume its natural shapelessness and stay in the dark for three days to heal itself. Now it had emerged at last, far smaller than its normal, healthy size, and it needed to eat before following Gillien and the lute.

What form would suit it best? The black bird had served it well, and Va'kul had discovered that it enjoyed flying. But flight took energy, energy the Changer did not have to spare at the moment. It recalled what it knew about creatures in this part of the world. Which would be the best hunter? Besides humans, it chuckled to itself.

The answer came swiftly. It was a form that would suit both of Va'kul's needs, to feed itself and to follow the bearer of the lute. It concentrated and its shape began to change. Its shovel-shaped paws thinned, grew longer. The stubby mole tail also lengthened and sprouted fur. A sleek, dark head replaced the naked muzzle of the earth-digger, grew ears and keen amber eyes. The oversized wolf lowered its massive, shaggy head and began to locate the scent.

There were not many humans out here, away from their crowded cities and towns. The scent of the girl, though faded, would probably still be clear enough to follow. Yes, it was here all right, as was that of her companion. Ears pricked forward, the wolf began to trot, its nostrils flaring as it followed the scent northward. Other smells mingled; rabbits, rodents, old fragrances of other travelers who had passed this way earlier.

The wolf halted abruptly. Another human scent crossed that of his intended quarry, even fresher than Gillien's traces. Horses and humans, eight of each, and not too far away. Va'kul paused, thinking. It had been charged with retrieving the lute and deciphering its message if possible. The new, alluring scents of the other humans beckoned. Va'kul reasoned that it would be stronger, better able to complete its task, were it fed.

Decision made, it veered off toward the east in the direction of the meat. Va'kul did not have to travel far to find the group, already camped for the night by a fire whose feebleness posed only a minimal threat. It waited in the shadows, fighting back its natural, almost overpowering desire to spring and feed. These were humans—the same species as the girl. Perhaps they knew something about her. It would be wise to listen before killing, and wisdom was one reason Leader had appointed Va'kul to this task.

From the safety of the darkness, it watched the humans. There were eight of them, and Va'kul had learned enough about human society to know its dregs when they showed themselves. The men were dirty, and Va'kul's lupine nose wrinkled at their rankness. They did not seem to particularly like one another's company. One of them seemed to have a badly damaged scalp. Va'kul wondered if the man had been wounded by one of his fellows.

Though this man was listened to as if he were the leader, his fellows seemed to tease him about his injury. Clearly, the man, who had a full beard and a nose that even Va'kul recognized as ugly, led by force and not respect.

"That girl sure did for you, Barak!" one of them laughed.

Va'kul pricked his ears forward. A girl had damaged the man so badly? Such behavior seemed to indicate Gillien. They were in the same general area . . . The shapeshifter listened harder.

The man named Barak swore. "Damn mute-girl. If Carm hadn't stopped me, *I'd* have made her scream for mercy."

Va'kul's hopes faded. No, one thing Gillien Songespynner was not was mute. He listened to the chatter for a few moments, until it was clear that these humans had nothing of import to say.

Then it sprang with silent speed, a monstrous lupine figure out of their worst nightmares; swiftly it fell upon the bearded leader of the group and feasted while the survivors fled in terror. One horse remained, tethered securely, and screamed its terror while Va'kul devoured its master before turning its dreadful attention upon the animal.

The clean bones of horse and man, along with the few bits of indigestible metal and other items, were all that remained when Va'kul had finished. The wolf was huge now, its senses sharp and alert. Rarely had it ever dined so well, and it brimmed with energy and enthusiasm.

Gillien, her friend, and the instrument so keenly desired by the Sa lord Kertu might have a few days' lead on the Changer. But it was fed and eager to begin the chase anew. The scent was hot in its nostrils as, silently, it raced after its prey.

"If you keep poking your head out," said Taran drily, "someone will eventually see you. The purpose of a hiding place is to hide, Daric."

The warrior turned and glared at the Sa elf. Taran returned the look with a raised eyebrow and a slight hint of a smile. Tavi looked from one to the other, his bright eyes intelligent and curious, but knew better than to say anything. Daric swore under his breath and stepped back from the ledge, for he knew Taran was right. His impatience might yet give them away—but it was hard, too hard, to be calm and logical when those bastards had Gillien.

The rescue party had taken all six horses in the Lamp's stable. Tavi had insisted on it. "There will be others besides Gillien," he pointed out. "If we're trying to free a whole party, anyone traveling on foot will slow our progress."

Taran had scowled. "I care not for your slaves. The lute wishes Gillien, and Gillien is whom I plan to free."

Daric had said nothing, but privately shared Tavi's view. They each had their own mount and guided one other horse. They had not traveled as fast as Daric's fear wished him to.

Tavi was no horseman, and with three riderless beasts to control, the trip had been perforce slowed. It had taken five days.
Daric knew he could have made it in three. Even so, the three
travelers had arrived here two days ago, well ahead of the slaver
party, Tavi assured Daric.

Tavi seemed to know his way well enough, pointing out land-
marks and guiding his companions confidently in a northeast-
erly direction. "Here," the boy had said when they reached the
plains, "is where the slaves will change hands."

"Why not over there, near the forested area?" asked Taran
suspiciously, pointing to the thick growth of trees about a mile
to the north. "It would mean greater safety for the Ghil. I cannot
imagine them taking any unnecessary risks."

"No, but the humans would never agree to that," Tavi replied
promptly. "Too easy an ambush—the Ghil could simply take
the slaves, attack the slavers and pay nothing for them."

"What direction will the slavers be coming from?" Daric
asked Tavi.

The boy pointed west, towards the open plains. "From there.
They don't take the Queen's Road—they ride around it. The
Ghil will be coming from the east."

"We must find a place to hide," said Daric. "It is far too open
here. Either the slavers or the Ghil, with their keen sense of
smell, will discover the horses almost at once."

He shielded his eyes with his hand and gazed at a ridge that
jutted up sharply, east of the plain. "I think we should make our
encampment there."

Taran nodded his head. "I was about to suggest the same
thing. We would get the horses out of range, have an excellent
view of the exchange, and be able to ambush from a height." He
laid a slender hand on the bow he had strapped to his horse's
back. "It would be perfect for an archer."

"A swordsman would need to be closer," said Daric. "But as
you pointed out, we would see them with plenty of warning.
Now all we need," he said with a touch of dry humor, "is a way
to get us and the horses up there."

Taran gathered his reins. "I am a stranger to this country, but no stranger to the vagaries of lands and mountains. I will find us a place."

Without another word, he coaxed his horse into a canter and headed toward the ridge. Puffs of dust rose under his mount's feet.

Tavi and Daric exchanged glances.

"I don't mean to be rude," said Tavi hesitantly, "but I thought I'd like elves better than I like him. They always sounded so nice in the folktales the Blesser used to tell us."

Daric chuckled. "Me too, Tavi. But Taran knows what he's doing, and I'd rather have him on my side than with the opposition. Come on."

By the time they had caught up with Taran, he had already found the beginning of a path of sorts that seemed to lead up the cliffside. The warrior and the young Tender waited impatiently with the horses while the elf explored the path, seeing if it would indeed take them where they wanted to go and if there would be a place to camp once there. Taran returned two hours later with good news. After that, it was simply a matter of getting the ponies up far enough to get them out of sight—or scent—of any approaching Ghil or slavers. The small party continued climbing until they reached the small cave Taran had discovered, where they could make camp. The elf had insisted on going over every inch of the cave personally before he agreed to use it as their site.

And here they had camped for two days. There was ample small game so they did not go hungry, but there was precious little to do to calm the tension that all, even Taran, seemed to feel. Tavi whittled and hummed to himself, when he wasn't asking questions of Daric or gathering a small mountain of rocks—his weapon of choice. The swordsman paced like a mountain cat in a cage as the hours dragged by. Taran kept to himself, checking his weapons and only occasionally joining in the conversation. Most of the time the elf sat quietly, holding Singer in his lap, but never playing a single note.

For Daric, the final day of waiting seemed to enjoy stretching itself out, and night came only with the greatest reluctance. The moon was bright and the plain was clearly illuminated. Now, safely protected by the shadows, the three could stand near the ledge and watch. Singer was propped up against the stone, out of harm's way. Daric did not want to look at the instrument much; its silence only served as a reminder that Gillien was not present to make it sing.

"Come on," Daric muttered to himself. "Where are they?" He turned suddenly on Tavi, his big hand on the pommel of his sword. "If you've tricked us, boy—"

Tavi flung up his hands in protest.

"My lord, no, I swear! They will be here. It's early still, and the Ghil are creatures of darkness."

Daric swallowed hard. Yes, creatures of darkness. He knew, better than the boy, what darkness was their home—and what darkness skulked in the hearts of the men who sold their own into a version of the Nightlands.

"I want to believe you, boy," he said, "but if this is a trap, by Death's breath I'll skewer you like a piece of meat on this sword before any of your friends can find you."

Tavi sat half in moonlight, half in shadow, but the fear on his face showed plainly.

"My lord," he repeated, his voice quivering, "did you think I did not know that? They will be here, with your lady—and they will not know of our presence. That, I pledge with my life."

Daric grunted noncommittally. He glanced up at the sky. "Dawn is not that far away. Look how far the moon's moved. If we don't see both Ghil and slavers soon—"

Taran's cool voice interrupted him. "While you two wolves bicker, the herd approaches."

He stood on the lip of the ledge, his slim figure lit by the moon. His shadow pooled in an inky black puddle beneath him. Turning to look at Daric, his large eyes glittered in the milky illumination. Without another word, he pointed.

Daric was instantly at his side, heart racing. He stared where the elf pointed, trying vainly to see what Taran had indicated. He tasted disappointment, like cold ashes, in his mouth.

"Gods curse you, elf, for playing with my emotions that way! Just because you don't have any—"

"I do not toy with you, human," replied Taran, a cold edge of irritation lacing his smooth voice. "It is not my fault that your eyes are inferior to mine. Keep looking where I have indicated. You will soon behold what I now see."

Daric bit back his impatience. "What are you seeing?" he asked, somewhat subdued. He did not take his eyes off the plain, but saw out of the corner of his eye that Tavi had come to stand beside him.

"There are three carts, each pulled by two horses," said Taran. "The slaves—I cannot see clearly how many—are in the carts. Six men walk beside the carts and horses; two others, it would appear, have their own steeds and are riding alongside. They appear to be slowing down . . . they have halted."

"You can really see all that?" Tavi asked, awed. Taran nodded, not bothering to even look at the boy. His eyes were on the horizon.

Daric shook his head. Even though he now knew exactly what to look for, he still could see only the vaguest hints of small dots on the horizon. The elf's vision was uncanny.

Then the full import of Taran's words hit him. "They've stopped?" he asked, dismayed. "But they're so far away—at least a mile! I had thought . . . Damn it!" He whirled and began to descend the way they had come.

"Daric, you fool!" exclaimed Taran, appearing at his side at once. "What are you doing?"

"They're too far away!" Daric's face was flushed and he glared murderously at the elf. "Gods, we have to hurry or the transaction will take place before we can even *reach* Gillien! And if those things get ahold of her . . . "

Daric's anger needed an outlet; he turned his rage on Tavi. "You said that it took place here!"

Tavi shook his head frantically. "I knew it was on this plain, that was all, my lord! I couldn't be sure where precisely . . . it was dark!"

A hint of emotion flitted across Taran's face. "No wonder your race breeds nearly as fast as the Ghil," he said, "if you are so quick to blame your children for your problems!"

Daric's voice came out in a growl. "Now listen to me, you gods-cursed son of a—"

"No, Daric Rhan, *you* listen to *me*!" His tone of voice was harsh enough to get Daric's attention. "We do not lose our advantage by rushing in to die like some mad knight in a child's bedtime tale! We wait. They will come to us."

Daric shook his head. "You can sit and wait here and hope that they'll march straight into your arms if you want. I'm going to—"

Moonlight glittered on steel, steel that had sprung out of nowhere and was now a bare inch away from Daric's naked throat. Long years of training froze Daric at once, although his anger still seethed within him.

"You will go nowhere, except perhaps to the Nightlands," hissed the elf. "I have my orders, and I will obey them."

There was a slight movement behind Taran. Daric kept his face from revealing his pleasure. Brave young Tavi had seized a large stone from his pile and was slowly approaching the elf from behind.

Taran, his gaze locked with Daric's, didn't budge, but his words crushed Daric's hope.

"My ears are as sharp as my eyes, little human, and you have seen me fight. Take one more step and I shall slay you and your friend before either of you takes another breath."

Tavi froze. He looked at Daric helplessly. Daric nodded.

"Do as he says, Tavi." Reluctantly the boy lowered his arms and tossed the rock back on the pile.

"All right, Taran. Will you at least explain to me why you're doing this? What's all this about orders?"

Taran searched Daric's face for a long, tense moment. At last he nodded and sheathed his sword. "Very well. Take hold of the lute."

Daric's black brows drew together. "If you think I—"

Already knowing what Daric was going to say, Taran interrupted him. "My request is not frivolous. I have told you it is magical, and my orders are to keep it safe and obey its desires—in that order. Take hold of the lute. I think you will learn something."

Daric glanced over at Singer. It still looked like an ordinary lute. He only half-believed Taran's claim that the thing was magical, but now he thought he had best humor the elf. He strode over to Singer, gazed down at it, then, shrugging to himself, picked it up.

And nearly dropped it.

Worry. Fear. Gillien! . . . Keep safe. Wait . . . wait . . Impatience. Tension. Gillien!

"By the gods," he breathed, "it *is* magical! And . . . it cares about Gillien."

"Yes, it does, which is why we are on this foolish quest to begin with," said Taran with exaggerated patience, as if he were speaking to an exceptionally slow child. "The lute—Singer, as it seems Gillien has dubbed it—wants her back safely. It is also instructing me to wait. So . . . we wait. Do we not, human?"

Daric glanced from the bizarre instrument that fretted in his hands to Taran, and then back to Singer again.

They waited.

The moon crawled over the ebony sky like a pallid turtle. Daric chafed, but stayed quiet. He continued to hold the lute. Only Singer seemed to be as concerned about Gillien as he was.

Silent as a shadow, Taran was on his feet, his bow in his hands and his quiver at the ready.

"The wait is over," he said. "And this you must forgive me for, Daric Rhan. I knew something you did not, and withheld that information. I judged it the wise thing to do. Behold—but stay back away from the ledge. You as well, young human."

He melted into the shadows like the ghost of an elf, one slim hand pointing directly downward to the base of the ridge upon which they stood.

Tavi gasped softly, and Daric felt the hairs on the back of his neck spring erect. The lute, which he was still holding, emitted loathing.

The humans could not see as well as Taran, either by day or by night, but they could see well enough to be repelled by the sight. Below them, crawling up from the foot of the cliffside like shadows given flesh, were the fluid shapes of five Ghil warriors. They scuttled like the rats they resembled, creeping out of their confinement.

Sweat broke out beneath Daric's arms. Beside him, his voice soft as silk, Taran confirmed his suspicions.

"I knew they would wait here until they judged the time to be right. My people know the Ghil, Daric. We know their ways. When I saw this cave-riddled ridge, not so very far from the plains, I knew that they must needs hide from the sun here. A few hundred feet beneath us there is most likely a vast maze of underground tunnels leading back to their cities. Have no fear for our present safety—had they known we were here, they would have attacked ere now. That was why I checked the cave so thoroughly. It would not do for our hiding place to open onto the Ghil's tunnels."

Gently Taran laid a hand on Daric's bicep, and his face was almost apologetic. "Had you known, you might have wished to go after them, and thus destroyed what slim chance we have of recovering Gillien."

Daric took a deep breath and suppressed his anger at the trick. Taran had acted wisely, though he underestimated Daric's cool head in times of crisis.

"Had you explained your reasons, I would have agreed. I understand military tactics—and the habits of the Ghil."

Taran raised a silvery eyebrow. "This is so. Your calmness does much to recommend you. Let me tell you the rest of my plan, then."

Daric gritted his teeth. "I would appreciate that. But first let me put this damned lute away. I can't think clearly with it buzzing around in my head this way."

He made to set the lute down when it issued a final plea. Daric was surprised for a second.

"All right," he said, "I'll make sure that you go straight to Gillien as soon as we get her away from those . . ." There were no appropriately vicious words for the slavers. He put Singer down and turned his attention to Taran.

"Very well, elf. Enlighten me."

Beside her, the little girl named Althea slept deeply. Gillien envied the child. The young ones would come out of this the best, she thought to herself. Already, in five days of slavery, some of the children had perked up enough to laugh and play, though such activities were quickly stopped if the slavers chanced to notice them. The suffocating blankets had been removed once they were far away from civilization. The children ate with good appetites when the slavers permitted their "property" to eat; they slept soundly, even when the carts rolled over rough terrain.

The youth on her left, Althea's brother Arval, was not faring as well as his sibling. Taciturn and withdrawn, he had not volunteered his name to Gillien as Althea had done. Gillien had learned it only because the girl continued to address her brother by his name when he persisted in ignoring her.

The old man, who had also not volunteered his name, would probably lose his mind after not too many more days, Gillien thought. He had become more and more withdrawn as the trip progressed, refusing to even smile when little Althea tried to play with him.

Gillien glanced over at the captives in the other carts. They were probably doing about the same, she mused bitterly—souls filled with hope or despair, resilience or fragility.

Her neck was stiff. She rolled her head around her shoulders, trying to loosen the taut muscles. For the success she got, her muscles might as well have been chiseled stone.

Carm and some of the other slavers were milling around, checking the carts every now and then. She caught snatches of conversation: *Ghil . . . almost dawn . . . good haul.*

Her lips thinned and a sudden, unexpected rush of anger crashed over her like a wave upon the shore. Gods, how she hated these men, hated everything they did, everything they stood for. She wanted to do something, anything, to fight them *now*, escape *now*, but wisdom kept her quiescent. Now was not the time, and odds were, she'd only have one chance.

Althea moved, whimpered in her sleep. Gillien's face furrowed in sympathy. Gods, if only her voice would come back.

Suddenly the slavers' idle chatter ceased. They stood stiffly, gazing out toward the ridge that rose in the east. Gillien followed their gaze. Her chains rattled, alerting her fellow prisoners, and those who still had enough interest in their surroundings also turned to see.

Five black shapes, moving with fluid speed, came at them across the plain. Gillien swallowed hard. She'd seen creatures like that before, when she and her family had been down on their luck and had played in filthy taverns for their coins. Once, a rat had actually scampered over her foot. She'd jerked her boot back with a slight cry of startlement—an ejaculation that had gotten her and her family summarily dismissed without recompense. Next time that had happened, she'd just kept on singing, a false smile plastered on her face as the vermin milled about her feet.

These rats, though, were not as small as her hand. They were as big, bigger, than she herself was. Big, and fierce, and graceful in a horrible, feral fashion. The moon's light caught the glitter of naked swords, of bits and pieces of human clothing adorning the black-furred pelts of the running creatures. Sweat began to trickle down her back.

"Dear gods," moaned Arval, shocked out of his silence for the first time on the dreadful trip.

Althea roused, rubbed the sleep from her eyes to the accompaniment of clattering chains, and followed her brother's gaze. Her eyes widened and she began to scream.

The other children picked up on her terror and added to the chorus of fear. Growling to themselves, the slavers tried to quiet the wailing children—and adults—but to no avail. The attempts were half–hearted and were eventually abandoned. The gags had been removed days ago; they were no longer within human earshot, and, Gillien mused darkly, surely the Ghil did not care if their appearance frightened their slaves.

She licked lips gone dry with fear. *Steady, Gilly,* she told herself. *No good to anyone at all if you're so scared you can't think.*

She could hear them now, hear the clicking, chittering sounds that passed for speech among their kind. A few yards distant, they halted and gathered to confer. One of them rose on its hind legs and looked straight at her. Even at this distance, its black eyes shone in the moonlight. It said something to its fellows, and its teeth gleamed as well.

Gillien gasped soundlessly as a hard stick was shoved into her midsection. "Get out," ordered one of the slavers. Gillien moved to obey, but was only able to move a foot or two before the rope tied at her waist pulled taut. She turned and looked over her shoulder.

Arval was not moving. He was kneeling over the old man, who appeared to still be asleep.

"Come on," Arval moaned, gently shaking the man. "Please, please wake up . . ."

Tears stung Gillien's eyes, surprising her. She was past weeping for herself, but not for others, it would seem. Even in this darkness, she could see that the old man would never move again. When had Lady Death come for him, she wondered; as the slaves sat quietly, waiting for the Ghil? Or just now, as he saw for the first time the obscene faces of the things who would be his new masters? Gillien desperately hoped the former.

"Damn," came Carm's voice. He jumped into the cart and went to untie the rope from the corpse's waist. "Come on boy, move along now."

Something snapped in Arval. His lips curled back from his teeth in a horrible snarl, and with a wordless cry of outrage he sprang for Carm's unprotected back.

It would not have lasted long, no matter what had happened next. Carm was bigger and better versed in fighting than the boy, and in a heartbeat his compatriots would have beaten Arval to a pulp. As it was, Arval didn't even reach the slaver. Gillien tackled him and seized the youth about the waist. They fell heavily to the floor. Arval's eyes went wide, thinking she had betrayed him. "You bitch!" he spat, and got in one good swipe across her face. Her head jerked hard to the side with the force of his blow, then three other slavers were there, dragging him off her and beating him cruelly. Carm was visibly shaken; clearly he had not been expecting any sort of attack from the formerly silent, sullen youth. He rose unsteadily and regarded Gillien with a shrewd glance.

"Don't know what you're about, little mountain cat, but

anks. Just for that, I'll separate you and yon scrapper." He
nt over her and quickly untied the rope that bound her and
rval. "There."

She didn't look at him. She had not stopped Arval from at-
cking Carm for the slaver's sake, but for her own. The more
ooperative she was, the less they would look to her for rebel-
on. Little Althea was still crying and pressed hard against
illien for reassurance. Her arm around the girl, Gillien slid out
f the cart.

And came face to face with a Ghil. She gasped. Althea didn't
ake a sound; the child was too startled to scream.

The Ghil warrior, a male, stood a foot taller than she. He
nelled of rot and filth, laced with the scent of fresh earth. His
reathing was wheezy and his breath foul, and Gillien tried hard
ot to vomit from the stench.

He reached to touch her with pink fingers, and she automati-
ally stepped back. She could retreat no further; her back
ressed hard against the wood of the cart.

"No 'fraid," said the Ghil in what passed for a soothing tone.
Not hurt good slaves. Only bad slaves. You good slave, yes?"

Gillien felt sick, but tried to conquer her fear. Althea
queezed her hand so hard that Gillien thought her bones might
nap. She nodded.

The Ghil narrowed his large black eyes. "Yes?" he repeated,
nnoyed.

Carm stepped in. "She can't talk," he volunteered, pointing to
is throat and shaking his head. The Ghil chirped in amusement,
ot the attention of his fellows, and conveyed the information in
is own language. More chirping, and nods of approval. The
hil placed a possessive hand on Gillien's shoulder.

"No talk, is better! 'ow much?"

Gillien did not have any desire to know how much she was
orth to a giant rat, and deliberately focused her attention else-
here. She had been right; there were five of them. Two were
emales. One of them had a slit in her belly that writhed and
ulsed. An instant later, as Gillien watched, a naked, blind crea-
are stuck its head out and hissed before returning to the safety
f its living nest.

Vomit rose in Gillien's throat. Folklore and legend had sai
nothing about this. She swallowed hard, tasting the bitterness o
her partially digested meal, and forced it back down to her un
happy stomach. She had a good idea that if she showed disgus
things would go harder for her.

Five Ghil. Two females. The one with the . . . babies . .
seemed to be in charge. The females carried swords and ha
more decorations than the males. The leader even had a jewe
glittering in one of her large, naked ears.

The males carried spears. Three spears, two swords, Gillie
noted, forcing herself to be calm. Eleven prisoners, all chaine
hand and foot. Her plan could possibly succeed . . . but so much
of it depended upon the reactions of her fellow slaves. Sh
glanced around.

Poor Arval could barely stand; his face was bruised an
bloody. The children were silent, shocked figures in the moon
light. The women and the men were little better. Only she
Gillien, seemed to have her wits about her. Very well. If he
plan worked, she might be able to give them back their will to
fight.

Oh, gods, please . . . she prayed, to whoever might be listen
ing.

At last the exchange was done. The slavers dumped the body
of the old man out for the scavengers without a qualm. Gillie
winced as she heard the body hit the earth. Perhaps it was bette
this way, she thought grimly. Better to die now among men than
later among rats. The slavers then climbed into the carts them
selves, and with much laughter and counting of coins, they
turned and began to move back toward the west.

Gillien watched them go, then jumped as she felt the hot stin
of a whip across her legs.

"Walk!" snapped the leader female, whiskers twitching in
displeasure. "Lazy slave, not get food!"

Gillien bowed her head and began to keep pace with the oth
ers. Soon, she would have to make her move, and she fought a
terrible, crippling fear that she might not succeed.

Byrn, my Byrn,
Great kingdom by the sea;
Byrn, my Byrn,
We'll fight and die for thee!

—chorus, *Byrn, My Byrn*

CHAPTER SEVENTEEN

"Gillien yet lives," said Taran, a hint of pleasure warming
is normally cool voice.

"Where?" Daric's pulse raced as he tried to search out
illien's slim figure among the approaching slaves.

When Taran had voiced his plan, it had seemed like a sound
dea: wait until the trade-off had actually taken place, the
avers had gone and the Ghil, returning to the fissures from
hence they had come, had approached to within arrow and
word reach. Even now, the concepts seemed solid, but Daric
ound it increasingly hard to sit by and simply wait for the little
and of monsters and slaves to get within reach. The knowl-
dge that Gillien was indeed among their number sparked re-
ef, but also apprehension. He knew what slavers did to
omen and, occasionally, to men. He knew, though he had
ruggled against and even tried to drown the memories with
quor, what that sort of abuse and debasement did to the
uman spirit.

"Ah, Gilly, please be all right," he murmured under hi
breath as his worried gaze searched her out.

"She seems relatively uninjured," commented Taran.

Daric didn't answer. The moon had chosen that moment t
clear a cloud and he could see the tiny figure that Taran ha
told him was Gillien.

She was far from all right.

She walked slowly, her slim, strong body not striding alon
with head held high, as he remembered her. She . . . shufflec
and the movement was not entirely due to the chains that encir
cled her ankles. Daric had walked in just such shackles, an
he had managed to stride, until his body and mind had bee
violated.

Her eyes were on the ground, and her shoulders sagged. Fo
a second, Daric's vision blurred. It took him several blinks be
fore he realized that tears had sprung to his eyes.

"Oh, Gilly, I'm sorry," he moaned softly.

Taran spared him a quick glance. "Wait," he hissed. "The
come closer. You go down and wait in the shadows. Tavi and
will remain here. Do not attack until I give the signal."

"And what will that be?"

A knowing smile curved the elf's lips. "You will recognize i
when it comes."

Surreptitiously, Gillien glanced up at the sky. The smalle
stars had disappeared, though the sky did not seem to be
lighter. Dawn was only about an hour away.

They had been marching for a while, long enough, she
hoped, that any noise would not draw the slavers back. In truth
she did not think that, having gotten what they wanted from the
Ghil, they would be in any hurry to help them fight their prop
erty.

The cliff ridge loomed ahead. The Ghil on Gillien's righ
chittered happily, and suddenly Gillien realized that the ridge
far from being a simple landmark, was their destination. She
wanted to wait, to gather her courage a little more, but in a very
short while her chance would be gone. Soon they would ente
whatever dark and twisted tunnels the Ghil had wrenched from

the mountain rock, and they would never see the stars, or
moonlight, ever again. Now, there were only five Ghil. This
was the time; now, before they got so close to the creatures'
lairs that others would hear and come to lend their aid.

It was now or never. Gillien, more afraid than she had ever
been in her entire brief life, closed her eyes and said a heartfelt,
silent prayer. Then she took a deep breath, steadied herself, and
opened her mouth.

Nothing came out.

She almost choked as fear shuddered through her, fear of yet
another failure, perhaps the most disastrous yet. She could not
remember the last time she had sung without accompaniment
of some sort, and the thought led of course to the magical lute.
She had let Singer down—she had been a poor guardian. Now,
its music was probably silenced forever, just as her voice was
perhaps silenced forever. Again she opened her mouth, and this
time a harsh croaking sound emerged.

Little Althea looked up inquiringly. Her small face was
white in the moonlight, her large, expressive eyes dark hollows
in her pretty face.

"You all right?" she whispered.

Gillien smiled. Yes, she was all right, and the Nightlands
take her, she was going to get them all away from these cursed
monsters or die in the attempt.

She breathed in again, closed her eyes, and began to sing.

> Thy fields are green and fertile,
> Thy rivers deep and wide,
> Thy forests rich with deer and hare
> Thy people full of pride.
>
> What country blessed with bounties
> Is the one of which we sing?
> 'Tis Byrn the Fair, 'tis Byrn the Just,
> So let our praises ring!

Her voice was thin, shaky, quivering with uncertainty. It
bore very little resemblance to her normal clear, powerful so-

prano, but it was enough to cause a reaction of some sort, which was all she wanted.

There was a harsh chattering among the Ghil. They'd apparently never heard anyone sing before and had no idea what it was. When Gillien paused for breath before breaking into the chorus, she could hear the rattling of chains as the slaves, startled out of their mindless shuffling, lifted their heads to see what was going on.

> Byrn, my Byrn,
> Great kingdom by the sea,
> Oh, Byrn, my Byrn,
> We'll fight and die for thee!
>
> We pledge allegiance to our lords,
> Our country and our king,
> Before the Seven Gods we bow,
> Their praises we do sing.
>
> But never shall a Byrnian
> Submit to slavery,
> We serve with pride and serve with joy
> But a Byrnian's heart is free!

The slaves had slowed. All of them were listening now, their backs straight and taut, waiting to see what would happen next. Chittering angrily, the leader female scampered over to Gillien and struck her with the whip. Gillien gasped at the stinging pain across her bare legs.

"You sposed silent!" the Ghil reprimanded. "No make noise!"

Gillien's eyes burned from the pain, but she noticed that some of the other slaves were murmuring angrily. "Come on!" she cried, rebellion flaring. "We are Byrnians! We are not slaves to giant *rats*!"

This time when she sang the chorus, other voices joined with her—cautiously, softly, but others were singing.

> Byrn, my Byrn,
> Great kingdom by the sea,

Byrn, my Byrn,
We'll fight and die for thee!

The Ghil were seriously distressed now. They had drawn
their swords, but were naturally reluctant to use them. Gillien
knew she was the best deal they'd gotten, and when the lead female brandished her weapon and screamed for silence, Gillien
merely grinned and sang even louder.

Beside her, little Althea was joining in—getting the words
wrong, but belting out the song with gusto. Everyone knew
Byrn, My Byrn. It was sung over babies as they slept, sung in
the fields at harvest, during ceremonies high and low. Song, as
Gillien had good cause to know, went deep into the minds of
her countrymen. She had prayed that her plan would work, and
seeing anger fill formerly empty faces, she felt hope rise inside
her.

This time when the leader struck with the whip, Gillien
grabbed it and pulled. Caught completely off-guard, the rat-
thing stumbled forward. Swift and confident, Gillien moved to
attack. She used the metal manacles about her wrists as a
weapon, striking the creature's head. The Ghil went down for
an instant, giving Gillien just enough time to get the leader's
sword away from her.

Trying her best to keep Althea out of the way, Gillien raised
the sword and attempted to impale the prone Ghil with it. But
the creature, now realizing just what kind of foe she faced, was
prepared with an attack of her own, and Gillien cried out as a
powerful tail slammed into her midsection. She stumbled and
fell.

Althea screamed. The Ghil leader, all teeth and claws now,
leaped to her feet and hovered over Gillien. Gillien covered her
head with her hands and braced herself for agony.

The attack didn't come. She heard a strange, stinging sound
that seemed vaguely familiar. Cautiously, Gillien raised her
head.

The Ghil leader stared down at her chest. A slim, feathered
arrow protruded from it about five inches. Angrily, she clawed
at it. The young in her belly pouch squirmed frantically. The

Ghil grasped the arrow and tugged, but succeeded only in snapping the thin shaft. Again Gillien heard the sound. The Ghil spasmed as a second arrow embedded itself in her throat.

Recovering her senses, Gillien rolled out of the way, scrambled to her feet, grabbed Althea, and dove to the right as the dying Ghil collapsed to the earth. She kicked and squirmed, sending small droplets of blood flying.

Gillien looked around frantically. "What in the Nightlands—" Arrows were everywhere. Even as she watched, confused and frightened, more whizzed past. Stones, too, sailed through the air to crunch on Ghil skulls. Had the slavers returned? The slaves seemed to be uninjured and had apparently rallied, fighting back with stolen swords, fists and chains. Two Ghil lay dead, one felled by the arrow, the other run through with its own sword. A third writhed on the ground, its muzzle crushed to a bloody pulp.

A sharp, animal howl shivered through the air and Gillien's heart slammed against her chest. A figure exploded out of the shadowy darkness, its sword moving so fast it seemed a blur as it flashed in the moonlight. The roar modulated into a human voice and joy flooded Gillien as she heard Daric cry, "Let them *go*, you bastards!"

Gillien wanted to cry aloud herself, to let him know how very glad she was that he was alive, and *here*, and had not deserted her after all. Instead, she flung back her head. Her throat opened and the song flooded out as if it had a life of its own.

> So hear us, gods, protect us all,
> From king upon his throne
> To lowliest of vassals,
> For this land is all our own,
>
> Let never one dark shadow fall
> Upon this land so free,
> Byrn the Fair, O Byrn, the Just,
> We'll fight and die for thee!

Another Ghil fell to Daric's sword. Heartened, the slaves renewed their attack on the last one of their inhuman masters. Gillien thought it an odd, violent harmony between her powerful, pure song and the sounds of steel biting flesh, of arrows slicing through the air to land with a dull *thock* in leathery Ghil bodies, the shrieks of the dying rat creatures.

Ghil bodies lay like large, black lumps on the earth. The small creatures housed in their mother's pouch were still mewling. Snarling savagely, Arval fell to his knees beside the dead Ghil leader and shoved his hands into her pouch. He clutched one writhing, hairless creature in his hand, placed it on the earth, and smashed its skull with a rock. Then he went for the rest. His mother rushed to him, embracing the boy hard, then helping him with his cruel but necessary task.

At last it was over. Gillien stood panting, surveying the scene. One of the slaves, an older woman, lay dead with her captors. The others had survived and were running to one another, crying and laughing at the same time.

"Gillien!"

Daric's rough cry made Gillien start. The warrior ran toward her, bloody sword still in hand.

"Thank the gods you're all right! When I learned you'd been taken, I—"

Her heart spasmed. Suddenly it was not Daric, but Barak racing toward her, naked, his maleness engorged and ready for another assault, her blood covering his thighs . . .

Gillien cried aloud, an animal sound of fear and loathing, and cringed, her arms flying up to protect her head.

"No!" she yelped, "don't . . ."

Daric halted so suddenly he almost tripped and fell. When Gillien chanced another look at him, he was only Daric again. His face was unreadable in the dim light.

He stepped forward, slowly this time. "Let me get those chains off you," he said quietly.

Gillien swallowed hard. Even having him close to her, touching her in an attempt to remove her bonds, made her want to either fly or attack. She concentrated on other things.

"How did you know where to find us?"

"The Tender knew where the exchange site was," Daric explained in that same quiet, neutral tone. "Here, you're free now. I'll go take care of the others." He walked away without another word.

Gillien gazed after him, her emotions riotous. She was about to call him back, apologize, when a smooth voice she had not heard before captured all her attention.

"Gillien, I am Taran. I have something I think you will want to see."

Gillien turned to behold a Sa elf, his silver hair lit with cool moonlight. That was enough to capture her attention, but the unusual being lost it at once when Gillien realized what he was holding.

"Singer!" she cried, hot tears of joy spilling down her cheeks. "Thank the gods . . . Singer . . . I'm so sorry . . . please forgive me . . ."

She seized the lute and held it tightly. Its response bathed her in warm, loving sensations. There was nothing to forgive. It had missed her, too, it told her; had feared for her safety, was happy that she was well.

She felt something else from it, too, a need that had to be answered, a need that she would be more than happy to fulfill. But Taran's voice, cool and logical, came to her ears and halted her when she would have begun to play the instrument.

"These Ghil are dead," said the elf. "But others lurk below the ridge. It is not yet day. We have brought enough horses so that the weakest might ride. I suggest that once the chains have been removed, we put distance between ourselves and the Ghil. There will be time enough for celebration when daylight rules the skies."

Gillien saw the faces of her companions fall, then harden with resolve. Taran was right. There was no point in rejoicing when recapture was imminent, and there was a good chance that the clamor of battle had been heard.

She was placed on a horse, little Althea seated in front of her. Daric, Taran and Tavi saw to it that all of the children and the weakest adults had mounts before Tavi swung up behind Arval. Daric and the surviving man slave planned to walk.

Taran was already on his horse. "I shall watch for attack," he said. "The rest of you continue on."

And so they did, although the act of sitting astride the horse, gentle though the animal was, brought tears to Gillien's eyes. Over the last few days the pain between her legs had begun to abate. Now, the agony returned full measure.

Perceptive Althea noticed and asked Gillien, "What's wrong?"

Gillien shook her head and forced a smile. "Nothing, sweet. Nothing's wrong at all. We're free, aren't we?"

They rode for about an hour, Daric and the other man jogging to keep up, until the morning grew sufficiently bright for all to feel secure in its light. Then everyone tumbled off their horses, hungry, aching, and laughing with delight at their escape. Silently, Gillien slipped off her mount, reaching back up to lift Althea to the ground. She wanted to help tend the injured, light a fire, cook the meal, but Singer called, and she needed desperately to answer.

She'd had enough of pain, of cruelty, of hunger and despair, of blood and death. Singer offered a brief reprieve. They would all understand. Eagerly, Gillien slipped the leather strap over her shoulders, positioned her fingers on the strings, and began to play.

Singer's song filled the air. For an all too brief time, chatter and laughter played joyful counterpoint to the lute's music and Gillien's full, vibrant voice. Daric and Tavi, more grim-faced than the almost giddy former slaves, treated those with injuries and passed around food and water. At last, Singer having quieted, Gillien placed the lute carefully aside and shyly came to join them. Arval and Althea ran up as she approached, the little girl flinging herself at Gillien's legs and almost tripping her.

Gillien didn't mind, smiling as she sat down beside them. They were free . . . though she, at least, had paid a terrible price. The thought sobered her, and even Singer's gentle nudge at her mind did not lift her spirits this time. Singer was safe, and they had bought their liberty, but she had still been ruined. When Daric came to sit beside her, nervousness clutched at her stomach and she edged away.

Arval ate heartily, and again Gillien marveled at the re-
siliency of the young. Gone was the silent, withdrawn, bitter
young man who had sat stonily at Gillien's side for the past
several days. He was now talking animatedly between mouth-
fuls of stew, recounting his family's capture and the rest of the
dreadful ordeal as if it was part of a grand adventure that had
happened to someone else long ago.

". . . And then I heard this song. I thought it was Lady
Death's wolves come for me, singing their song and getting
ready to bear away my soul. But then I realized the song was
about Byrn, and I looked over and there was—and there she
is!" he yelped, grinning as he realized Gillien had come to join
them by the fire. "The wonderful bard who had no voice. I
thought you were mute!"

"I was," admitted Gillien as she ladled herself a bowl of
stew. "I got my voice back. But I didn't save you. All of you
joined in . . . we all fought back."

"How did you know it would work?" Daric asked, tearing
off a hunk of bread and handing it to her. "You didn't know we
were there, ready to add our weapons to your voice."

She didn't look at him as she accepted the bread. "Songs are
powerful things," she answered. "I had hoped the others would
hear the song and remember who we were—Byrnians, born in
freedom. There weren't that many Ghil. If we all rallied, we
stood a good chance of killing them before they killed all of
us." She hesitated, then added, "Many of us—maybe all of
us—would have died if you hadn't been there, Daric. Thank
you—and Taran, too, for—" She started. "Where is he?"

Daric rose and looked around. The elf was nowhere to be
seen. Daric sighed. "He said he would watch our backs for us.
He probably still is. He was sent to guard the lute, Gillien. Now
that you've got the lute back, I think he wants to stay hidden
again. I must say, I'm not surprised."

The thin line of worry between Gillien's eyebrows disappeared. She cradled the lute.

"Yes. I've got Singer back. And I never want to let it go
again!"

She closed her eyes happily, and missed the look that flitted across Daric's face. The warrior rose, took a small stick from the fire, and began to sketch a map in the earth. Everyone craned their necks to watch.

"We're here," said Daric, making an X. "About a mile north, we ought to hit the King's Road. The nearest village is Geshim, about ten miles to the west along the King's Road." He sketched it, then glanced around at the eager faces. "Anyone live there?"

One of the women nodded enthusiastically.

"Good. Then you'll be home in a few hours. Gillien, Geshim is directly on the way to Kasselton. We should stay at Geshim tonight. If we rise early and press hard all day tomorrow, by nightfall we'll be in the city—and near the end of your journey."

The thought gave Gillien little pleasure. Soon, she would be saying goodbye to Singer forever, and she found the idea distressing. *I don't want to give you up*, she thought fiercely.

The lute reassured her, hinting that such a parting might not be necessary.

She smiled at that. Rising, she looked around. Nine expectant faces looked up at her—nine people she had helped regain their freedom. Daric, his face closed, regarded her coolly. The Tender was squirming with happiness, his eyes big and bright.

Her thighs still ached; the place between them throbbed and reminded her that despite her accomplishments, she was still nothing in the eyes of the world.

Maybe it was time to ignore the eyes of the world.

She strode over to one of the horses and swung herself into the saddle, ignoring the sudden sharp pain as she sat on the sensitive place. She lifted her chin.

"Well, what are we waiting for?" she queried, and launched into *Byrn, My Byrn*. As the sun continued its climb across the sky that morning, Light smiled down on a small band of survivors, singing songs of their homeland as they walked.

Behold our table laden
With fruit of tree and vine.
Partake of golden wheaten bread
And taste the sweet red wine.
Our larder's filled with winter stores,
A fair and welcome sight,
For the harvest has been gathered in
And we celebrate tonight.

—from *The First Harvest*

CHAPTER EIGHTEEN

The inconceivable had happened—the trail had gone cold. Va'kul, swift and powerful with its new strength, had followed it easily to a holy house that was chill and deserted. It waited in the shadows, watching, alert for the arrival of any humans, but it readily became apparent that this place would not be visited by anyone soon. Only the dead were to be found here now; a big man who stank of sweat and fear, another man in sacred vestments stiffening on the floor.

The warrior's scent was here in abundance, traceable from the holy house to the stables. From there, mixed with the odor of horseflesh, it continued on in some other direction, Va'kul cared not where. But that of the bearer of the lute was subdued, confused with too many other complex scents of humans, beasts, and materials to be traceable.

It was unimaginable. Yet it had happened. Va'kul had lost the trail.

It took to the sky then, transforming itself back to the shape of a bird, its black wings beating against the air with a numb steadiness. Anxiously, Va'kul cast its gaze about for hours that night, hoping beyond hope that it would see its quarry wandering carelessly out in the open, or at least find some hint, some clue, as to where she had vanished.

The search proved futile. Va'kul abandoned it, changed direction, and flew toward Kasselton and its teeming thousands. The next night, too, it searched, and the next, and the night following as well, this time posing as a nondescript man; but his explorations yielded nothing. Bards were common as dirt in big cities, even female bards. And a lute, though an expensive instrument, was not so rare as to have provoked commentary.

Now, eleven full nights after he had fought with the girl on that dreadful evening, Va'kul wandered down the road that led out of the great gates of Kasselton. His stride was determined, the expression in his human eyes sharply at odds with the jowly, benevolent mask he wore. Time was short. He knew what he had to do.

He did not know when Gillien would be arriving, but knew that she would eventually come to this city. The Sa leader Kertu had been convinced that Jencir would try to take the lute to the Queen-mother, the Falaran elf, Ariel. Surely, Gillien would, too.

Kasselton was enormous. He could not possibly search it all. Yet he must, if he were to complete his mission and uphold the honor of his people.

The brisk pace of his stride was not suitable to his round, heavy body. Sweat began to gleam on Va'kul's brow.

His steady gait had taken him out of the city limits now, out past the softly rolling farmland and into the outskirts of the enormous forested area the Byrnians called the Great Green Sea. That was good. He needed privacy and darkness, a sanctuary, to do what he must do.

He changed again, now that he was well away from discovery, into the sleek, fleet-footed form of something resembling a deer. There was no one to convince, to fool, out here in the forest, so Va'kul did not have to waste precious energy on getting the details correct. The Changer wanted the creature's speed, not its liquid brown eyes, majestic rack, or smooth brown hide. The thing it became was the rough framework of a deer, without grace or harmony or beauty of any sort. Once, Va'kul's pride would never have let it opt for only a partial change. Now, it gave such a haphazard transformation no thought at all.

It gathered itself and bounded through the undergrowth on long legs, its vision untroubled by the dark canopy of trees whose leaves increasingly shut out any light from moon or stars. Ferns bowed softly beneath its undetailed hooves as it moved ever deeper into the forest, in search of sanctuary.

At last it found what it had been seeking—a place where rock and earth came together to form a cave. Cautiously, Va'kul stepped forward, sniffing for the scent of any forest creatures. If this had once been anything's lair, it was long ago. Even the few bones of hare and wild pig scattered about were old and half-buried in forest detritus. Stepping gingerly on its delicate legs, Va'kul investigated. This cave was not particularly deep, or particularly large. It did not need to be. It only needed to be large enough, and quiet, away from prying eyes.

This would do. Even the entrance was small, and therefore easier to barricade. Resuming its natural form, Va'kul oozed into the cave through the footwide fissure, its shapeless body flowing like oil into every crevice, until it was well away from any hint of light from the outside. It extended a limb, pushing out fingers with which to seize rocks and earth, and began to seal the hole shut. In a few moments, Va'kul was effectively sealed inside.

The Changer thought over the last three weeks. They had been . . . remarkable, amazing, unlike anything it had ever experienced before. It had taken on so many different shapes: male human, female human, horse, bird, wolf, stag, monster, thing of nightmares. What a challenge that had been, and how exciting! And it had survived, had never been threatened, nor even suspected, by anyone other than that clever child who bore the lute. She alone had eluded it. Va'kul felt something stirring inside it; it recognized the emotion as hatred.

Each time, its disguise had been better, cleaner, more accurate. It had grown used to using the terms "I," "you," "me," "we," and other strange words that marked the delineation between one entity and another. It wondered if it alone, out of all its kind, now finally understood what it was like to be an individual—to be "I."

Now, it was preparing to surrender those feelings forever—to "die," as humans called it, in order to continue searching for the lute. It felt an odd pang, and realized that it did not *want* to lose these wonderful sensations. It wanted to abandon the quest for Gillien and her instrument. It wanted to continue to explore the delights of different forms. It could do it. It could simply . . . vanish, not return to its people. Leader would be angry that it had broken faith with Kertu, but what of that? What was Kertu, in the end, to the Changers? What was one elf-lord to a race of beings so united in their thoughts and essence that they were, in a sense, one?

Beings that Va'kul alone could teach about the wonderful concept of "I"?

No! it raged silently. *Do not wish to . . . I do not wish to die!*

But even as it mourned the inevitable loss of its recently evolved identity, it knew that this was necessary. It could not simply walk away from its people. The race was everything. The individual, literally, meant nothing to the Changers, whatever Va'kul had experienced over the last few days. It had to fulfill the bargain its Leader had made to the Sa king. And that meant . . . an ending.

And so Va'kul gently, but deliberately, closed the door on all thoughts of *I* and *me*. There was no room, no time, for such distractions.

It turned its consciousness inward. It lost sense of time, of place; it no longer felt the rock pressing, forcing it to alter its shape to fit the hole. It simply was.

And then, it was not.

The soft, shapeless mass began to quiver. With a slurping sound, the thing's weight edged away from its center, shifted toward the sides. In the cool darkness of the cave, two bulges writhed, connected only by an ever-narrowing band. There came a sharp sound as the band snapped. For a moment, two separate lumps sat and quivered, grew and shrank slightly. Then they, too, began to bulge and writhe, and the moist sounds of division rose again.

The little farming community of Geshim might have lost only one of its own to the slavers, but all of the former captives were welcomed as if they had been born and bred in the village. Gillien and Daric, in particular, were given a hero's welcome. The local inn and the Lamp of Traveler almost quarreled over which of them would have the honor of hosting "the liberators." In the end, the tavern won the privilege, and graciously offered to play host to all the "lost children" who had so miraculously escaped the claws of the Ghil. The innkeeper provided the ale, and the generous farmers donated all the food.

It made for a cheerful occasion at The Happy Sow. Daric and Gillien, flattered but uncomfortable with the sudden adulation, had sought refuge at a corner table. There was music and laughter, and even a little bit of dancing—the sounds of mirth and laughter, the raucous noise of grateful celebration.

Daric's brown eyes surveyed the scene, still alert for any threat to Gillien or the lute even here in this apparently pastoral setting. Young Arval was across the room, sampling the local brew and apparently having too much of a good thing. His smile, though foolishly wide, was free of any darker shadow. There was time yet for him to find the comfortable balance between tipsy and drunk, Daric mused. Althea was constantly underfoot, making new friends everywhere she went. The mother of the pair sat quietly, neither aloof nor gregarious, merely happy to see her children behaving like themselves again.

Tavi had departed a few hours earlier, in the company of a kindly-seeming Blesser of Traveler. Daric had taken the elderly man aside and explained the circumstances, emphasizing the boy's courage and desire to do the right thing. The man had nodded with comprehension and compassion, and when Tavi approached and asked shyly, "Is there anything I can do to earn Traveler's forgiveness?" the man had replied with the perfect words.

"Traveler has already forgiven. But you must work hard to thank him for that forgiveness, my boy."

The light in Tavi's eyes, made brighter by the sparkle of tears, had touched Daric's heart. He was glad the boy had come to a safe place. No one that young should have to traffic with slavers.

The music continued, but Daric no longer paid heed to Geshim's joy. He focused his attention on the slim figure sitting in front of him at the rough wooden table. She wore a brown dress, old and torn, but clean. Her bard's medallion, left behind at the false Lamp of Traveler, and retrieved by Daric, hung about her slender neck. All the former slaves had been given new clothing, happily donated by the town. As Gillien's gender had been revealed already, it was too late to continue the charade, and she had accepted the old dress with thanks. Her beer sat in front of her, untouched. Daric had requested wine, and water to cut it with. It was bland, but pleasant. Best of all, he found it did not command his attention the way the young minstrel did.

He could be silent no longer. "Gillien, what's the matter?"

Gillien's attention surged suddenly to the present. She started, glancing down at Daric, and then away. The swordsman might suspect what had happened to her when she was with the slavers, but she felt certain that if she met his eyes, he would know beyond a doubt. She couldn't bear that—couldn't bear for Daric, too, to think of her as despoiled property.

She swallowed hard before answering. "I'm not looking forward to arriving at Kasselton."

His eyes narrowed. "Why? It's the end of your journey. Soon it'll all be over."

She sighed. "It's all going to come out. I won't be able to hide anymore. And I'm afraid of what might happen when my real identity's known. Remember, I'm not just the lute's guardian, I'm a runaway from the law. Plus, I spent most of my time on this journey wearing men's clothes, pretending to be a boy. That's illegal too." Her lively face was still, as if it had been sculpted out of stone.

Daric waited patiently.

"Daric . . ."

His answer was swift, tense. "Yes, Gilly?"

"I want you to promise me something." She chanced a look at him behind lowered lashes. His face was open and un-guarded. He seemed anxious, worried. Why? He had rescued her; both she and Singer were safe—if not unharmed.

"Anything."

Daric's voice was soft but held a slight tremor. Exhaustion, Gillien thought with sympathy. She had forgotten that he probably hadn't slept much over the last few days, either.

"I want you to take care of Singer. You have to take it to Queen-mother Ariel for me if . . ." She couldn't bring herself to say it.

"If you're arrested," he finished swiftly before she could speak. "Gillien, I know you're innocent. I've seen the killer. I can get you—"

"Daric, they won't bother with a trial if they really think I killed all those people!"

Her voice climbed higher with the strain. A few curious folk turned their heads in her direction and she forced herself to be calm, bringing her voice down to a softer level.

"They'll hang me the minute they know who I am, if word has traveled this far. And I'm sure it has. Bards do so love a good story," she said with a trace of disgust. Singer lay at her feet, its neck against her calf. It sent her a sensation of gentle reproach and warm confidence. She closed her eyes in pain. She had to, *had* to, ensure the instrument's safety, even at the risk of her own.

"That won't happen. I won't *let* it happen."

"Daric, if it happens, it happens. What I need from you is a promise that you'll carry out this mission for me if . . . if . . . I mean, what about that creature? We haven't seen it in days. Maybe it's here, waiting to ambush us." She grew frantic at the thought. "Gods, Daric, please, please be careful. You know what to look for. Check everyone's hands, everyone's, mine included if I've gone out of your sight for a minute, please? Promise me, Daric, promise me you'll take care of Singer!"

Daric's dark brown eyes searched Gillien's for a moment, before she looked back down at the lute at her feet. He sighed heavily.

"I think everything's going to be all right," he said, "but I do promise to take care of Singer."

"And you'll check everyone's—"

"Yes, yes, I'll check everyone's hands after nightfall, I promise. Now, calm down and drink your beer."

She did so, and pleasure flitted across her face. "Mmm, that's good." Daric smiled slightly. "What?" Gillien asked.

He brushed a finger at his mouth, the smile deepening. "You've got a mustache," he said with a hint of laughter.

"Oh." Gillien wiped at the foam that clung to her upper lip and grinned, ducking her head a little in embarrassment.

Daric's heart turned over. That was the first gesture he had seen since her terrible ordeal that spoke of the Gillien he remembered. Sudden hope flared in him, hope that the cheerful, enthusiastic girl she had been had not entirely been obliterated at the hands of the slavers.

She had, as of yet, said nothing about what had happened during those few dreadful days. She had spoken openly enough about her tactics to free her fellow slaves, had not been silent when recounting the loathing she felt of the monstrous Ghil—a loathing that Daric shared, right down to the bone. But of her time as a captive in the hands of men crueler than the Ghil, she said not a word.

Daric had not pressed her, though her rejection of him hurt. She was herself only when she had the lute in her arms, when she could lose herself in her music and Singer's warm affection. She had not touched Daric, had flinched when he came too near. It was only now, when she felt safe in a crowd of people she trusted, that she even deigned to talk with him on any personal level at all. Was it him she didn't want? Or did her recent ordeal make her shy of being alone with any man?

Daric didn't know, and the not knowing tore at him.

He badly wanted to tell her that he knew what had happened, that it did not matter to him, that she was no less a wonderful person, a wonderful *woman*, in his eyes. That in fact, her courage had made him admire her even more. But there were ghosts and shadows still hiding in the depths of her eyes. Gillien would have to come to terms with them herself.

For now, though, she was as happy as she could be. Singer was at her feet, quiet now; a glass of fine, free beer was on the table in front of her, and she got a foam mustache again as she took another sip.

For now, Daric let that be enough.

They were up early the next morning, on horses that had been rested and fed. Gillien was quiet as they rode, intent on making good time. The competition was to be held tomorrow evening, and Gillien wanted to make sure that she was able to get an audience with Queen-mother Ariel before performing. What talk there was, mostly initiated by Daric, was low, brief, and to the point. Other than a few stops to rest, eat, and relieve themselves, they stayed on horseback. The two continued along the King's Road for about fifteen miles from Geshim until it intersected with the Queen's Road. The small stretch that led directly to Kasselton at this point was called the Royal Road, and was only about seven or eight miles. They would reach the city before dark.

As they approached the main gates of Kasselton, Gillien tensed. Singer sent messages of calm and she felt Daric's anxious gaze on her, but she could not let go of the trepidation that seized her. In the distance, far above the town that nestled at its feet, stood The Castle. Lesser homes, Gillien knew, had names, but not this one. This was *the* Castle, residence of the King of Byrn. Its cold gray was a somber contrast to the vibrant hues of the twilight sky. Gillien, who had performed in Kasselton before but never at the court of the King, felt that there was no delicacy to this ancient building, no lines of grace or harmony about it. Even its four turrets were squat, ugly things rather than soaring towers. Then again, it was a war fortress, built to repulse invasion in long-ago times before the Ghil had been driven away. Had Gillien arrived here as she ought, with her proud family surrounding her, a bard just like any other bard, she might have viewed it differently. Now, The Castle's semblance of frowning unwelcome merely mirrored her own fears.

"Courage, Gilly," Daric suddenly said. Gillien dropped her gaze from The Castle and her heart skipped a beat. The gates stood open—huge, painted doors whose colors had once been red and yellow—Byrn's colors—but whose hues had faded with years of weather to dull rust and ocher. Between them, Gillien could catch a glimpse of a bustling city inside. The noises of vendors hawking their wares, laughter, barter, and the sound of an infinite number of horses and human feet reached her ears. Over all hung the smell of a city—smoke and dust, spoiled food and mouthwatering fare, mixing in a strange, unique combination.

But Gillien had no eye or ear for the sights and sounds of Byrn's largest city. Her eyes were fastened on three men in livery striding through the crowd to meet them. Their par-ti-colored tunics in hues of red and yellow, and the no-nonsense swords at their sides marked them as royal guardsmen. The girl stiffened in her saddle, and her hand tightened around the cloth-swathed bundle that was Singer.

"Oh, gods, they're wearing gloves," she whispered.

"It's daylight still. It's all right," Daric pointed out.

Gillien swallowed, nodded. "Remember your promise, Daric."

"I've not forgotten."

The guards had reached them now. One of them grasped the reins of both horses. It was subtle movement, but it spoke volumes. Gillien swallowed hard.

"Please state your business in Kasselton, sir," said the first man to Daric.

"I'm the one with the business," Gillien said, fishing out her medallion from between her breasts. "This marks me as a competitor in the Byrnian Bardic Competition. I also have to—"

"The only bard yet to arrive is one Gillien Songespynner,"

the man interrupted, narrowing his eyes as his gaze roamed over Gillien's rough clothes. "From Hallenore. Is that you, miss?"

At first Gillien blushed at the contempt he displayed at her poor garb, then she grew annoyed. "The pendant marks me as the winner of the Borderlands competition."

The guard checked, nodded, and handed it back to Gillien.

"News of your doings precedes you, milady."

Gillien's heart climbed into her throat. "And what doings might that be?"

"Your escape from a dreadful fate. Rumor has it that you and your family—my condolences, by the way, miss—were the first victims of Mad Reeve Herrick. They say that he made a bargain with the Nightlands King, selling his soul and becoming a monster. But here you are, alive and well. So, tell me, milady bard, how much of the tale is true?"

The faces of her dead family filled Gillien's mind. In a cold voice, she said, "I don't know, sir, but my family is gone. That much of the tale is true."

The guard looked slightly uncomfortable. He cleared his throat. "Well, you're continuing the drama by arriving a scant few hours before your performance. I probably shouldn't keep you much—"

"What?" yelped Gillien. "Isn't today Loesdae?"

"Nay, milady, today is Healsdae. And you have only a little time to prepare," said the first guardsman.

"But I . . . listen to me. I must have an audience with Queen-mother Ariel. It's vital that I—"

But the guard's harsh bark of laughter cut her off. "D'ye hear that one?" he said to his fellow guards. "Rides up here all fire and pluck, and wants to see the Queen-mother!"

He turned back to her, and the cruel grin faded as he saw the intensity on her face. "You've had a rough time of it, that's for sure. Come, little miss, time to come with me. We'll put you with the other bards, get you all cleaned up and presentable. Then, after you perform, I promise you'll get a chance to talk with Her Majesty."

"But—"

"It's the best I can do, milady," said the guard, reaching to take the reins from his fellow.

"Where will you be taking her?" Daric demanded.

The first guard threw a glance up at the warrior. "I'm taking her to stay with the other bards," he explained with slow exaggeration, like an adult speaking to a slow child. "You can't go with her. I'm afraid you must watch the performance like everyone else. I'd suggest staking out a place now in the line if you wish to be inside. There's only limited space in the public galleries."

Daric's black brows drew together. "My duty is to safeguard the girl," he began, "and no scrawny, self-important, livery-clad—"

"Daric." Gillien's voice was weary, resigned. "I think . . . I suppose I'll be all right."

Daric fell silent. "You . . . you will be careful?"

"Certainly," she assured him, hiding her fear of these brusque men behind a veneer of calm. "It's almost over, Daric. Almost over." As she said the words, she felt a huge sense of relief mixed with anxiety. Through its swath of cloth, the lute sent her a gentle reassurance as the men in livery escorted her to a noble's house, where she would be prepared for the gala evening to come.

The last leg of the journey is the hardest.

—Byrnian saying

CHAPTER NINETEEN

It was amazing what a bath and the right clothes could do, Gillien thought as she surveyed herself in the mirror.

From the moment she had arrived, harried and tired, Gillien had been the object of several women's attention. She had not even been permitted to bathe by herself. Her body had been vigorously scrubbed and her ragged hair had been washed and trimmed into submission by a heavyset woman who clucked over the chopped locks in dismay. Clothing had been procured, gods alone knew how, that miraculously fit. She'd fought against the tight corseting—"I'm a singer, and you have to breathe to sing!"—with only moderate success. She still had to wear it, but the woman had reluctantly agreed not to lace it as tight as it would go. Over her head went undergarments, underskirt, and overtunic. Pretty, delicate shoes were slipped onto her feet, then came more fiddling with her hair and also her face. Now Gillien stared into the mirror at the young woman who stared back.

There was no trace of "Garen" left. Gillien's bright eyes had been encircled with kohl. Bleached flour, delicately applied, blanched the warm brown tone her face had gotten from years out under the sun. Her lips were reddened, as were her cheeks. The shortness of her hair was concealed by a veil of white silk, held in place by a delicate chain atop her head.

Her slim body was encased in silk as well, pink and white and trimmed with lace. The corset made her waist appear tiny, and her small breasts seemed larger when crushed together and pushed up by the undergarment. The women had despaired of her hands—too rough and hard, and oh, those dreadfully short nails!—but had dutifully painted the pared-down ovals with a bright red stain.

Gillien felt like an imposter.

Nothing of what she wore, on face or on body, reflected who she was. She might look like a fine lady, might even look beautiful, but she certainly did not look like Gillien Songespynner. Her hands were not meant to have painted nails—they were meant to play an instrument, toss a dagger, put a pony through its paces. How could she ride in such a dress, when she feared it might tear or get soiled by mud? Throw her head back in full-throated song, when the circlet might fall off?

"The sooner all this is over, the better I'll like it," she said softly, turning away from the glamorous woman who wore her face but had nothing at all to do with her.

She was forced to ride sidesaddle on a palfrey with no spunk, waving to the crowds that gathered to line the roads winding up into the castle grounds. Of her fellow bards, on that ride she saw only glimpses of scared, nervous faces, beautiful clothes and a collection of instruments. She clutched Singer close, and tried to steady herself, listening to the silent messages of comfort and encouragement the lute emitted.

After an afternoon and evening of breakneck rushing, things suddenly ground to an utter halt. Whereas she had had no time, hardly enough to swallow some bread and fruit while they fussed at her, now time seemed to crawl as she stood quietly with the other six bards in the castle's courtyard. There

was plenty of time to worry, and wonder if the dreadful creature had managed to catch up to her—and to Singer. She'd
tried to catch glimpses of the hands of those around her and
been largely thwarted. All the guards wore gloves as part of
their uniform; she'd have to simply trust that they were what
they appeared to be. Trust, and be ready to run if it proved otherwise. As for the other bards, Gillien had seen a few hands
here and there, holding instruments or nervously fiddling with
hair or garb. Some, she knew by those brief glances, were exactly who they said they were and nothing more. Others she
shied away from and hoped for the best.

The cobblestones hurt her feet through her flimsy slippers,
and she shifted her weight from side to side. She was aware
that the movement revealed her tension, but didn't care.

Sometime in the busy evening darkness had fallen and the
temperature had dropped. Gillien was slightly chilly in the
beautiful but thin garb she wore. Orange torchlight was the
only illumination. Gillien held Singer closely against her
body and took in the scene with apprehensive eyes.

The seven bards from the seven regions of Byrn had been
herded to stand here in the courtyard, outside of the Great
Hall. Together with a few guards who looked dreadfully
bored, they all waited at the bottom of a stone flight of steps
that led up to the hall. They ranged in age from a boy of about
seven, who was no doubt the possessor of an exquisite soprano, to an old man with gray hair and a stoop. There were
only two women, Gillien and a very comely girl with black
eyes and a haughty demeanor who was about two years older
than she. Gillien had tried to engage her in friendly conversation but had fallen silent before the aloof, hostile stare. None
of the other minstrels seemed interested in conversation, either. The young man standing next to her, handsome in a
sullen, overdressed way, kept shooting her furtive glances.

It was just as well professional jealousy temporarily
eclipsed bardic curiosity about Gillien's recent history, she
thought to herself. The last thing she wanted to do was go into
detail about her ordeal. She sighed slightly, leaned against the
chilly stone wall, and cradled the lute to her. She made sure

she was close to one of the torches, just in case she needed its light—or its fire—for defense.

Two guards waited with the group at the bottom of the stairs; a third stood at the top, at what Gillien presumed was the entrance to the hall, waiting to give the signal.

The minutes dragged on. Finally Gillien, her nerves strained taut, decided she just couldn't wait anymore. She tugged at the sleeve of the nearest guard. He glanced down at her without interest.

"Please, sir, is there any way I could get a brief audience with Queen-mother Ariel? I have a message for her. It's very important."

The man stared, then he and his companion laughed aloud. Some of the bards joined in, gazing at Gillien with thinly veiled contempt.

"Of course you do, miss," chuckled the guard, "and I'm the Queen's paramour!" The chuckles exploded into laughter, and Gillien felt her cheeks grow hot. The guard gentled a bit. "You'll have a chance to talk with her at the reception afterwards, dear."

The lute sent her sympathy and calmness. She tried to listen to its silent message, tried to relax, but at that moment the guard at the doorway finally glanced down and waved them forward up the stone stairs.

Gillien's stomach clenched, and she started to push forward through the small gathering of bards, eager to surge up the stairs. One of her fellow musicians, clearly angry at being up-staged, grabbed her elbow and twisted her around to face him.

"We go in order!" snapped the young man.

Again embarrassment flooded Gillien. She started to step back, her eyes lowered in chagrin, when she noticed the youth's garb.

He wore a parti-colored tunic of black and red, stockings, thigh-high boots, and carried a small hurdy-gurdy. What froze her heart for a long instant was the fact that this young man, a bard about to perform, was also wearing black leather gloves.

There was no time to even think.

She brought her arm around and down, twisting easily out

of his grasp as Kellien had taught her to do. Two bards—the
boy and the snobbish young woman—stood between her and
the stairs. Utterly disregarding courtesy, she barreled between
them. The young woman she elbowed hard in the ribs, the
young boy she knocked to the cobblestones.

She heard the woman squeal in vexation, heard the boy start
to cry with childish sobs. But her path was now clear. Grabbing her skirts with one hand and Singer with the other, she
ran headlong up the stone steps. She did not glance behind;
she did not need to. The cries of annoyance and insult suddenly became shrieks of genuine terror. A terrible roar, a roar
she had heard too many times before and knew she'd hear in
nightmares for the rest of her life, went up a scant yard behind
her.

"Here now, what—" began the guard at the top of the stairs,
not immediately seeing what was happening down in the
courtyard.

Inspiration came. Gasping, Gillien yelped, "Just part of the
act. Let me through, I'm missing my cue!"

She shoved past him, her words delaying him just enough
so that when he recovered his senses she was well inside. She
skidded to a startled halt as she found herself not in the Great
Hall, as she had expected, but in the buttery—an area where
the wines and ale were kept as the servants prepared to bear
them into the Hall proper.

Clutching Singer, Gillien glanced about wildly. Wooden
shelves reached up to the high stone ceiling, and each shelf
sported a host of bottles and jugs of different sizes and colors.
The timber floor was swept clean, bare of rushes or any other
sort of floor covering. Three yards straight ahead Gillien saw a
flight of stairs that led down, probably to the kitchen area. Beyond the stairs, on the other side, was the pantry, another small
room built along the same lines as the buttery. Instead of bottles,
the pantry was filled with loaves of bread and other dishes waiting to be served to those who sat in the Great Hall.

Where in the Nightlands *was* the Great Hall? Gillien wondered wildly. She could see no door, but about a yard to her
right, a prettily decorated screen blocked her vision.

Everyone in the buttery and the pantry had halted, staring at her.

"Just what do you think you're doing?" shrieked a heavyset older woman. Her broad face was flushed with indignation, and her beefy arms bore a silver tray stacked with filled goblets.

Gillien couldn't spare time for an answer. She ducked beneath the serving woman's arm and tried to scurry past her. A young page tackled Gillien with more enthusiasm than skill, ducking his head and ramming it into Gillien's midsection. The girl went sprawling and crashed into one of the bottle-laden sideboards as she fell. Bottles hurtled to the stone floor, crashing around her, spraying her with wine and bits of broken glass. Gillien, the wind knocked out of her, gasped for air like a fish out of water. She tried to fling up her arms, to protect Singer and shield her eyes from fragments of glass at the same time, and fell heavily on her back.

She still couldn't breathe. As she stared helplessly upward, her mouth working but not taking in any air, the faces of the servants went from angry to terrified. Screaming, they fled, some down the stairs, others shoving aside the screen and fleeing into what Gillien now realized was the Great Hall itself.

In the doorway to the buttery, where Gillien had charged in but a second or two earlier, stood the Changer. The nightmare creature still wore the face and body of the young male bard. But no bard of Byrn had four arms that ended in sharp, hooked claws that gleamed with poison. The thing bellowed its anger, and its teeth suddenly sharpened and grew. One appendage shot out, lengthening as it went, reaching for Gillien's legs.

Breath came back to Gillien in a painful rush. She snatched her legs away, barely avoiding the sharp, glistening spike that slammed into the wooden floor just an inch away. She stumbled to her feet, cutting palms and soles on the bits of broken glass and leaving smudges of blood as she followed the servants and crashed through the screen, knocking it down in the process.

For a fraction of a heartbeat, as she untangled herself from the wreckage of the screen, Gillien stared wildly at the interrupted glory that was The Castle's Great Hall.

She'd performed in plenty of halls in her eighteen years, but this one was enormous. It was, she judged, at least fifty yards long, the width perhaps half that. A vaulted ceiling, high enough to accommodate a gallery crowded with onlookers on either side, soared over the rows of tables at which the guests had sat. The tables, fifteen in all, must just a few moments ago have been glories of fine linen, beautiful plates, and graceful candlelit dining; the guests composed, perfectly groomed, coiffed and clad. Banners draped along the galleries and hung from the ceiling were a riot of colors, adding to the festive air. The hall was warmed and to some degree lit by two huge fires, burning in fireplaces centered beneath and slightly behind the galleries.

Now, though, what had been all gentility and rich grace was a mob scene. The shrieking, sobbing servants had interrupted the gathering. Nobles were shaking the servants, trying to get coherent words out of them. Over to the right, at least one table had been overturned, and more than one bottle of wine had spilled. No one could hear anything—everyone, from richest noble to lowest vassal, was shouting and demanding to know what was going on.

An aisle had been cleared between the groupings of tables—the aisle that Gillien and her fellow bards ought to have marched cheerfully down. At the far end, Gillien glimpsed the High Table, elevated on a raised dais. Briefly Gillien saw the Royal Family—King Evrei, on his feet and shouting orders that could not be heard; his wife Queen Aceline, her small fists crammed to her mouth and her eyes wide with fear; Prince Cathal, the Heir Apparent, shrieking as loudly as his little sisters; and in the center, in the place of honor, Queen-mother Ariel.

Alone of them all, Ariel was silent. Her eyes fastened on Gillien, who stood temporarily frozen at the end of the hall. In some dim place in her mind, Gillien acknowledged the elven Queen-mother as the most beautiful thing she had ever seen. Ariel was almost impossibly tiny, a child-woman, shorter by well over a foot than Gillien. As she rose from behind the table, Gillien saw that she was dressed in a sumptuous gown of clinging blue silk. A circlet of gold adorned with rubies sat atop her hair, but her own beauty outshone any she could possibly wear. Her skin was pale, almost white, and her huge gray eyes were wide with utter shock. Hair the color of pale gold cascaded down her back. She stood with her hands at her heart, an exquisite statue of astonishment.

Show me! shrieked Singer silently. *Show me to Ariel!*

The silent plea jolted Gillien from her paralysis. She trusted Singer utterly. She raised her right arm, brandishing the beautiful instrument like a club. Blood oozed from her sliced palms, staining the instrument, and her wounded feet marked her trail as she began to run down the center of the Great Hall.

"Ariel!" she screamed at the top of her lungs. "Ariel!"

The sound of her name seemed to free the elf-queen from her own moment of shock. Now Ariel, too, broke into a run, racing toward Gillien with an unseemly yet graceful speed, her slim arms outstretched, crying out something in Falaran that Gillien could not understand. Guards, fearful for their Queen-mother's safety, ran to stop her. Gillien could not make out the words, but Ariel shook off the hands of her would-be protectors with sharp words of command and continued to run.

Thwarted in their attempts to stop the Queen-mother, the guards flanked her instead. Their swords were out and there was a grim set to their mouths as they ran. Their job was to protect, and while they could not disobey an order, they could and would continue to stay glued to the elf-queen's side.

Out of the corner of her eye, Gillien caught a blur of movement coming at her. She did not think. With deep instinct, she suddenly swerved to the left, jerking her head around to see who had tried to waylay her.

The thing had completely shed its mask of humanity. It was a large blob of shapeless, sand-colored substance that had several appendages of all sizes and shapes. Each one of them ended in a barb or point of some kind, and Gillien had to leap directly over a twisting limb to keep the dreadful poison from coming into contact with her body.

But . . . it's still back there, isn't it?

Still running, she had to look, had to know if her horrible suspicion was true—that there was, suddenly and inexplicably, more than one creature here who was willing to murder to intercept Singer. Yes, there it was, only a few steps behind her, almost on top of its shapeless kin, racing down the aisle, the ghastly combination of minstrel and monster that had first revealed itself just seconds ago outside on the steps. How could this be? And then the dreadful truth hit home.

This time, the demon hadn't come alone. This time, it had brought another of its kind.

The cacophony of human voices raised in fear was joined by another sound, the shriek-growl that Gillien associated with the creature in pursuit of her. A hand fell on her shoulder and she screamed. She immediately dropped to her knees and rolled, executing the tumble despite the cumbersome dress she wore. She glanced back to see a guard drawing his sword.

The man's face shimmered, melted like hot wax. A third monster! She couldn't move, was frozen with horror, and stared stupidly up at the creature as it raised its sword.

"Keep running, Gilly!" came a familiar voice. She glanced up to see Daric standing on the railing of the gallery, ready to jump.

"Daric!" cried Gillien, horrified. The guard-thing paused, glancing upward with an utterly nonhuman face. Daric gathered himself and leaped upon it, sword drawn and at the ready. Monster and swordsman fell, but Daric was on top and sprang away before the creature could attack. The thing snarled and pressed its attack, wielding its sword with more power than any human could summon. Daric was hard-pressed to even defend himself, much less mount a counterattack. The brutal clang of steel hurt Gillien's ears.

"*Run!*" bellowed the swordsman, parrying another blow. He lost his footing but rolled to his feet, narrowly avoiding the monster's killing blow.

Gasping and crying, somehow Gillien got to her feet and again began the seemingly endless race down the hall toward the beautiful elven woman. She prayed Daric would remember the creature's poison and keep out of its fatal reach. Her feet cried out in agony with each step, but she did not slow.

Another voice, clear and musical and strong, soared above the pandemonium.

"Blessers, call sunlight! Call fire! They cannot stand it!"

And suddenly Taran was there, materializing out of the crowd, running at Gillien, his hood swept back from his silver hair. His fine features were set as if in stone, and his eyes were grim and determined. Too late, Gillien realized that another monster-human, this time wearing the velvet doublet of a noble and sprouting the face of a Ghil, had leaped in front of her. She cried out, tried to halt, but her feet would not obey her. She could not stop as the Ghil-monster raised its sword and dove at her.

Then she felt a strong shove and stumbled aside, falling on one of the benches. She glanced back, gasping and panting. Taran stood where she had been just a second ago, had interposed his body between her and the creature's blade. Gillien watched in horror as the bloody tip emerged from the back of his cape. The elf did not die at once. His handsome face worked, and he emitted a strangled, gurgling noise as blood dripped from his suddenly ashen mouth. Impatiently, the Ghil-monster tugged its weapon free. It brought back its arms, rich with inhuman strength, and swung the sword cleanly across Taran's shoulders.

The severed head sailed a good distance, propelled by the force of the blow, spinning and splattering blood as it went. Gillien tasted bile and watched, riveted with horror.

Do not let his death be in vain! cried Singer.

It was like a slap in the face. Recovering herself, Gillien leaped over Taran's fallen body, her attention fully on completing her mission.

Ariel had almost reached her. Gillien could see the Queen-mother's lovely face in detail now, see the red mouth slightly parted, see the slender hands reaching out for the gift that Gillien had vowed to bring her.

And then something strong, ropy, and definitely not human wrapped itself around her leg. The Ghil-monster, not even bothering to chase her, had suddenly grown a Ghil tail. The powerful limb, pink and scaly, had seized her ankle and would not let go.

Gillien felt herself falling as if in slow motion. With all her remaining strength, she drew her arm back and flung the lute toward Queen-mother Ariel. She kept her eyes on it as the hard floor rushed up to meet her, watching it in fascination as it turned slowly over and over in the air.

Ariel reached up a slender hand and sprang upwards. Her fingers closed around Singer's neck. Suddenly, the hall was bathed in a purging, blinding flood of light. The Blessers of Light who had shown up for the event had called upon their god, and he had answered. Other men in court who knew how to use hand and head magic, and they were not an inconsiderable number, had heard Taran's dying cry as well. Still others, possessed of no magical abilities but keeping cool heads, had taken the oil lamps and flung them into the fires. They had created light, both sunlight and fire, and the hall was suddenly unbearably bright.

Gillien squinted against the brilliance, but thought, in the instant before she hit the floor, that the radiance surely must have dazzled her eyes. She thought she saw, as Ariel's small white palm closed about the lute, that the image of Singer had blurred, shifted. Ariel no longer held the neck of the lute. Instead, she clasped the hand of a beautiful, golden-haired young man who now stood beside her.

Then, the overly bright hall went black.

*And The Lady placed the mark of Her favor around his neck.
"Rise, Elf-friend," She bade him, and he was the first of that
title.*

—from *The Book of The Lady*

CHAPTER TWENTY

Gillien woke to a dull, throbbing pain that sat atop her head
like a malicious cap of pure agony. Her eyelids fluttered open,
and for a long, strange moment, she couldn't place where she
was.

A silken nightdress modestly covered her neck and arms
and, she presumed, the rest of her body. She was ensconced in
linen bedclothes, tucked in cozily with beautifully embroidered blankets up to her chin. At her feet, the luxurious pelt of
a mountain cat stretched the width of the bed. The bed itself
was so enormous she felt nearly swallowed by it and the seemingly dozens of pillows.

The softness of the down pillows did nothing to mitigate the
pain snarling behind her temples. She turned to better inspect
the hanging fabric that canopied the bed and whimpered as the
movement brought a fresh onslaught of agony.

At once, the canopies were drawn back to reveal the face of

a woman of middle years. A red wimple covered her head and bespoke her rank as a Blesser of the goddess Health.

"Well, you've decided to join us again, I see," said the woman, smiling. "How do you feel?"

Gillien winced. "My head hurts. And I'm thirsty."

"Half a moment, and I'll attend to both."

The draperies fell back into place with a soft rustle, and Gillien heard the Healer moving about in the room. The woman was saying something in a low voice to one of the servants, but Gillien couldn't quite make out the words.

She had guessed where she was by now; in one of the solars in the castle. Memories were coming back, and her last waking recollection caused her heart to jerk suddenly.

"Singer!"

She flung the covers off and swung her legs to the floor. The movement caused waves of torment to crash through her head, and she gasped.

The Healer, hurrying up with a goblet in her hand, clucked her tongue disapprovingly.

"Get back in bed, young miss, or I'll put you back myself."

Gillien brought her legs back up under the covers obediently, but was full of questions.

"Please, Blesser, where's Singer—my lute? Did Queenmother Ariel get it? How long have I been here? What happened to—"

"Drink this and then we'll answer questions," replied the Blesser in a tone that brooked no argument. The goblet she handed Gillien was filled with a fragrant warm liquid. Gingerly, she sipped at it and wrinkled her nose. It was bitter, but the Blesser arched an eyebrow. Gamely, Gillien downed the beverage. Within a few seconds, the pain ebbed.

"Better?"

"Y-yes," replied Gillien, surprised.

"Good. Then you'll be ready to receive your guests." The Blesser pulled back the remaining draperies and Gillien got her first good look at the solar's opulence.

The large, glass-paned windows were open, permitting a warm breeze to circulate through the room. The walls were not bare stone, but rather sported paneling that reached halfway up the walls. The rest of the walls were plaster, painted with scenes of lords and ladies wandering through landscapes of fields, forests, and gardens. The wall on Gillien's right was mostly taken up by a large fireplace with an ornate mantel. In front of the fire was a small table with two benches. A game of Fox and Geese had been set up, and interrupted. A beautifully carved chest sat at the end of the bed. Exquisitely woven rugs covered most of the wooden floor.

Gillien had barely taken in the room when there came a light tapping at the door. The Blesser gave Gillien a reassuring smile and opened the door.

Standing in the doorway, a smile on her exquisite features, was Queen-mother Ariel. She wore a gown that was clearly meant to be far simpler than her formal garb of the other evening—how long ago was it, anyway? wondered Gillien—but was still lavish by Gillien's standards. Her hair, unbound and without a crown, fell to her waist in a rivulet of silver-gold. The elf-queen moved into the solar with a rustle of silk. The fragrance of jasmine enveloped Gillien as Ariel drew up a small stool and sat beside the girl.

She knew it was impertinent, but Gillien couldn't help but stare openmouthed. Smiling gently, Ariel leaned forward and placed a whisper-soft kiss on Gillien's forehead.

"You have done me and your country a great, great service, Gillien Songespynner," said the elf-queen in her musical voice. "There is no way we can properly repay you." The smile deepened, and a hint of a dimple appeared in Ariel's creamy cheek. "I know humans very well indeed, and I know that you must be fairly bursting with questions. But before you ask them, there is someone you must meet."

She turned to the Blesser and nodded. The Healer disappeared into the corridor for a moment, and then returned with another Falaran. He stood taller than Ariel, perhaps Gillien's height, and was as beautifully clad. His features were delicate and yet bore a masculine strength that Ariel's lacked. He resembled Jencir in build and movement, but his face, though equally handsome, was different.

He wore a short white tunic with a blue surcoat, hose, and matching slippers. Atop his golden head was a gold coronet. Small rubies glowed like embers, but the primary gem was a great blue sapphire. It seemed somehow familiar to Gillien, though she knew she had never seen the crown nor its wearer before.

When her eyes met the elf's, though, she felt as though she had been seized by the power in their gray depths. Joy blazed in those eyes, and eagerness was written as clearly on his beautiful features as words on parchment. Jencir, even at his most agonized, had never displayed such obvious emotion, and she wondered at the cause in this unbelievably handsome elf-lord.

"My cousin Ariel is slightly in error," he said in a voice like sunshine given substance.

Gillien started. She knew that voice, somehow . . . but when? How?

He appeared to have read her thoughts. "We have met before. I am Prince Liandir Kalessor Falahi, heir to the throne of the elvenland of Falarah." He placed a hand on his chest and bowed deeply. "But you might know me better under the name that you yourself gave me, Gillien—the name of Singer."

Gillien stared in silent shock. Her mouth worked, but all that came out was a broken questioning sound. "Wha—"

Liandir moved swiftly, sitting next to Gillien on the bed. He glanced over at his cousin the Queen-mother, who nodded that he might continue.

"A meeting was held a few weeks ago in my country—in essence, a council of war. The Sa elves are mistrustful of the humans, and they planned to secretly station soldiers at the Byrn-Falarah border." His face sobered. "Soldiers who probably would do more than guard. We feared that they were not simply preventing an attack, but rather planning one. I knew that I had to get a message to Byrn, and soon, before the amassing of Sa troops got out of hand.

"Like my cousin, I am fond of your race, Gillien." His gaze

softened, and his smile brought the blood to Gillien's cheeks
for no reason that she could explain. "I would not have such a
thing happen to your countrymen. I am, however, known for
my sympathy toward humans, and any message I tried to send
would surely be intercepted. The only way to warn your people was to send a message that couldn't be traced—a magical
message.

"The Court Wizard, Calleo, is a dear friend of mine, and he
was able to transform me into the lute you knew as Singer."

Gillien stared at Liandir's crown. She knew now why the
sapphire was so familiar. She had seen it a hundred times, nestled at the base of the instrument's throat. She recalled what
she had said to the lute, what she had done in front of it, and
blushed even redder. Good gods, what Liandir had seen of
her!

"Jencir smuggled me into Byrn." Now Liandir looked away
and swallowed hard. When he spoke again, his voice was
thick. "His task was to get me safely to Ariel, so that I could
warn her and she could warn her people. But Jencir was slain
by the Changer sent after him, living only long enough to pass
me along to you."

"Oh, Highness," breathed Gillien, sympathy overriding her
discomfort. "Was he your friend, then?"

"My best friend."

"I'm so sorry. I didn't know him well but . . ." Gillien ran
out of words. She reached and pressed Liandir's hand in wordless sympathy. The elf's warm, strong hand squeezed hers
tightly.

"Jencir died in the service of his country, and he did well in
choosing you to be the bearer of the lute." He forced a smile
through his sorrow. "Both of your missions were successful,
as you see."

Gillien chewed her lip thoughtfully, glancing from one elf
to the other. "But . . . there's so much I don't understand."

"Ask away, my dear," Ariel invited with a sweet smile.

"How did you know?" Gillien asked her. "How did you
know the lute was Liandir?"

"We are elves," the Queen-mother said, as if that would explain everything. Gillien shook her head, indicating that she still didn't understand. Ariel continued, "Only mortals can perform magic, and only mortals can be deceived by it. Elven eyes can see through illusions."

"You mean, it looked to you like I was carrying Liandir by his legs or something?" asked Gillien skeptically.

Both Falarans laughed, Liandir heartily, Ariel more softly. "Nay, nothing that droll. No, I merely . . . I simply *knew*. I cannot explain it better than that. I saw a lute, as did all present, but I knew that it was my cousin. And elves, though we do understand humor, would never play such a trick merely to amuse. There was some dire reason why Liandir had chosen to be transformed into the instrument. That was why I ran to meet you."

"I had to get to Ariel, you see," Liandir said. "Both to warn her of the potential invasion and to regain my form. Ariel's touch negated the spell. Calleo and I knew that would happen. Had I not gotten to her, or to another wizard who had both the skill to see through the illusion and the power to dispel it, I could very well have been an instrument forever." Mirth sparkled in his silver eyes. "Not that, in your hands, that would have been so dreadful a thing. I regret to stay that my voice was much sweeter when I was a musical instrument than now."

Gillien thought of her hands on the lute, her hand now in Liandir's warm palm, and quickly changed the subject. "What about the creature, the, what did you call it . . ."

"The Changer?"

Liandir turned away and rose. He began to pace, every line of his body radiating tension. "No, I do not suppose that humans have ever heard of the Changers. I must confess, I was not expecting one to be involved in this."

"But what *are* they?" asked Gillien, exasperated.

"What exactly, no one knows," replied Liandir in clipped tones. "They are not mentioned in *The Book of The Lady*, nor in any tome of which we have heard. But they are there. They are an old race, ancient, really; able to change shape at will. Their primary prey are the Ghil, and for many hundreds of thousands of years, they have kept the incredible numbers of the Ghil in line. You humans ought to thank them, Gillien. The way the Ghil breed, they could easily overcome your people—and perhaps even ours—by sheer numbers alone."

Numbers . . . "I always thought there was just one of . . . of the Changers after me," Gillien said, her voice soft and sober. "But at the competition, they seemed to be everywhere."

"I would assume that there was originally only the one," said Liandir. "They reproduce by dividing. It is my suspicion that the Changer, near the end of its quest and unable to have acquired what it was sent for, reproduced itself—thus increasing the odds of killing you and taking the lute . . . taking me."

"Did you catch them all?"

Liandir shrugged, a gesture that made him seem suddenly very human to Gillien.

"We cannot know. No one knows how many times a Changer may replicate. We killed four, and so far have seen no traces of any others. We can only hope. The thought that Changers may be roaming Kasselton is . . . disturbing.

"They have never before taken any part in any conflict," the elf-prince continued. "Had Taran lived, he might have been able to enlighten us as to why, now, they sent one of their own to fight with the Sa."

"Yes, what part did Taran play in all this?" Gillien was sitting up now, all eager curiosity. The covers fell away from her slim frame. "Wasn't he a Sa elf?"

"Yes," answered Liandir. "He was. He was also a friend of mine and chose to aid me and my quest to warn the people of Byrn."

"But . . . why? Just because he liked you?"

Liandir shook his head solemnly, and when he next spoke his voice was filled with respect. "Taran was one of Kertu's elite personal guards. But he knew that such enmity between our people—human and elf—was wrong, went against the teachings of The Lady. Kertu could not be permitted to continue with such a plan."

Gillien was silent, staring at her hands. "I don't think he liked us much."

A smile curved Liandir's lips. "That he did not, I am afraid. Taran was not fond of your race."

"Then . . . why? Why would he die for us?"

"Because it was not right to attack innocents, when The Lady had shown us that the way was peace. Taran knew that, and that is what he died for. He was a brave elf indeed."

Gillien was quiet for a moment, trying to absorb everything she had just been told. The two Falarans respected her silence. After a few long moments, Gillien discovered she had not run out of questions.

"How long have I been unconscious? And what's been happening while I was here?"

"You have been healing for almost a week," said Ariel, gently squeezing Gillien's arm. "You had a dangerous blow to your head. When you recovered from that, the Healer chose to keep you asleep so she could tend to and heal your other wounds more swiftly. Another day, perhaps, and you will be on your feet."

"The Byrnian Bardic Competition was canceled this year," added Liandir. "With one competitor slain by the Changer who assumed his form, and with you unable to perform, King Evrei decided not to continue. If you wish to replace that copper pendant with the gold one that signifies Byrnian Bard, Gillien, you will have to start all over again next year."

Gillien fingered the copper disk that hung from the chain about her throat.

"It doesn't seem that important, now," she said softly. "I mean, it's an honor, but . . ." Her voice trailed off as she saw in her mind's eye her family, Jencir, the young blesser Cadby, and all the others who had suffered and died so that Gillien might get Liandir to the Queen-mother. She hoped that their sacrifices had been worth something.

Again, Liandir seemed to sense her thoughts. "Human troops are being amassed at various border towns. Byrn is preparing for war—war that we desperately hope we can avoid. The Sa were counting on being able to surprise Byrn. That element of surprise is now lost to them, as is the time they had bargained on having to prepare." Liandir arched an

eyebrow and smiled. "And perhaps more elves will feel like
Taran than King Kertu thinks—that his plan is wrong and
must not be allowed to continue."

"Do you . . . do you really think so?"

"I cannot know. But I do hope so."

Liandir glanced over at Ariel, who nodded and then rose.
Liandir reached inside his tunic and withdrew a beautiful silver medallion. Curious, Gillien leaned forward to look at it. It
was flat and circular, but words were inscribed on one side,
though she could not read them, and there was a profile of a
man on the other.

"I brought this with me in the hopes that I would find one
who might be fit to wear it," Liandir explained, running his
slim fingers over the medallion's surface. He glanced at
Gillien and smiled, the light in his eyes shining. "I did not
dream that I would be so lucky as to find someone like you,
Gillien Songespynner. This," he said, gazing with affection at
the medallion, "is the symbol of Elf-friend. Have you heard of
this, Gillien?"

She shook her head.

"Long ago," said Liandir, "there lived one of mortal blood
who had great love for the immortal kind. He was our friend,
and The Lady loved him for his wisdom, gentleness, and
courage. She gave to him a medallion like this one, and called
him Elf-friend. Since that time, there have been a very few
whom we have called Elf-friend. There is no higher honor that
we of elven blood can give to a mortal. Bow your head,
Gillien Songespynner, and receive our honor."

For a heartbeat Gillien stared, shocked. Tears welled in her
eyes as the import of the honor sank in, and she humbly
bowed her head. Liandir placed the medallion over her neck,
his warm hands brushing her neck softly as he did so.

"'Our thoughts go with thee, Elf-friend, wherever thy path
may take thee,'" he quoted the inscription. Through her shimmering curtain of tears, Gillien gazed at both elves, smiling
shakily.

"And now," said Ariel, "I shall leave the two of you to chat
some more. Again, Gillien, I thank you, Elf-friend." She turned

and left, leaving the faint scent of jasmine to linger in the air for a moment longer.

Liandir watched her go, and for a moment continued to stare after her, as if suddenly shy and reluctant to talk to Gillien alone. Gently, she tugged at his sleeve.

"You don't have to stay to keep me company, Prince Liandir," she said. "I'm all right, really."

He looked confused for a second, then chuckled warmly. "No, Gillien, you misread me entirely. I would stay with you, if you like." The elf glanced away, then back at her. Gillien's heart sped up at the expression on his pale, perfect features. His emotions were entirely clear on his face.

"Gillien, I must speak what is in my heart. For a long time, we traveled together, you and I. You spoke to me as you probably have never spoken to another living soul, for you did not know that I was other than what I appeared to be—a simple, albeit magical, instrument. I know your heart. I have seen it, heard it, felt it when you touched me."

He reached again for her hand with his, and it was warm and strong as it closed about her fingers.

"Gillien . . . the heart that I saw, heard, felt, *knew* . . . that strong, brave, lonely heart of yours has won me. I am in love with you. Your touch did not lie; I know that you care for me as well. You have held me to your breast and told me that you did not wish to part. Gillien . . . we do not have to.

"I ask you with all honor, respect and fear . . . will you stay, and be my bride?"

The day was beautiful, the sky a gorgeous, cloudless blue. Daric's garb was clean, sumptuous and well tailored. The body they attired was strong, healed from its wounds, bathed, massaged, and well fed. The armor he carried had been created to fit him perfectly by royal armorers who had worked through the nights this past week to ready it for him. Between his legs was a fine chestnut gelding, with a mouth soft as butter and the strength and speed of a beast out of legend.

Daric Rhan felt absolutely wretched.

With each clop-clop of the horse's hooves, he traveled

down the Royal Road, farther away from The Castle and closer to his new station at the Borderlands military base. It had seemed the right decision, both politically and personally. He had looked the demon in the bottle in the eye, and denied it its power over him. He had confronted the Ghil—both their real, smelly, dangerous bodies and the ghosts of the past that had haunted him. He had faced his numbing terror of slavers, and freed an innocent young woman from their abuses. He felt more alive, more in control of himself, than he had in years. It was time, now, to put his skills to work in a good cause.

His talk with Liandir had convinced him that joining the troops amassing at the Borderlands was a good cause indeed. After hearing what the Sa elves were up to, and what Liandir—and that strange, surly Taran—had done, had sacrificed, to warn the Byrnians about them, Daric knew that he had to offer what assistance he could to ensure that the Sa would not win, should war break out.

Liandir. It was impossible not to like the prince, when one realized everything he had done to protect a country full of strangers. And personally, Liandir was a kind, warm soul, witty and engaging. He truly was the lute sprung to life—graceful, beautiful, wise, and so filled with devotion toward Gillien . . .

Daric recalled the lute's anguish when Gillien had been in the hands of the slavers. Daric had *felt* Liandir's fear and pain, felt it shiver up his arm as he held the instrument and reach his heart, pure and uncomplicated and genuine. Both warrior and prince had sat for hours at Gillien's side, hoping she would regain consciousness. Naked emotions played on Liandir's face—fear, hope, and, unmistakably, love. Clearly, Liandir had been "blessed" by his goddess with feelings and passion—for Gillien.

And Gillien . . . what, who had she wanted when she had been freed from the slavers? Not Daric and his rough embraces. She'd wanted Singer, the lute, the beautiful elf-prince who could comfort her with feelings that bypassed human expressions and touches, with a song that no mortal could make.

When the Healer said that Gillien was out of danger and

would wake on her own within an hour or two, Daric knew that it was time to leave. He took his departure, accepting the gifts of clothes and armor and horse, and left Gillien to awaken in the arms of the elf-prince who clearly adored her. It was, after all, what she wanted.

His horse tossed his head and whinnied, ears swiveled back. "What is it, boy?" Daric asked. Then he, too, heard the sound of hooves on hard-packed earth. He drew rein. The gelding halted obediently, and Daric turned to see who was galloping up behind him so fast.

Three riders, two in the immediately recognizable red and yellow livery of the royal household, headed toward him. The third wore male garb as well, but as the three drew closer Daric recognized the third rider as Gillien. She rode That Damned Beast, who, for the first time since Daric had clapped eyes on the animal, was behaving perfectly.

As she drew nearer, he saw that there were still bandages on her head, but she looked healthy. In fact, he thought dismally, she looked beautiful. The garb, while male in fashion, had been styled for her figure, and no breeches she had worn while fleeing the law and bearing the lute to its—his—destiny had fit so well, no tunic been so gracefully filled. Strapped across her back was a lute—not nearly so beautiful as Singer had been, but clearly a valuable instrument just the same.

She pulled That Damned Beast into a trot and drew alongside him. Gillien was panting a little from the exertion, and her eyes searched his. When she'd caught her breath, though, her first words were to her escorts.

"Thank you. I'm all right now."

The men glanced from her to Daric. "Are you sure, my lady?"

"Quite sure. Please thank the Queen-mother for me again."

Bowing, the men turned their steeds around and trotted back toward Kasselton. Gillien turned her full attention to Daric.

"So," he quipped, trying to hide his emotions, "who's the lute this time?"

"You left without saying goodbye," she retorted, ignoring the jest.

"I thought I left you in good hands. Safe hands." He paused, then added softly, "In the hands of the one who loved you."

She looked away at that, down at the horse's ears. She patted That Damned Beast's neck awkwardly.

"The lute was a going-away present. Liandir gave it to me. It's just a lute, don't worry."

"Yes, what *about* Liandir?" It was rude. It was forward. Daric couldn't stop himself. He had to know just what was going on here, had to know the facts before his own hopes set him up for disappointment.

Gillien's features worked. At last she said slowly, "I was born under the sunshine, not under a roof. I've never lived in one place for more than two weeks at a time. I don't know how to. Staying at The Castle, or traveling back to Falarah—Daric, I'd have been a mountain cat in a cage."

"You'd have had the freedom to wander. I doubt Liandir could deny you anything." He hated the way his voice sounded in his own ears—angry, jealous, hard. He liked Liandir, had tried to be happy for Gillien. But he couldn't, not really. Now, he made his voice hard, trying to quell his hope that maybe, just maybe . . .

"I might have, but I wouldn't have felt that I could. Life as a princess, life as an elf's bride . . . Daric, it never could have worked, even if . . . well, it couldn't. So I left."

She sighed, straightened, and looked him in the face again. "Where are you going?"

"To the encampment at the Borderlands point," Daric replied. "And you?"

"Same place. I'm a royal bard now, see?" She became again the girl Daric had fallen in love with, her eyes widening with childlike pleasure as she indicated the baldric of yellow and red that went from shoulder to hip. "I'm going to play for the troops. A little light music is always welcome, right?"

Daric nodded, but didn't reply. He sensed there was something else she had to say, and prayed that it was what he wanted to hear.

"And," she added, softly, "I came to find you."

He couldn't breathe. He managed to whisper, "Why, Gilly?"

"I . . . I don't know . . . how much I can offer you." Her voice, too, was thick. She glanced away, clearly trying to hide the pain in her eyes, but Daric had glimpsed it.

"I'm not . . . what . . . who I was before . . . Things happened to me when I was a slave, Daric, things that . . . that might m-make you not w-want me."

His heart ached in sympathy for her, for he knew exactly how hard those words were to say.

"Gilly, you don't have to say another word. I know."

She jerked her head around at that, and there was a hint of anger in her face. "You may think you—"

"No, Gilly," he said, his own tongue stumbling over the admission. "I *know*. It . . . I . . . ."

He wasn't as strong as she was. He couldn't say the words. He tried again.

"I know what they did, and I know how you feel because . . ." He swallowed hard, forced it out. "They . . . they did it to me too."

He saw her face change as comprehension dawned, saw tears of empathy well in her beautiful blue eyes, spill down her cheeks.

He squeezed his horse, drew it alongside That Damned Beast. Wordlessly, he extended his hand. She stared at it, her gaze roaming over the scarred palm, the callused fingers, the nails that had been cracked or torn, the fingers that were powerful enough to snap her slim neck. Tentatively, she placed her own hand—gods, so small, so pale—in his brown palm.

"Something like that . . . it's not our fault." He realized as the words came that, for the first time, he truly believed them. "It's not our fault," he repeated. "It is never, *ever*, the hurt one's fault. I know that if you could have stopped it, you would have. I know that the same holds true for me. But we couldn't. We just . . . couldn't. I kept thinking that somehow, I could have, I should have . . . and that made me drink, and drink hard, because I just couldn't keep thinking about it, and the drink made me forget. But when they got you . . . Gilly, I couldn't forget. I had to come and at least try to stop . . . I'm sorry. I couldn't stop it. Can . . . can you forgive me for that?"

"Daric . . ." A sob escaped her lips. "I never blamed you for that, never . . ."

"I care about you." He wanted to say *I love you* but he couldn't, not yet, just as she couldn't give her body to him yet. "What—happened—it doesn't matter to me. I want you, and I'll wait until you want me, too." He forced a smile. "It's not like that, not when there's caring and gentleness. When you're ready, I'll prove that to you." She stiffened, and he added, "And for now, I'm happy just to know that you're here. That's enough."

Her smile was like the sun to him, shining brightly through the tears on her face. She squeezed his hand, hard.

"Maybe . . . maybe you won't have to wait all that long."

They smiled at one another, then let their hands go. Squeezing their horses into a walk, they rode slowly along the road.

Gillien removed the lute from across her back, settled it in her hands, and sweet music accompanied the rhythmic clop-clop of horses' hooves. It didn't have the achingly sweet purity of Singer's voice, but the tunes were light and eased away whatever tensions were left. It was her gift to Daric until she could bring herself to give more. Daric understood, and a slow smile touched his lips as she lifted her voice—strong, pure and sweet—in a song of joy.

EPILOGUE

Liandir sat alone in a small solar. The shutters were closed against the day's light, and a few candles provided warm illumination. The room was lavishly furnished, but the elf prince had no eye for the solar's beauty. His golden head was bent over a silver scrying bowl, watching the images of Gillien and Daric as they rode away.

"Does she know?" came a soft voice.

Liandir raised his head, blinking at the light from the corridor that threw Ariel's slim figure in the doorway into silhouette. He waved her inside, answering when she had closed the door and come to stand beside him.

"She knows I love her," he answered.

"But does she know . . . what that means?"

"No. And I hope she never does."

Gillien, he knew, understood that elves did not normally have strong emotions. What she did not know, and Liandir chose not to reveal, is the only time in an adult elf's life when one is able to experience strong emotions is when "The Lady comes," when that elf meets the person that he or she was intended to love throughout a lifetime. Gillien had been chosen by The Lady to be Liandir's mate, and Liandir had fallen in love with the beautiful, feisty young bard. Gillien, however, had learned to care for another, and refused Liandir's proposal.

As long as Gillien was alive, Liandir would be able to feel deep emotions. And as long as she lived, the elf-prince could love only Gillien Songespynner—love her enough to let her go.

Gently, Ariel rested a hand on her cousin's shoulder. Liandir knew that Ariel had once loved a mortal as he now did. Her love had passed on, leaving her only the memory of emotions. That memory was enough, though, for her to understand Liandir's present pain.

"I am sorry, cousin."

"Do not be. I would it had been otherwise, but . . . truly, I am happy in Gillien's happiness. She has been through so much, she deserves a little joy. Is it possible to mourn so much, and yet to feel such joy on another's behalf?"

"Yes. Emotions are strange things, Liandir. You can grieve and rejoice at the same time."

"Then I am happy for her in truth." He smiled up at his cousin, then his gaze wandered inexorably to the image of two lovers leaving him behind. A tear welled from his eye to splash into the water. Instantly, the image dissolved.

"Very happy," he whispered, smiling.